Reflections in Time

Gwyn Jones

Copyright © 2024 by Gwyn Jones

All rights reserved.

Published in 2024 by Neuadd Press, an imprint of Write Now! Publications.

IBSN 978-1-912955-66-4

No part of this publication may be reproduced, distributed, or transmitted in any form or by any means, including photocopying, recording, or other electronic or mechanical methods, without the prior written permission of the publisher, except as permitted by U.K. copyright law. For permission requests, contact gwynjonesauthor.co.uk

No part of this publication may be reproduced, distributed, or transmitted in any form or by any means, including photocopying, recording, or other electronic or mechanical methods, without the prior written permission of the publisher, except as permitted by U.S. copyright law. For permission requests, contact Gwyn Jones.

The story, all names, characters, and incidents portrayed in this production are fictitious. No identification with actual persons (living or deceased), places, buildings, and products is intended or should be inferred.

Book Cover by White Rose Publishing

Dedication

In 1965 my primary school teacher, who had never heard of dyslexia, told my mother I was educationally sub normal.
My mother disagreed.
Reflections in Time, is dedicated to my Mum, Judith Alice Jones, who always believed in me.

Acknowledgements

The plot of Reflections in Time was hatched in Schiphol Airport when a flight home was delayed. I had never written before but once the story was in my head I found myself spending more and more time day dreaming about the next twist in the plot or tapping away on my laptop. I was writing for my own amusement and had no inclination to publish so when the final chapter was completed I filed the document and forgot about it.

When my mother died I remembered she had wanted me to publish the book, so having recently retired, I decided to give it a go. I sent a synopsis and sample chapters to a bunch of agents and publishers and waited. Nothing happened so I resolved to join a local writing group and discover why my wonderful novel had been ignored.

The people at, Write Now, were brilliant, their feedback was constructive and honest. Every fortnight I'd read them an extract from my precious manuscript only to receive copies littered with corrections and suggestions. Looking back I cringe at my earlier work and realise how much the group has contributed to the development of my writing. Many thanks all of you, particularly Wilf and Ruth who read my first draft from beginning to end and who gave me sound advice and encouragement.

A special thank you to my editor, Isaac Jones, who, without me feeling a loss of control, guided me through the structural edits and honed my novel into the finished article. Isaac you showed tremendous tact and insight throughout the process, I'm sure you have a successful career as an editor ahead of you.

I would also like to credit Sienna Rose of "White Rose Publishing" who produced my cover design and formatted the text. She is a consummate professional and went above and beyond to bring my vision to fruition.

Finally thank you to my wife Sally who listened patiently as I read her each new installment. She has always encouraged my creativity and never complained at how much time I spent closeted in my study writing.

Prologue

Myrleduin knelt in the centre of the great hall. Although his eyes were closed, he knew everyone was scrutinizing his slightest gesture. He tried to block them out and concentrate on the singing.

The Men of the Knowledge had gathered to witness his initiation. With the exception of a handful of Druids who were attending to duties on the mainland, the whole community was packed into the building. The power in their massed voices was visceral and their chanting rumbled like a gathering storm.

Knowing it might be the last time he would worship in their fellowship, Myrleduin drank in the experience. He had prepared for this day for many years but, now it had arrived, he wasn't sure. He was under no illusion that the tincture of henbane and willow bark would control the pain, but he wasn't afraid, it was just that he didn't feel worthy. What if the Goddess rejected him and his sacrifice was in vain?

The opening ceremony was drawing to a close and this was the final psalm. He'd chosen it himself. The brother who sang it had a beautiful voice, but it was the words that spoke to him. The song was a lament. It told how the Ancient Ones had left their mountain home, taking their ancestors with them, and of how the Gods wept as they wandered through the abandoned pastures. The poetry was exquisite. As the final notes drifted up into the thatch he brushed away a tear.

The Master reached down and placed his hand on his acolyte's shoulder. Myrleduin looked up. The High Priest was old and his skin was mottled with age, but his steel grey eyes were clear and bright. "Are you ready?" he asked.

Myrleduin held the Master's gaze for a moment then nodded.

One of the brothers stepped forward and handed a knife to the Master. The curved blade was small but razor sharp. The tension in the hall was palpable.

Myrleduin swallowed. He couldn't take his eyes off the knife, it seemed to have a life of its own.

Another brother placed a bowl on the earth floor between the Master and Myrleduin. When he saw the Chalice, Myrleduin felt his guts churn. The Cup of the Goddess was a thing of beauty, but tonight, knowing what was about to come, it was a thing of menace. The figures dancing around its body seemed to mock him. *Are you sure?* They seemed to say.

"Hold him," ordered the Master.

The brother who had brought the knife moved to grasp Myrleduin's hand, but Myrleduin shrugged him off. "I chose this path," he said.

The Master nodded. "Nothing worthwhile comes without a price."

"Do it," said Myrleduin, and bowed his freshly shaved head. He flinched as the Master made the first incision.

Myrleduin could feel the sting of the blade as it crawled across his scalp. He blinked as blood pooled in his eye. Gripped by a morbid fascination, he watched the blood drip into the chalice. *I must keep still,* he told himself.

As the Master worked, carving the marks of a Watcher into his skin, one of the brothers dabbed the wounds with a cloth dipped in salt water. When the Master had finished working on his scalp, Myrleduin lifted his head to allow him to operate on his face. At some point the chanting started up again. The sound gave him the strength to endure.

When the design was complete, the Master laid aside the knife and a brother came forward with a bowl containing ink. As the black sticky paste was rubbed into the wounds, it was as much as Myrleduin could do not to cry out. His face and scalp were on fire. He tried to remain still, but the pain was too much and his head began to spin.

"Help him up," snapped the Master. "It is time to finish this."

As his mentor reached between his legs with the knife, Myrleduin fainted.

When he regained consciousness, he found himself standing, supported on either side by two burly brothers. All around the hall, the Men of the Knowledge were stamping their approval. Myrleduin raised his head, his face streaked red and black. His mouth twitched in a mirthless smile. He had triumphed.

The Master allowed the cheering to continue a while, then he raised his hand and the hall fell silent for his address.

"My brothers," he began "Many of us have gazed into the Chalice but few of us have been blessed with the gift to see within its waters. Myrleduin is one of those so blessed. Myrleduin has completed his training and put himself forward for the office of

Master of the Cup. Tonight, in accordance with our customs, his body has been cut and marked as a Watcher. The Chalice will now pass into his care."

The Master turned to look at his former pupil and smiled. Myrleduin detected a new respect in his demeanour. "May our new Watcher be our eyes and ears in the Otherworld and may the Goddess guide and protect him." The Master turned to face his congregation and raised his arms. "Now let us sing our thanks to the Father and Mother."

As the brothers chanted, Myrleduin stared at the Chalice. Even now, shivering with shock and sweating with pain, the urge to fill the bowl with consecrated water and stare into its depths was hard to resist. The Master had cautioned him about these cravings during his training and stressed the need for self-discipline; Watchers who spent too much time gazing into the water risked their sanity. He would allow his wounds to heal and gather his strength but then... who knew where the Chalice might take him?

Chapter 1

"Arrgh!" James clutched his buttock. "I've got cramp."

Ed, his eighteen-year-old brother, six foot three inches of ill humour and hard muscle, dug him in the ribs. "For fuck's sake stop wriggling, James!" The two oversized brothers had been squashed in the back of the car for six hours and tempers were beginning to fray.

James elbowed his elder sibling in retaliation, then arched his body to ease the discomfort in his cramping muscles. "My bum's in agony," he moaned.

"Why can't you two act your age?" snapped their father. "You're not kids anymore!"

James' mother, Anne, glanced at her tired and irritable husband. "Pull over, Richard, and let them stretch their legs."

James fought his way out of the car crammed with the paraphernalia needed for a four-week summer holiday in Wales. He lurched stiff legged towards a stand of trees behind the lay-by. It had been an awful journey; Mum wouldn't stop quizzing him about his exams or banging on about using his inhaler. It was doing his head in. Even Dad was getting in on the act.

James found a tree out of sight of the road and relieved himself against its trunk. As he was zipping up, a pinecone whistled past his ear.

"You OK?" Ed asked.

James grimaced, "What do you think?"

"Mum can't help it, James. She worries about you."

"I'm sixteen for Christ's sake! It's all right for you; you're off to uni. I've got two more years of this."

Ed gave his brother a hard look. "She just finds it hard to let go. She'll get over it. More to the point, what's bugging you? You've been a pain in the arse all day."

James pulled out his phone and showed Ed the text he'd received from the Rugby Academy the night before.

Ed frowned. "You can't blame them. You've spent more time on the touchline than on the pitch."

"I know, but it's all I've got. I'm crap at exams. Rugby is the one thing I'm really good at."

"But it's not a total rejection. They've invited you for more tests so they must think something of you."

"But we all know what the tests will say, Ed. I've got bloody Asthma."

Ed placed a reassuring hand on his brother's shoulder. "It is what it is mate. Just give it your best shot, take your inhaler like Mum says, and hope for the best."

James nodded glumly.

"Look on the bright side," grinned Ed. "We'll be dropping you off in an hour. You'll be having a great time kayaking and potholing, and I'll be stuck in St Dog's with Mum's nagging."

By the time the boys got back in the car, tensions had diffused, and the family sat in silence as they wound their way through the Welsh countryside.

James gazed out of the window. Ed was right, it wasn't a definite no from the Academy, he'd have to chill out and wait for the tests. He took a deep breath. Just being in Wales among the quiet wooded valleys and small steep-sided grass fields helped. It couldn't be more different from the frenetic roads and flat landscape where he now lived.

He thought of his Welsh grandma and the holidays he'd spent in her cottage in West Wales. She'd died last year, and it still hurt every time he thought about her

Mamgu had been a great storyteller, and one of his fondest childhood memories was listening to her read Welsh myths and legends at bedtime. He still had the illustrated book of stories of the Mabinogi she'd given him one Christmas. He'd loved that book. He must have read it a hundred times, enchanted by extraordinary stories of giants who made themselves into bridges, magical people who could turn into animals, and a wizard who made a woman from flowers. Looking out at the wooded valleys, James was a child again, transported to a world where druids and other strange characters peered out at him from the trees.

He must have dozed off at some point. He was woken by the sound of rubber windscreen wipers squeaking as they smeared splattered insects and Welsh rain across the toughened glass.

He sat up and looked out of the window. Bugger! He needed the weather to be nice; nearly all the activities planned for the week were outdoors. He listened to the rain drumming on the windscreen. It was hard not to be depressed; this summer had been the wettest on record and the forecast was for more rain to come.

"It won't last long," his mum promised brightly. James looked despairingly at her and sank into his seat.

Fifteen minutes later, the car turned off the Fishguard road and started the descent to Abereiddy.

It was still tipping it down. James peered through the misted passenger window as a clutch of cottages came into view, huddled behind a stony beach. At the far side of the cove, the carcasses of other buildings poked out of the scrubby vegetation. The tumbledown walls which were all that remained of a once thriving slate mining industry gave the place the appearance of a ghost town.

"This must be it," said James' dad, and took a left through a rusting iron gate onto a rutted track.

Myrtle House, the down-at-heel base of Abereiddy Adventure Holidays, was almost unrecognizable from the images on their website. The dilapidated Victorian farmhouse occupying an area of flat marshy ground behind the breakwater looked far less grand in real life, and the photographs hadn't included the twisted heaps of redundant agricultural machinery stacked against the outbuildings.

"What a dump!" remarked Ed, but James wasn't interested in his brother's opinion; he'd seen the Morris' car parked on the far side of the redundant cow yard.

"Put your coat on!" shouted James' mum as he slammed the car door and sprinted for the shelter of the front porch.

As James' hand closed around the brass doorknob, the door flew open and he stumbled into the bosom of a girl around his own age. Flustered, he pushed her away. "Where's Tom?" he demanded.

The girl ignored James' abrupt manner and pointed upstairs, "Getting changed. He'll be down in a minute."

Delyth stared after James as he ran up the stairs. She had known James Cordle all her life. Their families were close friends, and until four years ago they had lived in the same village in Mid Wales. As children, she and her twin brother, Tom, had played with James, and he'd become a second brother, but when the Cordles moved to Suffolk and Tom and James started boarding in the Cotswolds, they'd grown apart. Now whenever the three of them were together she found they had little in common. All the boys seemed to be interested in was rugby, computer games and field sports. Recently, after showing Emma photos of dead animals the boys had posted on social media, she'd decided to take her friend's advice and distance herself from James. She'd even left their WhatsApp group.

"Delyth?" The rest of the Cordle family had crowded into the narrow hall and Delyth turned to find Anne staring at her. "My goodness, you've grown up so much since I last saw you. You look lovely."

As Anne hugged her, Delyth blushed. Her heart was racing from the thrill of having James fall into her arms. Evidently her feelings for him couldn't be ignored. "Thanks," she replied, trying to recover her equilibrium.

Delyth and Anne pulled apart as Tom appeared at the top of the stairs. He was an energetic looking boy with dark, wavy hair. "Hi Auntie Anne!" he shouted. Unlike Delyth, whose Welsh accent had been teased out of her at school, Tom retained a pronounced Welsh lilt. "Rick told me to tell you he's walked up the hill with his mobile to see where you'd got to. He said he'd be back in a minute." He ducked back out of view without waiting for a reply.

Upstairs, James started unpacking. "I saw your text," said Tom as he came back into the room. "You didn't get a place then. I'm sorry."

James grimaced. "Thanks, but I don't want to talk about it." He banged his luggage on the floor to emphasize that the Elite Rugby Academy was off limits for further discussion.

Tom sat on his bed while James disembowelled his overstuffed and battered suitcase on the floor and strewed the contents around the room. Even though they'd not seen each other since the end of term, the boys barely spoke, their conversation limited to a few gruff comments on the fishing gear Tom had purchased and whether James had packed the beer he'd promised to purloin from Ed. People who didn't know them might have formed the opinion that they weren't on good terms, but that couldn't be further from the truth. James and Tom got on like a house on fire, they just didn't talk much. They didn't need to; they knew each other so well they could almost read the other's thoughts.

Having inherited his looks from his Welsh ancestry, Tom was the polar opposite of James physically. Short for his age with a wiry physique, he lacked James's size and strength, but made up for it in speed and agility. The two boys were also opposites in character and disposition; Tom's quick wit and enthusiasm being complemented by James' pragmatic approach to life and dogged determination. Together they made a formidable team.

"I'd better say goodbye to Mum and Dad," said James. He tossed an armful of socks and pants into a drawer and slammed it shut. "You coming?"

"Yeah," said Tom. "I'll introduce you to Rick."

Chapter 2

By the time Tom and James got downstairs, introductions were already underway, and Anne and Richard Cordle were making it abundantly clear they weren't impressed with the tall, bearded individual standing before them.

"We can't get a signal down here," Rick explained, waving his mobile, "so we walk to the top of the valley to pick up messages. We can get 4G up at the crossroads but nothing down here."

"What's wrong with FaceTime or WhatsApp?" asked Richard. "I assume you have broadband here."

Rick looked sheepish "The service was terminated last week," he confessed. "There was a misunderstanding about the bill."

Anne had heard enough, "What happens if anything goes wrong? You can't be cut off from the outside world when you're in charge of other people's children."

"It'll be okay Mum," James cut in, "Auntie Mags will be here, and it's not as if we're kids anymore. Anyway, this is supposed to be an adventure holiday!"

"You were saying only yesterday that the boys were spending too much time on the phone," said Richard, "and I agree. It won't do James any harm to do without a phone for a few days."

Anne looked appraisingly at Rick McFarlane, the proprietor of Abereiddy Bay Adventure Holidays. His face had featured on Mags' Facebook account for a while now, but it was the first time she'd seen him in the flesh, so to speak. If you ignored the beard and the scruffy clothes, he was good-looking enough, sexy even. She could see why Mags found him attractive, but she didn't trust him. He seemed the reckless type. On the other hand, Rick had been an officer in the army and Mags insisted he ran the activities safely. James wouldn't starve either. Her sister might be a rotten judge of men, but she was an excellent cook.

"Okay," she said, still harbouring misgivings. "We'd better be on our way or it'll be dark before we get to St Dogmaels."

"Are you sure you wouldn't like a cup of tea?" asked Rick, "Mags will be back in half an hour. She'll be disappointed to miss you."

Anne pursed her lips and glanced at her husband. "No," she said shaking her head. "We're late already. The M25 was an absolute nightmare, and we'll have to air the sheets when we get in. We'll be down for four weeks. Mags and I can meet for a coffee in Newport. Tell her I'll message her, she'll understand."

Rick shrugged his shoulders.

Anne gave Rick a final searching look then turned her attention to her son. "Are you sure you haven't forgotten anything, James?" she said, holding out a preventer inhaler.

"Come on, Mum!" Ed had a girl and a pint waiting for him in Cardigan and didn't intend to be late. "James is a big boy; he can look after himself."

James knew exactly what and with whom Ed intended to be up to that evening. He grinned, grateful for his brother's intervention.

Anne handed James the inhaler and raised her eyebrows in defeat.

James was sufficiently relieved to allow his mother the rare opportunity to kiss him in public. He knew she could be as awkward and stubborn as him, and it wouldn't have surprised him if she'd kicked up even more of a fuss.

His dad winked at James as he disappeared out of the door and escorted his wife out to the car.

As the Cordles' car disappeared up the drive, the boys went back upstairs to finish unpacking.

Rick retreated to the refuge of the kitchen. When he walked through the door, Delyth had the kettle on.

"I take mine with milk and no sugar," he grinned and plonked himself down on a battered old settee next to the Rayburn.

Delyth scowled, irritated at being treated like a servant. Rick didn't notice.

She pursed her lips and reached for an extra mug from the dresser.

The handsome owner of Myrtle house smiled benevolently at his new slave. He didn't regard himself as a misogynist, but he'd been brought up by two older sisters and an overly maternal mother who'd overindulged him. So he'd grown up with an over-inflated ego, out of step with most men his age, and accustomed to being waited on by women. The continuance of this entitled demeanour was facilitated by a boyish charm that he'd deployed to devastating effect on a series of doting girlfriends; the latest and he hoped the last of which was Mags.

Rick stretched out his feet and watched Delyth make the tea. He found himself thinking about Mags.

She'd been good for him. They'd only been together a year, but she'd brought order to his life. Without Mags sorting out the day-to-day admin, the holiday centre at Myrtle House would be a shambles. It wasn't as though he didn't have experience. Ten years in the Paras more than qualified him for leading the adventure activities, but an aversion to paperwork and an offhand manner with customers let him down. Forgetting to set up the direct debit for the Internet package was just typical. In his eyes he'd never had any problems with the kids though. Normally by the end of the first day all the boys thought he was the coolest thing since ice cream and half the girls had a crush on him. By the time Mags arrived, Delyth had put a mug of tea on the table and was foraging for biscuits.

"Don't spoil him," said Mags, "he won't eat his tea." Delyth moved to put the lid back on the tin, but Rick made a grab and came out with a chocolate hobnob.

"Don't listen to her," he grinned, "I need the energy and..."

"No ands!" said Mags firmly. "Out of my kitchen and let me get on." She glanced out of the window. "The rain's stopped and the meal won't be ready for at least an hour. Why don't you take Delyth and the boys to the beach while I finish off here?"

Ten minutes later, Delyth, Rick and the boys were walking towards the beach carrying costumes and snorkelling equipment. After the rain, the evening air was cold and still. Wisps of mist were beginning to settle over the marshy ground, and in the distance Delyth could hear the soft hush of waves breaking on the beach.

The moist conditions had encouraged some of the less attractive wildlife in the area to make an appearance. Slithering on the grass on either side of the track, dozens of enormous slugs had emerged from hiding to graze on the damp vegetation.

To Delyth's dismay, the slimy brown molluscs hadn't escaped the attention of the boys, and Tom, aware his sister hated slugs, had balanced a particularly large specimen on the end of his flipper.

"Catch Delly!"

Delyth squealed.

"Cut it out!" snapped Rick.

"Sorry," said Tom. He let the slug roll off the fin of his flipper and squashed it under his flip-flop.

Delyth looked away, her brother's casual killing of the defenceless creature disgusted her. She was reminded of the ruthless efficiency with which Tom and James dispatched rabbits when she stupidly agreed to go ferreting with them. For days afterwards, shocked that two people she loved could enjoy something so horrible, she could hardly speak to them. When she'd told Emma she said James and her brother were sadists and should be prosecuted. But her dad, a Welsh hill farmer, had laughed. "You've been watching too much Walt Disney!" he'd said.

Later Tom tried to explain. "The rabbits were eating the farmers' crops, and what's the difference between killing a wasp and killing a rabbit? It's not like we're killing people."

She could never imagine killing anything, but her mum's rabbit pie was delicious. Not that she'd ever admit that to Emma, she'd be disgusted. Emma was a vegan. *Thank goodness she's coming*, Delyth thought, *I don't want to be here on my own with the boys. When they're together they pick on me.*

"Come on, Delyth!" shouted Tom. "Last one in is a chicken!" The stillness of the tiny bay rang to the shrieking laughter of the three friends as they sprinted into the sea.

Rick sat down on the shingle, content to watch the youngsters have fun and absorb the magic of the place.

After a few minutes he pulled off his socks and shoes and wriggled his toes, enjoying the sensation of the cold pebbles on the soles of his feet. He'd be thirty-five this year and had been coming here since he was a child, but he never seemed to get tired of the place.

He guessed part of the attraction was his childhood memories in this bay. The family holidays in their old caravan parked in the field behind Myrtle House. Collecting driftwood with his sisters. His mother cooking sausages on the beach. The other attraction was more difficult to explain; he felt he belonged in this wild place that was constantly changing with the moods of the sea and sky, and yet seemed timeless – unchanged for thousands of years. Buying Myrtle House after he'd left the army and starting up the holiday business was the best thing he had ever done.

Hell, he thought. *I'm broke, and we've only got four kids booked this week, but what a fantastic way to earn a living! Life is good.*

Chapter 3

James groaned. He often found it difficult to wake up, but this morning he may as well have had his head nailed to the pillow. The previous evening, he and Tom had drunk the cans of lager he'd secreted in his suitcase and fiddled with Tom's fishing gear for hours, so it was well after midnight when they turned off the lights. But it wasn't the booze or the late night that was the problem.

Tom had fallen asleep immediately, James remembered, but he had lain in the dark for what seemed like eternity, tortured by the snores from Tom's end of the room. Then, when he finally drifted off, he'd had the most terrible nightmare. He closed his eyes and tried to piece together what he'd dreamt. As the images coalesced into a coherent picture, he gasped out loud and sat bolt upright in bed.

"What the fuck's going on?" demanded Tom, wide-awake.

"Sorry," said James trying to compose himself, his heart pounding. "I had a bad dream."

"Oh for God's sake," sighed Tom and pulled the sheet over his head.

James closed his eyes, hoping to doze off, but it was not to be. Within seconds of his head settling into his pillow, the door burst open, revealing a smiling and annoyingly lively Rick.

"Out of bed, lads," he bellowed. "Breakfast awaits!"

"Oh my God," muttered Tom. "He must be joking."

By the time the boys stumbled into the kitchen, their breakfast was congealing.

"Don't you dare!" said Mags, noticing Tom's expression as he prodded his fried egg. "If you were down on time it would have been perfect."

Delyth, who was buttering her fourth piece of toast, nodded. There was no way she'd have been late for a cooked breakfast.

James sat down, poured a dollop of tomato ketchup over his sausage and egg, lowered his head and shovelled the food into his mouth as fast as he could. Mags stared, torn between horror at James' disgusting table manners and delight at how much he was enjoying her cooking.

When even James decided he couldn't accommodate another round of marmalade on toast, Rick banged the table with a teaspoon and stood up.

"You were all tired last night, so I thought we'd leave it until this morning to welcome you and establish a few ground rules for your stay." He paused to make sure everyone was paying attention. "First off, Myrtle House is Mags' and my home, and while you're here we want you to treat it as your home too. But remember, Myrtle House is a home, not a hotel, so, as I'm sure you already know, everyone is expected to muck in and help with the chores."

Rick grinned. "We expect you to keep your rooms tidy, make your own beds, and do your share of the washing and clearing up after mealtimes." He ignored the groans. "I've pinned a rota for the washing up on the noticeboard in the hall. Unfortunately, because there are only four of you this week, you'll be doing the washing up either at breakfast or dinner every day. You'll be given a packed lunch as we will be out during the day. Failure to do your chores will mean you'll not take part in some of the activities. Tom and James will be washing and clearing up after breakfast this morning. Any questions?"

Rick sat down but held eye contact with James. Rick gave this little speech for every group of kids and each time he did it he made a point of picking out the leader and asserting his authority. It was something he learned in the army. He didn't do it for fun, some of the stuff they did could be dangerous if the kids ignored his instructions.

Rick held his stare until James dropped his eyes. "OK then, lads, I suggest you get cracking, and when you're finished, come through to the lounge. We'll go through the week's activities and discuss what we'll be doing today."

"Just one question, Mr McFarlane," said Delyth, holding up her phone. "I've tried messaging Emma but there's no reply. Do you know when she's getting here?"

"Her dad asked us to pack her lunch, so I assume she'll be out in the kayaks with us this morning. And," he smiled again, "I'd prefer you called me Rick."

When the two boys were alone in the kitchen, they surveyed the pile of dirty plates and cooking utensils gloomily. "Why don't they get a dishwasher?" moaned Tom.

James eyed the greasy pans. "Shotgun I do the wiping," he said quickly. The ensuing struggle, standard procedure between them for deciding who was washing or wiping up, involved a tea towel fight. The fight, as usual, ended in Tom agreeing to wash.

"I've seen a few posts on Instagram but what's she really like?" asked James once the hilarity had subsided and they began to get on with the clearing.

"A spoilt bitch," replied Tom, knowing that James could only mean Emma. "She thinks because her dad's an MP she can order everyone about."

"If she thinks she can play Miss Bossy Boots with us she can think again," said James truculently. "Her hotshot daddy won't be around this week, so she'll have to muck in with the rest of us."

Tom smiled; there'd be fireworks when Emma and James finally met. Emma had stayed with his family last summer and by the end of the second day he'd almost wished he were back at school. Tom didn't like to admit it, but it wasn't that Emma had behaved particularly badly that upset him, it was because she'd bruised his ego.

He and Emma were the same age, but last year, having gone through puberty early, she'd been taller and stronger, so Tom, a late developer, had suffered a series of humiliating defeats as Emma had outswum, outran and outplayed him all week.

As the boys packed away the last of the dishes, a green Jaguar swept into the old cow yard.

Delyth rushed across the hallway and pulled open the front door as the car came to a halt.

An overweight man in a tweed sports jacket heaved himself out of the cream leather driver's seat. "What a hell of a place!" he complained, examining his surroundings with distaste. "No wonder the satnav couldn't find it, we're in the middle of bloody nowhere."

"Don't make a fuss, Daddy," said the tall, blonde girl who stepped out of the car after him, deftly keeping her platform heels out of the muddy puddle next to the passenger door. "They said this was going to be an adventure holiday, so you can't expect the Hilton."

"Emma!" squealed Delyth excitedly, running over to her friend.

"Hi, Delyth," replied Emma.

Through the kitchen window, the two boys watched the girls hug, Tom with studied disdain, James with undisguised interest.

The difference between the girls was striking. Emma was tall and athletic, her figure precociously sexy for a girl of fifteen. Delyth, in contrast, was short and chubby. The difference in their physiques was accentuated by their clothing.

Delyth invariably selected clothes for their practicality and ability to disguise her excess weight, which on this occasion featured a sloppily hand-knitted cream sweater, old jeans, and cheap trainers. Her thick black hair was pulled back and secured in a ponytail with a cheap hair band.

There was nothing about Emma's clothing that could be considered practical for an adventure holiday. Not unless it was a romantic adventure. She had arrived in a very bright, very tight, very pink T-shirt, over which she wore a tastelessly large gold cross on a chain that dangled between a pair of large breasts. Her tailored flared trousers were kept clear of the mud by a pair of gravity defying platform shoes, and her long blonde hair looked like she'd just walked out of the hairdresser. Everything about her screamed expensive.

James couldn't take his eyes off the new arrival. "You didn't tell me she was *that* hot," he told Tom, gawping through the window.

"Wait 'til you meet her," replied Tom. "You'll hate her."

James stared out of the window and made no further comment.

The girls made their way into the house, leaving Emma's father struggling with the suitcases.

Rick intercepted them in the hall. "Hi! You must be Emma," he said holding out his hand. Emma shook his hand politely,

"Delighted to meet you," she said in a studied upper-class accent. "I'm so sorry we're late," she added levelling a cool gaze at Rick.

REFLECTIONS IN TIME

Blimey, thought Rick, *here's trouble.* "We're planning a kayak trip this morning," he said. "Why don't you unpack, and we'll meet in the lounge in thirty minutes. Delyth, do you mind showing Emma up to your room?"

The two girls climbed up the stairs, leaving Emma's father to huff and puff his way after them with the suitcases. Forty-five minutes later, Rick and the boys went outside to fetch the kayaking gear. They left the Right Honourable Benjamin Kingsley-Smith perched on an ancient Chesterfield sofa, waiting for his daughter.

The kayaks were kept with the other equipment in a large barn on the far side of the yard. Rows of rusting steel cubicles, each one with its own drinking trough and wooden feeder, betrayed that the building once housed the Myrtle herd of Friesian Holstein dairy cows. Rick had removed one of the rows of cubicles and concreted over the floor to create a large open area where the adventure holiday equipment was laid out in regimented lines.

The barn was an Aladdin's cave; the sheer variety of things stored there was bewildering. The boys pushed past four Mirror dinghies, their masts and red sails neatly stowed, and made their way towards the kayaks hung on a rack which Rick had welded the previous winter.

"Leave the big sea kayaks," said Rick. "We'll take the Daggers today. Pick out five and carry them out to the yard. I'll fetch the splash covers and paddles. When we've got everything outside, we'll fit you out with wet suits."

The girls arrived while the boys were trying on wetsuits. Emma giggled as James and Tom wrestled with the rubbery neoprene and stiff zips. The only suit that James could get over his broad shoulders was too tight around the crotch. To James' chagrin, it was purple with pink stripes.

"Very fetching, darling," smirked Emma. Delyth laughed out loud and even Tom smiled. James' coloured with embarrassment and he glared at Tom, seething at his lack of solidarity.

"They don't have anything that fits," he complained.

"Sorry, I couldn't resist teasing," said Emma, holding out a perfectly manicured hand. "You must be James. Delyth has told me *everything* about you. My name's Emma."

"Hi," said James, then without further comment he picked up his head protector and life jacket and stalked out. Tom shrugged his shoulders and followed.

"He's not very sociable," said Emma, staring at James' back as he disappeared out of the door. "Have I upset him?"

"No, he's just shy. He never says much, at least not when I'm around," answered Delyth, sorting through the rack for a suit big enough to fit round her thighs. Like James, she was out of luck. The only one that fit was tatty and the zip was corroded.

"This will have to do," she groaned.

But Emma was already kitted up and was exploring the other equipment in the barn. "Look," she exclaimed picking up a respirator, "they've got proper diving stuff!"

They were still poking through all the gear when Rick came in for dry bags to store the food and spare clothes. "Now you can see where I spend my money," he said. "We cater for most water and climbing sports as well as a few other amusements.

He took out a key and unlocked a steel cabinet revealing a rack of paintball guns and box after box of plastic jars full of luminous orange paintballs. "This is what we're playing with tonight," he smiled. "Now if you're ready, I don't know about you, but I fancy a paddle."

Chapter 4

Carrying the Kayaks to the beach was harder than Delyth had anticipated. It was just before eleven; the sun was beating down, and the black rubber of her wetsuit was absorbing its energy like a solar panel. She felt her skin prickle with sweat. She'd always regarded herself as a sporty type, but recently the weight had crept on.

Now, having carried her kayak fifty metres, she realized she was badly out of condition. By the time she reached the beach, her face was bathed in sweat and the others were already at the shoreline. She dropped the kayak and sank onto the pebbles. Suddenly, she heard feet pounding across the shingle.

"Hi," said James. "I thought you needed some help." Delyth felt a powerful hand grip her arm and heave her to her feet.

"Amazing," she murmured, as James gripped the kayak by the rim of the cockpit and carried it down the beach with nonchalant ease. She stared at James for a few moments, then followed him to the shore.

Rick had lined up the kayaks on the shingle just out of reach of the sea. He waited for Delyth to join them and motioned everyone to sit down. "You've told me you've all handled a kayak before, but we have to go through the drills." He tapped his head. "First of all, make sure the chin strap on your safety helmet is properly secured. You can't swim or paddle if you knock yourself unconscious. And it might seem obvious, but I'll say it again: no matter how good a swimmer you think you are or how hot it gets, do not remove your life jacket until we're back on shore."

Emma rolled her eyes and made a face. Rick caught her out of the corner of his eye and stopped talking. He gave her a hard stare. Emma looked down sulkily.

"If it's okay with you, Emma, I'll carry on," he said, still staring at her. Order in the ranks restored, Rick put his kayak in the shallows and demonstrated how to get in by using the shaft of the paddle to steady the craft. Then he got them to step into their splash covers and climb in the cockpit. With a few wobbles, they all managed to clip on their splash covers and paddle out to the deeper water. Rick herded his little flock like a mother duck, his paddles efficiently driving through the clear green water. Rick kept them together in a quiet corner of the bay while he demonstrated, and they practiced a series of safety drills and manoeuvres.

Very quickly, James realised Emma was more skilful than he was, and although his strong shoulders powered him through the water, her better technique allowed her to keep up, her kayak gliding effortlessly at his side.

The final exercise was an Eskimo roll. James watched closely as Rick demonstrated the move; he'd never tried the manoeuvre before and was determined to get it right. Rick made it look easy. James ran through the technique in his mind. Stretch forward, hold the paddle out straight, lean over to the right, dip down under the water, drag the paddle towards you and flip back up.

"Who's going to go first?" grinned Rick.

Before James could volunteer, Emma took two quick strokes forward then neatly rolled the kayak over. She was under for a second or two then bobbed back to the surface, grinning triumphantly.

"She's done this before," muttered James, who was plucking up courage to try it himself.

Tom looked on, his eyes twinkling. He'd been humiliated by Emma last year; it appeared James was going to get the same treatment.

James took a couple of strokes, leant forward as he'd been taught, twisted over and flipped upside down.

The shock of the freezing water hitting his face momentarily disorientated him. He gripped the paddle and dragged it through the water, twisting his body in an attempt to complete the three-hundred-and-sixty-degree turn. He got his left shoulder and head out of the water but, hard as he tried, he couldn't get upright and slipped back under. James gritted his teeth and tried a second time; once again he failed to complete the turn and remained upside down, his paddle flailing. He'd been underwater for forty seconds and his body was screaming out for oxygen.

Then James felt his asthma take hold and he let go of his paddle.

Despite the danger James remembered the safety drill, grabbed the release tab on the splash cover and pulled. But instead of coming away from the rim of the cockpit, the cover snagged. He pulled harder, but it wouldn't budge. With his chest bursting, James felt the strength seeping out of his arms.

There was a bang as Rick's craft knocked against James'. The sound, which reverberated under the water, meant help was at hand and helped James fight down the urge to panic. He pulled again, this time the cover snapped free, and he rolled forward and shot to the surface. He felt somebody grasp his life jacket as he tried to fill his lungs with air. Desperate for oxygen as he was, the iron grip of asthma refused to allow him the air his lungs craved. He willed himself to relax trying to steady his racing heartbeat. At last, his airway opened, and the first draught of air flooded his lungs. He gasped again; the air wheezed as it made its way down his windpipe.

"Where's his inhaler?" yelled Rick.

"It's in his kayak! In the dry bag!"

"Then get it," said Rick. "Link paddles with Emma, roll it over and pull the bag out!"

Tom and Emma went through the drill they'd practiced a few minutes earlier. Despite the tension, they worked well together, and within moments James' kayak was the right way up and wallowing in the calm water. Tom reached into the swamped craft and hauled the bag from behind the seat. He quickly located the inhaler and placed it in James' outstretched hand.

James depressed the canister on the inhaler with his forefinger and put the mouthpiece between his lips. He hesitated a moment, waiting for his next breath, then inhaled. He felt the ice-dry chemicals on the back of his throat and relaxed, allowing the drug to take effect. He laid back, supported in the water by his lifejacket and Rick, who was holding his collar. Gradually colour was restored to his face and his breathing returned to normal.

"You okay?" asked Rick.

James nodded weakly then cleared his throat and spat. The sputum left a green trail down the front of his dayglo orange lifejacket.

Delyth looked on, blinking back her tears. Seeing James suffer an asthma attack always upset her, but to see him trapped under the water and witness his distress had been awful.

James looked up and saw the pity in her face. He shrugged off Rick's supporting hand. Without any explanation, he abandoned his kayak and swam for the shore. Frustration at his asthma and anger at failing to complete the exercise consumed him, driving him the fifty metres to shallow water. Once ashore he marched up the beach, pulled off his life jacket and head protector, and flopped down on the shingle. He lay there inert for a several minutes, letting the warmth of the midday sun soak into him.

West Wales was dressed in its Sunday clothes. It was high tide; the sea was a Mediterranean shade of turquoise and sparkled in the sunshine. There were young families on the beach and the children playing in the shallows made the bay ring with squeals of delight. James, even in his foul mood, couldn't fail to appreciate the beauty. He sat up, unzipped his wetsuit top, and watched the other members of his party paddling towards the beach. *They've emptied the water out of the kayak*, he thought as he watched it bobbing along behind Rick on the end of a piece of rope. He made no effort to help as they pulled the kayaks up onto the beach.

Tom was the first to reach him and grimaced as he handed over the dry bag containing his lunch. "You dickhead," he said. "You almost drowned yourself."

"It wasn't my fault," replied James, opening up the bag and inspecting the contents. He selected a cheese and pickle roll. "The splash deck cord got stuck and I got asthma."

Rick and the girls joined them. Rick didn't look pleased.

"Why didn't you bale out sooner?" Rick demanded.

James, his mouth full of cheese and pickle, shrugged.

Rick sighed and sat down to eat his lunch. He could see the dynamics of this group developing and he didn't like it.

Chapter 5

Emma picked at her lunch in silence. Everyone else was chatting but she wasn't in the mood to join in. She glared at Delyth; she was fawning over James like a lovesick puppy. She felt sorry for James – it must be awful to have asthma – but the way he ignored her was getting under her skin.

She glanced at James stuffing a sandwich in his mouth and talking at the same time. She didn't think he was gay. She was puzzled. It wasn't just that he didn't fancy her. His studied indifference bordered on being downright rude. She bit into her chocolate muffin angrily.

She'd taken an unflattering photo of Delyth in her wetsuit and thought about sharing it on Instagram. She was sure her friends would like to see Delyth flopped out on the beach like a stranded seal!

Tom glanced at James. His friend had recovered from his asthma attack, but the incident had shocked him. He was also concerned about the girls. They'd been over the moon when they first saw each other this morning, but relations had become decidedly frosty. Emma was sulking and Delyth stared daggers at her whenever she glanced in James' direction. Tom sighed. It was going to be an interesting week.

After lunch, Rick addressed the group. "If you guys are sure you are up for it, we'll get the kayaks back in the water and make our way to the Blue Lagoon." Rick looked at James and Emma. "This isn't a race. I want everyone to stick together. We don't want a repeat of this morning's drama, so take your time and enjoy the scenery."

He'd hardly finished the sentence before the kayaks were clattering down the beach and hitting the water with a hollow thud.

Tom was the first into his kayak; it felt better to be doing something rather than dwelling on what had nearly happened to James. He pulled his splash cover over the cockpit and waited for Rick to give the signal to paddle into deeper water.

As they moved off, the spirits in the group lifted and everyone was chatting excitedly as they paddled towards the headland. As they rounded the head, however, the mood changed, becoming more reflective, and the conversation petered out as they began to appreciate the wild beauty around them. Soon the only sounds were the cries of the gulls and the rhythmic splashes of paddles dipping into the water.

Tom craned his neck to gaze at the cliffs towering over him. He'd regularly sailed this coast with his dad, so he'd seen these cliffs from the sea many times. They never ceased to fascinate him. They reminded him of a multilayered sponge cake. The upper cliff was topped with meadow grass icing sprinkled with hundreds of thousands of sea pinks and vivid blue harebells. Below the icing was a thin layer of chocolate soil and partially sorted alluvium, which sheared away to a massive sponge slab of grey vertical slate. Then, as the cliff plunged into the sea, the tide revealed a final layer of crusty yellow barnacles.

As Tom paddled under the shadow of the cliff the water took on a mysterious oily appearance. Suddenly his eyes were drawn to a dark object in the water; "Look!" he shouted, pointing towards a narrow inlet. "A seal!"

They all turned to where he was pointing.

A bull seal, anxious to see who dared enter his sea-weedy fiefdom, was swimming directly towards the Kayaks, snorting indignantly. He halted twenty metres or so in front of the interlopers and surveyed them with a pair of huge eyes. For a few magical moments the seal stared at them unblinking, then without warning it slipped lazily into the depths.

"It looked at me like my dad's sheepdog," observed Tom, struck by the intelligence in the seal's coal black eyes.

He and the others scanned the patch of water where the seal had disappeared, hoping for a second glimpse. Then, unexpectedly, just as they were giving up hope, it popped up a few feet from Emma's kayak.

Emma was so surprised she almost capsized.

The seal was unimpressed and watched her curiously.

Tom, keen for a better view, paddled closer. His kayak banged into Emma's.

Startled, the seal slid beneath the surface. This time it didn't reappear.

"You idiot," snapped Emma. "You frightened it!"

"I didn't mean to," retorted Tom defensively. "We're bound to see another one anyway."

They hung around the headland for a while, hoping another seal would turn up, but none did. Disappointed, they paddled on.

When they entered the entrance to the lagoon, Tom looked down. The water in the passage was crystal clear and the seabed was easily visible under his kayak. Beneath the boat, a forest of eelgrass waved gently in the current like strands of brown liquorice. Tom peered into the depths and was rewarded by a flash of silver. A bass, he thought.

Distracted by the wonders beneath the surface, he hadn't noticed the inlet had narrowed and a swell drove the prow of his boat against a jagged rock. He looked up, startled. Suddenly he was fending off the rocks with his paddle. Once inside the lagoon, however, the water was flat calm, and he paddled to the far end with ease. He beached his kayak next to the others on a rocky shelf.

"This is epic," said James, gazing around the vast amphitheatre where the lagoon lay. He wasn't given to superlatives, but he was seriously impressed.

"That's where they dived off in the YouTube video," said Tom, pointing.

They looked up at the massive cliff where the world diving competition had been held. It looked implausibly high.

"Shit," said James, "I think you're right."

Delyth was intrigued. "This lagoon wasn't made by the sea, was it?"

Rick smiled. "It was a slate quarry," he said, pointing to an obviously manmade stone wall which rose vertically out of the water at the other end of the lagoon. "But the slate was poor and expensive to extract so they flooded it. It's an amazing place to scuba dive; the water's twenty metres deep in places."

Emma wasn't interested; she'd spotted the jumping point at the top of the tower. "Bet you daren't go off the top, James!" she taunted.

James eyed the jump. It was at least fifteen metres high. "Is it deep enough?" he asked.

Rick eyed him seriously. "It's deep," he said, "but it's a hell of a drop."

James nodded. "Alright," he said, stepping carefully over the sharp slates towards the water, "let's see who's chicken!"

A few minutes later, James, Tom and Emma were clambering up the rocks at the base of the tower.

"You nutter," hissed Tom. "We'll break our necks!"

James didn't reply. Instead, he followed Emma's shapely, wet-suit-clad behind as she nimbly scrambled up the path to the top. The three would-be heroes stood on the grassy outcrop that led to the top jump and waved to Rick and Delyth, spectating from the beach.

James, who'd removed his ill-fitting wetsuit and was just wearing swimming trunks, peeped over the parapet. The water looked very far below; he was having second thoughts. He glanced at Emma.

Emma was grinning. "You're scared, aren't you?" she taunted. Without any hesitation, she ran shrieking into the void.

"Shit," said Tom as a loud splash told them Emma had hit the water, "I guess we've got to do it now!"

James crept gingerly towards the edge and looked down. Emma was treading water and looking up triumphantly. "Damn!" He curled his toes over the stone at the top of the wall and his heart began to race.

"Go on, chicken," shouted Emma. "Jump!"

James hesitated. Suddenly his legs felt like jelly. He teetered for a few seconds then made up his mind.

"Geronimo!" he yelled, and leapt off.

In mid-air, the sensation of exhilaration was incredible. Then *WHACK!* He hit the water arse first. The pain took a moment to kick in, but as he surfaced through a mist of bubbles, the backs of his legs felt like they'd been hit by a cricket bat.

"I bet that hurt," Emma smirked.

James forced himself to smile and swum over to Emma. "Not really," he said, wishing he'd kept his wetsuit on like Emma had, "We'd better hang around while Tom has a go."

Tom had other ideas; he'd seen how hard James had hit the water. He shook his head.

"No way!" he said, backing away from the edge. He slunk down the path to the lowest jump off point and plopped back into the water while Emma made clucking sounds.

James fumed; there was no need to humiliate his friend. Emma needed a lesson; he shoved her head under the water.

He was sure most boys his age would take a ducking as it was meant, a warning, but James got a lot more than he bargained for with Emma. She rose to the surface screeching, and lashed out. One of her manicured nails cut into the skin just below his left eye, drawing blood. "Fuck off," she yelled.

"She's gone mad!" James yelped.

For a moment the two of them glared at each other, treading water, then James turned and swam back to the beach, leaving her fuming in the icy water.

Delyth met him as he made his way up the stony beach. She held out his towel. She was white-faced. "Are you OK?" She couldn't tear her gaze away from the blood oozing from under his eye.

"Fine," replied James. "Just keep your crazy friend away from me." Then, wrapping the towel round his waist to conceal the bruises on the back of his legs, he dabbed his eye with a corner of his towel and sat down next to Rick.

"I shouldn't have ducked her," he admitted, "but I never thought she'd react like *that*."

Rick smiled dryly. "You've just learned a couple of important lessons: one, never jump off high places without a wetsuit, and two, women can be dangerous."

James grinned. "How did you know I hurt my backside?"

Rick grinned back. "I jumped off there in a pair of speedos when I was about your age and I couldn't sit down for a week! Now get yourself dressed before Catwoman over there decides she's cold and swims back."

Catwoman was freezing in spite of her wetsuit, and was regretting losing her temper. She knew she'd been an idiot and didn't want to face everyone, so she swam round and round the icy pool while she thought things through. Delyth would forgive her, of course – she always did – but the boys were a different matter.

She supposed she'd have to apologize to James, but it wouldn't do any good. He and Tom would be horrid to her the rest of the holiday. It was lucky she hadn't posted that photo on Instagram, she thought, she'd need Delyth on her side if she was going to survive the week. By the time she'd plucked up courage to swim to the beach, her fingers were numb.

Rick met her at the waterline. "I'm sorry," she said.

"You'd better save your apologies for James," he told her.

She looked towards the boys. James had an awful scratch on his face. She tried to catch his eye, but he ignored her, pretending to fiddle about with something in his kayak.

Emma shrugged and turned to Delyth for support "I suppose–"

She never finished the sentence; the look Delyth gave her stopped her in her tracks. Her usually placid friend's eyes blazed.

"You bitch!" Delyth stomped away to join the boys.

Emma suddenly felt very alone. She wished she hadn't come.

Chapter 6

By the time they got back to the beach, the day-trippers had left and a gang of seagulls had moved in to comb for titbits. They flapped off, screeching, as Rick and the youngsters dragged their kayaks up the sand.

The paddle back had been uneventful, but strained, and Emma had hung back, looking subdued. The atmosphere remained frosty while they stacked their kayaks on the racks in the old cowshed until James removed his wetsuit. Everyone dissolved into laughter.

"What's the matter?" demanded James, then the realisation dawned and his face went scarlet. "It shows does it?"

"Shows!" Tom laughed. "I thought you'd hit the water hard, but I didn't realise it was that hard. Your bum's as red as a beetroot."

James made a playful grab at Tom, but he darted through the door and ran across the yard, hooting.

One of the girls carried on sniggering. James wasn't amused.

"You've had your fun," he snapped, turning on Emma, then stopped in his tracks. It wasn't Emma laughing. The spitting cat that'd attacked him a few hours earlier was looking at him with sympathy.

"Does it hurt?" she asked.

The angry words froze on James' lips as he noticed how green Emma's eyes were.

Delyth stopped laughing. She'd seen the look that had passed between the two of them.

James broke the silence. "I'm starving," he stammered. "I expect Mags has got tea ready." He turned abruptly and marched out.

In Myrtle House, tea was indeed ready, if *tea* was an apt description for the mountain of food laid out on the kitchen table.

"Grub's up!" yelled Mags. A cloud of steam enveloped her as she drained potatoes through a colander.

The kitchen quickly filled with people, drawn by the tantalising aroma, and they jostled for space around the table.

James found himself next to Emma and spent the first half of the meal ignoring her. Only after he'd inhaled a plate of chicken casserole, mashed potatoes, and peas, did he acknowledge her presence.

Emma had only eaten a few mouthfuls of potato and nothing else. "Aren't you hungry?" he asked.

"I'm vegan," she explained. "Eating meat is against my principles. And I hate peas."

James, an avid country sports enthusiast, resisted the temptation to share his view of 'veggies' as he called them; he couldn't cope with another temper tantrum.

Emma pushed her plate away and looked around the kitchen. She was bored. Tom, Mags, Delyth and Rick were chatting amongst themselves, leaving her and James alone at the other end of the table.

She gave James a speculative glance. If you ignored his atrocious table manners, he was good looking – handsome even – but there was something about him that seemed to bring out the worst in her. She'd sat next to James at dinner tonight intending to apologize, but now the moment had come, she couldn't resist provoking him.

On a whim she leant forward and rubbed her knee against the inside of James' thigh. She almost laughed out loud as James' eyes widened in shock and his face went pink. She pressed her knee against him again just to let him know it hadn't been a mistake, then moved her leg away. James didn't say anything, but Emma knew he had enjoyed the contact despite his blushes.

Well at least that question is answered, she thought, watching James attack a bowl of apple crumble and custard, pretending nothing had happened. *He does fancy me, he's just shy.*

James couldn't wait for the meal to end, even though he'd have to face the washing up. He was totally confused. Was Emma coming on to him for real or was she just amusing herself? And how did he feel about that? He fancied her – who wouldn't? She looked stunning – but the girl was a brat.

James didn't have a clue when it came to girls, especially ones as self-assured as Emma, so when he and Tom were left alone in the kitchen to clean up, he told Tom what had happened at dinner and asked his opinion.

Tom was aghast. "Steer clear is my advice. She's as mad as a box of frogs."

"You have to admit she's hot."

"Yeah well so is that oven over there, but I wouldn't go sticking my hand in it."

James touched the scratch under his eye ruefully. "Point taken. I guess she's done enough harm already."

Rick, ducking his head into the kitchen, interrupted their conversation. "There's time for a quick game of paintball before dark. Are you interested?"

James had been itching to play paintball ever since he found out Mags' boyfriend had the equipment. Paintball had all the ingredients he liked; dressing up in combat gear, running around in woods, shooting guns that splatted paint; what could be better?

James grinned, girl troubles forgotten. "You bet!"

When he and Tom burst into the storeroom, Mags was handing out guns, masks, overalls and ammunition to the girls. The excitement in the converted cowshed was infectious.

"Wow!" said Tom when he received his weapon. "I didn't realize they were automatic!"

"Just don't be too gung-ho." Mags smiled, handing him a container of orange balls, "You get 500 shots free, then after that it's five pounds a bottle."

When they'd been kitted out, they trooped down to the ramshackle portacabin Rick had rigged up as a day centre for the paintball. Wearing camouflaged overalls and daft face masks, James thought everyone looked like extras from a *Star Wars* movie.

Rick and Mags were waiting for them in the portacabin; they were wearing bright yellow waistcoats.

Rick talked them through the safety aspects. "The guns are powered by compressed air and have an effective range of thirty metres," he explained. "At that distance the paintball will burst on impact but won't hurt if it hits your clothes. But at close range the balls sting and can leave a bruise even if they hit your overalls." He paused. "A sting or two is all part of the excitement. The important thing is to wear your mask, because if a ball hits you in the face, you could lose an eye."

James glanced at the others. Delyth was fidgeting nervously with her gun and he could see sweat beading under Tom's mask.

Rick continued: "For safety reasons, we have a 'two strikes and you're out' policy. Anyone seen shooting people at close range or not wearing their mask will be asked to leave the game and return to the safety zone. But anyone shooting people at close range or not wearing their mask for a second time won't take part in any further paintball activities during their stay at Myrtle House. Is that clear?"

Rick gave the thumbs up and everyone returned it except Tom, who couldn't see a thing because his mask had steamed up.

After signing a form that felt like a death sentence, they filed out of the safety zone into a muddy enclosure featuring a clumsily painted sign that proclaimed 'PRACTICE AREA.'

Rick lined them up in front of some targets nailed to posts. Most looked like bull's-eyes, others were soldiers with circles on their chests; all of them were smeared with orange goo. It looked like dayglo blood.

James thought the whole set up was crummy.

"You can load your weapons and remove the safety stoppers," Rick told them, "and fire when you're ready."

James methodically decanted his paintballs into the hopper of his gun, taking care not to break the balls as they entered the chamber. Then he removed the barrel stopper and waited. Tom and Emma were already peppering the targets with orange blobs, but he held his fire, watching their shots and gauging the elevation required to hit each target. He heard swearing and grinned.

Delyth had forgotten to take the stopper out of her barrel and jammed the gun with a sticky mess of paint.

When James decided he was ready, he shot with clinical efficiency and, after a couple of ranging shots, he was hitting the targets with deadly accuracy.

Rick watched James with interest. "You've done a lot of shooting, haven't you?"

James nodded. "Rabbits mainly. Don't tell Emma. It's my dirty secret."

Rick laughed. "Well stick that stopper back in. We're going to the safety zone while I tell you about the first game."

Sitting on logs inside the netted confines of the safety zone, Rick explained: "The first game is simple. I'm going into the woods to hide. When I've gone, Mags will give you a map to show where I am. You'll all be on the same team, and your task is to find and shoot me."

Tom groaned. He didn't fancy a shootout with an ex-paratrooper.

Rick smiled and carried on. "If you're hit, raise your hands above your head and return to the safety zone to wait ten minutes before returning to the game." He gestured towards Mags. "My good lady here will act as marshal." Rick stood up. "I guess I'll see you later." He beamed, then hurried out into the wood.

"We'll give him ten minutes," said Mags, handing James the map.

James spread the A4 photocopy on the ground and motioned for the others to gather round. Emma ignored him and sat down on her own, leaving the others to pore over the map.

"I've got an idea," James said. "According to the map, Rick will be hiding here." He pointed to a spot on the map. "Why don't you guys make a diversion by attacking Rick from the front here, while I sneak round the edge of the wood and shoot him in the back."

"Well there's a surprise," Emma said. "Fancy you wanting to be the hotshot."

Sarcasm always put James' hackles up. "Look," he said, "if you want to be the one to shoot Rick, that's cool with me. But cut it with the wisecracks. It's pissing me off."

There was an acrimonious silence as James and Emma eyed each other. Before Emma could reply, the ten minutes were up, and Mags gave a blast on her whistle. Emma rushed through the gap in the netting and dashed into the wood.

"Let her go," said Tom, pulling on his facemask. "She'll be back soon. Listen! She's making as much noise as a charging rhino. Rick will hear her a mile off."

James walked slowly out of the netted zone and looked around. He loved woods, and this one, with its twisted oak and ash sculpted by the winds from the sea, looked magical in the golden evening light. He knelt down and rubbed mud into his hands and neck, and the parts of his face not covered by his mask. He glanced at Tom; he was doing the same.

"What are you doing?" asked Delyth. She looked horrified.

"Camouflage," James told her. "Your face and hands are the first thing anyone sees. The mud takes the shine off your skin and makes you more difficult to spot."

Delyth looked at the peaty black muck the boys had smeared on their skin with distaste. "You must be joking."

James grinned; his teeth looked very white against his muddy face. "Don't worry, you're not expected to do it. Tom and I know we're mad. Are you ready?"

Delyth returned a wan smile. She looked very uncertain.

"We'll stay off the path," James told them, wading into the undergrowth at the side of the track, "and split up when we get nearer Rick."

Tom and James moved with quiet efficiency through the tangle of nettles and rosebay willowherb. Delyth stumbled behind, less interested in remaining silent than not getting covered in mud or stung.

Eighty metres into the wood, they heard the hollow popping sound of paintball shots being fired. James held up his hand. Up ahead they heard a high-pitched squeal followed by muted swearing.

"Emma's been hit," said Delyth, shocked.

"Serves her right," whispered James. He popped his head above a mossy rock. SPLAT! A paintball whizzed past his ear and hit the tree trunk a few centimetres to his left. "Bloody hell!" He dropped to the ground and wriggled behind a rotting log. "That was close. Where is he?"

"It wasn't a he," said Tom, "it was Emma. She took a pot shot at you. I told you she was a cow."

James watched Emma slink back to the netted area, her gun held over her head.

"Ignore her," Tom said. "Maybe kicking her heels in the safe zone for ten minutes will cool her down."

James glanced at Delyth. She'd scratched her ear on a bramble. "Are you alright?"

"I'm fine, don't worry about me."

James knew Delyth hated every minute of this, and he admired her for joining in. He'd have to remember to be nice to her when they got back to Myrtle House.

"James, look at those drums," whispered Tom.

James peered through the trees; a line of blue oil drums had been placed in front of a log pile. "You think that's where he is?"

"It's where the map said he'd be."

James nodded; he'd gotten his bearings and knew what they should do. "Tom, you creep up to those logs. And Delyth, can you get behind that tree over there and fire at those drums? I'll stay here and figure out where he is."

James watched Tom leopard crawl across the boggy ground towards the log pile. As the cold mud soaked into his overalls, Tom glanced back at James, his disgusted expression was a picture and James had to bite his sleeve to stop himself laughing out loud.

When they were in position, Tom and Delyth rained a hail of paintballs at the drums. There was a moment of silence then suddenly a series of well-placed shots had Tom pinned down behind his log pile. The shots were coming from the base of one of the oil drums. James spotted a flash of yellow. *The tape around the end of Rick's barrel,* thought James, and slithered forward, using a tree to keep him out of Rick's line of vision.

SPLAT! SPLAT! SPLAT! "Aaahhh!" Tom was hit.

James watched him stand up and hold his gun over his head. As Tom trudged past on his way to the sin bin, James had an idea. "Drop your gun," he whispered. "You can pick it up later."

Tom did as he was asked, and James sent a barrage of shots at the drums to attract Rick's attention. Soon shots were splattering orange paint at the base of the tree where James was hiding. James grinned as he propped up Tom's gun so the yellow tip of the barrel was visible. He crawled to a safe distance and doubled back around the edge of the wood to get behind Rick's position.

Rick was firing sporadically, and, although he was screened by the large log, James noted the ex-para had taken his bait and was shooting at the barrel of Tom's gun. James took a deep breath and slithered towards the log shielding him from Rick. He moved carefully, methodically removing twigs from his path that might snap and give him away.

Bang! One of Delyth's shots connected with the oil drum.

Nice one, Delyth. That'll keep him occupied.

Rick was just the other side of the logs. James peeped over the top his gun raised ready to fire. Rick was lying with his back exposed, his gun pointing at a yellow dot at the base of the tree where James had been lying five minutes earlier.

SPLAT! An orange blob appeared in the centre of Rick's back.

Rick and James span around in shock.

"Beat you to it, hotshot!" Emma said gleefully.

James was furious. "You're meant to stay in the safe area for ten minutes!"

"Sorry," said Emma, grinning from ear to ear, "I'm not good with rules. I thought you'd need help."

"I didn't need your help," James replied coldly. "You knew I was about to fire."

Emma smiled sweetly. "Sorry," she said, "I couldn't resist." She walked off.

"It's only a game," said Rick as he and James followed Emma back through the wood. "You'll get your chance to get even. The next game is all against all!"

James tried to heed Rick's advice, but when he got back to the safe area he was still seething.

Before he went in, Tom waylaid him. "It's time to teach that bitch a lesson," he whispered. "Delyth and I have agreed to work together, if you join us, it'll be three against one. We'll let Emma rush off ahead then we'll ambush her. What do you think?"

James thought this sounded like ganging up on her and hesitated. He didn't approve of bullying.

Tom was adamant, "She needs a lesson, James. She's really upset Delyth."

James pulled off his facemask and sighed. "I suppose you're right," he agreed reluctantly. "But no shooting at close range. I don't want her to get hurt."

As the boys entered the netted area, Emma stared at them defiantly.

Delyth sat with her head bowed. She'd been crying. James said nothing and sat down. The two girls had clearly been arguing.

Rick, conscious that the light was fading, didn't waste any time explaining the next game. "As you already know, this time it's all against all. You'll all leave the safe area at the same time, but there'll be no shooting until I blow the whistle. This gives everybody two minutes to hide. I'll blow the whistle again twenty minutes after the first one; that will signal the end of the game and for everyone to return to the safe area." He looked at his watch. "Are you ready... go!"

Emma was the first to react, sprinting into the wood like a scalded cat, unaware that the others were hanging back. James watched her disappear, glanced meaningfully at the others and advanced into the combat zone, his gun slung casually over his shoulder. Twenty metres in, he sat down on a tree stump and waited for the others.

"Hide up on either side of the path," he said as Tom and Delyth approached. "When Rick blows his whistle, I'll let off a few shots to attract her attention, then we'll wait. Don't shoot until she's walked right into the trap, but when I give the signal, let her have it!"

Delyth was angry but was having second thoughts about bushwhacking her friend. *Emma needs bringing down a peg or two*, she thought, *but I hope we don't upset her too much, or the next few days are going to be absolute hell. Maybe it would be best to leave the shooting to the boys. They'll never know if I just fire in the air.*

When the whistle went, Emma found herself near the line of yellow tape that marked the limit of the combat zone. Although certain she was well away from the others, she dropped to the ground and crawled into the thick undergrowth.

She was in a foul mood; the row with Delyth had upset her. It wasn't like Delyth to argue, but what really rattled Emma was she knew her friend was right; she was behaving like a bitch. She'd been like this ever since she'd found out about Dad's affair.

The problem was there was no one she could talk to about it. Mum was no good; she was hiding in her gin and tonics and refusing to accept anything was going on. And Dad... he went ballistic and threatened to disown her if she told anyone.

"Ouch"! She dropped her gun and sat up clutching her hands.

"Fucking nettles!" She extricated herself from the stingers and lay down. She was close to tears.

In the distance, she could make out the pop pop of paintballs being fired. She was of half a mind to walk back to the safe zone and let the others get on with it, but then the competitor in her kicked in.

I'm not a loser, Emma told herself, *and just because Dad's a pig doesn't mean I have to be.* She got to her feet cocked her gun and headed towards the action.

Tom was the first to hear Emma coming and hissed a warning. James gave him the thumbs up and ducked behind a tree stump.

Emma had no inkling they were there until a paint ball smacked into her facemask. She dived to the ground and wiped her visor, but all this did was smear gooey orange paint across the Perspex obscuring her vision. Unable to see, Emma was helpless as James and Tom rained shots at her, hitting her in the legs, buttocks, and head. They only stopped when she started screaming and threw down her gun.

"You bastards!" She sobbed as the realisation that they'd planned the ambush in advance sank in.

"You started it," retorted Tom unpleasantly, "we finished it." He looked at James for support.

James shook his head, seeing Emma spattered in orange paint and blinking back tears, he suddenly felt ashamed. "She's had enough," he said turning away, "Let's get back to the–"

SPLAT! SPLAT! Paintballs smacked into both boys' backs. James turned to gape at Delyth in disbelief.

"Looks like I won," she said coolly.

Before either James or Tom could reply, Mags appeared. Her mouth was set in a hard line. "That was out of order," she said as Emma bolted towards the portacabin.

James blanched – Mags rarely got cross. "It got out of hand," was all the excuse he could muster.

It wasn't until they got back to the safe area that they noticed Emma was missing.

"Stupid bitch," complained Tom.

"You can hardly blame her," snapped James. "We were pretty mean to her back there. She'll come back when she's ready."

Half an hour later and with the light fading, Rick was worried. "Mags just texted me. Emma's not at the house. I guess we'd better look for her before it gets dark."

James glanced at Tom. He looked pensive, and James suspected his friend was feeling as guilty as he was. As they spread out and combed the woods, James kept Rick and Tom within sight, but after encountering a dense patch of brambles he found himself detached from the others and outside the taped off combat area. He was standing on a muddy track, which meandered deep into the wood away from the paintball area.

Something in the undergrowth at the side of the path caught his eye. He stooped and picked it up. It was a discarded facemask. The Perspex was smeared with orange paint.

"She's been this way!" he shouted. He waited for a reply, but none came. "RICK? TOM?"

Shit, he thought, *I've lost them. Now what?* He'd have to make his way back to the safe zone or continue to follow Emma's trail into the wood. Despite the poor light, he decided to press on. It was slow progress, shuffling along the track bent over like an ape as he scanned the ground for evidence of Emma's presence.

After five minutes combing the vegetation, he was rewarded with a pile of orange paint balls next to an area of flattened bracken.

He stopped and listened; she was close now and he didn't want her to hear his approach. *I'm not letting her run off again or we'll be here all night.* His patience was rewarded by snuffling noises.

James crept silently towards the sound and found himself on the edge of a large pool. In the half-light the pool was as black as one of the crows that sat like sinister sentinels in the trees behind Myrtle House. A thin mist was forming over the glassy surface of the water.

James felt a prickle of alarm; the uncomfortable notion occurred to him that the wheezy snivelling noises might not be Emma. *For God's sake get a grip*, he thought. A bat hunting for moths flitted across the pond.

After a minute or so his eyes adjusted to the mist and poor light and the swirling shapes on the far bank coalesced.

Emma was sitting hunched over on a fallen tree trunk. Her head rocking as she sobbed into her hands. Her paint ball gun was propped up against the log. Her hair looked like a bird's nest.

James swallowed. This was his fault. The girl was a pain, but he'd behaved like playground bully. He was about to walk over to console her when Emma squealed and jumped to her feet.

James watched as Emma stared into the pool, her body rigid with shock, then lurched forward towards the water. For a split-second James thought she was going fall in, then at the last moment she clutched an overhanging branch and pulled herself back from the brink.

From where he was standing at the far end of the lake, James saw a dark shape break the mirrored surface of the lake, then it was gone, leaving ripples in its place. James stared at the inky water, unsure what he'd seen. Then Emma started screaming.

Galvanised into action on seeing a damsel in distress, James burst from his hiding place and threw his arms around the terrified girl. Emma, however, was not your average damsel. She lashed out and hit him on the side of his face with the back of her hand. Stunned, James let go and stepped back before she could whack him a second time.

"Emma! It's me, James!"

Emma screamed even louder.

"Listen, It's okay. Calm down. And, please, don't hit me again."

Emma blinked, wild-eyed, then, realising it was James, stopped screaming.

James stretched out his hand, but Emma sniffed and brushed it aside.

"Did you see her?" she demanded. "In the lake?"

"See what? There was a fish, I saw the ripples."

"There was a face in the water!"

James shrugged and picked up Emma's paintball gun. "It's dark. It's easy to imagine stuff in a place like this."

"No!" shouted Emma. She was on the edge of hysteria. "I saw a girl in the water, I thought it was my reflection at first... then she looked right at me and..." She saw doubt in James' face and the words dried up.

James went to place a comforting hand on Emma's shoulder, then thought better of it. He tried a different tack. "Emma," he said slowly, choosing his words carefully, "whatever you saw has gone, and it's no use speculating what it was. I don't know about you, but I'm hungry. Why don't we go back to the house and find some food?" He smiled encouragingly. "Mags will run a hot bath. You'll feel better once you're clean and warmed up. You coming?"

He reached out his hand and this time Emma accepted it.

Chapter 7

It was pitch black when Emma and James got back to Myrtle House. They were both exhausted. Blundering about in a darkened wood full of stinging nettles and brambles was no joke, even for James, who was used to a beating line. For Emma it was a nightmare. Her face was scratched, and she'd managed to turn her ankle, but she was determined not to complain.

As they turned the knob, the door was yanked open and Mags gushed all over them as she herded them into the kitchen. Tom and Delyth were waiting.

Tom watched them enter and raised an inquisitive eyebrow. "Been having fun in the dark?" he asked.

James ignored the insinuation. "You'd better have left enough food, Tom."

"You don't think I'd let you go without," interrupted Mags. "Now stop stirring, Tom. Run up the hill and tell Rick that Emma and James are back safe. He's worried sick and it won't help if he phones the police and they start asking awkward questions. Go on!" she encouraged. "Chop chop!"

As Tom bolted for the door, Mags turned her attention to Emma and James. "You two look like you've been dragged through a hedge," she said. "Lets strip those filthy overalls off you."

This time it was James and Emma's turn to run for the door. For, tired as they were, there was no way their teenage egos would allow them to suffer that indignity.

By the time Emma returned to the kitchen, bathed, her hair washed, and prerequisite beauty products applied, James was wolfing down a huge bowl of apple crumble and custard. She wanted to talk, so she sat next to him, but James carried on eating and barely acknowledged her presence. She bit her lip in irritation; she was desperate to discuss what they'd seen at the lake.

Delyth put a plate of meat free sausages and chips on the table and walked off without a word. Emma watched her disappear into the hall in silence, then stabbed one of the sausages harder than necessary.

James glanced up from his pudding. "She'll get over it," he said. "You alright?"

"Yeah, fine. This cut stings though," she said, stroking a scratch on her cheek.

James raised his eyebrow ruefully; he'd inspected the cut Emma had inflicted under his eye with her fingernails. It was a lot worse than Emma's scratch.

Emma's cheeks coloured and she pushed her chips around the plate.

James looked at her questioningly. "Do you want to talk?"

Emma hesitated. What she'd seen at the lake earlier in the evening had shaken her, and, beneath the veneer of confidence she projected, she was afraid. She wanted to talk about it, but was having second thoughts. Could she trust James? "No, I'm fine. Really."

James shrugged, picked up his bowl and walked over to the sink. She looked at her plate; the vegan sausages were awful; she couldn't face another mouthful. The clanking of dishes indicated James had made a start with the dishes. She couldn't remember ever doing the washing up herself. *Why don't these people have a dishwasher?*

Left alone at the table, she kept returning to what happened at the lake. The vision of the girl in the water had been so vivid it was hard to believe she'd imagined it. Even now, sitting in the cosy kitchen, she only had to close her eyes and she could see the girl glaring at her accusingly out of the black peaty water. Emma shook her head. If only the girl hadn't looked so much like her.

"Emma? Emma?"

She returned to her surroundings with a jolt and looked up.

It was Rick. "You look like you've seen a ghost." His voice was gentle. "You'd better get to bed." He glanced at James. "And the same goes for you. Mags and I will do the washing up."

When the kids had gone to their rooms, Mags handed Rick a mug of Horlicks and they slumped down on the pine rocking chairs next to the Aga.

They sat sipping the hot milky brew for a while before Rick broke the silence. "At least Tom caught me before I rang them."

Mags put her mug down. "Is that supposed to be an apology? You lost it this afternoon and you're supposed to be the one who keeps his cool."

"Sorry, Mags, I panicked. But after last time I thought I'd better report it as soon as possible."

"Report what? The girl was missing less than two hours. If you phone the police every time one of the kids goes off for a sulk, they'll close us down."

Rick winced, "You're right, Mags, but I think that creep is still out there. And I'm worried that one day he'll get bored with watching and he'll do something to one of the girls."

"The police have searched the lake and woods twice now and found nothing. They'll take a dim view if you call them out on a third false alarm."

"But those girls swore they'd seen someone watching them at the lake and their description of the guy was–"

"Teenage fantasy," Mags interrupted. "Half-naked stalkers covered in tattoos don't disappear into thin air. If he existed, the police would have found him by now."

"But–"

Mags gently touched Rick's lips with her finger, "No more buts, Richard McFarlane. There have been silly stories about that lake ever since I can remember. And that's what they are: silly stories. Now finish your drink and come to bed with me."

Rick smiled. "That's the best offer I've had all day."

The Watcher hunkered down and stared into the water in the iron chalice. He had to focus very hard, as the flickering candlelight barely penetrated the darkness in the cave. He'd drunk from the spring about an hour ago and was waiting for the trance that would take him far beyond this place and time.

It was cold as death in the cave, but as the sacred water took effect, sweat beaded on the Watcher's shaved pate and dripped down his tattooed face. Now his mouth felt dry, and his tongue darted nervously across his upper lip. Breathing slowly and rhythmically, the watcher fixated on the surface of the water in the cup as the Men of Knowledge had taught him. It wouldn't be long now.

As the vision materialised, the Watcher took a sharp breath, his pupils dilating. A girl had appeared in the reflection. As she walked towards the lakeside, her long hair shone golden in the evening light. He'd watched other young girls drawn to the lake on earlier visits to this strange world, but this time it felt different.

The girl loosened the collar on her extraordinary clothing. The Watcher's pulse raced as he glimpsed the sign on her necklace glinting between her breasts. Surely this young woman was the one.

He muttered a fervent prayer to the Goddess. The girl was close now; if she was the chosen one, it wouldn't be long before she passed over to his world. And when she did, he would be waiting.

The subject of her disappearance the previous night was not mentioned when Emma came down to breakfast the following morning. *Thank goodness,* she thought. She hadn't slept last night, brooding over the row she'd had with Delyth and what had happened at the lake.

Tired and emotional, she sat eating her breakfast while the others chatted excitedly. She remained uncommunicative for most of the day and, although the snorkelling and rock-climbing Rick had arranged were activities she normally relished, she couldn't seem to enjoy herself and didn't join in with the banter.

It was teatime before her mood had lifted sufficiently to speak to James. "I thought I'd better thank you," she said awkwardly, when nobody else was listening.

James looked up, surprised. "What for?"

"For coming to find me last night. And for not saying anything of course," she replied.

"There wasn't anything to say; we shouldn't have upset you like that. It was the least Tom and I could do to try and find you."

"I meant about the girl in the lake," whispered Emma.

"What? Do you still really think that's what you saw?"

"Yes!"

James was dubious. "I admit it was weird at the lake last night, but the eyes can play tricks in situations like that." He stuffed another forkful of potato in his mouth and looked at Emma thoughtfully. He could tell she wasn't convinced. "Tell you what," he offered, "why don't you and I check out the lake tonight. If we find nothing, it'll put your mind at ease."

Emma was taken aback. The thought of returning to the lake in the dark filled her with dread, but James had laid down a challenge. "I'll do it," she said. "Meet me on the front porch at twelve-thirty. And bring a torch."

James checked his mobile. It was twelve-forty; he'd been waiting for ten minutes. He was about to go back to bed when the front door creaked open. It made him jump.

"I thought you'd got cold feet," he whispered as Emma stepped onto the porch.

She ignored him. "Have you got the torch?"

James nodded and motioned her to follow him across the yard. *Click!* A security light flicked on and illuminated the front of the house.

"Shit!" muttered James. He scurried round the back of the cowshed and ran into a tangle of scrap metal. Emma could hardly suppress her sniggers as James emerged on the far side of the farmyard nursing his shin. "Do you think anyone saw us?" he whispered.

"Or heard us more like," smirked Emma.

James was embarrassed. "I guess nobody shouted or turned the lights on, so we carry on."

"Agreed," said Emma, but James was already picking his way along the track that made its way into the trees. As she entered the wood's dark embrace, Emma shrank towards James. She had a rotten sense of direction at the best of times, but in the pitch black she hadn't a clue. "Where are we?" she whispered.

"It's difficult to explain. Just keep close,"

James had made an idiot of himself blundering into the plough in the cow yard, but in the woods he was in his element. He knew exactly where he was and effortlessly guided them to the trail that led to the lake. At the end of the track, they stopped while James flicked the torch across the open ground in front of the lake. Nothing sinister appeared in the beam, so they crept across the clearing to the edge of the pool. There was no mist this time. The gentle onshore breeze rustling the trees had cleared away the cold, moist air before it condensed. Without the mist, the pool didn't look like it belonged in a horror movie anymore.

"Go on then," urged James. "Take a good look."

Emma glanced nervously at James, then stared at the spot where she thought she'd seen the girl.

The water looked completely different. The lake had lost its dark, mirror-like sheen, and the ripples created by the breeze obscured any reflection. She studied the water for some time. When she was sure she'd looked her demons in the eye, she turned away.

"I've seen enough," she said quietly. "I want to go back now."

James looked at her with respect; he knew how scared she'd been the previous evening. It must have taken a lot of guts to come out tonight. He wanted to tell her so but couldn't find the words. He shrugged his shoulders and walked back the way they had come.

They walked back to the house in silence, but as they moved through the wood, he became increasingly aware of Emma's presence. He found himself listening for the sound of her breath. At one point, as they ducked under a wire fence, they brushed against each other and he caught a whiff of her scent. When it was time to go back into the house, they stood awkwardly together on the front porch.

James, not a good communicator at the best of times, was tongue-tied.

Emma, aware of the effect she was having on him, took a while to decide what to do. At last she stepped forward and kissed James on the cheek. "Thanks," she said, and then was gone.

Delyth heard Emma sneak back into bed and pretended she was asleep. She'd witnessed the kiss through the bedroom window. She bit her lip and fought to control the rage that boiled inside her.

Chapter 8

When James opened his eyes, Tom was awake and being annoying.

"Well," Tom demanded, "did you and Emma go to the lake last night?"

"Yeah, but nothing happened. We just walked to the lake and walked back again."

Tom gave his friend a searching look and James wished he'd not confided in him.

Tom grinned. "You fancy her, don't you? Well, well," he said, warming to the subject, "James Cordle has finally gone gooey over a girl!"

James whacked his pillow into the side of Tom's head. "Piss off."

Tom didn't respond, he sat on the edge of his bed, smirking.

To James' dismay, Tom was still smirking when Emma sat next to him at breakfast.

Delyth didn't seem to share Tom's good humour, and James caught her scowling at him and Emma more than once. She looked overwrought. He wondered what had gotten into her.

After breakfast, Rick briefed them on the activities for the day. "We're going to use the climbing drills we learned yesterday," he announced. "The difference is that some of the climbing will take place inside a cave. The plan is to abseil the cliff at Carn Lwyd on the far side of the headland down to the cave entrance."

James looked at Tom. He was surprised his friend didn't look more enthusiastic.

"I want you all to see the Blue Cavern at the end of the cave complex. That'll mean a tricky climb up a vertical chimney near the cave entrance, as well as squeezing through a tight passage into the Blue Cavern itself. It'll be a challenge for some of you," he glanced at Delyth who looked down at her feet, "but believe me, the Blue Cavern is worth the effort."

"How long will we be in the cave?" asked Tom.

"The entire complex only extends a couple hundred metres into the cliff, so it won't take long. I reckon about an hour and a half to explore everything and climb back to the top."

Rick laid out a large chart on the kitchen table. He'd highlighted the cave in red felt tip. They could see it was very close to the Blue Lagoon where they'd kayaked to on the first day. A dotted line denoted where the cave ran under the headland.

"What's that?" Delyth pointed to a mark on the map in a field close to the headland.

"It's a hill fort," answered Rick. "There's quite a few round here. Mags told me they date from Iron Age times."

"That's over two thousand years ago," said Delyth. "We did a history module on prehistoric Britain last term."

Rick folded the map; history wasn't his strong point. "We'd better pick up the kit from the barn," he said. "Mags will make the packed lunch while we get organized."

James glanced out of the window. The clear blue sky of the previous day had gone, obliterated by banks of amorphous grey cloud. Over the hills, the clouds had turned to charcoal, and a washed out grey haze indicated it was already raining. He grimaced. *Hell!* he thought. Surely it wasn't going to rain again.

By the time they trooped out of the front door and charged across the yard, raindrops were exploding on the concrete.

In the barn, Rick was issuing equipment. "It'll be wet and cold in the cave, so you'll need these." He said, dumping a pile of orange overalls on the floor. "These are cave suits. Wear them over the top of your clothes; it'll keep the mud off."

In the ensuing scrum, James was surprised to find an XXL that accommodated his massive frame. *We look like painters and decorators,* he thought, as everyone lined up to receive bright yellow hard hats, head torches and caving belts. Rick checked their equipment one by one, connecting the wire which ran from the battery on their belt to the LED head torch, and flipping the switch to make sure it worked. When the checks were complete, the team of painters and decorators looked more like overexcited Welsh miners.

Before they left, James placed his mobile phone, an inhaler, and his Swiss army knife in his bumbag and clipped it on. He wasn't anticipating an emergency, but he liked to be prepared.

Tom was unhappy. When they finally set off for the headland, it wasn't just raining. It was pouring. It was the sort of persistent heavy rain that only fell in the western fringes of the UK. "Yuck," he shuddered as they trudged up the stony path that wound up the hill on the far side of Abereiddy Bay. The path, eroded by the feet of thousands of summer visitors, was already slippery and was fast turning into a stream.

The rain ran off Tom's hardhat, dripped onto his collar and then found its way inside his cave suit. He wiped his forehead with the back off his hand and focused on the bobbing figure of Rick bounding up the path ahead. Tom was fit, but he struggled to keep up with the ex-paratrooper, who, despite carrying a mountainous rucksack filled with climbing gear, was yomping up the steep slope with no sign of slowing.

At the top of the hill, Tom gave up trying to keep up and stopped for a breather. He looked back to see how the others were faring. James and Emma were keeping up but Delyth, accompanied by Mags, was lagging behind and appeared to be struggling.

"We'd better wait," he suggested as James and Emma squelched up to him.

"Don't bother," grunted James, "they'll catch up later. Anyway, I'm keeping clear of Delyth. Something's got into her this morning; she was crabby as hell with me at breakfast."

"I got the same treatment," agreed Tom. "I asked her to help strap my battery on and she nearly bit my head off."

"Probably wrong time of the month," offered James, who'd googled pre-menstrual tension after listening to his parents rowing.

Emma looked at the boys pityingly; she had a shrewd idea what was wrong. Delyth hadn't said anything, but the look her friend had given her as she sat next to James at breakfast had spoken a thousand words. Delyth knew she'd met James last night and was jealous.

Emma squinted through the rain at Delyth and Mags. They were deep in conversation. Emma sincerely hoped Delyth hadn't ratted on her about going out last night. "They can look after themselves," she said. "Let's see if we can catch up with Rick."

Chapter 9

It was another twenty-five minutes hard walking before they caught up with Rick. He was standing nonchalantly at the top of the headland next to a large coil of blue rope secured to a metal stake, which he'd driven into the ground at the edge of the cliff.

"Nice weather for it." He smiled.

James crept towards the edge and peered over. The sea was a long way down and the rock face was slippery. "He's mad," he muttered.

"No offence taken, James," grinned Rick, who could lip-read. "It looks far worse than it is. Mags will make sure you're properly clipped in, so if you follow the drills we practiced yesterday it's perfectly safe. Once we get inside the cave, it won't matter if it's raining."

"It matters to me," insisted Mags, who, together with Delyth, had joined the conference at the clifftop. "I'll have to wait up here until you come back out."

Rick looked thoughtful. "Mags," he said, "I know it's not usual but why don't you wait for us to get to the bottom then make your way back to Myrtle House? We'll be in the cave at least an hour and we can take the goat track back up to the top. Why wait here and get cold?" He looked at his watch. "It's eleven-thirty. If we're not back by two, come and find us."

"Are you sure?" While Mags was keen to get back to her warm kitchen, it would be highly irregular to leave Rick as the lone adult leading the expedition.

"It'll be fine," replied Rick firmly. "I've been in that cave dozens of times." He clipped on his harness and lifted his arms to let Mags check the buckles. "I'll nip down first. When I give the signal, send the others down one at a time." He pecked her on the lips. "See you later," he said, and stepped over the edge.

Less than a minute later the rope went slack and a shout from below signalled Rick had reached the beach safely.

Delyth watched with growing consternation as Tom, James and Emma disappeared over the cliff and descended towards the misty sea. She'd abseiled before and this was not a particularly difficult descent, but she couldn't shake off a sense of foreboding. Now, as Mags tightened the harness around her middle, the palms of her hands had grown damp with sweat.

Below there was a chorus of shouting. "Come on, Delyth, you can do it!

"Come on!"

"Just go for it!"

Mags was more sympathetic. "You don't have to do this, Delyth. We can walk back to Myrtle House and have a nice cup of hot chocolate if you want. The others won't mind."

"But I will!" insisted Delyth, taking deep, long breaths. "Thanks for the offer, but I'm doing this."

"Alright," said Mags, looking at her shrewdly. "I'll see you in a couple of hours and then you can sit down and tell me what's really bugging you."

Delyth grimaced. "Thanks, Mags," she replied. "Don't worry, I'll be fine."

She grasped the rope, gritted her teeth, and leant back until the harness took her weight. Then, just as she'd been taught, she passed the free end of the rope through the cleat and backed over the edge.

The first part of the descent was relatively easy. Here on the upper cliff, low-growing wild sloe bushes and heather clung to the loose shale and cushioned the impact of her boots from the rock. Then came a heart-stopping moment when the upper cliff gave way to a sheer rock face that left Delyth hanging in space. She hesitated a moment, allowing her breathing to return to normal, then kicked away from the cliff, passing the rope through the cleat. She swung in a downward arc, initially away from, then back towards the rock face. At the moment of impact, she bent her knees to absorb the shock, and repeated the process, lowering herself in a series of graceful sweeps until she felt the gravel of the beach crunch under her boots. Exhilarated, with legs like jelly, she looked expectantly at the others.

"Well done, Delyth!" yipped Tom, relieved his sister was down in one piece.

"Brilliant!" said Rick, impressed Delyth had even attempted the drop let alone executed a textbook descent.

Delyth unclipped the harness, which was tight around her midriff. She looked at James.

James felt obliged to add to the plaudits, "Well done," he offered.

Delyth brushed back her damp hair. For the first time that day, the ghost of a smile played around her face. One kind word from James and life seemed rosier.

The beach on which they stood was never going to be the sort that featured in a tourist magazine. There was no expanse of golden sand, only a small bank of dull grey pebbles swept into a tiny inlet on the southern flank of the headland. The tide was out, exposing smooth, slippery rock which slid into the sea like the flanks of a giant whale. The rock was grey, the sky was grey, and it was still raining.

"This is it, folks," Rick announced, pointing to the top of the beach, where the gravel disappeared into an inky black crevice in the cliff face. "I suggest we do a final check on the gear, connect up the head torches, and head on in."

Rick watched carefully as the youngsters went through the routine checks and tested their torches. When they'd finished, he examined the four young faces looking up at him expectantly. "Don't worry," he said, "I take groups into this cave all the time. It's not a technically difficult climb, but none of you have been potholing before. So if the enclosed space freaks you out, it's no big deal. Let me know the moment you feel panicky, and I'll bring you out straight away."

Satisfied by their nods, Rick shouldered his pack and led the youngsters up the beach towards the cave. He was confident in his ability to lead an excursion like this and didn't anticipate trouble.

Although he had never been into a cave of any significance before, Tom thought the trip would be a doddle. The entrance was large enough to allow the group to stroll in side by side, so Tom had no qualms about following the others into the cave. However, the cave quickly narrowed, and as the gravel floor rose steadily upward, Tom noticed with alarm the watermark of barnacles and squidgy red anemones that encrusted the dank walls closer to the ceiling. He spied a tangle of driftwood wedged into a rocky crevice just above his head, and a long-lost buoy peeped out at him like a bright orange party balloon. He decided he wouldn't like to be here at high tide and followed the others up the gentle incline into the darkness. Further in, the gravel gave way to soft sand and Tom became aware of a very nasty smell. In the enclosed space, the cloying, sweet aroma of fish was overpowering.

He gagged. "What the hell's that stink?"

Rick pointed his head torch at the legs and shells of crabs strewn over the cave floor. "This is where the seals haul up and eat," he said. "And this," he indicated a treacly black lump on the sand, "is where they go to the toilet."

"You're joking," said Emma.

Rick grinned. His teeth gleamed in the torchlight, "Don't panic. They won't be at home right now, all the racket we made on the way down here will have scared them off."

Horrified by the prospect of stepping in seal shit or meeting an angry seal, the youngsters' advance slowed. Soon there was barely enough room for them to grope forward one at a time.

Tom bumped into Delyth; the people in front had stopped. They'd come to a dead end, and the cave roof seemed to have disappeared. Tom looked up, and a large drip of water hit him in the eye. He wiped his face with the back of his hand and squinted upwards. All he could see was a mist of water droplets falling out of a black nothingness. Disorientated, he stumbled on a boulder and fell against the cave wall. He lay dazed, trying to work out where he was. Gradually, it dawned on him that they were standing at the bottom of a massive vertical tube. He sat up. The walls were starting to close in. He bit his lip. His stomach churned.

"Are you alright, Tom?" asked Rick.

"Yeah. No problem," he replied groggily. "I just slipped."

Satisfied his young charge was okay, Rick pointed to the vertical pipe. "This is the chimney I was telling you about," he explained. "We have to climb about fifteen metres to reach the horizontal main passage."

"I thought you said it was going to be easy!" exclaimed Delyth.

Rick smiled. "It's easier than it looks," he assured. "Look." He turned his head so the lamp on his helmet illuminated the far corner of the vertical shaft. Despite the dripping water, they could make out steps chiselled into the slate. "Nobody knows who carved these steps or how old they are. Local legends say this was once a sacred place used by druids. More recently, I'm told, the cave was used by smugglers to store contraband." He laughed. "Don't get too excited; you won't find any treasure. Too many people have already looked!"

Rick patted Tom on the back. "I'll take the lead, you follow. Keep an eye out for the iron rings driven into the rock. When you reach the first ring, clip it to your safety line. Do it with each ring as you go up, then if you slip, the most you can fall is a couple of metres."

Tom gave Rick a thumbs up, but a growing sense of panic was making his insides bubbly. He let out a nervous fart. It echoed in the darkness. The whole group, including Rick, dissolved into laughter.

"You dirty boy!" sniggered James.

"Shut up!" yelled Tom, mortified.

James made a raspberry noise and everyone except Tom laughed helplessly. Tom had to sit out the indignity in silence, vowing not to chicken out of the climb – a thought that had seemed very appealing a few moments earlier.

Rick waited for the merriment to cease, then started up the steps, Tom climbing defiantly behind. In the early stages of the climb, the steps had been hacked deep into the rock, so the going was easy, and Tom was able to put his claustrophobia to the back of his mind. However, the further he ascended, the narrower the pipe became and the more claustrophobic he felt. To add to his woes, as he climbed higher, the steps got shallower, and the water that had been dripping on his hard hat became a steady flow exploding into droplets all around him.

With the water obscuring his vision, his foot slipped on the wet rock and he almost fell. He clung to his safety rope, heart hammering. Reason told him he wasn't going to fall, but the black empty space below him beckoned. He counted to ten and took a deep breath.

"You're doing well, Tom," Rick encouraged. "It's not much further."

Tom looked up. A stream of cold water hit the peak of his helmet and made him gasp for breath. He could just make out Rick's face through a curtain of droplets. He was looking down from the top of the pipe, his arm outstretched. Somehow, Tom found the courage to climb one more step, then another and another. Finally, Rick grabbed his harness and hauled him onto a ledge that opened onto a horizontal passageway. Breathing heavily, Tom crawled into the passage to wait for the others.

One by one, Rick hauled them out onto the ledge. Last up was Delyth; she'd had a bit of a scare, having tangled her safety rope around her ankle but she was still smiling when she made it to the top. Tom looked on glumly, everyone apart from him seemed in high spirits.

"That was brilliant!" enthused James.

"Yes, great!" lied Tom, wishing he was back in Myrtle House.

Rick seemed to be enjoying himself as much as the kids. He squatted down next to them, smiling broadly. "Sorry about the water," he said. "It's not usually this bad; it must be the rain we've had in the last few weeks. I'm sure the next section will be dry but prepare yourselves; the roof gets very low just before we get to the main cavern." He looked at his watch, "We'd better press on if we want to stay on schedule." Still grinning, Rick stooped under the low roof at the entrance to the passage and beckoned them to follow.

Tom hung back, making sure he was last. If there were any nasty surprises, he didn't intend to be the first to face them. As he waited for the others to file forward, he looked back at the shaft. The flow of water coming down the pipe had increased and was dislodging stones from the cave roof. He thought about mentioning this to Rick but decided not to make a fuss.

They'll think I'm scared, he thought, and scurried after the others before he lost sight of them.

He caught up with Delyth at the tail end of the group.

"Are you alright?" she whispered as he approached.

Tom hesitated. He was slightly tempted to confide to his sister how frightened he was. Ultimately, he decided against it. "I'm fine," he replied stubbornly.

Delyth wasn't convinced. "Make sure you keep up," she said. "I don't want you to have an accident without us knowing where you are."

Tom knew she meant well, but her concern had touched a raw nerve. "Quit nagging!" he snapped. "I can look after myself."

Delyth didn't reply, she knew her brother was scared but knew not to injure his male pride.

Tom, being shorter than the others, was able to walk upright along the horizontal passage for a bit, but eventually he too was forced to stoop to stop his helmet banging against the ceiling. It was then that the walls began to close in again. To keep his mind off his claustrophobia, he focused on what was directly in front of him, which happened to be Delyth's bum. This would be funny in other circumstances, but all he could think about was getting out of the cave. About a hundred-and-fifty metres from the pipe they came to a halt, and Tom face planted into his sister's muddy bottom. Bunched together in the tunnel, Tom felt his boots slide underneath him. Water was seeping out of the rock walls and pooling on the cave floor to form a thin, muddy soup.

"This is where the passage gets tight," shouted Rick from somewhere up ahead. "If anybody's not sure about this, I suggest we all go back out now."

"We can't back out now," said Emma. "You said the cavern at the other side is the best part."

"Yes, but not everyone might want to crawl through to get there," explained Rick diplomatically. "It's extremely cramped, and there's a lot of mud and water down there." He peered back down the passage at the others. "Does anybody want to go back?" He waited for a response. "Delyth are you sure you want to do this?"

Delyth thought for a moment, not wanting to let the others down. "I'll have a go as long as everyone else is happy." She shot a glance at Tom.

Tom ignored her and remained obstinately silent. Inside his stomach was churning.

Rick nodded. "It's too low to crawl. The technique is to slide in headfirst on your backs. Keep your hands by your side and use your feet to wriggle forward. The really tight section is only a couple of metres, then you're though into the Blue Cavern. I'll go through first, and then you follow one at a time."

Tom watched in horror as Rick and his friends disappeared one by one, headfirst into the slimy tunnel. *It isn't much bigger than a badger hole*, he thought. *Or a coffin.*

Delyth was the last to go. "You don't have to do this, bro," she said, reaching out to stroke his cheek.

Tom pushed her away, afraid he would cry. Delyth shrugged and put her head into the hole. Tom closed his eyes as his sister wriggled out of sight. He was alone in the passageway, and absolutely terrified.

At the other end of the tunnel, Rick, James and Emma found themselves in a vast open space. They were plastered with muddy slime that coated their hands, face, and clothing, but that didn't seem to matter. All three were gazing in wonder as the light from their headlamps danced over the cave walls.

Emma was the first to speak. "It really is blue!

James could scarcely believe a space this big could exist below the ground. "You could fit a church in here."

"Impressive, isn't it?" Rick grinned, his eyes white in his mud-splattered face.

"Very!" added Emma, whose appearance would have shocked her antiseptically clean mother. Then she noticed the bizarre formations protruding from the cave floor. "What are those?"

"Stalactites, stupid," chuckled James.

"Actually," said Rick, "the ones sticking up are stalagmites and the ones hanging down are stalactites."

It was too much detail for Emma, but she was intrigued by the colour. "I thought Stagladites or whatever were supposed to be white, not blue."

"You're right," agreed Rick, ignoring her mispronunciation. "The blue staining is algae or fungus; I can't remember which. Apparently it's very rare. Usually there are just a few small patches of it; I've never seen it covering everything like it is today. It makes the place look amazing, doesn't it?"

The conversation was interrupted by Delyth's arrival at the tunnel entrance. She struggled to her feet, then slipped, wallowing in the mud. Trying not to laugh, James pulled her to her feet then returned to his study of the cave. He squinted at one of the stalagmites poking up out of the floor. *It's like a weird candle,* he thought, *stuck to the rock by melted wax.*

He touched the shaft of the rock formation in wonder.

"It looks like a willy," Emma confided to Delyth in a stage whisper. There was muffled giggling. James flushed and hastily removed his hand, grateful the girls were unable to see his blushes in the dark.

While the sniggering subsided, James rummaged in his bumbag and pulled out his knife. He flicked open the blade and ran it over the surface of the stalagmite. He inspected the end of his knife then wiped some of the sticky blue film onto his finger and sniffed it like a dog. "It's not algae," he said finally. "It's too dark in here. Algae are plants, they need light. It must be a fungus."

"Or bacteria," added Delyth. "I wonder if it's poisonous?"

"Who cares?" laughed Rick. "None of us plan on eating it."

They fell silent for a while, playing their torches around the cave, enjoying the way the cave walls glistened blue in the lights.

James came to a sudden realisation. "Where's Tom? He should've come through by now."

Crouched the other side of the tunnel, Tom could hear them talking. When he heard his name, he finally plucked up the courage to make a move and inched towards the entrance. He placed his head inside, lay on his back, closed his eyes, and squirmed forwards. Trembling, he groped the smooth rock with his hands and wriggled further until his entire body was inside the passage.

Tom took a deep breath and wriggled again, but instead of moving forward, the peak of his helmet scraped on the roof, then snagged. Then he made a big mistake – he opened his eyes.

All he could see was slimy black rock two centimetres in front of his nose. He pictured thousands of tonnes pressing down on his chest, squeezing the air out of his lungs, crushing the life from his body. Then panic took over and banished rational thought. Whimpering in terror, he thrashed against the confines of his imaginary tomb, bruising his knuckles on the hard stone.

Somehow, he managed to get out of the narrow tunnel into the horizontal shaft where he had sat a few minutes earlier. He could hear worried shouts from the other end of the tunnel, but he'd had enough, and bolted back down the passage towards the exit.

They could hear Tom thrashing about in the tunnel from inside the cavern. For a few moments the animal squeals of fear paralyzed them.

Rick reacted first. "Stay right here," he barked. "I'll go and see what's happened." He looked at the youngsters' anxious faces and his voice softened. "Don't worry. I expect it's the confined space that's upset him." He stuck his head into the entrance. "You enjoy looking around for a bit, I'll shout when I want you to come through."

James, Delyth and Emma watched in silence as Rick disappeared out of sight.

Once in the tunnel, Rick sensed Tom wasn't there and began to get concerned. "Tom," he shouted, "can you hear me? Tom?" There was no reply. "Shit," he muttered, "the little bugger's scarpered."

By the time Rick had squirmed back into the open passage, Tom had already reached the ledge overlooking the pipe. Breathing heavily from the run down the passage, he looked down into the abyss. Despite his agitation, the drop caused him to pause and think about his next move. He looked up. there was a lot more water coming from the roof than before. He wondered what it meant.

A geologist, had one been there, would have explained that months of heavy rain had percolated through the porous shale above his head and had then hit a band of clay that overlaid the impermeable rock below. The clay, sandwiched between the two layers of rock, was now so wet it was ready to liquefy.

Tom, blissfully unaware of the danger, ignored the water pouring from above and decided to risk the descent.

He felt around the ledge for the end of the safety rope and clipped it to his harness. He was so preoccupied with the rope he didn't notice Rick was standing behind him until he spoke.

"Tom," Rick said quietly, "what are you doing?"

Tom never replied, because that was when the saturated clay above their heads turned to liquid mud.

There was a deafening rumble, and Tom felt the ground under his feet tremble. Then a spurt of water erupted from above and the ceiling over the pipe collapsed.

In moments of mortal danger, they say the brain is capable of processing information many times faster than normal, which is why people who have experienced extreme situations often say they felt like everything slowed down. It certainly felt like that for Tom, who witnessed hundreds of tons of rock and sloppy mud hurtling past his nose in super slow motion. He remembered a powerful draft of air created by the vacuum caused by the falling rock rush out of the passage behind him and lift him off his feet.

If Tom hadn't been attached to a safety line, he'd have been sucked into the abyss. Instead, the rope snapped taut and held fast, leaving him dangling over the edge. Rick was less fortunate. With no safety rope to hold him, he didn't have a chance. The rush of air picked him up like a doll and propelled him into the stream of falling rock and down the pipe.

Tom was suspended over the void for what seemed like an eternity as the falling debris petered out and came to a stop. Dazed and confused, he didn't have the wherewithal to call out.

To add to his woes, his helmet had been dislodged during the fall, so he had no light. Hanging in the dark, all he could do for a while was cling to the rope.

He forced himself to assess his situation. He could feel a trickle of blood on his forehead, and his shins hurt like hell, but he was pretty sure he wasn't badly injured. *I've been bashed up worse playing rugby*, he thought grimly.

Gritting his teeth, he swung his feet sideways to get a foothold on the side of the pipe, but after several unsuccessful attempts, he came to the conclusion that his only chance of reaching the ledge was to climb the safety line. He gripped the rope and started trying to haul himself up. In PE lessons Tom could climb a gym rope with ease, but this was a very different proposition. Not only was the rope thinner, which left painful friction burns on his hands, but he was exhausted. After a couple of minutes of arm wrenching exertion, he was forced to accept he wasn't going to make it.

Finally, hanging inert in defeat, he had an idea.

Chapter 10

Inside the Blue Cavern, James, Emma and Delyth waited. They were cold, wet and irritable.

"Where the fuck are they?" James demanded.

"Maybe Rick decided Tom needed to get out," offered Delyth.

"More like he's giving him a talk about how he shouldn't worry about being shit scared," said Emma.

"Shut up!" snapped James.

They fell silent when they heard the sound of rushing air, followed by a deep rumble that echoed around the cavern.

James' heart hammered. He looked at the others. He could see fear in their eyes.

"What was that?" Delyth squeaked, a note of panic in her voice.

"It sounded like an explosion," said James, worriedly.

"It can't be." Emma's tone was disbelieving.

"You got a better explanation?"

Delyth grabbed James' arm. "Go and look." her eyes were wide. "Please, James."

James stared at the exit hole.

"Rick told us to wait," Emma reminded them.

James thought for a moment, nodded and sat on a rocky outcrop. The girls followed his example.

The silence was deafening. After a few minutes, Delyth began to sob.

Emma's arm crept around her friend's shoulders, their quarrel forgotten.

The rock was hard; James shifted in an attempt to ease the discomfort. He was scared, but he was trying not to show it in front of the girls. Suddenly he sat bolt upright, alerted by a distant noise. "Did you hear that?" he whispered.

"Hear what?" said Emma.

"Shhhh!" he hissed. "It's a whistle!"

They strained to pick up the sound. This time they all heard. The shrill, high-pitched noise was clearly a distress signal, and, by the way it was repeated, whoever was blowing it was desperate.

"They must be in trouble," said James.

Delyth's sobs grew louder.

James ignored her. He needed to assess the situation. "If there's been an accident, we need to find out what's wrong," he said, then added: "We'd better stick together."

"Tom!" wailed Delyth. Her cries were deafening.

"For fuck's sake, calm down!" snapped Emma. "We can't hear ourselves think!"

James placed his arms around the hysterical girl's shoulders. She clung on. Her hands were shaking. "Delyth," he said firmly, "if Tom's in trouble, we need your help. You need to stay strong."

She wiped her eyes and sniffed. James, sensing she'd regained control, took the lead. "Come on," he said grimly. "We'd better face whatever's out there."

"I'll go first," offered Emma.

James glanced at the girl he'd written off as a brat with new respect. He nodded. "Thanks," he said, "I'll help Delyth."

Emma ducked through the exit. She had no difficulty in wriggling through the narrow tunnel and was soon in the horizontal shaft. There was no sign of Rick and Tom, and the whistle blower had stopped, so she crouched on her haunches and tried to forget how cold and filthy she was. She wiped her hands on her boiler suit; it was dripping wet, and the damp was beginning to seep through into her clothes. She shivered, wishing she were lying in a hot bath back at Myrtle House. The fantasy was interrupted by grunting and blowing noises. Emma imagined Delyth wedged in the tunnel like cork in a muddy bottle and smiled. Then the seriousness of their situation sunk in. *What if we're stuck in here?* she thought.

Emma was still pondering the gravity of their predicament when Delyth joined her in the open shaft; she didn't even laugh when James got mud in his mouth as he slid out of the tunnel. As they huddled together deciding what to do, her mood was grim. "What do you think happened?" she asked James, ignoring Delyth, who seemed content to let the others take the lead.

"We can't be sure," replied James. "But the person who blew that whistle is in trouble. I vote we press on, but be careful, in case there's been a fall."

Emma nodded; even with his face plastered in smelly mud, James inspired confidence. "What happens if somebody's hurt?"

"We'll do what we can," answered James pragmatically. "What else can we do?"

Not waiting for a reply, James led the girls back down the shaft in the direction of the pipe.

Tom's heart was racing, and the blood pulsing in the little arteries in his temples made him feel his head would pop. He'd been suspended from the safety rope for twenty minutes, and the harness was cutting into his armpits. The combination of swinging in mid-air and the pressure of the harness around his ribcage made him feel sick. With claustrophobia adding to his woes, he abandoned the whistle to conserve his energy. All he could do was cling to the rope, hoping James would come and get him out of there.

He was at the end of his tether – literally – when a ray of light illuminated the wall of the pipe just above his head. "James!" he wheezed, breathing restricted by the harness. "I'm down here!"

The beam of light bobbed up and down on the wall but there was no reply. At last, he grasped the whistle, put it to his lips and blew three long blasts. Within moments he was bathed in light. He looked up, shielding his eyes from the powerful headlight directed on him, and then his body sagged with relief.

James was on the ledge a few metres from the pipe when Tom blew the whistle. The blast was incredibly loud in the confined space, and he rushed to investigate. At this stage he had no inkling that there had been a rock fall, so it was a shock to find the chimney filled with debris. Stunned by what he was seeing, it took a few seconds for him to register that Tom was looking up at him out of the pipe. There was no sign of Rick.

"Tom, are you okay?" he called. "Hold on. We'll get you out of there."

James knew he needed to get his head together. *Don't babble*, he told himself, *do something!*

He grabbed the safety line and pulled. Emma rushed to help, but it was soon clear that it wasn't working, and they let go of the rope.

"Help me!" begged Tom. "My chest hurts."

"Are you injured?" asked James, at last thinking clearly.

"I don't think so," gasped Tom. "The harness is cutting in, but I don't think anything is broken."

Emma and James peered into the hole.

"The rubble's just below his feet!" exclaimed Emma. "We're being prats, why don't we just cut the rope and let him drop? Once he's on the top of rock fall, he can walk to the side and climb up the steps."

James scratched his head. Emma was right, the scree had filled the pipe to within three metres of the ledge. Tom wasn't hanging over a ten-metre drop; the top of the fall was less than a metre beneath his feet.

James wondered why he hadn't noticed. "Good idea," he conceded, "but we'd better lower him gently. We don't know how stable that rubble is." He called down, "Did you hear that, Tom?"

Tom grimaced and looked down at the rubble, which was now illuminated by James' headlamp. He hung his head in silence. In his mind, he saw Rick being sucked into the pipe by the rush of falling debris.

"Tom," repeated James, "we're going to lower you down!"

Tom nodded weakly, "Hurry up, I'm being crucified."

James gave Tom the thumbs up, grasped the safety rope and braced himself while Emma unhitched the braided nylon cord from the iron ring. Fortunately, the debris lodged in the pipe was stable. If it weren't, they'd have been in trouble, because when the rope was free James was almost pulled over the edge and Tom fell like a sack of potatoes. When Emma and James looked down the pipe Tom was lying in a heap on the rocky trash which blocked their escape.

This was too much for Delyth. She'd been crouching a little way down the shaft too afraid to look . Now she rushed forward. "Tom! Tom!" she shouted, her voice squeaking with emotion.

"He's fine," James said, grabbing her arm to prevent her falling over the edge. "He fell about twenty centimetres to his death."

Sure enough, when Delyth looked, Tom was already on his feet and rubbing his chest where the harness had cut into him.

Tom gazed up at his sister; he looked shaken but he managed a weak smile. "Don't look so worried, sis. I'm alright."

James was brutally sensible. "For fuck's sake, stop pissing about. The whole lot might collapse."

Tom's face dropped. He scurried to the edge of the rock screed and clambered up the steps cut into the walls of the pipe. After hanging helpless for what seemed an age, his escape turned out to be ridiculously easy, and it was less than a minute before he joined them on the ledge.

Delyth embraced her brother, and this time Tom clung to her.

When he disengaged, Tom's face was ashen. "Rick is dead," he said. "He fell down the chimney when the roof collapsed."

The others stared at him in silence. They'd all worked out that Rick must have fallen down the pipe, but hearing it confirmed was a shock.

"Rick found me as I was about to climb down," Tom explained. "The water was pouring through the roof, then rock and mud started falling, it happened so fast. One moment he was standing next to me, then the rocks hit him and he fell." Tom's face twitched and tears rolled down his cheeks. "It's my fault," he said, his voice cracking. "If I hadn't panicked, Rick wouldn't have been killed."

"That's enough." James' voice was firm. "It's not your fault. What matters is how we get out of here."

"But what about Rick?"

"If he's under that lot, there's nothing we can do; we've got enough to deal with ourselves, like how we get out."

"But that *is* the only way out," argued Tom, pointing to the pipe. "There must be a hundred tonnes of rock and mud down there. It would take weeks to dig ourselves out!"

"We'll be dead by then," said Emma. The magnitude of what she had said was left hanging in the air.

James was the first to break the silence. "We need to stay positive. Mags will raise the alarm when we're not back on time. In a couple of hours there'll be a small army out there clearing the rubble. Two days max and we'll be out of here."

"How long will the torches on our helmets last?" asked Delyth, who surprised everyone with how calmly she accepted the situation.

"Rick said three hours," replied James, "so we should use the lights sparingly to conserve power. We've got the torches on our phones, but I vote we reserve those for an emergency."

"Agreed," said Emma. "We'd better switch the lamps off now."

James and Delyth nodded, and they were plunged into darkness. They sat waiting for their eyes to adjust. Nobody spoke.

Tom gripped Delyth's hand. He was normally the positive twin, but the prospect of spending hour after hour in this pitch-black hellhole was unbearable. He tried to think how lucky he was not to have been killed, but it didn't allay his guilt. He'd panicked like an idiot and Rick had paid the price. Now, with the darkness pressing in, the urge to run had returned. Delyth squeezed his hand. He rewarded her with a brittle smile, then realized that she couldn't see, and the gesture was wasted. He wondered if he could ever get used to this new black existence.

Tom lay in the dark, brooding and listening to the others breathing, for what seemed an age. He was about to check the time on his phone when Delyth spoke. "I'm thirsty," she said. "My bottle's empty."

"Mine too," said Emma. "We'll have to fill them up soon, I watched one of those survival programmes – you know the one where people get dropped on an island? One of the guys on there said you can go without food for a month, but only two days without water."

"Water's not a problem," said Tom. "There's loads of it. It's why the roof fell in!"

"I can't hear any water now," Emma observed. "The fall has turned the tap off."

James flicked on his headlight and pointed it upwards. Emma was right; the stream that had been gushing down from the roof had dried up.

"Told you," said Emma.

Tom stared up into the void. "Do you think it's stable now?"

As if somebody had heard him, some rocks clattered noisily into the pipe. They came to rest on the spoil heap where Tom had been standing earlier. They all jumped.

"That was a warning." James said. "More could come down any moment. I'm going back to the Blue Cavern. It's safer, and there's water."

"You must be joking!" Tom couldn't think of anything worse than attempting to crawl through to the cavern a second time.

James was insistent. "I'm not sitting here with my fingers crossed, hoping I don't get buried. I'm going back. There's a pool in there and water dripping off the stalactites. We can fill the bottles as much as we want."

Emma glanced up at the void above the rock fall. "I'm coming with you. We can't stay here."

"Me too," said Delyth.

"Well?" James looked at Tom.

Tom couldn't think of an idea he hated more, but he couldn't think of anything else, so he nodded.

"We should leave a message for the rescuers," Emma urged. "They need to know we're further inside."

"Good idea." James looked at the others enquiringly. "Anyone got a pen and paper?"

Tom's anxiety made him pissy. "For Christ's sake! Do you really think we'd bring fucking stationery down here?" He patted his pockets as if he were searching. "Nope, nothing."

Emma sniggered.

"Well you think of a better idea then, smartarse!" James snapped.

The atmosphere became charged. The two girls, shocked to see the boys argue, said nothing.

Tom's eyes flashed, then he shrugged his shoulders in surrender. He knew his friend was rattled. He recalled how three bullies had cornered James in the playground on his first day of school. James was outnumbered and much younger than his tormentors. He must have been very frightened, but instead of running away he launched himself at the older boys and snapped one of their fingers. From that day nobody picked on James. And he, as James' friend, lived under his protection. When James felt threatened, it was best to back off.

Delyth intervened. "What about making a message with stones?" she suggested. "We could make letters or maybe an arrow pointing down the passage."

"Neat," agreed Emma. "There are loads of stones."

The mood of the group lightened as they busied themselves collecting rocks and arranging them on the ground. They felt better doing something. Anything was better than sitting in the dark. When they'd finished, they stood back and admired their work.

Written in capital letters the stones read: WE ARE HERE, followed by a large arrow pointing down the horizontal shaft.

"They'd be blind if they missed that," said James. "Anyway, we'll hear them break through."

"If they break through, you mean," muttered Tom.

Chapter 11

Mags luxuriated in a piping hot bath. *I'm too long in the tooth for running up and down these hills*, she thought. She pinched a roll of fat on her belly. *I'll have to go on a diet!* Her friends were green with envy when they found out about her relationship with the dashing army officer, but she was about to hit forty and was finding it hard to keep up with her younger partner. Her sister had been disapproving; what a pity she wasn't here when Rick and Anne met. Rick had told her about the hard time she'd had given him. *Little prude*, she smirked. *I bet she fancies him.*

Then she remembered she said she'd phone. She hauled herself out of the bath and grabbed a towel, then realised her mobile was downstairs. *Anne will have to wait*, she thought. *If I don't get lunch on soon they'll be back before it's ready.* She hurried to her bedroom to dress.

Thirty minutes later, Mags was bustling around the kitchen like a woman possessed. She glanced at the clock on the wall; it was one-thirty. Lunch would be ready at two. She'd timed it to a tee, she thought smugly. When two o'clock came and went, and they hadn't arrived, she stirred the mashed potatoes irritably and took the pans off the heat. *That man would be late for his own funeral!* she thought. By three o'clock, Mags was concerned. *They should've been back over an hour ago*, she thought. *I hope everything's alright.*

Mags glanced at her mobile. She considered calling 999, then thought better of it. There'd been a terrific fuss over the stalker at the lake last year, and stupid stories about the lake being haunted. Any more adverse reports concerning Abereiddy Adventure Holidays could finish the business. She had only one option, she would have to see what had happened herself.

Mags yanked her boots on; they were still soggy from the morning. *Yuck!* she thought, as she stepped off the porch. *This is the last thing I want to be doing.* The rain had stopped, but the soothing effects of the bath quickly evaporated as she plodded up the hill. Her boots slithered on the muddy path, and she slowed. They were probably perfectly safe, so there was no point risking a twisted ankle. When she reached the cliff that Rick and the kids had abseiled down and saw the rope still attached to the metal stake, her heart sank.

"Rick, can you hear me?" she shouted down at the beach. "Rick? RICK!"

She tried to remain calm, but her instincts were telling her to press the panic button. She reached into the pocket of her anorak and pulled out her mobile. The screen displayed a single signal bar. Should she ring 999? She hesitated, then slipped the phone back in her pocket. She paced the cliff edge. *If this is a false alarm, Rick will kill me.* She decided to check the cave herself.

The descent didn't faze Mags – she was an experienced climber – but she was on her own, so she took her time, carefully picking her way down the cliff face. The instant her feet hit the beach and she'd detached the rope from her harness, she sensed something was wrong.

The cove was deserted. The only sign of life was a flock of oystercatchers *peep-peeping* as they foraged amongst the seaweed for sand hoppers and shellfish.

The tide was coming in fast. The rocks at the bottom of the beach had already disappeared, and water was creeping over the gravel towards the cave.

"Rick, can you hear me?" she shouted. The sound echoed off the cliff, and the silence that followed seemed to confirm her worst fears. She stood there for a desperate moment, straining to hear a response, then ran up the beach towards the cave.

Mags stopped at the entrance and peered into the gloom. "Rick! James! Can anybody hear me?" *Shit*, she thought, *I'll have to go in*. She fumbled for her mobile and switched on the torch. The beam was pathetic, but she wasn't fazed. She'd been in the cave many times, and she knew her way around.

She strode up the gravel into the dark. When she reached the point where the gravel turned to sand, she flicked the beam over the ceiling. This was where the roof got low. She wasn't wearing a helmet and didn't want to bang her head. With the beam waving around above her head she didn't see the rock on the floor and stumbled. She fell awkwardly, her phone falling from her hand.

She lay on the sand, stunned. She'd banged her shoulder, nothing serious. She sat up and groped for the phone. It was undamaged, and the torch was still on. She wiped sand off the screen and directed the beam into the cave. "What the..." Mags' voice trailed off.

When the penny dropped, she screamed and rushed at the heap of debris, scrabbling at the rock and wet clay with her bare hands. "Oh God! Rick! RICK!" Even in her distress, she realised her efforts were futile. It would take a big team to clear the rubble and mud.

Mags wiped her muddy, wet hands on her trousers and slid back down the pile. She needed to find a mobile signal fast.

She bolted for the entrance, splashing through the incoming tide, and squinting to protect her eyes from the afternoon sun. She pulled out her mobile and punched in 999. If there had been a signal, and she'd managed to get through, all the emergency operator would have heard was screaming. Because Mags had just seen that her hands and trousers weren't smeared in mud. They were covered in blood.

Chapter 12

As she followed James back down the passage, Emma was frightened. Really frightened. It wasn't easy to admit. She'd always regarded herself as pretty tough. *Or tough and pretty*, as she'd sometimes told herself in the bathroom mirror. She wondered if James was scared. If he was, he showed no sign of it; on the contrary, their plight seemed to give him a buzz. *He's either very brave or he hasn't any imagination* at all, she thought.

She shuddered, picturing a cold, miserable existence in the darkness, followed by a lingering death of hypothermia or starvation. Her sense of humour came to the rescue. *Mum would pay a fortune for this at a health spa*, she thought, spring water, mud treatments, a weight loss program, and best of all, no contact with Dad.

Her whimsy was brought to an end when she blundered into James.

"We've reached the entrance to the low tunnel," he said. "We'll wait here for the others."

As she huddled next to James, contemplating the slither through to the Blue Cavern, she was surprised and a little irritated at how easily she had accepted James' command.

"Hurry up, Tom!" shouted James. "We're ready to go through."

Tom scurried along the passage. "I'm coming!" He was terrified of going down that dreadful hole, but even more worried that the others might leave him behind.

"Are you sure you're up for this?" asked James when he caught up.

Tom bit his lip, "I'll do it this time, I promise."

"Good, you go first then," ordered James. "You'll be fine, just keep moving forward. I'll be right behind you."

Tom felt the full force of James' stare. He knew his friend was trying to help, but James could be intimidating when he wanted to be.

Tom nodded meekly and James softened his voice. "No messing about in there, all right?" he added as Tom slid out of sight.

Whether it was James' bullying tactics or an adrenaline burst, this time Tom managed the tight squeeze into the cavern without a hitch.

James quickly joined him. "Well done mate," James muttered as they squatted together on the damp cave floor.

Tom grinned weakly. "Thanks," he replied.

Tom would never admit it, but he hero-worshipped James. He knew only James could have forced him to go down that hole, and for that he was grateful. He also felt more confident he could now master his claustrophobia. *Good job*, he thought, *because for the next day or so I'm stuck here.*

The two girls emerged from the tunnel and looked expectantly at James.

"We'd better have a good look around," he suggested, "just in case there's another way out."

"Don't be thick," said Emma. "We all know perfectly well this is a dead end."

James' tongue poked angrily out of his mouth.

"Don't argue," snapped Delyth, her voice echoing in the enclosed space.

James was about to retaliate but thought better of it. "You're right, let's stay cool," he said. "This is going to be a long wait." He looked at Emma in the flickering torchlight. "I'm not stupid. I know there's no way out," he confessed, "but I'm crap at sitting still. It helps if I do something."

The angry spark went out of Emma's eyes, and she surprised herself by accepting the olive branch. "I'm sorry," she said, "I guess we're all wound up. You're right; we may as well have a look round. It won't do any harm."

James reached out to touch Emma's arm, then withdrew. "Fine," he mumbled awkwardly, "We'd better use one light at a time to save power."

On second viewing, James thought the cave looked as wonderful as the first, but knowing that this beautiful place could prove to be their tomb, the glistening blue rock formations took on a more sinister aspect.

James clambered over the slimy rocks, peering into every nook or crevice, probing for a potential escape route. The others followed dutifully. None of them believed there was any hope of finding another exit, but James was a force of nature. Nobody wanted to argue with him.

The cavern was enormous, and by the time James explored the far end of the cave, his torch was fading, so he didn't know the spring was there until icy cold water poured over the top of his boot.

"Urghhh!" James recoiled. "I'm soaked."

He swung the failing beam and illuminated a pool about five metres in diameter. Then the light went out. "Shit! Shit! Shit!" James shook his foot, trying not to fall in the pool. "That's all I need."

Emma switched on her lamp, and all four of them peered down the beam. The pool was deep, very deep, and once the ripples from James' foot had disappeared, the water was still and crystal clear.

"You were lucky you didn't fall in," said Delyth. "You could have drowned."

James brushed aside her concerns. "Shine the torch up here." He pointed to the cave wall. Water was dripping from a crevice in the rock.

"It's a spring!" Tom exclaimed. "A blue spring."

The water spread like a curtain over the surface of the rock and trickled into the pool. Where the water flowed, the rock was encrusted with slimy blue fungus.

James knelt down and scooped some water from the pool. They'd been in the cave for several hours now and his lips were parched. He sucked the water into his mouth. It had a faintly acidic taste, but it wasn't salty. "I think it's safe," he pronounced.

Emma wasn't convinced. Water always came from plastic bottles in supermarkets. "I'm not drinking that!" she said.

"You don't have any choice," Delyth told her. "We'll probably be down here for days."

Emma took a sip and wrinkled her nose, "It's ghastly," she complained. "I'd have to be dying of thirst before I'd drink that!"

"It may well come to that," said James grimly. "Delyth's right, we don't have a choice. This is all the water we've got. I think we ought to drink, then switch off the light and try to get some sleep."

"What time is it?" asked Tom. His stomach was telling him that too many hours had elapsed since breakfast.

James pulled out his mobile. "Ten past five," he said, his mind on the same subject. "Tea time!"

"Has anybody got any food?" Tom asked.

James perked up. "I bet one of you girls has got some chocolate?"

Emma shook her head, but Delyth looked sheepish.

"Come on what have you got?" wheedled Tom, guessing his sister had something stashed away.

Delyth reached in her pocket and pulled out a Mars bar. It had got squashed, and the wrapper was torn at one end. The boys eyed it greedily.

"Go on, give us a bite," begged Tom.

"No!" insisted James. "We'll save it for later. Perhaps we should cut it up and have it for breakfast tomorrow."

Tom groaned, but didn't argue. Delyth put the bar back in her pocket. James watched her hide the chocolate and tried not to think about food. He dreaded to think how hungry he'd be by the morning.

They sat on a flat, rocky ledge near the pool, each of them lost in their own thoughts. Emma was thoroughly miserable; the sweat between her skin and the waterproof lining of her cavesuit had chilled.

She rubbed her hands. She'd been cold for some time, but stress and the exertion of climbing through the cave system had pushed this to the back of her mind. Now the adrenaline had worn off, she was shivering, and her fingers felt numb. She stared at her hands; they were puffy, as if she'd laid in the bath too long. One of her nails was cracked and her pink nail varnish was chipped.

She removed her hard hat and ran her fingers through her hair. It felt limp, tangled, and gritty. *Don't be pathetic*, she thought, *who cares what I look like? Nobody's going to see me down here*. She shivered again and curled up into a ball.

"We'd better put the light out," she said bravely.

Delyth looked frightened. Tom put his arm protectively around his sister. She snuggled up to him. Her teeth were chattering.

"You're right," agreed James. Emma killed the light.

Chapter 13

The climb up the cliff passed in a blur. Mags, in her panic, had made the ascent at breakneck speed and only when she reached the top did she realise how tired she was. She collapsed, panting, on the damp grass, pulled out her mobile and stared at the screen. This time she had a decent signal. Ignoring the dried blood on her hands, she dialled 999 and waited.

"Thank God," she babbled as the operator asked what service she required. Somehow, she managed to gather her wits and explain the situation.

"Stay where you are," instructed the operator. "I've put a call through to Air Sea Rescue, they will be with you shortly. Have you got a friend who can look after you?"

"My- my sister," stammered Mags.

"I suggest you contact her and ask her to pick you up after the helicopter arrives."

Mags pressed the end call button and dialled her sister. No reply. "They must be on the beach." She considered sending a WhatsApp. The idea was enough to trigger tears. What should she send? There wasn't an emoji that remotely conveyed what she needed to say.

She lay on the grass, weeping, her thoughts jumbled. She was getting older, and Rick was the man who she hoped would give her the child she longed for. She couldn't bear to lose him. And how was she supposed to tell her sister that her boy was trapped and might be injured or even dead? The distant yammering of rotor blades jolted her back to her senses, and she struggled to her feet, waving madly.

"Here! Here!" she yelled, as the helicopter veered in her direction. It circled the headland before hovering over a flat meadow cut for silage. The meadow was sixty metres from the cliff, but even at that distance, Mags could feel the wind from the whirring blades. The noise was deafening.

She carried on shouting as the helicopter set down, and three helmeted men clad in orange flying suits disembarked. They pulled rucksacks from the aircraft and calmly jogged over to where Mags was standing.

The first to reach her was tall with an outrageous moustache. He held out his hand.

"My name's Peter Fenton," he announced in a clipped tone. "These gentlemen are Ron and David. I believe you have people stuck in a cave? Please, take your time, and tell me what you know."

If Mags had not been out of her mind with worry, she'd have laughed. Her world was falling apart and a bloke doing a Biggles impression was introducing himself as if they were meeting at a vicar's tea party. Somehow this was immensely reassuring.

Wiping her tear-stained cheeks, she explained the plan Rick had made to take the youngsters into the cave. She also described what she'd seen in the cave entrance and what she knew of the layout. Peter Fenton, obviously the guy in charge, took notes and, with Mags' help, sketched out a plan of the cave.

When they'd finished, Mags showed them the blood on her hands. "Get them out quickly," she pleaded, "One of them is hurt or..." She couldn't bring herself to say it.

Flight Lieutenant Peter Fenton sat Mags down and nodded at the man he'd introduced as Ron. Ron, a paramedic, took a silver lined blanket out of a rucksack and wrapped it round Mags' shoulders.

Fenton turned to winch operator David Edwards. "We're going to need backup," he told him. "If this lady's right, there'll be a lot of rubble to move before we can get them out. Rig up a tripod. We're going to need some heavy gear down there. And tell Owain to get down there and take a look." He jerked his thumb at a fourth man who'd appeared on the clifftop.

Fenton spoke into his headset. "Delta One, we have an uninjured female for extraction, and we're sending down a team for a recce. If we have any cave rescue specialists on standby, tell them to pack their buckets and spades; we've a bit of digging to do."

"Roger, Bravo One. Should they bring swimming trunks?" The female voice at HQ had a husky Welsh accent.

Fenton grinned. One day, he promised himself, he'd ask that little flirt in Swansea HQ to dinner. His reply was consummately professional. "Good point, Delta One. The tide's coming in; tell them to bring diving gear. Over."

"Roger. Over and out," replied the flirt in Swansea.

Fenton turned to see Dave assembling steel lifting gear and Owain strapping on his helmet and climbing equipment. Two minutes later, Owain was disappearing over the cliff edge.

This was Owain Morgan's first operation. He'd been out on a couple of false alarms, but this was the real thing, and he was determined to show his new team he could hack it. Keen to impress, he made the descent quickly, but hesitated as he reached the bottom. The incoming tide had covered the gravel at the foot of the cliff. Owain grimaced; he was going to get wet. *Bollocks. I should have put on a wetsuit*, he thought as he slid into the knee-deep cold water.

"Delta One," he said into his radio mic. "Descent completed. I'm standing in water. I can see the cave from here, and I'm going in."

Up on the clifftop, Dave couldn't resist a jibe. "Captain Keen has got his arse wet." He smiled.

Commander Fenton grinned back. "Don't get too comfy, Dave. You're next!"

Chapter 14

James lay in the dark and tried not to think about the cold. The foot which had gotten dipped in the pool was freezing, and his nose and ears were numb. He couldn't get comfortable, and, tired as he was, sleep was impossible. He could hear fidgeting and deduced the others couldn't sleep either. The darkness was oppressive. Even on the blackest night, it was possible to see something, but underground he literally couldn't see his hand in front of his face.

Worst of all, he felt like they were being watched. He knew it was stupid, but the feeling had been growing ever since they'd switched off the light.

"Don't be a dick," he muttered.

He tried to imagine being rescued to block out the disturbing thoughts but, try as he might, he couldn't shake off the feeling that someone or something was watching their every move.

"James," hissed Emma, "I can't sleep. I'm freezing. Do you mind if I cuddle up? James, can you hear me?"

James lay still, not daring to reply, as Emma crawled over and snuggled up. They curled together, shivering, Emma's back pressed against James' front. They lay there a while, sharing body heat, then James put his arms around her waist. Even muddy and cold, Emma was highly desirable and as he held her his pulse quickened.

Don't be a prat, he told himself, *this isn't the time or the place.* He closed his eyes. Emma had removed her hard hat, and the back of her head crushed against his face. Despite the grime, he could smell the shampoo she'd used that morning. The fragrance was intoxicating.

Emma lay there, unmoving. She understood the effect she was having, and, despite the cold, she smiled.

James woke out of a fitful sleep. His stomach felt tender, and he was sweating. He'd been dreaming again, and as on the previous two nights, his dreams had been vivid and distressing. The nightmare was always the same; he was in a burning room when a huge man wearing a metal helmet burst through the door. James remembered the man swinging a sword through the smoke, then the dream ended in a starburst of orange flames, followed by screaming.

James made a grab for his bumbag; his chest was constricting. After much fumbling, he located his inhaler, took a deep breath and held it for a few seconds, then exhaled slowly. The medication percolated deep inside his lungs, gently opening up his airways. He closed his eyes and focused on breathing as the asthma attack subsided.

"Are you alright?" Emma switched on her light.

James could see the concern in her face. "Yeah." He sighed. "I'm lucky I didn't have an attack earlier." He gave Emma a weary smile. "You can put the light out. I'll be fine in a minute."

Emma and James cuddled up again, but the excitement had gone; both of them were too miserable to think about anything other than staying warm. Soon Emma dropped off, but for James sleep remained elusive.

It wasn't the cold keeping him awake, it was fear. *I've got every right to be scared shitless*, he reasoned, *I'm trapped thirty metres underground. I don't know for sure if anybody is trying to get us out. There's no food and the batteries for the lights are running out. And on top of that I stand a good chance of getting hypothermia. I'd be an idiot if I wasn't scared.*

But deep inside, James knew this wasn't the whole story. There were warning bells going off in his head that told him something else, something very disturbing, was going on. James wasn't someone given to flights of fancy, but he was a hunter, and hunters learn to trust their instincts. And right now, all of James' instincts screamed danger.

He sat up and stared into the blackness.

It defied logic, but the impression that they were being watched wouldn't go away, nor would the conviction that whatever was watching was dangerous. The feeling was so strong at that he almost turned on the light to challenge the silent watcher.

Get a grip, he thought, *we've only been down here a few hours and I'm already going mad.* His stomach gurgled rebelliously, and his thoughts returned to more mundane matters, *I suppose its hunger pains*, he thought. *I haven't eaten for ages.*

Unable to sleep and unwilling to waste the battery in his phone to check the hour, James felt the time stretch out in the darkness. Hour after hour, he listened to Emma's rhythmic breathing while he lay churning things over. Suddenly his abdomen was gripped by cramp. The pain was excruciating.

He groaned.

Somebody switched on a light, and they all sat there blinking.

"What's going on?" asked Emma, startled.

"My insides are on fire," grunted James through gritted teeth.

"I'm not feeling good either," complained Tom, clutching his stomach.

"Don't tell me you're coming down with a tummy bug!" moaned Emma. "If you need the toilet it's going to be disgusting." Her nose wrinkled, "We haven't even got toilet paper."

"Thanks for the sympathy," snapped Tom. "If you don't stop whining, I'll shit right next to you!"

"Shut up!" yelled James.

Emma glared at Tom. His vulgarity had shocked her.

Delyth turned to James. "Have we got a bug?" she asked. "I feel awful."

"How the hell would he know?" butted in Emma. Although she was the only one unaffected by the mysterious illness, she seemed the most upset.

James began to chuckle. The others looked at him as if he were a madman. "You've got to see the funny side." He smiled bleakly. "Just when we thought things couldn't get any worse, we go and get a tummy bug. And there's no bog for three miles!"

Delyth changed the subject. "What time is it?" she asked.

Tom flicked on his mobile, "Two thirty-five in the morning," he sighed. "No wonder I'm knackered."

"It's too cold to sleep," complained Delyth.

"Well, what do you suggest?" replied Tom. "How about we turn off the light and play I spy?"

"Let's just settle for turning off the light," said James sensibly. "If the battery conks out, we'll be in an even worse muddle."

Once again, the four of them huddled together, trying to conserve body heat. For a few minutes nothing was said. The only sound was Tom's teeth rattling like an old-fashioned typewriter.

After a while, Delyth asked the question they were all thinking, "Do you think we'll get out of here?" Her voice was quiet.

"Yeah," said James, who was considering the possibility they might die of hypothermia. "I bet the cave entrance is crawling with people by now. They're bound to break though in a few hours."

Chapter 15

Rick slipped in and out of consciousness several times before his eyes finally flickered open. His first thought was that he was dead, then the pain kicked in and he knew the fall hadn't killed him. He was lying face-down, with his head twisted to one side. His body was squashed into the soft floor of the cave, and gritty sand clogged his left eye and partially filled his mouth. He managed to spit out some of the sand. The pain was incredible. He sobbed in agony as his smashed jaw grated against damaged nerve endings.

Shit! he thought *I need to focus*. He concentrated on the far wall of the cave, determined not to pass out again. Eventually the pain receded to a dull throbbing ache, and he was able to evaluate his predicament.

He was pinned underneath a slab of slate that must have formed part of the ceiling above the pipe. He couldn't feel his legs, and it occurred to him that his spine might be injured. He couldn't move his right arm. It was trapped under his abdomen, and from the pain in his elbow, he deduced he had broken at least one bone in that arm. The only limb he could move was his left arm. Slowly, he moved his hand towards his head and gingerly explored the sticky mess that was once his face.

He fought to quell the sobs of self-pity and pain, and, drawing on his army training, rallied himself to focus on survival. *I must be on the entrance side of the rock fall*, he reasoned, *or there would be no light at all. If I can hold on long enough somebody will come looking for us.*

Feeling started to return to his shattered legs. With the feeling came immense pain.

Please, God, help me.

He blacked out.

Owain Morgan waded into the cave and flicked on his headlamp. *Careful*, he told himself, looking at the ceiling nervously. *If there's been a fall, the roof may still be unstable.*

Although the sea was calm, the tide created a swell as it entered the confines of the cave, and Owain had to brace his legs to stop himself being buffeted against the cave walls. Fortunately, the cave floor shelved steeply, and after a dozen or so steps in the swirling water, Owain found the water was getting shallower. Even better, he could see dry sand on the floor of the cave up ahead. He sloshed through the remaining water and onto the dry cave floor, only to be confronted by a mass of rock and mud.

"Delta One, do you read me?" he asked into his mic. "I'm at the rock fall now…" His voice faltered. A sickly smell pervaded the damp air. He shone the beam over the debris. In the dim light, he picked out a dark stain on the sand adjacent to the fall. Stooping to investigate, he knew even before his fingers touched the sticky sand that the stain was blood. A lot of blood.

"Shit," he muttered, wiping the blood on his sleeve. "Delta One, get Ron down here ASAP, and tell him to bring the medikit and stretcher. I can't see a body, but there's blood everywhere. It looks bad; I'm going to take a closer look."

The blood was oozing from under a massive slab of rock at the bottom of the fall, so Owain began to clear away some smaller rocks to gain access to the slab. The rocks proved heavier than they looked, and, despite the chilly air in inside the cave, he was soon sweating from the exertion. He was relieved to hear Ron and Dave splashing into the cave, whistling like demented songbirds. They placed the stretcher they'd been carrying on the dry sand at the base of the rock fall, and unslung the rucksacks containing their equipment.

"The tide's still coming in," Ron observed dourly. "We'd better stash the stuff further up this lot." He pointed to the rock fall.

Meanwhile, Dave had noticed the blood. He stopped whistling and clucked his tongue. "Whatever we do, we'd better do it fast," he said, rolling on a pair of latex gloves. "I doubt anyone can survive losing that much blood, but if they are still alive, we'd better get them out quick before they drown."

"Help me shift these rocks!" snapped Owain, who was losing patience with his older colleagues.

Ron and Dave gave each other a knowing look as Owain started feverishly pulling aside more rocks. They'd worked together for years and knew this was going to be a long haul with some unpleasant surprises along the way. They worked steadily, clearing rubble from around the big boulder. Within minutes they'd opened up a gap, and Owain peered into the space under the slate slab. What he saw made him recoil in horror.

The casualty's head glistened red in the wavering light from the torch.

Owain's heart was hammering, and sweat was beading on his face. "I think I'm going to be sick," he choked.

Ron had no time for theatricals; they had a job to do and not much time to do it. "Get out of the way!" He shoved Owain aside and crawled under the slab, which pinned Rick to the cave floor like a mouse in a trap. In the cramped space, Ron assessed the extent of the victim's injuries as best he could.

The casualty was an adult white male; it was difficult to guess age because of trauma to the face. Remarkably, his torso was undamaged, and there were signs of shallow breathing. The major issue was that the rock, which had protected the man's upper body, had crushed both legs just below the knees, trapping him and causing massive blood loss.

Ron located the carotid artery; the pulse was weak. "He's alive, but we'll have to move fast or we'll lose him," he shouted. "He's lost a lot of blood; get a drip here fast."

"Don't just stand there!" yelled Dave. "Pass the bloody drip!" Owain jumped as if someone had stuck an electrode down his pants. He grabbed a plastic bag of plasma and pressed it into Ron's waiting hand.

Working feverishly in the dark and cramped conditions, Ron inserted the drip into Rick's forearm.

"What are we going to do about those legs?" Ron gazed dispassionately at his patient's shattered knees.

"We'll have to get him out fast," advised Dave. "The tide's coming in. He'll be submerged in half an hour." As if on cue, there was a swooshing, gurgling sound as the tide renewed its assault on the upper reaches of the cave.

"Shut up," replied Ron, unfazed. "I'm thinking."

"Well think faster," replied Dave. "This water is going to play havoc with my athlete's foot."

Ron snorted with amusement. "That's one problem this guy will never have to worry about," he riposted. "The only way to get him out is to cut him out. We'll never shift this rock in a month of Sundays, so we've got a choice. We let him drown, or we amputate both legs at the knee." Ron stopped; he had felt the casualty's body tremble. He looked up and was startled to find Rick's eyes open.

The eyes regarded him pleadingly. "He's conscious," Ron exclaimed loudly. Realising his patient had understood what they were proposing, he grasped Rick's hand. "If you want to get out of here alive, we've no choice. You understand what I'm saying?"

Another tremor ran through Rick's body, and it seemed to Ron that his patient was trying to communicate. But Rick was too weak, and his jaw too badly smashed, to say anything; all he could do was stare at his rescuer, his pupils dilated, his fear palpable.

Ron forced himself not to look away. He was a seasoned professional, but he had a lump in his throat when he spoke. "You have to trust us," he said quietly. "I'll give you a shot of something and you won't feel a thing. When you come round, you'll be safe in hospital. I promise."

He squeezed Rick's hand again. "Morphine," he hissed urgently, holding out his hand to Dave. "Hurry up, he must be in agony."

Dave passed the syringe and watched as Ron inserted the needle into Rick's forearm. "Well, at least he's out of it," muttered

Dave as Rick's eyelids fluttered and closed. "Let's just hope he wakes up."

Another surge of seawater gurgled up the narrow passage, this time to within a metre of the stricken expedition leader.

"He won't if you just stand there and yak," complained Ron. "Pass the medikit. We'll get the bleeding under control, then make a start on cutting him free. And for Christ's sake, get an oxygen mask on him or he'll drown."

Ron crawled further under the rock and examined Rick's trapped legs in the flickering beam of his headlamp. He'd assisted in roadside amputations before, but he'd always had a doctor with him, and it had never been in conditions like this.

Ron reached into the medibag and pulled out two lengths of webbing, each with a brass clasp on the end. He needed to apply a tourniquet on each leg. He gritted his teeth and burrowed into the shingle, wriggling towards where Rick's legs disappeared under the rock.

Icy water rushed under the rock, soaking through his boiler suit. Ron choked back curses and concentrated on the job in hand.

Working quickly, he scooped blood-soaked sand and shingle from under Rick's legs and passed the webbing around them just above the knee. Miraculously, he managed to tighten both tourniquets before the next tidal surge. "Welcome to the house of horror," he muttered as he tore open the plastic wrapping of a sterile scalpel.

"You okay down there?" inquired Dave, peering under the rock.

"Yeah, fine! You know me, never happier than when I'm hacking off some poor bloke's legs."

For once, Dave was serious. "Do you want help, mate?" he asked quietly.

"No, but thanks for the offer. It's a bit of a squeeze down here as it is. I'll be okay. It won't be a pretty job, but we'll get him out of here."

The extent of Rick's injury made the removal of the first limb simple. The crushing weight of the rock had all but severed the leg midway down the shin, so all Ron had to do was separate the remaining strands of muscle and sinew that connected the lower leg to the rest of the body. The injuries to the second leg were less serious, so Ron lost valuable minutes scrabbling at the shingle underneath the trapped limb in the vain hope that they could draw Rick out from under the rock without the need for a second amputation. The rising water soon forced him to resort to the scalpel.

The second operation was more challenging than the first. Not only was the leg less accessible and therefore less easy to work on, but it was intact, so as well as cutting the tough tendons around the knee, he had the sickening task of sawing through the knee joint. To make matters worse, the tide was continuing to rise, threatening to engulf them both. It was with considerable relief that an emotionally drained Ron called to his waiting colleagues.

"I've finished," he gasped as another wave hissed up the shingle. "Help me drag him out."

Dave caught hold of Rick under the armpit and gently pulled.

"For God's sake, Owain, give us a hand! Shove the bloody stretcher under him!"

Gradually, the limp form of the unfortunate expedition leader emerged from under the rock fall and was strapped onto the waiting stretcher.

Owain stared at the tattered stumps where Rick's lower legs had been a few minutes earlier. He felt bile rise in his throat again, and only just managed to avoid the embarrassment of being sick.

"You poor bastard," he murmured, reaching down to feel for signs of life. He detected a pulse, but it was weak.

They looked up; they could hear shouting and hollow splashes.

"Looks like the cavalry are coming," grunted Dave as a group of men in wetsuits waded into the cave carrying heavy equipment.

Ron regarded their approach balefully. "I don't envy them. I can't see this ending well. Even if they shift this lot, surely none of those kids could have survived."

Chapter 16

Like a flock of wet pigeons, the people gathered on the headland huddled against the evening rain. They looked utterly dejected as they waited for the casualty to be winched up the cliff. Clad in bright waterproofs and high visibility jackets, they were a dazzling contrast to the grey seascape.

"He's coming up!" yelled a man in orange overalls. "Everybody, stay back, we don't want any accidents."

There was a buzz of anticipation in the fluorescent ranks, but as the stretcher appeared at the top of the cliff, the crowd fell silent and stared at the inert body. The brief reverie was broken by the blink of a flashbulb. A reporter in a yellow anorak elbowed his way forward.

"How is he?" the reporter shouted as the media scrum closed in around the victim.

"You were told to stay back!" snapped one of the paramedics holding the stretcher, but the reporter was not easily put off. "How badly hurt is he?" he persisted.

"His condition is critical," said the other stretcher-bearer tersely, irritated at the media circus. "Now stand back and let us get the guy out of here!"

The reporter was about to follow the stretcher as it was carried to the waiting helicopter, but a meaty hand clasped his shoulder. Police Constable Evan Jones had had enough. He'd witnessed this type of journalist before, and he wasn't prepared to give him any quarter. The reporter took one look at the burly Pembrokeshire policeman and backed away. He stood mutely with the rest of the crowd, and watched the helicopter whirr its way East towards Swansea.

"Where's the nearest pub?" the reporter asked a cameraman as the helicopter disappeared over the horizon. "We may as well go for a pint; I can't see them getting those kids out tonight."

"If at all," replied the cameraman blithely, not knowing how close he was to being punched in the head.

Richard Cordle clenched his fists and tried not to let the media lowlifes upset him. *It wouldn't do to lose my temper*, he thought. It was easy for these parasites to be brutally realistic, but it wasn't their kid down there. His guts churned. He couldn't bring himself to think of James lying down there injured or even... No! He had to cling to the hope that James and his friends would walk out of there alive and well.

He'd left Anne and Ed at Myrtle House with Mags and hurried up the cliff path to the rescue scene. That had been two hours ago. He'd wanted to help in the cave but the copper wouldn't let him, so he'd been there ever since, standing in the pouring rain. It was uncomfortable; he was dripping wet, and he knew it was a waste of time, but anything was better than the raw emotion back at Myrtle House.

He shivered as the onshore breeze whipped around his soaking wet jeans. When he'd left Myrtle House, Mags and Anne had been in floods of tears, frantic with worry. He knew he should be with them, but the lonely vigil in the wind and rain was infinitely preferable. Truth be told, he was terrified he would go to pieces if he stayed with them.

"Are you okay, sir?" It was Constable Jones.

Richard nodded unconvincingly.

"It won't do any good staying out here; you'll catch your death. Why don't you let me take you back to Myrtle House?" He offered kindly. "I promised to let Miss Edwards know as soon as they got her partner out, so it's no trouble. I could kill two birds with one stone."

"I can't go home without him..."

The taciturn policeman gripped his arm supportively. "I've got three boys of my own. I can only imagine what you're going through, sir." Constable Jones sighed and continued in a low voice, making sure no reporter was in earshot. "From what I've been told, it's going to be hours, if not days, before they reach the kids. If they've not been hurt in the fall, these lads will get them out. But you can't stay here all night. Let's nip back to Myrtle House, I'll have my chat to Miss Edwards, and we'll both have a nice hot mug of tea. If there are any developments, you'll be the first to know, I promise."

Richard opened his mouth to argue but surrendered to reason. He allowed the constable to lead him away.

Mags shifted uncomfortably in the blue hospital visitor's chair.

She'd been sitting there all night. Her neck was stiff, and her bottom felt sweaty against the cheap vinyl upholstery.

She rubbed her eyes and sat up. She must have dozed off because somebody had draped a blanket over her knees while she slept. She looked across at Rick. She was relieved to see his chest rising and falling rhythmically, but his eyes were still firmly closed. Tubes poked alarmingly out of his nose and a transparent mask delivering oxygen was clamped over his mouth. His normally ruddy complexion was pale, his skin translucent under the harsh glare of the neon light.

A monitor bleeped insistently from somewhere behind Rick's bed. Mags reached out and squeezed his hand; it felt cool to the touch.

The patterned curtains separating them from the rest of the ward swished open, and a harassed looking nurse bustled in. She gave Mags a tight little smile, gave the monitor a perfunctory glance, then pressed her index finger against Rick's wrist. After recording her patient's pulse, the nurse turned to Mags. "Are you okay, love?" she inquired. She had a soft, lilting Valley accent.

Mags didn't answer, instead she asked the same question she'd already asked the surgeon and the procession of nurses who had attended her fiancé. "How is he?"

The nurse, like the rest of her colleagues, answered carefully. "He's lost a lot of blood; his condition is critical."

"That means he could still die, doesn't it?"

The nurse regarded Mags appraisingly, and then, realising platitudes were not enough, decided to be frank. "Yes, it is still possible he could die. The operation went well but he's very weak. The doctor said the next hour or so will be critical, but he should pull through." She placed a reassuring hand on Mags' shoulder. "Why don't you nip down to the cafeteria for a cup of tea and something to eat if you can manage it? I'll keep a close eye on him, I promise." She looked at her watch. "It's gone six. They'll be serving breakfast now."

Mags bit her lip and looked at the space at the bottom of the bed where Rick's feet should have been.

"I'd prefer to stay," she replied. "If he wakes up on his own and finds out his legs aren't there, I'd never forgive myself."

Chapter 17

The humming of the generator reverberated around the cave, its output powering the LED spotlights, which bathed the rescuers in cold white light.

It was late afternoon on the second day of the operation. Despite the hydraulic lifting gear that had been flown in that morning, the work was physically demanding and dangerous.

It was Owain's third shift clearing the rubble from the vertical shaft. Ron and Dave had flown out in the air ambulance with the casualty, but he'd decided to stay. He'd been told he could go home, but he'd been the first in and he wanted to see the job through. He was dog-tired and his wetsuit chafed his groin and armpits. He glanced nervously above his head and heaved at the steel bar. "Here she comes!" he shouted.

"Okay below!"

The boulder rolled down the slope and landed with a thud on the cave floor. A shower of loose earth and smaller stones skittered behind. Men scrambled to attach chains to the massive lump of slate, ready to winch it out of the way, while others shovelled the smaller debris. Everyone was aware it was a race to find the kids alive, but they were hampered by falling debris and progress was agonizingly slow.

Every time they removed waste from the bottom of the fall, a hail of rock fragments rained from above pinging off the cowering rescuers' hard hats. Occasionally the removal of a boulder caused a large portion of the fall to slump onto the cave floor at the bottom of the chimney. When this happened, hard hats were not enough, and the men had to scurry towards the cave entrance for safety. One of the team hadn't been quick enough and a large chunk of rock had landed on his foot. The guy had been lucky and, despite his shouts, he'd escaped with minor bruising.

"What pig of a job," muttered Owain, checking the chin straps of his hat apprehensively. He was putting a brave face on things, but he was tired, and scared he'd find himself under the next big rock fall.

One of the volunteers, a local builder, tapped him on the shoulder. "Owain," he said, his weather-beaten face dripping with sweat, "how much more have we got to shift?"

"Hard to know. They say the shaft is fifteen metres high, but we don't know if it's filled right to the top with this stuff."

"There's a shitload of rubbish out here." The builder jerked his thumb in the direction of the cave entrance. "We can't have much further to go."

"Let's hope so. Those kids can't survive much longer in this cold."

"Poor buggers," grimaced the builder. "They must be scared shitless."

"At least we've haven't found any bodies."

"Yet."

It was Owain's turn to grimace. He hadn't recovered from the shock of finding Rick, and he dreaded finding a corpse. He didn't know how he'd cope if he found a dead kid. The builder patted him on the shoulder and retreated towards the cave entrance.

Owain gritted his teeth and jammed the steel bar under another rock. This was going to be another long night.

The Right Honourable Benjamin Kingsley-Smith slammed the newspaper on the coffee table in frustration. The cave rescue had made front-page news. *Not surprising*, he thought bitterly. It wasn't often the daughter of a cabinet minister got stuck in a cave. And that picture of the expedition leader being loaded into the helicopter with his feet cut off would have been hard for any editor to resist.

"Do something, Benjamin!" wailed his wife.

He held his head in his hands. "There's nothing more I can do," he sighed. "I've spoken to the Chief Constable; he assures me everything humanly possible is being done to get them out."

"Then come with me to Wales and wait for her. You're her father for God's sake!"

"We've been through all this before," he replied, trying to remain rational. "We agreed it would be counterproductive for me to be there. All it would achieve is to turn it into a bloody media circus and hamper the rescue. God knows it's bad enough as it is. That confounded reporter from the Daily Mail has even interviewed Denise, though I can't see what light our cleaning lady could shed on the matter."

Mrs Kingsley-Smith wasn't in a fit state to argue; emotionally drained and in a near catatonic state, she sat on the leather sofa, tears smudging her carefully applied makeup.

Benjamin looked across at his wife. For once, he felt able to look at her without feeling exasperated or downright cross. Lucinda was still an attractive woman; careful grooming and an obsession with healthy living had delayed the onset of middle age. But the strain of the last twenty-four hours had etched lines in her face, and, for the first time, he noticed the skin under her chin had begun to sag.

They'd met at a college ball in Oxford. She'd worn a green gown that night. He remembered how she'd turned and smiled at him; she'd looked stunning. A lump caught in his throat. Emma looked so much like her mother had done.

He sat on the sofa next to his wife. Even now, he felt unable to hold her hand.

God, where it had all gone wrong? He remembered the early years – how happy they'd been. Then work had taken over, and, gradually, the fire had gone out. He couldn't even remember the last time they shared a bed.

It had been Emma that had held them together. Beautiful, high-spirited Emma.

Waves of despair washed over him. He laid his head on his wife's shoulder and surrendered himself to the tears.

"Bugger the party conference," he snivelled. "The Prime Minister will just have to manage without me."

Chapter 18

James switched on his head torch and crawled towards the pool. His gut ached, and, despite the cold, his skin was hot to the touch. He flicked his tongue over his parched lips; he had a raging thirst. *It must be a fever*, he thought. He dipped his face in the pool and gulped down the cold, refreshing water.

His thirst slaked, he dragged himself back to the others. They looked like they were asleep, but their appearance worried him. All of them looked pale, but Tom looked dreadful; his skin had the same opaque quality as a sheet of white plastic stretched to its breaking point. His eyes were closed, but under the lids, his eyeballs moved as if he were having a nightmare. James shook his arm and Tom rolled over, face-down on the hard, slimy rock floor.

Emma woke, disturbed by the noise. She took a moment as she recovered her bearings, then she saw James kneeling next to Tom. "Is he okay?" she murmured.

"He's having some sort of fit! I can't wake him."

"What should we do?" Emma asked, beginning to panic. She'd woken up feeling distinctly unwell and shivering with cold. She was sure she was coming down with the same bug.

"I don't know," replied James. "We'd better lay him on his side in case he chokes."

James recalled the first aid he'd learned at school and hauled Tom into the recovery position. He felt for a pulse with his finger and was reassured by a steady rhythmic throb.

The commotion woke Delyth. She stared blankly at James and Emma as they tended to her brother, then began to cry. Emma left Tom and tried to console her friend, but Delyth's sobbing became hysterical. She only stopped when she threw up on the damp floor.

Emma overcame her distaste and retrieved a hanky from her pocket, using it to wipe the puke from her friend's mouth.

Delyth continued to cry, but her sobs were more subdued. "I'm sorry," she snivelled.

"What for?" James asked.

"I ate the chocolate," she confessed.

"What?" James exclaimed, amazed. "We're trapped in the dark with food poisoning or whatever and you're worried about *a bar of chocolate?*"

"But I promised Tom I'd share it, and now Tom's ill!" The sobbing started again.

James shook his head. He'd never understand girls.

Emma intervened. "Delyth," she said firmly, "we're going to be here a while, so we need to stay calm. Tom will be okay. We've just got a bug or eaten something funny."

"He'll be fine," insisted James, hoping to reassure. "But we must turn off the lamp or the battery will run out."

Emma nodded and James flicked the switch. The darkness embraced them.

When the light went out, Emma huddled close to James, listening to the others breathing. Soon, the uncomfortable feeling they were being watched returned. She sat up and stared into the blackness. It didn't make sense; they'd explored every inch of the cave. Nothing could be in there with them.

She snuggled to James like a frightened child. The feeling of a malevolent presence in the cave was palpable. She thought about telling James, but decided against it. She'd made a twit out of herself over the girl in the lake; he'd think she was crazy if she told him there was something out there in the dark. *I'm being a silly girl*, she told herself, but the hair on the back of her neck said otherwise. She'd never felt so scared.

Her tongue was swollen and sticky. She fumbled for her hard hat and sipped the water she'd scooped from the spring. She touched her abdomen; her tummy was tender. *I'm coming down with the bug*, she thought.

She smiled ruefully. At home she'd be creating a scene and Mum would be fussing over her like a mother hen. Down here it was best to keep her thoughts to herself. Her companions had too much to worry about themselves to listen to any whinging from her.

A thought popped into her head. *Perhaps it's the water making us sick?* She considered the idea and then discounted it. In this little corner of Wales, miles from any pollution, what could possibly be wrong with spring water?

Had a mycologist been present, they might have recognized the rare fungal bloom that lent the cave walls their extraordinary blue colour. Had they done so, they might have warned Emma that the mycotoxins produced by the fungus that gave the spring water its distinctive taste were reaching critical levels in her blood. Now it was only a matter of time before the toxins disrupted the nerve endings in her brain and began to distort her thoughts.

Chapter 19

Across a vast passage of time, the Druid Myrleduin observed the young people from the vantage of his own toxin-induced dream. He'd been studying them ever since they entered the sacred cave, waiting for the spring water to work its magic. It had been a long wait, but as Emma's body became limp, he felt his pulse quicken. He watched in eager anticipation as her eyes snapped open and her pupils dilated.

As the toxin-laced water scrambled Emma's brain and her mind began to open, Myrleduin's tattooed face cracked into a smile, displaying a ragged line of broken and discoloured teeth. The Druid didn't often smile, but this was a moment to savour, for which he'd watched and waited so long.

When he'd first seen the girl at the lake and glimpsed the symbol of the Goddess around her neck, he'd thought she might be the one he'd been tasked to find. Now, gazing at her beautiful young body, he was certain. It would be difficult to imagine a vessel more worthy of the Goddess.

The water in the cup shook violently, obscuring the image. Something was wrong.

Myrleduin peered into the chalice. His brow furrowed as he searched for the girl, then his eyes widened in surprise as a spirit rushed towards him out of the swirling water. Then the being was upon him, picking him up and throwing him to the ground like driftwood tossed upon the beach in a storm.

Myrleduin was afraid. This was not meant to happen. A mere boy couldn't be this strong.

Myrleduin fought back, willing the errant spirit back to the future from whence it came. He fought with increasing desperation, summoning powers honed by a lifetime of training and self-imposed privation. He knew the stakes were high. It was risky to take the girl, but it would be madness to let the others pass across. He suspected even the Master could not foresee the consequences if that happened. But the spirit was too strong even for Myrleduin, and quickly broke through his defences. The druid gasped in shock as the young man glared at him out of the water.

Chapter 20

James succumbed to the toxin soon after the light was switched off. He lay on the cave floor like a discarded doll, his arms outstretched in a picture of mute supplication. His eyes were open; the only sign of life was the rapid movement of his pupils.

The dreams commenced immediately.

It was the recurring nightmare he'd endured ever since he arrived in Wales. He was in a thatched building, the thatch was alight, the flames roaring through the tightly packed reeds and licking around the supporting beams. The door burst open, and a giant armed with a sword and wearing a helmet stepped inside. The man was grinning, his bared teeth gleamed white through his tangled red beard. He raised his sword. His eyes glittered in triumph. And then he disappeared into a wall of fire.

This is where the nightmare usually ended, but this time, aided by the mind-bending toxin, it continued. The flames were gone, and the grinning warrior replaced by something else. Something dangerous. James couldn't see what it was, he only knew it was there, watching and waiting in the shadows.

The urge to run and hide was overwhelming, but James wasn't programmed to give in to fear. His instinct was to fight even in his dreams. As a child, James had faced fear many times; fighting for breath in the night while his terrified parents held a nebulizer to his face and whispered anxiously to doctors on the phone.

His dad had told him once that what doesn't kill you makes you stronger. It was a throwaway comment, but James had taken it to heart. Living under the cloud of asthma had been tough for a boy mad about sport, and there had been nights when he beat his head against his bedroom wall in frustration. But the fury born of frustration made him stronger, and over time James learned to temper his anger, forging an iron will that belied his shy demeanour.

Lying in the cave, his body inert and his brain scrambled by psychedelic toxins, James' only defence against the shadow waiting in the dark was the force of this will. Somewhere in the fog of his mind, James sensed the evil creep closer and turned to face the threat. He knew whoever or whatever it was meant him and his friends harm, and it made him angry. Really angry. He felt rage surge through him and rushed at the shadowy apparition like an avenging angel.

James awoke. He was back in the cave. He lay in the darkness for a while, not sure if he was still dreaming. He was breathing heavily, and his body felt as though he'd been circuit training.

He sat up and switched on his torch. The others were sleeping fitfully. He licked his lips; his mouth was bone dry, and his head was pounding. *I must be dehydrated*, he thought. He stood up and groped his way, stiff-legged, back to the pool.

The moment his fingertips disturbed the surface of the water, he sensed the presence of the Watcher. "I know you're there!" he whispered.

The challenge reverberated around the enclosed space, gaining volume with each echo. As the noise reached a crescendo, James sensed he was under attack and shone his torch towards the back of the cave trying to locate the source of the sound. He glimpsed movement and his anger returned, snuffing out the noise and hurling itself against the presence, which retreated into the pool.

In the stunned silence that followed, James, eyes blazing, stared into the water. He was searching for something, but what? He was about to look away when the ripples cleared, and, to his astonishment, a man's face appeared out of the inky depths. The face was old, and the head was devoid of hair and covered with extraordinary tattoos. His piercing black eyes were open and unblinking. For a few moments, James stared into the water in amazement, then a clattering broke the illusion.

James looked up, startled. An old man wearing a tatty woollen cloak was stooping to retrieve a metal pot, which was rolling noisily over the cave floor. The man whirled around, his movement faster than his wizened body might have indicated. Their eyes locked.

"What the..." James didn't complete the sentence; the malice in the old man's eyes froze the words in his mouth.

For a moment, James and the stranger stood transfixed, neither knowing what to do. Then the spell was broken and there was a knife in the old man's bony hand.

James had been in fistfights but never faced anyone with a knife, so as the blade flashed towards him, the shock made him slow to react.

The dagger thrust at his solar plexus was meant to kill, but James got lucky. He'd slipped his mobile into the chest pocket of his cave suit. The screen took the impact.

The crunch of broken glass was enough to jolt James into action. He grabbed his attacker's wrist, twisting his arm until he screeched in pain and the knife slipped from his grip. Aware he was fighting for his life, James ignored the old man's cries of pain and pinned him to the floor.

James pressed his knee between his attacker's shoulder blades and held the struggling man's arm behind his back. The man writhed under him; it was difficult to maintain his grip, the guy was smeared in some sort of grease. The smell of rancid animal fat made him gag.

"GOT YOU!" James snarled.

But the old guy wasn't finished. With sudden burst of manic strength, he broke free and made a grab for the knife. James got there first. James held the knife – he had the advantage now. He eyed his adversary warily, unsure what to do. The old guy was dangerous, but he didn't want to hurt him.

"Lie down!" James shouted. He had a vague idea to tie the guy up.

The man stared back; his flinty black eyes told James he would kill him if he could. He stood for a moment, weighing up his chances, then grabbed the bowl, bolted for the exit, and disappeared like a rabbit down a burrow.

The commotion had roused the others. They, like James, seemed to have made a miraculous recovery from the mystery illness.

Tom was the first to speak. "What the hell's going on?" he demanded. "And where did those lights come from?"

James looked around in bewilderment. He'd been too busy fighting with the man with the knife to notice the cave was lit up. He stared at the flickering candles, which were set in earthenware dishes all around the cavern.

"They must have been lit while we were asleep," said Tom.

"I saw the guy who put them there. He tried to stab me," explained James. "I don't know how he got in without us knowing, but he must be a tramp. He must've been living rough in here. He stank."

"I knew somebody was in here," Emma said, "I could feel it."

Delyth looked frightened. "You should've said something. He had a knife. He could have killed us while we slept!"

"But he didn't." Emma was dismissive. She turned to James. "Where is he now?"

"He went out through the passage." James held up the knife; the blade glinted in the candlelight. "I managed to take this off him."

They stared at the weapon, shocked by the size and brutal simplicity of the blade. "Bloody hell," said Tom.

James showed them his broken phone. "It did this."

Tom blanched. "You mean he stabbed you and the phone stopped the knife?"

James nodded.

"And he's sitting listening to us on the other end of that tunnel?"

James shrugged. "He must be. He can't go anywhere until the rubble is cleared."

"He might have another knife," Delyth said. "He could wait for us to fall asleep and cut our throats!"

James shook his head. "I don't think there's another knife, but we need to make sure he can't sneak back in."

"We could block the hole," said Emma.

"What with?" asked Tom. "There aren't any rocks big enough."

James had heard enough. "He's old, I've got his knife, what harm can he do? I'm going back through the passage to sort him out. We've got the rope; I can tie him up. The police can deal with him when we get out of here." He turned to the others. "Anybody coming with me?"

Tom looked at his feet. He wasn't afraid of the old man, he just couldn't face the narrow tunnel.

"I'll go," offered Emma. "My torch has the most power. Besides, anything's better than sitting here freezing to death!"

"No," said Delyth firmly. "We'll all go. You're right, anything is better than sitting here. And if this man causes trouble, there'll be safety in numbers."

James grinned. "Ladies first," he teased. Secretly, he was relieved he wasn't going to face the tattooed tramp on his own. The guy was no match for him physically, but James had seen the malice in those black eyes, and was under no illusion; the man was a psychopath and, knife or no knife, he was dangerous.

James tapped the smashed iPhone in his pocket. He'd had a close shave, but he wasn't going to let a nasty old man intimidate him. "I'll go first," he said.

James put on his helmet and slithered into the low passage. He moved cautiously, keeping the lamp on the tunnel ahead, ready to react should the bloke with the tattoos appear. Once he was through the tight section, he called to the others. "It's all clear!" He flicked the beam nervously down the horizontal shaft. "He must be up at the rock fall."

Muffled calls from inside the Blue Cavern told James the others had gotten the message. One by one, they wriggled down the slimy tube to join him.

Tom was last through. "I must be getting used to this," he muttered as James hauled him to his feet. "But I promise if we get out of here in one piece, I'm never *ever* going caving again!"

James laughed. "I can't see myself booking a potholing holiday either."

"Piss off," replied Tom. "I'll be fine."

"For God's sake," Emma butted in. "We need to find this guy. My battery could run out anytime. We don't want to meet him in the dark."

James nodded. He was getting used to Emma's brusque manner. "We'd better press on," he said, catching Tom's eye. As he spoke, James put his hand in his boiler suit pocket and offered Tom his pocketknife.

Tom glanced at James in alarm. It was a knife James used for skinning rabbits, not a combat weapon, but it was razor sharp. Sharp enough to slit open the belly of a rabbit... or a person if necessary. "Are you crazy?" he asked. "You're not really going to threaten an old man with a knife?"

"It's a toy compared with what he stabbed me with," James replied, brandishing the huge knife he'd taken from the tramp. "Believe me, he really meant to kill me!"

Tom took a second glance at his friend and flicked open the pocketknife. "Just in case," he said.

Emma switched on her mobile torch. "Ready?"

James nodded. They moved along the shaft as quietly as possible, listening for any sound that might betray the presence of the mystery assailant.

James took the lead, gripping the knife tightly. His palms were slick with sweat despite the cold.

The tension was unbearable. He was convinced his friends could hear his heart hammering against his ribcage, but he was determined not to let his anxiety show.

When they reached the ledge overhanging the vertical shaft, beads of sweat dripped from under James' helmet. There was no sign of their quarry. "Where the hell is he?" he whispered.

"You imagined it," replied Tom. "This place does your head in after a while. I've had some weird dreams down here."

"Me too," said Emma. "It's difficult to know whether you're dreaming or whether it's actually happening down here."

James shook his head. "I know what I saw, okay? There was a bloke, and he really did try to kill me! Anyway, how do you explain the candles? They weren't there when we went to sleep."

"If this guy exists," Emma said, making no attempt to keep her voice down, "he's standing on the rock fall listening to our conversation. There's no point having a debate, we just need to shine the light down there and say hello."

James stared at Emma. He couldn't fault her logic.

"She's right," whispered Tom. "We'd better have a look."

James nodded and together they peered over the edge. What they saw took them all by surprise.

Chapter 21

James pointed the lamp down the shaft. The beam disappeared into empty space.

"Where's it gone?"

Tom was open-mouthed. "They- they can't have cleared it that fast," he stammered. "There must have been hundreds of tonnes of rock in there."

"Maybe we slept longer than we thought?" suggested Delyth.

"Don't be daft," said James, alarmed. "They must have used digging equipment like they use in mines."

"But why didn't we wake up?" asked Emma. "If they had massive machines in here, we'd have heard."

"Not if we were drugged," said Delyth. "Maybe we didn't have a bug. Maybe we were poisoned."

"By the tramp, you mean?" asked Tom. He looked shocked.

Delyth nodded.

"But why didn't anybody find us?" asked Emma. "If they made the effort to move all those rocks, surely they'd search for us in the rest of the cave?"

"It doesn't matter now," said James. "Let's get out of here. We can find out later."

Tom stared into the hole. "What about Rick?" his voice trembled. "Do you think he made it?"

They went quiet.

James broke the silence; his expression was grim. "Like I said, we can find that out later."

Tom didn't reply. His shoulders sagged. He was close to tears.

James reached out and placed a reassuring hand on his friend's back. "It wasn't your fault. We have to get out of here while we can."

Tom didn't move. His shoulders still slumped, weighed down by guilt.

Emma intervened. "It can't still be raining," she said, trying to be positive. "I wonder if it's sunny outside."

Tom sniffed. His face was strained and his eyes glistened, but he managed a half-smile. "Thanks guys. You're right. Let's get the fuck out of here."

The climb down was dicey. The tramp, or one of the rescue team, had taken the rope they'd left on the ledge, and, inexplicably, someone had gone to the trouble of removing all the iron safety rings, so they were forced to make the descent without a safety rope, clinging to handholds and groping for each step with their feet.

James was the first to reach the bottom. The tide was out, and his feet touched soft sand. He peered towards the entrance. A tantalising ray of sunlight marked the exit of the cave. The urge to run outside was strong, but a sense of foreboding made him wait for the others. Something didn't feel right.

Tom was the next down. He looked around in amazement. "Where's the rubble?"

"They must have dumped it further down the beach," replied James.

Tom frowned. "Why would they bother?"

The girls seemed less concerned with the whys and wherefores of the rescue operation, when they reached the bottom of the chimney, they just wanted to get out. "Come on," said Emma, taking Delyth's hand, and led them out into the sunlight.

They emerged onto the beach, blinking like bedraggled owls. Cold and wet, they flopped on the pebbles to soak up the warmth of the sun.

James gazed down the beach at the incoming tide. It was one of those perfect summer days that transformed the grey, windswept Welsh coast into a Greek island. The sky was blue, the sea turquoise, and the water lapping over the pebbles was crystal clear.

James recalled the day they went kayaking. Was that only three days ago? It seemed much longer. He felt different too. Older maybe. *I don't suppose any of us will be quite the same after this*, he thought.

He looked up. Something in the water caught his eye. It was a tiny boat not much bigger than a child's inflatable dingy. He screwed up his eyes to get a better view. A man was hunched over the front of the craft with a paddle.

"Hey!" shouted James. The man turned back to the beach and stared. "That's him!" James yelled, pointing excitedly. "The guy who attacked me!"

"That's weird," said Tom, squinting at the bobbing shape. "The little black boat he's paddling is a coracle."

"Forget him," Emma said. "We can report him to the police when we get back to Myrtle House. The main thing is to let our parents know we're safe."

"And get something to eat," added James, brightening up at the thought of food and a hot drink.

Tom pulled his mobile out of his pocket. He switched it on and tapped in the pin number. He waited to connect to the network. "No signal," he muttered.

"Me neither," said Emma.

"Then we'll have to go up to the footpath and see if we can get a signal there," James suggested.

"I don't want to be negative," said Tom, "but we'll have to climb out of here first, and somebody's taken the rope!"

They stared up at the cliff. Tom was right; the rope they'd used to abseil to the beach was gone.

"Oh," said James.

"Didn't Rick say there was a track round the side of the headland?" said Emma. "We'd have to clamber over the rocks to get to it, but it's better than climbing the cliff without a rope."

Delyth groaned. "I'm not sure I can make it. My legs feel like jelly."

James was about to reply when Emma made another suggestion. "If you guys are too tired, you could stay here while I get help."

"No!" said James firmly. "We got into this together, we'll all walk out of this together. After all, it's not very far."

Delyth hadn't said anything, but she'd thought it was an excellent idea to stay on the beach while Emma went for help. She was banged up; two days in the cave had taken its toll. She couldn't ever remember feeling this tired, and she couldn't stop shivering. She wondered whether it was the cold or stress. *Both probably*, she thought miserably. She looked at her hands; they were white and puffy and, like the rest of her, covered in smelly mud.

"Can't we clean ourselves up first?" she asked.

"The tide's coming in," James said bluntly. "We need to get off the beach."

Delyth opened her mouth to complain, then saw the determined look on James' face and resigned herself to the mile-and-a-half walk back to the house. She even managed to smile as he helped her back to her feet. To her surprise, the clamber over the rocks was not as difficult as she'd anticipated. Once they were around the headland, they found the sheep track which wound its way up a narrow gully to join the main path at the top of the cliff.

It wasn't until they were standing on the main footpath that she noticed things were not quite as they should be. The outline of the coast was much as she remembered, but the land, with its patchwork of fields and dividing stone walls looked odd. With increasing disquiet, she began to pick out the anomalies. She wondered if the others had noticed.

Tom was the first to say something. "Where's the fencing gone?" he asked, pointing to where a sheep-netting fence had once divided the coastal path from the fields belonging to the nearby farm. The others stared in bewilderment. "And look at that field," he pointed to an area of rough pasture and scrub. "When we walked up here, that was a silage field. I remember watching them cut it."

Then Delyth looked towards the headland. Incredibly, it took her a few seconds to notice it, and when she did the shock made her gasp. "The tower's gone," she said, pointing to the promontory overlooking the Blue Lagoon.

They all stood rooted to the spot, staring in disbelief. The winch tower from the old slate workings had disappeared, and, incredibly, so had the entire quarry. The Blue Lagoon had gone.

"James," wailed Delyth, "what's happening? I'm scared."

James didn't reply. He'd noticed the lane leading from Abereiddy to St. David's Road wasn't there. Nor was the whitewashed farm that stood at the Maesglas crossroads.

He screwed his knuckles to his eyes and looked again. "It must be a dream," he muttered. Then, without saying anything more, he took off along the path like a startled rabbit. He didn't know why he was running or what he hoped to find, he just knew that something was terribly wrong, and he needed to know what. The others stumbled after him, strung out like runners in a long-distance race, Delyth bringing up the rear.

James didn't slow until he could see Abereiddy beach. The sight that greeted him stopped him in his tracks. Like the view from the headland, the landscape was both familiar and terrifyingly different. The contours of the land were the same, as was the shape of the bay, but where was the car park? And the ramshackle café? And the row of cottages behind it? And what the fuck was *that*?

Nestling in a clearing in scrubby oak woodland, where Myrtle House should have been, was a peculiar, thatched dwelling. The building was circular, and wisps of white smoke rose from the apex of the steeply pitched roof. In the distance he could hear somebody chopping wood. Suddenly wary of being seen, he ducked behind a gorse bush and crept towards the beach. When the others caught up, he was hiding in a strand of rosebay willowherb, peering towards the thatched hut. He motioned them to keep down.

"What's going on?" whispered Tom.

"I don't know," replied James, trying to hide the wobble in his voice.

Just then, a woman appeared in the clearing and walked into the hut carrying a basket of logs. She was lean and muscular. Her dark hair, streaked with grey, was plaited and wound round her head in a bun. The woman's clothing was extraordinary. She was wearing a dress that would have made Joseph's technicolour dream coat look plain. The garish yellow, red, blue and green weave was fastened at the shoulder with a large, shiny pin, and bunched around her middle with a wide leather belt.

Emma broke the stunned silence. "Woah!"

"She isn't wearing any shoes," observed Tom.

"Probably a New Age type," reasoned Emma. "My dad says they're scroungers."

"He would do," frowned Delyth.

"It's like one of those historical re-enactments," Tom said. "Like on the telly."

James' mind was reeling. His friends were missing the point. "Don't you get it? None of this should be here! We should be looking at Myrtle House, not a mud hut! Where's the house gone?"

"Are you saying we're lost?" said Delyth.

"I don't know what I'm saying, but it's like everything from the twenty-first century has gone. And the lagoon! How can a bloody great hole in the ground like that just disappear?"

There was a stunned silence. All of them trying to compute what James had said.

"Then we *are* dreaming," said Emma. "It would explain why there was nobody there when we came out." There was another period of quiet while they digested this idea.

James broke the silence. "If it's a dream," he said, "it's about something that happened before they dug the quarry and built houses. I expect we'll wake up back in the cave."

"There is another alternative," Tom looked grim. "Maybe we died in the cave."

"Shut up, you're freaking me out!" James snapped. "I'm definitely not dead, and I'm pretty sure I'm not dreaming. This is happening."

"Then perhaps this, whatever it is, is happening at some time in the past," reasoned Tom.

"You're telling me we've gone back in time?" James was incredulous.

"Well you tell me what's going on!" Tom's eyes flashed.

James, taken aback at his friend's outburst, had nothing to say. James was bright but brutally pragmatic, and not given to what he described as 'Tom's crazy ideas.'

"If this is the past, then it's a long time ago," said Emma. "Because that is an Iron Age roundhouse. I know because Mum insisted on taking me to a reconstruction of an Iron Age village a couple of years ago."

James was about to tell Emma she was bonkers when a stranger interrupted him.

"Pwy wyt ti?" the high-pitched voice demanded in Welsh.

All four of them jumped as though they'd touched an electric fence and turned to face their inquisitor.

"What's she saying?" hissed James as he eyed the sharp little dagger held by a girl of about his age.

"She asked who we are," said Tom nervously. "She's speaking Welsh, but her accent is really weird. What should we say?"

The girl was very pretty, and James suspected her sack-like woollen dress hid a good figure. Her dark eyes flashed fiercely, but he sensed she was as scared as them.

"Please," pleaded Delyth in Welsh, "we've had an accident. We're lost and we haven't eaten for days. We need your help."

The girl showed no sign of putting down her knife, but her expression softened. "You speak strangely," she said. "What tribe are you from?"

"What's she saying?" demanded James. The girl, who didn't appear to understand English, eyed James nervously.

"Don't be afraid," said Delyth, taking the initiative. "We don't belong to any tribe. We are alone and need your help."

"I said they looked nice, Tegwedd," squeaked a voice from just behind the girl, and a boy ran out from the bushes.

"Artur! I told you to stay where you were until I told you it was safe," scolded the girl.

The boy poked out his tongue, his freckly face so comical that everyone, including the strange girl, laughed. The tension diffused, the girl allowed the point of her knife to drop. "I am sorry; I have been less than hospitable," she said. "But your clothes are very strange, and we've had many troubles recently." She looked at them in turn, weighing them up. "You look tired. You must have travelled far," she observed. "My name is Tegwedd, and this is my brother Artur."

She looked at the boy and smiled again. "Run home and tell Mam we have guests," she said.

As the boy scurried down the path towards the thatched hut, she addressed her new acquaintances. "Come," she said. "I am sure my mother will be pleased to offer you the hospitality of our house. Once you have eaten and rested, you can tell us your story." With that, she stuck her knife into a leather scabbard at her side and followed the boy down the path.

"What's going on?" whispered James, frustrated that he couldn't grasp a word of what was being said.

"Her accent is awful, I can't understand everything she says, but she's going to ask her mother to give us some food," explained Tom. "I suppose we've no other choice than to go with her."

James nodded; he'd never felt this hungry in his entire life, and right now he'd have followed the Devil himself if he thought he was going to get fed.

Chapter 22

When they reached the thatched house, the hippie woman they'd watched earlier was standing in the doorway, holding Artur's hand. She frowned as the mud-splattered youngsters approached.

"Who are these?" she demanded.

"They are travellers who need our help," Tegwedd explained. "They mean us no harm. I thought they might bring news or something to trade."

The woman stared at the wayfarers waiting hopefully at the entrance to her home. Close up, James thought the woman's similarity to Tegwedd was striking. It was easy to imagine that a decade earlier she must have been a real beauty. The crow's feet around her dark, inquisitive eyes spoke of a hard life lived outdoors.

"What in the name of the Gods are they wearing? What tribe are they from?" the woman asked, staring at the orange cave suits.

When Tom translated the comment about their clothes, James smiled wryly; the hippie lady was wearing a startling hand-woven woollen dress decorated with yellow, red, blue and green patterns. The dress was pinned at the shoulder by a shiny copper clasp.

"They say they do not belong to a tribe," Tegwedd answered, "but two of them speak the tongue of the chosen tribes, so I'm sure they are not of the Du Tarian."

The woman looked unconvinced. "Everyone belongs to a tribe," she said.

"They haven't eaten for three days," pleaded Tegwedd.

The woman studied their exhausted faces, then relented. "These are troubled times," she told them by way of explanation, "but it would be uncharitable to turn you away with empty bellies." She motioned them inside. "My name is Heulwen. I am Tegwedd's mother. I offer you the hospitality of my home in the name of the Goddess Cliodna."

James hadn't a clue what she was saying. He took his lead from Tom, ducked his head under the thatched eves and followed him into the hut. As they entered Heulwen said something.

"She wants us to take our shoes off," Tom translated.

James sat down to unlace his boots and looked around. The interior of the building was simple, consisting of a single circular living area around twelve metres in diameter and open to the eves. Lined up against the wall opposite the entrance were three wooden cots spread with brightly coloured woollen blankets and rusty brown sheepskins. In the centre of the building, a neatly laid fire sent sparks crackling into the eves like miniature fireworks. The smoke drifted lazily to the apex of the roof and filtered out through the thatch.

James placed his boots near the entrance with the others and padded across the polished dung floor towards the fire. He took a place next to his friends on one of the wooden benches positioned around the hearth. Tired and hungry, the four bewildered teens gazed into the embers taking in their astonishing new environment.

"What are they doing?" whispered James as Tegwedd and her mother busied themselves around the room.

"I think they're making something to eat," Tom whispered back.

They watched Tegwedd ladle what looked like porridge oats from an earthenware jar into a heavy, black, iron pot. While Tegwedd carried the pot over to the fire, her mother delved into some earthenware containers and produced strips of dried fish and a bundle of knobbly white stuff that looked like dried roots. She then cut the ingredients into cubes and placed them in the iron pot. Finally, she went to the back of the room and grabbed a handful of unidentified dried plants from bunches hanging from the rafters.

"This is seriously weird," said Tom,

James grinned. "More like a horror movie."

Tom chuckled. "Eye of newt and wing of bat."

"Shush!" hissed Delyth. "You'll offend them."

"I don't think so," replied James. "They don't seem to understand English."

Emma watched Tegwedd pour water on top of the mixture and stir it with a wooden spoon. "There's no way I'm eating that!" They moved aside as Tegwedd lifted the heavy pot and hooked it to a chain suspended over the fire.

"You'll eat anything if you're hungry enough," insisted James, peering into the pot greedily.

Once they were seated back around the fire, Heulwen brought out an earthenware jar, and poured an opaque liquid into four decorated pottery cups.

She handed a cup to each of her guests. "Drink this," she said in her singsong Welsh dialect. "It will warm you in body and in spirit. Then you can tell me your story."

Delyth translated. "She says we can tell her what's happened when we've drunk this stuff."

"What is it?" Emma was less than enthusiastic.

Tom sniffed the liquid. It smelt alcoholic. "I think its booze!" he said. He brought the cup to his lips and took a cautious sip. He grinned. "Its mead," he said, taking another swig. "Dad made some once and I '*borrowed*' one of the bottles from the garage. Try some; it's fermented honey. It's delicious!" Soon everyone was drinking the sweet heady brew and smiling. It was their first pleasant experience since the rock fall.

Heulwen sat down with them next to the fire, "It's been a while since we've had visitors here," she said, pausing for Tom to translate, "we are eager for news. Tell us, have you travelled far?"

Tom glanced in askance at James who made a strange face and shrugged his shoulders.

"We've only come from the cave," said Tom. "You know, the one at the end of the headland." Heulwen frowned and Tom hesitated, not sure if he'd said the wrong thing, but he carried on with his story. "We were trapped in there by a rock fall, and we think our leader, Rick, might have been badly hurt or killed. We were in there for two days. It was freezing cold, and something made us ill. You must know something. There would have been police and rescue people parked up near the beach." He looked at Heulwen hoping for a response, but she remained silent.

Tom ploughed on. "Then James was attacked in the cave. The guy had a knife! We followed him out and found the rock fall had disappeared and everything was different. Now we're trying to work out what's happened."

Tom could see from the bewildered looks on Heulwen and Tegwedd's faces they were confused, so he tried a different tack. "Our mobiles aren't working," he said, "can we borrow yours? Our parents will be going crazy; we need to let them know we're okay."

Heulwen looked troubled. "You came from the cave," she said. "Only a man with the Knowledge – a Watcher – is permitted to enter the sacred cave. It is said that those who enter without the Knowledge risk losing their immortal spirit."

Tom translated this to Emma and James.

"I said she was a New Age type," whispered Emma. "I wouldn't be surprised if some of that dried stuff," he pointed to the bunches of herbs hanging from the eves, "is weed."

"I'm not so sure," said Delyth, looking frightened.

"Ask her where we are," said Emma. Tom nodded and translated.

This time, Heulwen was able to answer them. "You are at the shrine of Cliodna, the Goddess of the Lake," she explained. "Though little remains of our community. There were thirty people living here once, and pilgrims came to worship at the lake, but that is all finished. Since the attack, the pilgrims have stopped coming, and the villagers who escaped never returned to rebuild their homes. The three of us are all that remain."

Tom thought James might be right about Heulwen's' mental state, but curiosity got the better of him, so he asked the obvious question. "Who attacked you?"

Heulwen looked surprised. "The Du Tarian of course!" she answered, "But tell me what you were doing in the cave."

"We meant no harm," said Delyth. "We didn't know the cave was sacred to you. Where we come from, we don't have sacred places. Well, churches I suppose, but nobody minds if you go in them." Then a thought occurred to her. "Do you think that's why the old man attacked James?"

Heulwen looked up sharply. "What did this man with the knife look like?" she asked.

"I've no idea, it was James that saw him," replied Delyth.

Heulwen turned her dark, intelligent eyes towards James while Tom dutifully translated her question. James took a swig of mead and tried his best to give her an accurate description of the tattooed man.

Heulwen listened intently as Tom translated, but said nothing until James mentioned the bowl the old man had dropped. "What did this bowl look like?" she asked.

James shrugged. "It was made of metal, iron maybe, and heavy. It had pictures of people on it and a pattern around the rim. Crosses, I think."

Heulwen glanced at Tedwedd. She looked stunned. "So Myrleduin had the chalice after all," she said in hushed tones. "He must have hidden it during the attack."

"Or stole it back?" suggested Tegwedd.

"Who is this Myrleduin?" asked James, exasperated. He was impatient by nature, and having to wait for everything to be translated was driving him crazy.

Heulwen sighed. "Myrleduin is one of the men of the Knowledge. A druid. He once led the religious community here, but on the day the shrine was attacked, he ran away. Maelog, our chieftain, was furious and exiled him. Now, it seems Myrleduin has returned with the Sacred Chalice. What that means, I do not know."

"Nor do I," mumbled Tom. He thought Emma might be right about the 'wacky backy;' the woman was off her head.

While they all tried to make sense of what Heulwen had said, Tegwedd brought out some wooden plates. James watched as she ladled the contents of the cooking pot into the bowls. He was hungry, but the lumpy grey goo didn't look very appetizing. "Are there knives and forks?" he asked.

"Doesn't look like it," replied Tom, watching Artur shovelling his food into his mouth with his fingers.

"That's gross!" said Emma, watching James scoop a handful of the dubious looking mixture.

"Not bad," James pronounced. His mouth, full of food, resembled a cement mixer. "It's kind of a cross between paella and porridge."

James' description wasn't selling it to Emma, but she hadn't eaten for days. She picked out some black bits that looked suspiciously like shellfish and dug in. She surprised herself by finishing the whole portion. By the time they finished eating, the light was beginning to fade. Heulwen said something to Tegwedd, who got up and went outside.

"Where's she off to?" whispered Emma. Like James, she was frustrated not to be able understand what was being said.

"Her mam's told her to fetch the sheep home," replied Delyth.

"I'll go with her," said Emma quickly. "I need the loo."

"I'll come with you. You don't speak the lingo, remember? Anyway, I need to go too."

The girls nodded awkwardly at Heulwen and slipped outside.

Tegwedd had already reached the edge of the clearing when the two girls emerged from the hut.

"Wait for us!" called Delyth.

"Hi," Delyth panted when they caught up. "Sorry to bother you, but can you tell us where the toilet is?" she asked politely. "We didn't want to ask in front of the boys."

Tegwedd grinned. "It's at the back of the wood store," she replied and walked back towards the house. "I'll show you."

They followed her along a well-trodden path behind a smaller version of the thatched house. Half of the building was a wood store full of neatly stacked logs, the other half was a pen housing a fearsome looking pig. The pig rushed towards them, eager for scraps, then squealed in disappointment as they walked by.

A few paces past the pigpen, Tegwedd pointed to a small section screened by hazel hurdles, the area was open to the sky. In the middle of the enclosure was a hole in the ground framed by a crude wooden toilet seat. Flies buzzed around the hole. It smelt worse than the pigsty.

"You must be joking!" gasped Emma. "I can't go in there. We could catch God knows what!"

"Shut up!" Delyth hissed, noticing the look Tegwedd was giving them. "You're upsetting her. It isn't worse than the toilets at camp last year."

Emma grimaced; the camp toilets had been horrendous. It was one of the reasons she'd given up Girl Guides.

Delyth was undeterred. "It's better than going to the toilet in the cave."

Emma wasn't convinced. "Where's the loo paper?" she asked.

Delyth translated this to Tegwedd, who stared blankly. "What is loo paper?"

Delyth squirmed with embarrassment before asking the question that simply had to be asked. "How do we... well, how do we wipe our bottoms?"

Tegwedd gaped at her for a moment, then her mouth widened into a huge grin and she started to giggle. The giggling was infectious, and soon all three girls were laughing helplessly. Still chuckling, Tegwedd pointed to a basket placed near the hole. "Use the moss," she smiled. "Don't you have moss where you come from?" She reached in the basket and pulled out a handful of pale, springy plant material and handed it to Emma.

It felt dry, spongy, and thankfully not as scratchy as it looked. "I guess we don't have any choice," sighed Emma. "Let's hope we don't fall down the hole!"

Tegwedd waited at a discreet distance while her two reluctant guests completed their business. She then led them up a track lined by stone walls, which wound its way uphill to some grass fields overlooking the valley. At the entrance to one of the fields, Tegwedd lifted aside a hurdle and whistled softly. As if by magic, a huge dog appeared out of the shadows. Delyth and Emma froze as the hound slunk towards them, its lips curled back.

"It's alright, Bregg, they're friends." Tegwedd, crouched down. "Come here, boy."

The dog's hackles dropped and he bounded towards his mistress, wagging his tail frantically.

"Whew!" laughed Emma as Tegwedd stroked the dog's massive, hairy head. "I thought he was going to eat us. Now I think he wants to lick us to death!"

Guessing what Emma had said, Tegwedd smiled and spoke quietly to the dog, which dashed into the field and disappeared into the dusk. Soon they could hear bleating as Bregg chivvied his flock towards the gate. The little bronze bells around the sheep's necks tinkled as they ran.

Even Emma, who usually found farming boring, was captivated. The sheep were different from anything she'd seen before. Not only were they chocolatey brown, not white, but they were also smaller and more agile. More like goats, with fearsome horns that spiralled like ammonites.

The bleating press Bregg had packed into the narrow track forced Emma and Delyth to jump up on a dry stone wall as they passed. They stood on the wall and gazed in amazement as Tegwedd, Bregg, and the sheep tinkled their way down into the valley.

"My dad's a sheep farmer and I've never seen anything like that," said Delyth.

Emma was reminded of the illustrated children's Bible her mum had read to her at bedtime. "It's like something from the Bible." She wrinkled her nose. "I never imagined how smelly it must have been," she added, pointing to the dung the sheep had deposited liberally along the track.

Delyth wasn't interested in the sheep poo, she was scanning the coastline. "I can't see any lights. Not anywhere."

Emma nodded. "It's as if all the houses have disappeared."

"And did you notice there was no electricity at Heulwen's house?" said Delyth. "I looked and there are no sockets or telegraph poles. In fact, I don't think they've got any technical stuff at all."

Emma grimaced. "Tom may be right. Perhaps we really have gone back in time. If that's true, we'll have to get used to wiping our bums with moss and not having any Internet!"

Delyth didn't reply. She'd trod in something soft and was trying not to think what it might be.

By the time they reached the clearing, Bregg had cajoled the sheep into a pen. The pen, which looked like a giant basket, was constructed using wooden posts driven into the ground, around which someone had wound lengths of split hazel. Tegwedd ordered Bregg into the pen and secured the gate.

"Is he going to sleep with the sheep?" Delyth joked.

"Of course," said Tegwedd. "Even this time of year there are wolves. The sheep are safe with Bregg. He'd tear a wolf to pieces if it got close."

Delyth translated this extraordinary piece of information to Emma. They watched in amazement as the massive dog snuggled up against his woolly wards. "Wolves!" Emma said. "Now I know I'm going mad!"

Chapter 23

The girls were in a state of turmoil when they entered the round house. They found the boys making up beds from a stack of sheepskins and blankets at the far end of the room.

"We need to talk," said Emma tersely. "Tegwedd says there are wolves in the woods here, and the crazy thing is I believe her. This is freaking me out."

James and Tom glanced at each other.

"We've been talking while you were out," said James. "We've decided we're not dreaming this."

Tom's expression was serious. "I think this *is* reality. I think when we were asleep in the cave, something happened to us, and we ended up at some time in the past."

Delyth looked as if she was about to cry. "How can you be sure?"

Tom sighed. "We can't," he admitted, frowning as he struggled to form his thoughts into words. "When you're dreaming," he said, "and start to think you're dreaming, you wake up straight away. But we've been thinking we're dreaming ever since we came out of the cave, and we still haven't woken up. Therefore we're not dreaming and this is real." Tom studied his friend's faces waiting for a reaction.

Emma looked bewildered. "Are we going mad?" she asked.

James shook his head. "I agree with Tom," he confessed. He ran his hand over one of the sheepskins, "It feels too real to be imagination."

"Then we'd better work out how to survive," said Emma. "Tegwedd's mum isn't going to feed and look after us forever."

"Agreed," yawned James. "But I'm too knackered to discuss it now. Let's get some sleep and talk again in the morning."

James was woken by a grinding noise. He snuggled into his blanket and tried to doze, but the annoying grating sound made sleep impossible.

He propped his head up with his hand and looked around blearily. Somebody had built up the fire, and tongues of orange flame crackled around the newly laid logs. Early morning light spilled through the entrance to the house, illuminating the source of the awful noise. His curiosity aroused, James sat up.

Heulwen was knelt over a large block of stone. She was holding a smaller round stone in both hands and grinding it against the large block using a rhythmic circular motion. Every now and then, she stopped, reached into an earthenware pot, and poured a handful of grain into a depression in the large stone.

As he watched, Heulwen started to sing. He had no idea what this strange woman was singing, but he listened, entranced by the purity of her voice. Artur broke the spell. He threw another log on the fire sending sparks up towards the roof.

"Jesus," groaned James. "They get up early round here, don't they?"

He lay under the blanket, watching as Heulwen finished grinding her flour and began mixing it with water and other ingredients. Finally, she kneaded the dough into fist-sized balls, which she rolled onto a flat stone placed on the fire. Soon, the tantalizing aroma of freshly baked bread had James out of his bed and sitting next to the fire. Stirrings from other piles of bedding indicated the smell was having a similar effect on the others. A grubby hand reached stealthily towards the cakes.

"*Nadu!*" said Heulwen, rapping Artur on the on the knuckles with a wooden spatula. "Where are your manners? Guests first!" Artur looked crestfallen, and Heulwen's expression softened.

"Go fetch Tegwedd," she ordered, keeping up a pretence of anger. "Then you can have a cake."

Artur nodded and walked, head down, towards the door. But when his mother wasn't looking, he gave James a wink and skipped outside.

"Cheeky bugger!" grinned James. "He winds his mum round his little finger."

"Where's Tegwedd?" asked Delyth, who'd joined James, hovering over the bread cakes.

Heulwen gave her a look that said *you're late up*. "She's still milking the sheep. She should have finished by now, but she woke up late."

Emma glanced at James and turned her nose up. James tried to keep a straight face; he too found the idea of milking sheep disgusting. Why couldn't they milk cows like normal farmers?

As if on cue, Tegwedd appeared, carrying a misshapen leather bucket. She placed it on a wooden trestle and smiled at her guests. "I trust you slept well," she said, and curtsied in a manner that was suspiciously sarcastic. "May I offer you a drink?" She ladled some milk out of the bucket with one of the cups they'd drunk mead out of the previous night and offered it to James. The milk stank of sheep.

James took the cup in both hands and gulped back the warm liquid. "Delicious," he lied, wiping his mouth with the back of his hand and trying not to gag. The others followed suit, then sat down next to the fire, wishing they hadn't. Fortunately, the bread cakes were as good as they smelt and took away the sheepy taste of the milk. After breakfast, they sat outside and basked in the early morning sunshine, each lost in their thoughts.

James broke the silence. "So... what next?"

"We've got to work out how to look after ourselves and find out if it's possible to get back to our time," Emma replied thoughtfully.

"We'd better start by changing our appearance," said Delyth. "Tegwedd and Artur keep staring at our clothes. Not everyone may be as friendly as them. We don't want to draw attention to ourselves."

Tom laughed. "Look at us! People would stare if we were at home!"

"True," said Emma. "We look like we've been dragged through a ploughed field on a rainy day!"

"Getting clean isn't a problem," Delyth observed, "but new clothes are a different matter. Maybe we can swap something."

"Clothes aren't going to help if we get attacked by wolves," said James, "or those Du Tarian people Heulwen told us about. What we need are weapons."

"You've got the old guy's knife," Tom pointed out.

"A spear or a sword would be better."

"You've been watching too much Netflix," scoffed Emma. "What chance would you have against a trained killer? Or a wolf for that matter?"

James rolled his tongue, "We might not have any choice!" he snapped. "And that knife isn't much good."

"Cool it, James," interrupted Tom. "Nobody's threatening us at the moment. Why don't we chat to Heulwen and see what she says? She's weird but I'm sure she'll help if she can."

The two boys wandered back into the house to find Heulwen, leaving Emma and Delyth to their own devices.

"I need a wash," said Emma.

Delyth smiled. "That's the best suggestion I've heard all day. We crossed a stream when we fetched the sheep last night. It isn't far away."

When they reached the point where the track to the top fields forded the stream, they realized the water wasn't deep enough to bathe. Disappointed, they removed their boots and socks and dangled their feet in the babbling brook.

"Let's see if there's a pool upstream," said Emma. "I want to get these filthy clothes off and have a proper wash."

Forgetting Tegwedd's warning about wolves, she grabbed her boots and waded upstream.

"Ouch!" Delyth stubbed a toe on a rock. "Slow down!"

Emma grinned. "Don't make a fuss!" she shouted. After being cooped up in the cave, she was enjoying herself. It was a lovely morning. The sun was warm on her back, and the water gurgling over her feet was cool and refreshing.

Further upstream, the brook cut deeper into the land, and the rosebay willowherb and marshy grasses on either bank gave way to scrub oak, ash, and hazel. Here in the shade cast by the trees, the woodland floor was carpeted by moss and ferns. Emma was entranced. Surrounded by birdsong and the sound of running water, the glade was a garden of mystical creatures. She reached down and stroked the soft, springy moss growing on the side of one of the trees. It felt like the pelt of a huge beast. A thought shattered the fantasy. "Now we know where Tegwedd gets her bottom wipes from!"

Delyth sniggered.

As they rounded a bend in the stream, they were faced by a wall of sticks. Emma was flabbergasted, "What the hell is that?"

"Don't ask me. A dam maybe?"

Emma and Delyth scrambled up the sticks. Emma was the first to the top. Behind the wall of sticks was a pond. Delyth was right; it was a dam. Amongst a stand of birch saplings on the far side of the pool, a brown animal the size of a large cat sat up in alarm. Emma caught a flash of rodent teeth and a paddle like tail as the creature slithered down the bank and swam upstream.

Emma gasped in amazement. Even with her limited knowledge of natural history she knew what it was. She also knew they'd been extinct in the UK for centuries. "I've just seen a beaver!"

"What?" muttered Delyth. "Is that supposed to be some sort of joke?"

"I've seen a beaver! You know, the bucky-teethed things that build dams?"

Delyth wasn't interested "We can't wash in that," she said, pointing to the weed infested pond.

"Oh, come on. This is fun. I'm sure we'll find somewhere soon."

They splashed their way upstream until the trees opened out and they found themselves standing at the edge of a reed bed bordering a small lake.

The mirror-still water was cobalt under the clear blue sky. Swallows flitted over the surface of the lake, questing for insects. Hidden in the reeds, a mother coot called to her chicks. The girls gazed in astonishment at the little paradise they'd stumbled into.

"What's that?" Delyth said, pointing to a circle of wooden slabs the size of tree trunks sticking up out of the water on the far side of the lake. The posts, which resembled giant Jenga pieces, were linked to the shore by a wooden causeway.

"Who cares?" said Emma. "I'm going for a swim." Laughing madly, they plunged through the reed bed and flopped down on a grassy bank.

"Race you in!" shrieked Emma, which was the cue to strip off their clothes. Delyth stripped down to her knickers and T-shirt. Emma was less bashful, "There's no one around," she said, "no need to be so shy."

They hesitated at the lake's edge. Up close, the peat-stained water didn't seem quite so inviting.

Delyth scooped some up in her hands. It was the same colour as whisky. "I'm not sure this is safe."

"Don't be silly," said Emma and plunged in. After the initial shock, Emma surfaced, exhilarated. She swam away from the bank. The sensation of the soft cold water felt marvellous against her naked body. As she turned to swim to shore, she felt the trauma of the last few days being gently washed away with the grime from the cave.

Chapter 24

James and Tom followed Tegwedd along the track that led to the lake. They were in a sombre mood. Their chat with Heulwen regarding personal protection had been alarming, and now every bush seemed like a potential hiding place for a dangerous wild animal, or an even more dangerous person.

Heulwen had talked again about the Du Tarian attack and the abandoned settlement at the lake. Her mention of a temple at the lake had piqued their curiosity, so when Tegwedd said she was going there to gather willow, they volunteered to go with her.

They'd walked about half a mile when the ground either side of the track became marshy, and the oak woodland opened into an area of spindly saplings and waist-high vegetation.

As they entered the clearing, Tegwedd stopped. James looked up expectantly; he was sure she was going to say something important.

"This is where our village stood," she said, pointing towards charred posts peeping out of the weeds.

When Tom translated, James was amazed; he was expecting empty buildings. "Is that all that's left?' he asked.

Tegwedd grimaced; James could see the pain etched on her face. "The fire took everything. After they killed our men, they torched our homes. The fire burnt so brightly that long after night fell, I could see the enemy warriors and what they did to the women."

"Didn't they hurt you?"

"I was collecting moss in the woods when they attacked. I hid until it was all over."

James looked around the clearing. Somewhere amongst the trees a woodpecker drummed. It was hard to imagine brutality like that in such a peaceful place. James stared at Tegwedd. She couldn't have been very old when it happened. He wondered what she'd witnessed.

The girl seemed read his thoughts. "I watched as they raped the women. The Du Tarian were drunk and took turns. Heulwen was the high priestess, so she was the last. Their chieftain, King Darragh, singled her out and raped her himself. When he was finished, he beat her and left her for dead."

Tom was aghast. "Why did they come here?"

Tegwedd spat, the saliva balling as it hit the dusty ground. "They came to steal. The shrine was a holy place. Pilgrims journeyed here from far off places to worship and make offerings to the Goddess. The Du Tarian came here for gold, but they didn't know that gifts for the Goddess were always thrown in the lake. We kept nothing back for ourselves. My mother told them, but they didn't listen. When they couldn't find the treasure they craved, they burnt the effigy of the Goddess and slaughtered the menfolk."

James listened in horror as Tom translated. The story was so far-fetched, so completely crazy, that James was sure she was lying. Then he saw how Tegwedd's eyes glittered with rage. "Bloody hell," he murmured. "What sort of place is this?"

Then, as quickly as it had appeared, the anger in Tegwedd's eyes went out. "I'm glad I showed you this place," she said, "but I have already dwelt too long on the past. We have work to do." With that, she turned and walked out of the clearing. James and Tom stood for a moment, stunned, then trotted after her like sheepdogs.

The track led into a jungle of coppiced willows on an area of flat, marshy ground bordering the lake. The finger-thick shoots sprang from stumps to a metre above head height. The leafy tips rustled in the breeze.

They were about to start cutting when they heard laughter. Curious, James and Tom pushed deeper into the willow bed, towards the lake. They arrived at the shoreline as Emma emerged naked from the water. The two boys stood transfixed as she ran towards them, laughing, her lithe young body oozing sexuality. Then she spotted the boys standing open-mouthed on the bank and screamed.

"Sorry!" stammered James as Emma crossed her arms to cover her breasts.

Further up the shore, there were angry squawks as Delyth splashed towards them. "Bloody perverts!" she yelled. Under her t-shirt, her tummy and breasts jiggled up and down as she ran.

It wasn't a good look.

"How long have you been spying on us?" Delyth demanded.

"We- we weren't spying!" stammered James. "We just walked out of the trees and there you were. Ask Tegwedd."

They looked round. Tegwedd was kneeling on the grass staring at Emma. "Are you the one?" She trembled.

"Pardon?"

"You bear the sign of Cliodna, the Goddess. Are you the chosen one?"

"What's the matter with you?" said Emma startled. "I want my clothes."

Tegwedd was undeterred. "We had hoped you would come. We should have known when you told us Myrleduin had returned."

Emma wasn't interested; Delyth thrust her clothes into her hands.

"What's she on about?" asked James.

"Something about the sign of the Goddess," replied Tom, sneaking a peep at Emma pulling up her knickers. Delyth caught his eye. Tom looked away guiltily.

"Somebody ask what the hell is going on," begged James, who was pissed off at having to have everything translated.

Tom, embarrassed, let his sister take the initiative.

"*Beth sy'n bod,* Tegwedd?" Delyth asked, stretching out her hand to help the girl to her feet.

Tegwedd ignored her hand and remained on her knees. Her lips were moving. She appeared to be praying.

"Was it because we went swimming?"

Tegwedd glanced at Emma, who was hurriedly dressing.

Sensing she was close to the mark, Delyth carried on. "It was to do with Emma swimming in the lake, wasn't it?"

Tegwedd looked frightened. "The lake is a holy place. It's forbidden to bathe here."

Tom raised his eyebrows.

Delyth silenced him with a warning look. "I'm sorry. Emma and I didn't know," she said. "I hope you will forgive us."

Tegwedd looked surprised. "But your friend wears the sign of the Goddess. Surely you understand the significance of this place?"

"We told you last night, we don't come from here. You'll have to explain."

Tegwedd hesitated.

"What's she saying?" James demanded.

"In a moment, James. Let her talk."

"The Lake is a door to the world of the spirits. The Goddess Cliodna has guarded its waters since the dawn of creation." Tegwedd glanced at Emma nervously. "After the Du Tarian burnt her body at the shrine, the Men of Knowledge promised a girl would come to take her place."

"Who are these 'Men of Knowledge?'" asked Tom.

"Some call them druids. Even my mother fears them, and she is a priestess who casts the water herself."

Tegwedd's reply seemed to pose more questions than it answered, but Delyth stuck to her original line of questioning. "So why did you get so upset when you saw Emma swimming?"

"After the shrine was destroyed, the druids sang of a girl rising from the lake. Their song promised she was to be the chosen one, perfect in form and golden of hair."

Tegwedd stared at Emma, who was now clothed. "Now we hear the druid Myrleduin has returned, and a girl appears at the lake wearing the sign of the sword."

"I've heard enough," said Tom irritably. "She's as mad as her mum."

Delyth ignored him. "What sword are you talking about?" she asked.

Tegwedd pointed to Emma's cross.

"I think she means your cross," Delyth exclaimed.

Emma frowned. "This is crazy!"

"Go on show it to her."

Emma undid the clasp on the twenty-two-carat chain and held out her ostentatious gold necklace. "Is this what you say looks like a sword?"

The look of reverence on Tegwedd's face was an answer in itself. The cross was a stylized Latin cross, with the long axis extended. Held upside-down, the long axis became a blade, while the shortened axes became a hilt and cross guard.

James remembered something. "That metal bowl the druid had. It had crosses like that all round the rim."

Tegwedd was still kneeling. She looked confused and fearful.

Delyth crouched beside her. "Emma's necklace is a sign of our religion too. But for us it represents a cross, not a sword."

Tegwedd shook her head. She looked even more bewildered.

"You're wasting your time," interrupted Tom. "We'll be here all day if you try to explain the crucifixion. If this is the Iron Age, Jesus Christ hasn't been born yet!

"That's a pretty amazing thought, isn't it?" said Delyth. "But what should I tell her?"

Tom shrugged his shoulders. "Christ knows!" he said, then smiled at the irony of what he'd said.

Tegwedd gazed up at Emma expectantly.

Emma had had enough. "For God's sake, tell her to stop staring at me like that!" she exploded. "She's freaking me out! Tell her if she wants the bloody thing, she can have it." With that she flung her pendant on the ground and stormed off. Tegwedd jumped back as though the cross was an unexploded grenade and banged heads with Tom. They fell back on the bank, stunned.

James watched Emma bolt off along the shoreline and frowned. "See if you guys can get any more information out of

Tegwedd," he told Tom and Delyth. "I'll go and make sure 'the Chosen One' doesn't get in any more trouble."

As James walked off, Delyth bit her lip. She wondered what Tegwedd meant by Emma being the Chosen One. Chosen for what?

When James caught up with Emma, she was about to step onto the wooden walkway which connected the bank with the temple in the centre of the lake. "I don't think you should go out there," he said.

Emma stared back petulantly but said nothing.

"These people believe this place is holy. Who knows what they might do if they caught us intruding on their special place."

"Do you think it's special then?" challenged Emma.

The circle of massive oak pillars waited mutely for James' reply. "A few days ago, I'd have said it's bollocks, but now I don't know."

"Same here."

"Are you alright, Emma?"

Emma shrugged. "I'm scared. I think this has something to do with that girl's face in the lake at Myrtle House."

James held out his hand and Emma smiled shyly. Lost in thought, they strolled back to their friends.

"Where are they?" asked James. They were standing on the trampled area of grass where Emma had emerged from her swim. The words had hardly left his mouth when Tom emerged from the willow trees. Delyth was close behind. Both were breathing heavily.

"Tegwedd's run home," Tom panted. "And she's taken Emma's cross."

"Great!" said Emma. "I doubt I'll see that again. And I suppose she'll tell her mum I've been in their lake."

"It didn't take you long to get us in trouble," complained Tom.

"Button it, Tom," snapped James. "It's hardly Emma's fault. How was she supposed to know all that crap about not swimming in the lake?"

"So what do we tell Heulwen? Tegwedd said she was a priestess."

James sighed. "I guess a peace offering wouldn't do any harm. Why don't we bring back some of these willow twigs as we promised." He hefted the billhook Tegwedd had discarded in her haste. The curved blade was heavy and crudely made, but the edge had been sharpened. The ash handle was shiny with use.

"Let's see what this thing can do." James swung the blade at a thumb thick willow stem. He grinned as the blade sliced through the green wood, dropping the shoot in one swing.

Within an hour they'd collected four large bundles of willow, which they bound together with strips of twisted willow bark. Satisfied with their work, they hoisted the bundles over their shoulders and made their way back towards Heulwen's house.

Chapter 25

They had no idea what reception they might get from Heulwen, so the youngsters were nervous as they approached the enclosure that marked the boundary of her farmstead. From somewhere inside the compound, a dog was barking furiously.

"I don't think we should go in," fretted Tom. "That dog's a beast. If he'll attack a wolf, he could tear us to shreds!"

"Tom's right," agreed Emma. "We should wait here."

James was dismissive. "Bregg will be fine. There's no way Tegwedd would let him hurt us."

Tom raised his eyebrows. He wasn't going to argue, but he hung back as James unlatched the gate and entered the yard. The dog had been tied to a fence post. When it saw James, it lunged at him, snarling, its barking becoming even more insistent. The hairs on the back of James' neck began to prickle. Why wasn't anyone coming to investigate why the dog was making such a commotion?

He gripped the billhook tightly as he entered the house. It was a sunny day, so his eyes had to adjust to the gloom inside the hut. Tegwedd and Heulwen were standing at the centre of the room near the fire. Their bearing was stiff and Tegwedd looked frightened.

Sensing something was wrong, James' eyes darted around the room, but it was too late. A hand locked around his wrist and twisted the billhook out of his grasp. It clattered to the ground.

James reacted instinctively. He swung his free hand in a wild haymaker and felt his fist slam into soft cartilage. It was a lucky blow. As his assailant staggered back, clutching his nose, James took up a boxer's stance, eyes blazing.

A roar of laughter broke out, and James saw the warriors crowded at the edge of the room. Stunned, James looked around at the ferocious faces jeering at him from the shadows. He realized he was hopelessly outnumbered and dropped his guard.

A girl's voice shrieked a warning. James whirled around, but it was too late. The warrior he'd punched in the face was charging across the room. He launched himself at James' midriff, his head catching James squarely in the solar plexus. Winded, all James could do was wrap his arms around his opponent's chest in a desperate embrace while the warrior rained blows on his back. James knew that as long as he maintained his hold, the punches would be ineffectual, so he clung on, crushing his attacker's ribcage, driving the air from his lungs. As James squeezed harder, the warrior clawed at James' head desperately.

Suddenly James altered his grip grabbed a handful of tangled hair and jerked his opponent's head down, smashing it into his knee with devastating force.

James stood, panting, as his assailant slumped to the floor and rolled onto his back. Beneath the blood plastered on his face, James could see his attacker was a boy of about his own age.

The laughter stopped, and a deathly hush fell over the room as a huge man stepped forward. The man was wearing checked trousers and an equally garish woollen tunic. The sides of his head were shaved, but on top he had a shock of red hair which cascaded down his back in braided dreadlocks. His lip sported a long, carefully manicured moustache. Around his neck he wore a heavy band made from twisted strands of gold. The look, a fusion of punk, hipster and rapper bling might have looked comical if it weren't for the fearsome sword he held.

The man gazed down at the young man James had beaten and nudged him with his foot. "The pup has much to learn," he growled. He glared at James. "But what am I to make of you?"

James, pumped up at his triumph over the boy, glared back.

"Well, answer me. Who are you?" The warrior lifted his sword until the point touched James' Adams apple. "Tell me, lad, or I will slit open your throat like a solstice lamb."

"Stop!" screamed Tegwedd. "He can't answer. He does not speak our tongue."

"So he is Du Tarian!" The man glowered and nicked James' skin. A scarlet bead appeared on his neck. James, the sword still at his throat, stared back, wide-eyed like a cornered deer. .

"They are not Du Tarian," Tegwedd pleaded. "Let his friend speak for him. If you kill him without giving him the chance to explain himself, we are no better than the Du Tarian."

James was frozen to the spot. His hands were trembling.

The man frowned, his glittering blue eyes locked onto James.

James' shoulders sagged with relief as the man smiled broadly and lowered his sword. "Very well," the warrior said, lowering his sword, "The youth's courage has earned him the chance to persuade me to spare his life."

The warrior seated himself on a bench as James' three friends were thrown unceremoniously into the room; he was clearly the man in charge. "Which one of you speaks the tongue of the chosen people?" he demanded. Tom swallowed nervously and held up his hand.

The warrior smiled dangerously. "Tell your friend I am Maelog of Mynydd Ychydig," he said in a booming voice. "My people tended the land here and harvested the seas along this coast before the ancient ones dug the blue stones from the mountains."

"P-pleased to meet you," Tom stammered.

"Last night I heard a voice who said he was a messenger from the Gods. The messenger told me that the enemy had sent spies. He said a traitor was sheltering them at the Lake. Well," he said glowering at his captives, "what have you got to say?"

As Tom translated, Heulwen pushed her way through the warriors and stood in front of her chieftain. She was angry, and she didn't look like the sort of woman to be trifled with. "How dare you accuse me of being a traitor," she fumed. "The shrine of Cliodna may be destroyed but I am still her High Priestess. Whoever told you this is a liar!" Maelog remained silent, and some of the warriors shifted uncomfortably. A Priestess was a person to be feared. "The Du Tarian killed my husband and their chieftain raped me. Only a fool would think I would betray us to the enemy!"

The chief pursed his lips. "I did not say you were the traitor," he conceded. "But who are they and why are they here?"

"I don't know who they are or where they have come from," admitted Heulwen, deciding not to tell Maelog they had been in the cave. "But these people are not our enemies. Look at them! The Du Tarian would have sent seasoned warriors, or at least not sent them attired in such an outlandish fashion. No spy would draw such attention to themselves!" Maelog furrowed his brow. It seemed a compelling argument.

Tom was whispering a translation of the exchange to James and Emma when he stopped mid-sentence. "Hang on," he said. "Other than Heulwen, Tegwedd and Artur, the only person who's seen us here is the druid from the cave. It's him that's told the chief, it must be!"

"Why would he do that? It would be risky, surely? He's supposed to be exiled."

"Maybe he got someone else to tell him?"

"It doesn't matter," said Tom. "If Maelog suspected this mysterious messenger had anything to do with Myrleduin, he might be less likely to condemn us out of hand." They were so busy talking they were not aware that the room was watching them expectantly.

"Well?" said Maelog. "I asked you who you are. I'm waiting for your explanation."

Tom decided to take the initiative. He stood in front of the Iron Age chieftain and told him a pack of lies. "We come from the north," he began, making it up as he went, and hoping he would remember what he'd said later. "Our village was attacked by a Du Tarian raiding party and our parents were slaughtered. We escaped by the skin of our teeth, but as we watched our houses burn," he said dramatically, beginning to warm to his task, "we swore we would avenge our families!"

There was a murmur of assent from the assembled warriors. James sat listening and groaned inwardly. He hadn't a clue what was being said, but he knew bullshit when he heard it.

On a roll, Tom decided a bit of flannel was needed; it had gotten him out of scrapes in the past, and he calculated Maelog would be susceptible. "We came here," he went on shamelessly, "because we heard this tribe had a strong chieftain. A great leader whose warriors would drive back the Du Tarian." The warriors rumbled their approval some of them beating the flats of their swords against the sides of their feet.

Don't overdo it, prayed James, who never ceased to be amazed at his friend's capacity for persuasion.

"And now," Tom announced rashly, "we offer ourselves to you, to fight our common enemy!"

The chieftain sat aloof, but Tom sensed his flattery had hit the mark. Stroking his luxuriant moustache, Maelog pondered what Tom had said. "You speak eloquently," he conceded. "But why was I sent word that you were spies?"

Tom was in a quandary. He didn't know what the reaction would be if he mentioned their run in with the druid, but he felt he had to say something. He decided to take the risk. "Only one person other than Heulwen and her family knows we are here," he replied, pausing for effect. "His name is Myrleduin."

There were mutterings from some of the warriors and Maelog frowned, the whispered voice in the dark had sounded strangely familiar.

Tom swallowed. What he said next could mean life or death for himself and his friends. "My friend James fought off a man with a knife yesterday morning. He escaped, but we described him to Heulwen. He had very distinctive tattoos. She told us he was a druid and his name was Myrleduin. It must have been him who sent word to you, falsely accusing us of being spies. I have no idea what his motives were, but he clearly hoped he could trick you into doing his dirty work. If you kill us, you would be dancing to the tune of a man you thought you had banished into exile!" The muttering turned into an angry growl and Tom clenched his fists trying to disguise the fact his hands were trembling with fear. James and Emma exchanged worried looks.

"Maelog dances to the tune of no man, let alone the tune of a coward!" the Chieftain bellowed. Tom almost wet himself. "You strangers will come to the fort with me," he roared. Then, pointing his sword at Tegwedd, added, "And she comes too. If her mother has been lying, Priestess or not, the girl will pay the price!"

Chapter 26

The trek to the fort was made at a dogtrot and James kept glancing anxiously at Delyth, who was struggling to keep up. The roadway was no more than a muddy track, meandering southwards, hugging the contours of the coast. From the demeanour of the warriors walking with them, James found it hard to gauge what status they were being afforded by their new captors. They all seemed friendly enough, and there had been no attempt to tie their hands. Tom even seemed to be sharing jokes with two of them, who were trying to barter for his dayglo orange suit and boots. James counted sixteen men, including Maelog, who led the procession, standing proudly on a lightly-built carriage drawn by two ponies.

Mind-blowing, thought James, staring at the war chariot as it rattled its way over the bumpy lane. *It's like we're in a movie.* The smile that had begun to form on the edge of his mouth froze as his gaze rested on the young warrior he'd bested in Heulwen's house. The boy, despite a swollen and bloody nose, had striking good looks.

I bet I broke his nose, James thought with satisfaction, noting the arrogant swagger the youth affected. One of the warriors with Tom, a fearsome brute, made a comment, and there was a ripple of laughter amongst the other men. The youth coloured and glared at James. The boy didn't say anything, he didn't need to; the look was enough. James had made an enemy and was going to have to watch his back.

The track wound its way up a steep incline; Emma and Tegwedd paused to wait for Delyth. They'd covered about three miles over the uneven ground and Delyth's face was pink with exertion. Suddenly, Emma realized they'd become detached from the rest of the group and were receiving unwanted attention from a group of men in the vanguard. One of them, a warrior who looked like he'd put his face in a food processor, was making a point of walking just behind her, studying her bottom with undisguised lust.

When the guy made a clumsy attempt to grope her buttocks, she'd had enough. "Fuck off!" she shouted, and slapped her tormentor across his battle-scarred face. The blow landed with a satisfying crack. His look of surprise was a picture; he stroked his cheek, scowling, while his mates sniggered. For a moment Emma thought he was going to hit her, but instead he gave her a toothy grin and made an unsavoury gesture. This might have been the end of the matter if Tegwedd hadn't launched a stream of Welsh invective that had Emma's admirer incandescent with rage. Bellowing like an enraged bull and with the other warriors hooting with laughter, he grabbed Tegwedd round the waist and held her in a vicelike grip.

"Right you little bitch," he grunted, forcing a calloused hand between the struggling girl's thighs, "you need breaking in. And I have the very thing to do it with." Tegwedd let out a high-pitched scream as her attacker pinned her to the ground and started to unbuckle his belt.

Without warning, Maelog stepped into the ring of warriors which had formed around them. "Stop!" he commanded, holding his sword to the old warrior's throat. The man froze, then rolled off the girl. He stood up hurriedly, hauling up his flannel breeches.

"Sorry," he said, shrugging his shoulders. "She needs to keep a civil tongue in her head."

"And you need keep a civil cock in your pants!" roared Maelog. "However the girl may have offended your delicate sensibilities, her mother is a High Priestess and a clanswoman. The Tree God might hold sway in our land now, but I still fear the Spirit of the Lake. So unless the girl's mother proves to be a traitor, she remains under my protection. And that applies to the others. Understand?"

"Yes, my Lord," grunted the man sullenly.

"Good! Then we will continue." Maelog stepped back onto the running board of his chariot. "And let them go," he said to the warriors who'd restrained Tom and James during the incident. Then he turned to Tom. "We are not barbarian Du Tarian. You are now in my service, so unless you prove false, I offer you my protection. But remember, when the enemy comes, I expect your sword arm."

Tom didn't reply. Offering his sword arm sounded downright dangerous! *Trust me to open my big mouth*, he thought ruefully. *God knows what this maniac will expect us to do.* Tom was so preoccupied with the worrying consequences of offering his sword arm to the chieftain that when they rounded a bend, it was James who first saw the fort.

The stronghold stood, imposing, on the headland. The site's natural defensive position had been enhanced by an earthwork bank lined with stones and topped with a palisade of sharpened stakes buried in the ground like giant pencils.

To James, anxious about the girls' safety and preoccupied by the idea of escape, the fort looked like a prison. "Holy shit!" he gasped. "How did they build that thing? They haven't got any machinery."

"No idea," replied Tom, awed at the sheer scale of the construction. "They must have dug it and cut all the timber by hand. It must have taken years."

"That wall must be twenty feet tall," calculated James, already considering the possibility he might have to scale it in not-too-distant future,

"Easily! And look, that must be the main gate," pointed out Tom. "But what are those?"

James shielded his eyes from the glare of the sun and squinted at the pair of massive timber gates. Hung in the centre of each door he could see the skulls of what must have been giant bulls, their bleached horns gleaming in the afternoon sunshine. Then he noticed a row of smaller objects pinned to the top of the gates like a row of footballs. "Oh my God!" he exclaimed. "They're human skulls!

Tom's eyes widened, "Do you think they're cannibals?"

"Don't be soft." James laughed nervously. "All the same, we'd better not piss them off, or we might wind up as one of their trophies."

They didn't have much time to consider this before Maelog reached the gates. An old man peered myopically over the parapet. "What is your business?" the wizened gatekeeper demanded.

"In the name of the Gods, Cai! Open the gates, you blind old fool, or I'll cut your balls off!" Maelog thundered. "I'm too tired and thirsty to play games." Several warriors sniggered as Cai "the Gate" darted out of sight.

They listened impatiently to muffled curses from the other side of the gate, followed by the rasping of a wooden bolt being drawn back. Eventually, the gates swung open to reveal Cai the Gate. He was breathing heavily. He was accompanied by a scrawny youth, who, by his facial similarity, might be his son. Cai bowed obsequiously as his stone-faced chieftain looked down from his chariot and led the raiding party into the stronghold.

As they passed into the stronghold, Cai lifted a huge trumpet to his lips. The instrument, the Great dragonhead trumpet of Mynydd Ychydig, was designed to strike fear into the hearts of the enemy. Blown by Cai, the mighty horn sounded like an asthmatic fart, and James, despite his misgivings on entering the fort, couldn't help but smile at the expression of displeasure on the chieftain's face.

The trumpet blast, pathetic as it was, did rouse the inhabitants, and within minutes, dozens of people of all ages gathered to stare at the strange young people and their outlandish clothing, chattering excitedly.

The youngsters stared back with equal interest. One of the children, an impish girl about four years old, poked James' boot inquisitively before scampering back to her mother, fearful that the object of her curiosity would admonish her. James smiled and the child smiled back, her brown eyes twinkling mischievously. The touching exchange made James reflect that the inhabitants of this new world he found himself in were not so different from people back home. *They dress strangely*, he thought, *and have some very odd beliefs, but they are basically the same*.

The thought was comforting until it dawned on him that if he ever got home, things would never be the same. What happened in the cave and what seemed to be happening in this new world had altered his perception of life. He felt a lump in his throat. He missed his mum and dad. *Pull yourself together, James Cordle*, he thought. *God knows what's going to happen next.*

An uneasy hush fell over the gathering and James looked up expectantly. Like the parting of the Red Sea before Moses, the crowd drew back, allowing a man to walk unhindered towards Maelog and his captives.

The chieftain, standing erect, looked down at the newcomer from the vantage point of his chariot. The man stared back, undaunted. Tom nudged James in the ribs and made a face, and no wonder. All the extraordinary things they'd witnessed since leaving the cave hadn't prepared them for the manner in which this man was attired. Or not attired would be a better way of putting it.

All he wore was a loincloth scarcely more substantial than a G-string. But it wasn't his lack of clothes that blew their minds, or even his shaved head and meticulously plaited pigtail. What made the guy truly amazing were his tattoos. The whole surface of his body was covered with them. There was literally no area of skin that wasn't adorned with black, swirling patterns. This included his face, his scalp and even, James noticed to his horror, his eyelids. The tattoos made it difficult to determine his age, but going by the firm muscle tone and the fluid way he walked, James reckoned he was not much older than thirty. In his hand was a heavy wooden staff topped with a carved figure of a crouching bear. The staff was held like a badge of office, but it didn't take much imagination to appreciate it could be used as a weapon.

"I see you, Mordred," said Maelog coldly, his tone of voice making it clear that he wished the man was a thousand miles away.

"And I see you, Mighty One," replied the tattooed man, his words hanging in the air like a threat. The crowd watched the chieftain and druid in silence. It was like watching two wolves circle each other, each one waiting for the opportunity to seize the other by the throat.

Maelog's eyes narrowed. "Myrleduin has returned," he hissed. "We need to talk." A buzz of excitement spread through the assembly and, to the satisfaction of the chieftain, a look of alarm flitted briefly across Mordred's elaborately decorated face.

Keeping the initiative, Maelog pointed to his young captives. "Bring them to my house," he ordered. He stepped out of the chariot, then strode over to the largest roundhouse in the compound and went inside. Mordred followed the chieftain at a sedate pace, careful to maintain his dignity as spiritual leader of the tribe.

James observed Mordred closely. His instincts told him this was a dangerous man, a very dangerous man. A man to be watched. The guy's tattoos camouflaged any subtle facial movements, but they couldn't disguise the treacherous intent of the druid's eyes, which bored into the chieftain's back.

James' thoughts were interrupted by a prod between his shoulder blades, indicating that he was to follow the chieftain. As the youngsters filed into Maelog's roundhouse, the building was already filling up with people.

Chapter 27

From a dense thicket on the hillside overlooking the fort, Myrleduin watched Maelog lead the little convoy through the gates. He was worried; only the girl was supposed to come to his call. He pursed his lips; bringing across four of the strange folk was like dropping a pebble in a pond. He couldn't know how far the ripples would reach and what the repercussions might be.

It was the one called James that troubled him. The boy's spirit had taken him by surprise in the cave and almost overwhelmed him. He must make sure this dangerous young interloper didn't interfere with his plans for the girl.

It was his fear of the boy that prompted him to persuade Maelog that the young strangers were spies. It had been childishly easy to slip, unnoticed, into his gullible brother's roundhouse and whisper his doom-laden message to the chieftain in his drunken stupor. Security had become lax since his retreat into exile, and that idiot Cai hadn't even bothered to draw the bolts across the main gate.

Myrleduin shrugged his bony shoulders. It didn't need a Watcher to foretell what would happen when the Du Tarian returned. Maelog's fortress would fall and his people's blood would be spilt, staining the fields their forefathers had hewn from the forest.

Myrleduin sighed; things could have been so different.

He and Maelog had been close once. There was a mere one year between them, so they'd grown up together. As young men, they'd been inseparable – hunting, fighting, drinking, and womanising. The big, boisterous Maelog and his wiry, clever younger brother, Myrleduin.

Then they fell in love with the same girl and, to Maelog's dismay, Heulwen chose Myrleduin, with his dark good looks and charismatic personality. Initially there was no animosity, but as months passed, Maelog found it more and more difficult to accept Heulwen's rejection, and the seed of resentment grew in his heart.

Myrleduin remembered the look of anger and bewilderment on his brother's face when he told him he'd decided to commit himself to the life of a druid and reject the pleasures of this world. Maelog, a simple man, couldn't understand why his brother wanted to forsake the woman they both loved. But then, Maelog didn't have the imagination to comprehend the power that could be wielded by a man with the Knowledge.

Months later, during the early days of training, he was given word of Heulwen's pregnancy and hurried marriage to Morgan. It seemed that Maelog, much as he loved Heulwen, had been too proud to marry the woman his brother had cast aside, and was unwilling to bring up his brother's child as his own.

Myrleduin remembered the harshness of the treatment he received as a novice. Even the tough life of a warrior had not prepared him for the hardships he endured on his lonely path to Knowledge. Under the guidance of the Master, the physical pain and mental exercises had brought a spiritual dimension that was beyond the experience of ordinary men. Above all, it gave him the power he craved. To look beyond the here and now of the physical existence and over the horizon of tomorrow.

Unconsciously, Myleduin's hand went to his empty scrotum, from which the Master had plucked his testicles. There had been little pain at the time, he remembered; soporifics administered by the druids and days of meditation before his initiation had seen to that. The pain had come later as he meditated in the solitary darkness of his cell, sweating the infection from his fever-wracked body.

When he'd returned to his tribe as a Watcher three years later, his spiritual journey complete, the power in him was manifest to the people, and many made the pilgrimage to the shrine at the Lake to hear his teachings and worship the Goddess. Even Maelog was in awe of him and eagerly sought his advice, although there was no warmth between them.

Myrleduin closed his eyes, a smile playing about his lips. It had been a golden time for the people of the Lake. The community had flourished under his leadership and, much to his delight, Heulwen had found the grace to forgive him and work at his side.

The smile became a frown. *A flower is at its most beautiful just before its petals fall*, he reflected. *How apt that our crowning moment came just before we were crushed.*

The Du Tarian had arrived a few days after the Summer Solstice, the night Heulwen was anointed as a Priestess. He remembered that balmy night; it seemed that Cliodna would pour out her blessings on them for eternity. How was it that he, a Watcher, did not foresee the axe that was about to fall?

Myrleduin cast his mind back to the morning the raiders landed on the beach. It had been a chilly start to the day, and he'd been making his way toward the cave for the dawn ritual. The sea had been oily calm, and a sea mist had rolled in with the tide.

The mist had been thick that morning and had obscured the approach of the enemy, so the first he knew of their presence was a hollow thud of an oar against the side of a boat and muttered curses. At first he'd thought it was Morgan, returning from his fish traps. Then he realized the whispered voices, which carried clearly over the still water, were not speaking his own tongue.

In the thicket, Myrleduin rolled on his side. The ground was hard, and the prickly twigs that had fallen from the hawthorn bush under which he hid were pressing into his scrawny backside. He'd seen fifty winters, well past middle age, and the privations of his calling had taken their toll on his body.

I'm getting old, he thought. There was a time when he could wait in complete stillness for hours. Now, increasingly, he longed for a dry bed and the comfort of a warm fire. But the guilt of what had happened would not allow him rest.

Seven long, bitter years had passed since that fateful morning, and he could still see the warriors creeping up the beach, their war shields, painted with pitch, slung over their backs, and their swords, as yet un-bloodied, in their hands.

He still didn't know why he'd failed to raise the alarm. As a young man, before he devoted his life to the Goddess, he'd been a brave and determined warrior. So why was it when the Du Tarian ran up the beach, he'd slunk back to the cave, leaving everyone he cared for and the Goddess he had sworn to protect at the mercy of the enemy?

There were times when he tried to rationalise his actions, reasoning that he could not have warned them in time, and hopelessly outnumbered there was nothing he could do. But in his heart, he knew it was because he'd been afraid. He'd hidden in the cave until the following morning, then concealed the chalice before venturing out to investigate.

Like the morning that had preceded it, the morning after the raid had been still, with not a breath of wind to ruffle the becalmed sea. The only sound was the haunting peep-peeping of a flock of oystercatchers as they skimmed the surface of the sea. The sense of peace had been so complete that he'd wondered if the warriors had been a figment of his imagination. But when he'd rounded the headland, the ominous pall of smoke hanging over the valley had shattered that illusion.

Suddenly his own safety had seemed unimportant. He had to find out if his friends had survived. On a flat area at the top of the beach, he encountered the first body. It was Morgan; he lay sprawled, facedown, on the coarse, marshy grass. His head had been crushed and flies buzzed around his hair, settling to feed and lay their eggs on the congealing blood and brains.

In his hiding place, Myrleduin shifted uncomfortably on the hard ground. Shocking as it was, the discovery of Morgan's body was nothing compared to the horror at the lakeside.

His abiding memory was the smell of burnt flesh. He hadn't eaten roasted pork since.

He'd paused at the edge of the village; a makeshift pyre had been constructed over Cliodna's shrine. As he approached, noxious smoke billowed into his face. Gasping for breath, he watched as the flames licked around twisted black objects that once had been friends and clansmen.

He remembered wandering around the remains of the village, picking over the smouldering wreckage, desperately hoping that the Goddess' sacred body had survived. When the sun had reached its zenith, he'd abandoned hope and wandered grief stricken back towards the beach. It was there that he'd found Heulwen and Tegwedd kneeling over Morgan's corpse.

He'd watched them in silence, listening to their cries, not wishing to intrude on their grief. As mother and daughter tended to the body sprawled on the grass, he felt a stab of envy for the man his daughter had called father. Had he not chosen to follow the chaste life of the initiated, it would have been him, not Morgan, who would have demanded their love. Now the shrine had been destroyed, and with it the earthly body of the Goddess, his sacrifice seemed futile and his life bereft of purpose. No one would grieve when he passed.

"Coward!" Heulwen's voice, ugly with anger and grief, had pieced him like a lance.

"Forgive me," he'd pleaded, hanging his head. His lack of denial made his guilt obvious.

"Where were you when we needed you? We trusted you. You who claimed to hold the secrets of the future. Did you not foretell this? Or did you choose not to tell us?"

"In the name of Cliodna, believe me," Myrleduin had implored, "I swear this was hidden from me! I knew nothing of this until they were upon us."

"And then you hid!"

Myrleduin had shrunk before his former lover's withering gaze.

"How could you?" she'd sobbed. "You sacrificed our love for your precious Goddess! You let them cut away your manhood, and for what? When Cliodna needed you most, when *I* needed you most, you ran and hid." Then Heulwen's expression had darkened, and her next words had become etched into Myrleduin's memory. "They tossed Our Lady Cliodna's body on the fire like a dry twig," she'd raged, "and threw the corpses of our men on top. Then they raped the women. Tegwedd hid in the woods above the village, but they caught me." Myrleduin recalled his shame as Heulwen's eyes had dropped to her torn dress and he noticed the livid bruises along the inside of her thighs. "Darragh, their chieftain, was the first," she'd told him, "I couldn't stop them!" Then Tegwedd had wrapped her arm around her mother as the tears flowed. "And now this..." Heulwen had sobbed, pointing to Morgan's fly ridden corpse. "He was a good man, and now he is gone."

"Morgan is not gone," Myrleduin had answered gently. "His spirit still lives."

The force of Heulwen's reply had shocked him. "You pious, patronising bastard! I'm not listening to your druid lies any longer! Go, and never come back!"

Myrleduin sighed. That was how he'd left her seven years ago, eyes ablaze with hatred and contempt. A day later, Maelog sent him into exile, branded as a coward, his life and reputation in ruins.

There was no sign of movement from inside the fort, so Myrleduin settled down to wait for nightfall. He wondered what the pretender Mordred would make of the four strangers. He had already decided he would gain access to the fort under cover of darkness and find out.

He had plenty of time to reflect as he waited. The years of wandering that followed his exile had almost broken him. He'd lived like a wild animal, scratching an existence on the fringes of society, begging for food, shivering under hedges in winter. But the suffering and the aching loneliness had not been in vain. Away from any distractions other than filling his belly and staying warm, he'd had time to meditate and search for answers in the swirling waters of the chalice.

It had been clear from the start that the shrine at the lake must be restored. Rebuilding the shrine itself was a simple matter. Timber and reed were easy to find, as were willing hands to hew the wood and craft the thatch. Replacing the sacred effigy of the Goddess was a different matter, and it demanded deep magic.

He'd travelled to the Holy Isle and sought wisdom from the Master. A girl would be chosen, the druid had told him. It had been prescribed in the 'Psalm of Transfiguration.' She would be perfect in form, so the ancient song foretold, a fitting sacrifice for the Goddess.

"A Golden Virgin bearing the Sign of the Sword."

Her body would be placed in the sacred lake, where the alchemy of holy water would purify the flesh, and the spirit of the Goddess would inhabit it. When the body was lifted from the water, it would be transformed. An incorruptible, physical embodiment of the Goddess.

He chanted the words of the psalm,
"One score years shall she lie in the lake,
A Holy Temple for the Goddess to make,
Then shall She be raised Incorruptible and Pure
To dwell with her people and bring Life once more."

Once he learned the truth, Myrleduin had sought the girl. The search had ended when he'd seen Emma at the lakeside. The sign of Cliodna she wore around her neck confirmed it. Emma was the one who must be sacrificed. Praise the Gods he'd found her at last.

Chapter 28

The atmosphere in Maelog's roundhouse was electric. James didn't have a clue what was being said, Welsh was gobbledygook to him, but the chief and the man with the tattoos were clearly having a row. The argument became particularly fraught when the name Myrleduin was mentioned.

From the finger pointing and gesticulations, it seemed that the argument concerned him and his friends. Eventually the two men reached an agreement.

Tom, ashen faced, leaned over, and whispered in his ear. "The tattooed guy wants to throw us in a pit full of spikes, but Maelog says he won't do that because that's just what Myrleduin would want him to do."

"So what are they going to do with us?"

"The girls will be staying with Tegwedd's aunt in the village. You and I are going to live with the warriors here at the fort. Apparently we're to be trained in the arts of war, whatever that means."

"What? Learning to use swords and stuff?"

"Hell if I know! I suppose we'll find out soon enough," he added as the ugly warrior who assaulted Tegwedd indicated they were to follow him.

There was no time to speak to the girls before they were hustled outside, but James caught Emma's eye, and she managed an encouraging smile. He felt a lump in his throat.

She's got guts, thought James. It was only a few days ago he'd written her off as a spoiled bitch. The vision of Emma emerging naked from the lake popped into his mind again. He tried to erase the image; it was going to be difficult enough to survive in this dangerous new environment without mooning over a girl.

The two boys were escorted to a small group of dwellings located at the centre of the fortified area near Maelog's house. The huts were of a very similar construction to Heulwen's roundhouse at Aberieddy: a circular wattle and daub wall with a thatched roof stuck on the top like a dunce's hat. Wisps of smoke from a fire in the centre of the building rose ethereally up from the thatch. As they ducked through the low entrance, a group of young lads looked up at them curiously. Their hideous escort grunted something to the occupants of the hut and stalked out. As he left, one of the boys made a comment, precipitating a bout of muted sniggering.

Tom, smiling, turned to his friend. "It looks like this is our new home," he explained. "They call the ugly guy 'Mochyne.'" Tom grinned. "It means 'Pig' in Welsh."

"Are you a spy from the North?" asked the lad who'd made the others laugh. He was small and wiry like Tom, with dark, inquisitive eyes.

"We come from the North," Tom said, repeating his earlier lies, "but we're not spies. Our village was destroyed by invaders and we fled south. We've come to offer our services to fight the common enemy."

"Is it true your friend beat Rhydderch?" asked one of the other boys. "We heard you broke his nose!"

Tom glanced nervously at James, who towered over the other boys in the room like a Goliath. Outnumbered and unsure of the reception they were receiving, he noticed his friend was balling his fists, ready for a fight.

Tom thought he'd better try to defuse the situation. "If you mean the boy he hit at Heulwen's house, he was only defending himself."

"Then it is true." The lad grinned, looking at James with respect. "How about that? That bastard Rhydderch got a bloody nose!" He laughed, holding out his hand to James.

"My name is Carrad. Welcome to the house of training. None of us here care for the chieftain's son. He's a bully, and many of us have suffered at his hand. It was about time somebody brought him to heel, but be careful. He'll make a dangerous enemy."

As Tom translated, James relaxed. His hands unclenched and a broad smile lit up his face. He grasped Carrad's hand, and suddenly he and Tom found themselves surrounded by boys crowding forward to introduce themselves and offer their congratulations. It was as if James had scored a winning try in a rugby match on the first day of joining a new school. He was an instant hit.

They spent the rest of the evening sitting around the fire chatting with the lads, trying to ascertain the rules of this new school and sussing out the characters that would play a part in their new lives.

Carrad and his friends explained that all boys born into the tribe were expected to spend at least two years in the house of training when they reached adulthood in their fourteenth year.

They lived together in the apprentice's hut, learning the art of war under the watchful eye of Mochyne, who, from the tales recounted by the boys, was a cross between a drunken housemaster and a psycho karate instructor. As they listened to the laughing apprentices, the life of these young warriors sounded idyllic. Each morning there were one or more sessions of weapons training then the rest of the day they were free to do what they wanted, including hunting and fishing.

It's like being at a school with games every day and no academic lessons, thought Tom, enthused, *brilliant! And they're even allowed alcohol! Mochyne encourages them to take part in warrior drinking games. Imagine teachers at school giving boys booze. Crazy!*

According to the lads, food was the major plus point of being a warrior, as, unlike the rest of the people in the village, warriors were provided with meat or fish every day, cooked by one of the women.

Iron Age society, thought James wryly, hadn't embraced women's equality; he wondered how the girls were faring.

Chapter 29

Sitting cross-legged on a moth-eaten sheepskin, Delyth wasn't happy. She'd spent an uncomfortable night in an unspeakably itchy bed, only to be woken up at dawn to fetch water from the spring half a mile down the valley. "Why is it us girls that have to get the water?" she moaned, rubbing the nape of her neck where the heavy clay container had chafed.

"It's a maiden's duty to carry water for the family," admonished Tegwedd. "Did your mother not teach you this?"

"We didn't have to carry water back home," explained Delyth. "There were pipes which brought water into our houses. We could have as much water as we wanted just by turning a tap. We had hot water taps as well, so we could have a bath or wash our faces whenever we wanted."

Tegwedd stared at her new friend; she didn't have a clue what she was talking about. What was a pipe? Or a tap for that matter? And why would you need hot water to wash your face? She had many questions she'd like to ask her strange new housemates.

She glanced at Emma. It was a pity she didn't speak their tongue, she wanted to ask about the charm. The sign of the Goddess marked Emma as a special person, but how did she come by it? Was she a priestess amongst her people, or perhaps a princess? Tegwedd touched Emma's cross, now hanging round her own neck. She knew she should return it, but something stopped her. It would be safer if she looked after it for now.

A diminutive woman bustled into the roundhouse and interrupted Tegwedd's thoughts. "Who told you girls you could sit on your arses?" the woman demanded in a tone that inferred she would stand no nonsense. "The sun has risen and there is no flour to bake the men's bread," she scolded. "You girl," she pointed to Emma, "there's barley in the jar behind you. Bring it here and make a start on the flour."

"She doesn't understand you," explained Delyth. "Let me fetch it." Hurriedly, she located the large earthenware container behind Emma's bed and attempted to drag it to the centre of the room. But Delyth had underestimated the weight of the storage jar, which tipped on its side, spilling its precious contents over the smooth mud floor.

"Stupid child!" shrieked the woman. "That's the last of the grain. We'll have no more till harvest!"

"I-I'm sorry," stammered Delyth. "It's too heavy."

"Get out of the way!" ordered the tiny woman, who, much to Delyth's surprise, grasped the rim of the heavy jar, heaved it upright, then dragged it towards the centre of the hut. "Now sweep up that grain and put it on the stone," the woman said, patting the dust off her hands. "We need flour enough to bake bread for fifteen men." Then she turned to Tegwedd and her expression softened. "Come girl," she said, a suggestion of a smile crinkling the lines at the side of her coal black eyes. "You'd better help me fetch the wood. Tell me, how is your mother? I haven't seen my cousin in many moons."

"She is well, Aunt, and sends you her best wishes."

Emma and Delyth watched disconsolately as Tegwedd and her feisty little aunt gossiped their way towards the trees lining the valley bottom.

"Now what?" asked Emma.

"Make the flour, I guess," replied Delyth, looking dubiously at two cylindrical blocks of granite lying on the floor next to the hearth. She picked up the larger of the stones. It was extremely heavy. She turned it over. "Look," she said, "this side is hollowed out; we put the grain in here and use the other stone to grind the barley into flour."

Emma curled her lip. "I suppose you're right, but it sounds incredibly boring."

Delyth ignored her. "Scoop up a bit of barley, Em, I'll have a go."

Emma dipped her hand in the jar and drew out a handful of grain. "Ergh," she said, "it's mouldy." Both girls peered suspiciously at the handful of barley. The grains were thin and coated in a sooty substance. Emma rolled the barley in her palm. "Gross!" she exclaimed, pointing to a small, elongated brown object. "That's mouse poo!"

"Just pick out the poo and put the grain on the stone." Delyth sighed. "Birieth said this is the last of the grain, so we've got no choice."

Wrinkling her face in disgust, Emma picked out the offending mouse turds and poured the grain onto the grindstone.

"Right!" said Delyth, placing the quern stone on the top and rubbing it from side to side energetically. "How long will it take?" she asked breathlessly.

"It won't take long if we take turns," suggested Emma.

Delyth's enthusiasm was already evaporating. "It must be your turn soon then. My arms are killing me,"

"Don't moan. We've only just started."

Emma's words were prophetic. When Tegwedd and her aunt returned some time later, the girls had only managed to produce a couple of handfuls of coarsely ground flour.

"What have you been doing all morning?" enquired Aunt Birieth, fixing her beady eyes on Delyth and Emma.

"We tried our best," insisted Delyth defensively. "We've never done it before."

"Don't–" Aunt Birieth was about to say 'lie to me,' then she noticed the blisters on Delyth's palms. She examined the girls' hands. "These have never seen hard work!" she said disapprovingly. "You may have been noblewomen amongst your people, but you live in my house now, and I expect you to do your share of the work."

Delyth translated.

Emma shot Birieth a rebellious look.

Birieth got her retaliation in first. "And tell your friend if she wants to eat tonight, you'll finish the flour."

It was mid-afternoon when Birieth told them they had done enough. Delyth and Emma sank down on the grass at the front of the house. Both girls were close to tears. Their arms felt like jelly and their knees were numb from kneeling on the hard floor. Worst of all, holding the grindstone was like handling sandpaper, and had rubbed the skin off their soft hands. Their palms were a mass of blisters.

"I'll have to pop it," whimpered Delyth, gingerly touching a hot, angry pustule on her right hand.

"Whining isn't helping!" retorted Emma.

"I can't stand much more of this," Delyth persisted. "We're supposed to do this every day."

"We have no choice!" said Emma. "We can't run away, we've got nowhere to run! If we want to stay alive, we'll *have* to grind the corn, fetch the wood, fetch the water..." A thought struck her. "And by the way, if we're going to be stuck here, you'd better teach me Welsh. I can't stand listening to you wittering to Tegwedd and not being able to understand a word."

The girls' conversation was interrupted by footsteps; they spun around, hoping it might be James or Tom, and found themselves face to face with the chieftain's son.

"They tell me you girls are not used to work," Rhydderch smiled, his eyes lingering on Emma's chest, "so I've come to see what you *are* good at." He let the words hang like a threat.

Emma stared back. She'd seen his type before. Rhydderch was a misogynistic bully. He was good-looking enough, striking, in fact, if you ignored his swollen nose. But there was something about his face that rang alarm bells. It was the mouth, she thought. It was an arrogant mouth. A cruel mouth.

Rhydderch smiled at her insolently, revealing a row of even white teeth.

"You have fire in your belly," he said, acknowledging Emma's defiant stare. "That can be attractive, but take care; a girl must know her place."

"Don't bother to translate," snapped Emma as Delyth started to open her mouth, "I can imagine what this worm is saying. And tell him to stop staring at my tits. It's not polite."

"I don't think that would be a good idea," said Delyth. "He could make a lot of trouble for us."

"Please yourself," replied Emma, "but I'm not staying here to be leered at by this creep. Come on, let's go back inside."

Emma started to get to her feet, but Rhydderch pushed her down with a disdainful shove. "I'm talking to you, you bitch," he snarled, his white teeth bared.

Emma reacted like a cat that'd just realised it was at the vets. Spitting with rage, she sprang to her feet.

"Stop that! Now!" The authority in the voice was unmistakable. All three youngsters froze. "Get inside, girls!" commanded Birieth, her five-foot-nothing frame bristling. "And Rhydderch, your father will know of this. I heard every word you said. These girls may not be of this tribe, but they are noblewomen and have been afforded the hospitality of your father. You *will* accord them respect!"

Rhydderch gave Birieth a hard stare, then nodded his head. He would love to smash his fist into this little woman's face, but he feared his father, so he would bide his time. One day he would rule in his father's place, and then he'd give this impudent woman what she deserved.

"Bastard!" whispered Emma to herself. "I wish James would give him another hiding." Then she brought herself up short. *I don't need a knight in shining armour*, she told herself, dispelling the fantasy of James rushing to her rescue.

Chapter 30

For James and Tom, the day began in a leisurely fashion. Unlike girls their age, young warriors were not expected to get up early to fetch water. They lounged around while a bossy woman called Birieth served them jugs of water and flat cakes made of oats and honey.

The arrival of 'The Pig' shattered any illusions that they were at a holiday camp. "Get your arses outside!" he screamed, the veins on his bull-like neck sticking out like purple spaghetti. Suddenly there were youths running in all directions, hastily grabbing swords, shields, and bits of kit that looked like protective clothing. James and Tom lined up with the other boys on an area of grass in the centre of the fort.

The Pig surveyed his wards critically. His piggy little eyes homed in on the two newcomers. "You boy," he addressed Tom, knowing he understood Welsh, "tell your big friend I want to see what he can do." He handed James a sword and an oval shield.

James took the sword in his right hand and swung it clumsily. Then he picked up the shield. He had no idea how to hold it, and it took a bit of fumbling about before he realised how the arm straps worked. It was obvious he didn't have a clue what he was doing, and some of the boys started to snigger.

"Come on, boy!" bellowed the Pig. "Hold that shield arm up!"

James, not knowing what his thug like instructor was saying, stood immobile, looking confused.

"Watch out!" yelled Tom, as the Pig whirled a long wooden staff in his hands and brought it crashing down on James' shield. James buckled under the force of the blow, but just managed to keep on his feet.

The Pig laughed. "I thought you were the big hard man, surely my little twig didn't hurt you?"

James stared back at the battle-scarred warrior defiantly. He didn't understand Welsh, but the meaning was clear. The Pig intended to test him.

If he wants me to wimp out, he's going to be disappointed, decided James. *He's going to beat the crap out of me, but if I back down now it'll be worse in the long run*. James gripped the sword, which already felt like a lead weight, and instinctively brought his shield arm up. Then, transferring his weight to the balls of his feet, he focused on his opponent's eyes. Something he had learned in the boxing ring.

"That's better," smiled the Pig disarmingly. Then, without warning, he slashed his staff towards James' exposed right flank. The ash pole had been whipped down at incredible speed, but James had seen a flicker in the warrior's piggy eyes and anticipated the attack. It gave him just enough time to parry the stick with his sword. He was not so lucky with the third blow, which came from nowhere, thumping him on the side of his head, making him stagger back, his ears ringing. Then the staff caught him at the back of the knees and suddenly it was all over, and James found himself sprawled out on the hard ground.

The Pig stood over him. "You have much to learn," he grunted, "but you have quick hands. I will make a warrior out of you." He turned to the rest of the boys, who were watching in silence. "Now we will begin," he said.

Their first morning weapons drills made the first rugby training session after the summer break seem like a picnic in the park. The Pig was relentless. One by one, they went through a series of weapons drills, each more energy-sapping than the last. Tom and James found themselves unable to match the stamina of the other boys.

The final exercise was a killer. The Pig lined them up and told them to hold out their sword with their arm extended. Any boy who dropped his arm before being told had to run twenty times around the perimeter of the fort, holding his shield over his head. Both Tom and James had to suffer the ignominy of running round the fort.

Later, flopped out on a piece of grass, James rubbed his aching forearm. "I'm knackered," he complained. "I don't know how the other lads hold up those swords for so long. My arms are killing me."

"Same here." Tom had a nasty bruise on his shin where the Pig had whacked him with the ash spear shaft. "But remember this is our first time. Those lads have been doing this every day for a year or more."

"I suppose," agreed James. "I just don't like looking like an idiot."

Tom looked up at his friend. "Looking like an idiot is the least of our worries. I don't care if I make a prat of myself. Think about it James; we're not practicing for a sports match. That psychopath is teaching us how to kill people!"

"Or teaching us how to stay alive."

"It's the same thing," Tom insisted. "I just don't think I could kill someone."

James shook his head. "You sure we're not dreaming?" he asked, the enormity of what Tom had said sinking in.

"I thought we'd agreed all this is for real."

"I know. It's just that everything is so crazy, it's easier to pretend it's not really happening." James swallowed; the vivid images he'd seen in his dreams had started bouncing around inside his head again. He paused as he brought his thoughts under control. "Tom," he said at last, staring into his friend's eyes, "I do get it. I know this training means we might have to stick a sword in a person sometime. I just haven't worked out how that makes me feel."

Tom said nothing, he just stared at James.

The conversation was brought to an end by Carrad. "The boys are going swimming," he said, running up to them. "You coming?"

Chapter 31

It was another glorious afternoon, and James lay on the beach in his twenty-first century boxers. He looked down at his body. Apart from a few yellowing bruises, courtesy of the Pig, his skin was bronzed and the muscles beneath were toned from daily weapons drills. He took a deep breath of sea air. He couldn't ever remember feeling this fit back home.

"Hi there."

James sat up and hurriedly pulled on his breeches. He didn't want the girls to see him in his ragged pants. He shaded his eyes and squinted in the direction of the sound, "Oh is it just you?"

Emma smiled. "Just me?" she teased.

"What I meant was, is Delyth not coming?"

"I know what you meant," smiled Emma. "And no, she isn't. She started her period this morning and they've shut her in that awful hut."

James didn't respond; menstruation was something he'd rather not talk about.

"They treat us like we've got a contagious disease. Girls in that condition are unclean apparently. We are forbidden to prepare food or touch anyone. The only saving grace is..." Emma stopped. "Where's Tom?"

"The Pig caught him and Carrad fooling around. He's made them muck out the stables."

"Ouch." Emma grinned. "In this heat?"

James smiled. "They'll stink."

"So, it's just us this afternoon?"

"Looks like it."

Emma raised her eyebrow and gave James an appraising stare.

James felt his face colour. He'd spent the morning sparring, but the look she gave him disarmed him faster than the warrior he'd fought. It was her green eyes, he thought. He could lose himself in those eyes.

Emma released him from her stare and smiled. "Birieth has packed some oatcakes. Let's wade round to second beach for a picnic. It's nice and secluded."

"Sounds great," said James, who didn't appreciate the implication of the word secluded.

Emma brushed her fingers on James' shoulder. "Come on, silly," she said, hitching up her skirt. "We haven't got long, I have to stoke the fire for the meal tonight."

James stared at her legs as she waded into the shallows. He followed her into the water.

His fire was already stoked.

The glacier-white pebbles of second beach sparkled in the afternoon sun, but James scarcely noticed. Emma dazzled brighter. He couldn't take his eyes off her as she swayed up the beach.

"This will do," she announced, plonking down on a ridge of dry stones. "Sit down, James. I don't know about you, but I'm starving."

James sat on the gravel and caught a whiff of her scent. The smell was intoxicating.

Emma unwrapped the linen parcel she'd been carrying and held out an oatcake.

"Thanks," said James. He munched the oatcake mechanically. His appetite seemed to have deserted him. He ate in silence, his eyes fixed on the pebbles.

When he looked up Emma's eyes were twinkling. Well?" she said.

"Well what?"

Emma laughed. "Well aren't you going to kiss me, you doughnut? We both know you want to."

James opened his mouth to reply, but Emma leant across and kissed his lips. Her mouth was soft and warm. He kissed her back.

Chapter 32

Mordred squatted in the shadows of the oak grove and contemplated his god. The Tree God Tanu, hewn from a giant inverted oak stump, stared back. From under his hair, a tangle of serpent like roots, the God's expression was disapproving. The druid came here to meditate and offer prayers every day. News of Myrleduin's appearance at the lake had added urgency to his prayers.

In the seven years since Myrleduin's exile, Mordred, born a humble fisherman's son, had risen to become the spiritual leader of the tribe. He'd won the ear of the chieftain by claiming to be a man of Knowledge. A man able to read the water and divine the future. Only he knew it was a lie. Now Myrleduin, a true Man of Knowledge had returned, he was afraid. Would Maelog forgive his errant brother and welcome him home? If so, Mordred would lose his position.

Mordred stared into his God's implacable wooden eyes. He'd prayed a thousand times for the gift of second sight, but this morning was like all the others, and his prayers floated unanswered into the leafy canopy. A magpie cackled from the edge of the clearing. Its harsh cries seemed to mock him.

Suddenly, the resentment boiled over. "Why do you ignore my prayers?" he raged. "I would use this gift for your glory; surely you do not doubt me? I who have brought you the gifts you hunger for?"

The God's inanimate eyes glared back, unmoved.

"What more do you desire?" he pleaded. "Haven't you had enough blood?" The dark marks staining the upper part of the God's face glistened in the half-light.

Mordred hung his head. He knew his prayers lacked conviction. He wanted to give his spirit up to his God, but he'd always had doubts. Doubts that crowded in like unwelcome guests. Did Myrleduin have doubts, or was his faith as unassailable as it seemed?

Mordred spat on the ground, as if to expel the bitter taste of jealousy. Why was it a coward, an exile, who had the gift and not he? And why was it that he, Mordred, was condemned to live the life of an impostor, pretending to be communing with the Gods, while living in fear that one day the people would discover the truth?

Mordred sat back on his haunches and drew a stick across the dusty soil. It couldn't be a coincidence that Myrleduin had chosen to return at the same time the strange young people had appeared in their land. He suspected they were important to Myrleduin, which was why wanted Maelog to have them killed. But who were they and what was their significance?

Mordred's tattooed eyebrows furrowed, then he stabbed the stick into the ground in frustration. Without the gift of the Knowledge, he would have to wait and see.

From his hiding place high on Mwnt Dinas, Myrleduin poured the sacred water from the chalice into the fire. He watched it boil and hiss into the still air. He chuckled to himself. He'd been watching Mordred, enjoying the spectacle of the fraudulent druid reaching out to a power he neither understood nor believed in.

Myrleduin rubbed his aching back. He might be old and raddled, but he was no fool. When the time came, he would crush this young charlatan like a beetle under his heel.

Chapter 33

As Tom and James walked along the seaweed-strewn beach, the sun-kissed days of summer seemed a long time ago. The autumn storm had abated, and the choppy sea was brown with silt. A persistent drizzle cloaked the hillside above the beach in mist. The boys had discarded the orange cave suits they'd worn when they arrived in the Iron Age and were dressed in clothing that befitted young warriors. If their twenty-first century friends could have seen them now, they'd have creased up. Both were wearing multi-coloured check trousers made of finely woven wool and similarly patterned tunics, bunched at the waist by a wide leather belt. Incongruously, they still wore their modern socks and leather walking boots.

Tom pulled his woollen cloak around his shoulders and shuddered. "It never stops raining," he grumbled. "I swear if I get any wetter I'll grow webbed feet!"

James grinned. "I thought you men from Breckon were used to a bit of rain," he replied in halting Welsh dialect.

Tom frowned. "It's not the rain that's getting me down," he said, "it's us. We're changing, and I'm beginning to forget about how it was in our world."

James shrugged; little beads of rain rolled off his shoulders and dripped down his cloak. "Don't be a drama queen. We've been here three months and we've discussed this all before. We can't look back. Our past life has gone. We've got to make the best of our life here; it's not all bad."

Tom sat down heavily on the wet shingle and looked out to sea. "I miss Mum and Dad," he admitted.

"You've got Delyth," reminded James.

"Yeah, but I hardly ever see her. The girls always have chores to do. God knows how they put up with it. I'd go mad if I had to slave away like them. I know the Pig doesn't give us an easy ride, but at least we get some free time."

"Well at last you agree we've got something to be thankful for," retorted James.

"I'm sorry," sighed Tom. "But on days like today, it's impossible not to miss home." He flicked a heap of seaweed with his right foot and watched as a swarm of sand hoppers danced about in panic. Then he grinned, "Right now I could do with a big mug of hot chocolate and a huge fat Mars bar... you know, the king-size ones."

"Pillock," said James amiably. "You've got chocolate on the brain."

"It's hard not to think about chocolate when you might never taste it again."

"I miss a hot bath," admitted James.

Tom sniggered. "Your mum would never believe you said that, James Cordle. Anything else you miss?"

"Boxer shorts," said James, laughing. "Going commando in these itchy trousers is killing my balls."

Tom laughed and sprang to his feet, his black mood lifting. "Race you up the top!" he shouted, and sprinted up the beach.

"You're on!" James pounded after him, pebbles clattering.

A couple of months earlier, James' asthma would have made the run to the top of the cliff seem like Everest, but the affliction that had dogged him throughout his childhood had miraculously disappeared.

He'd first noticed the change when, like all the other young warriors, he'd helped bring in the harvest. They'd followed the men with the scythes, toiling in the hot, dusty fields, stacking the freshly cut barley and tying it into neat stooks. Running up and down the steep fields and breathing dusty chaff would normally have been guaranteed to trigger an attack, but to James' amazement, nothing happened.

At first he'd put it down to coincidence. He'd occasionally have days at home when he didn't need his inhaler. Now he was sure something was different. Today for example, with a cold mist hanging over the hills, any vigorous exercise would have left him reaching for his inhaler, but he felt fine. He sucked in the fresh sea air and ran on, relishing his newfound freedom.

Why had the asthma gone? Had he just grown out of it? The doctors said he might. Or was it something about this place? Perhaps it was true that kids back home were eating or breathing stuff that caused it? Whatever the reason, it was a good job his asthma had gone, because his inhaler had almost run out.

James thundered up the path; he was faster than Tom on a straight sprint, but Tom was as agile as a wild goat and had the advantage on the winding stony track. By the time James reached the top, Tom was already sitting on top of the stone wall that marked the perimeter of the top pasture.

"Slowcoach!" grinned Tom, then his smile froze. "We have company."

James reached for his knife, then let his hand drop. He recognised the tall young warrior strolling across the meadow towards them. "Rhydderch!" he muttered. "That's all we need."

Tom and James watched the chieftain's son approach in stony silence.

Rhydderch was the first to speak. His tone was arrogant, though his eyes were wary. "I see your time with us has done nothing to mend your manners. Have you not learned how to greet a nobleman? Surely you will have remembered how to show respect to your betters?"

James stared at the chieftain's son, his face hard set. "I only give respect to those that earn it," he said in perfect Welsh. "And your crooked nose should be a reminder that you are not my better."

Rhydderch stared back at James. He would love to beat him to a pulp and make him beg for mercy. He'd thought about it often, but he knew what James was capable of and was afraid. Afraid of those powerful fists and the indomitable will that lay behind those pale blue eyes.

He'd witnessed that iron will on the training field. Particularly in the early days when James hadn't yet acquired basic weapons skills, when, time and time again, the Pig had tried to beat James into submission, only to find him getting back to his feet and coming back for more. At first the old warrior had reacted with amused indulgence, but this quickly turned to respect as the outsized young man with incredible hand-eye coordination started to master the art of warfare. Now, after three months training, none of the boys would dare take on James, and Rhydderch suspected even the Pig was beginning to avoid sparring with the young giant who fought with white hot ferocity.

"You'll live to regret those words when I become chieftain," Rhydderch muttered darkly.

James laughed. "Then let's hope your father lives to a ripe old age."

Rhydderch felt the urge to crash his fist into James' face but thought better of it. Instead, he smiled tightly and walked away. He could afford to be patient; there were other ways of exacting revenge against this upstart, more pleasurable means. Mordred had promised to persuade his father to let him have the girl.

James and Tom watched him disappear.

"Scumbag," said James contemptuously. "Pushing people around and making big threats, but when it comes to the crunch he's got a yellow streak a mile wide. No wonder everyone thinks he's a worm."

"You need to be more careful," Tom admonished. "He might not be flavour of the month with his father now, but the chances are Maelog will still name him as his successor, and then the boot will be on the other foot."

"I'll worry about that if and when the time comes," James replied defiantly, but the seeds of doubt were there. Things were different here, he thought. At home there were laws to protect people's rights. Here people didn't have rights. The law was what the chieftain decided. Maelog had the ultimate power of life and death over everyone in the tribe.

James found the idea preposterous; why people were prepared to bow and scrape to an idiot that spent half his time hunting and the rest of the time pissed on barley beer was beyond him. But then, things were not quite as they appeared. Maelog did not make day-to-day decisions; the council, a small clique of men and women appointed by the chieftain, made those. These councillors, according to the custom of the tribe, were responsible for carrying out the edicts of the chieftain, and for collecting tithes from the farmsteads within the tribal territory.

Under a strong chieftain, the system worked well, but Maelog, despite his prowess as a warrior, was a weak leader, easily bored and lazy. In recent years, he'd left the council a little too much to their own devices, and many of the councillors, including his wife, had fallen under the sway of the druid Mordred. Maelog, without realizing it, had become a puppet king, with the manipulative Mordred pulling the strings.

It makes British party politics look functional, thought James wryly.

Delyth and Emma were waiting for them at the gate to the top field. The boys ran down the hill towards them, making the little brown sheep canter about in alarm.

"Hi there!" James almost careened into Emma. "How's it going?"

"Oh, not too bad. We've been out shopping and we're on our way to the hair stylist," joked Emma, slipping her arm around James' waist. "How about you?"

"Well... you know, playing tennis an' stuff."

Emma silenced him with a lingering kiss.

Tom raised his eyebrows and steered Delyth to a discreet distance away from the two lovers.

"You're looking okay, Sis," he commented approvingly; "You've lost weight."

"Thanks" said Delyth, taken aback by a flattering remark from her brother. "I can't believe how much fitter I feel."

"It's the constant physical work," replied Tom. "James and I have spent the last couple of days ploughing the field in front of the fort. You wouldn't believe how hard it is to keep a straight furrow and control that stupid ox. My arms feel like they've been stretched on a rack, and God knows how many calories I've burnt."

"I thought you said you liked the outdoor life," teased Delyth.

"I do, but it gets tough now and then. What about you? Are you still missing home?"

"Not as much as in the beginning. I think I'm getting used to it, and the exercise is good for me."

Delyth hopped up on the top of the wall and looked out over the sea. She loved being here after a storm when the waves crashed up the beach. She inhaled the ozone-rich air. For once in her life, she felt truly alive. She missed her parents, of course, but strangely not much else. The absence of social media had been a bit of a shock at first, like most of gen z she'd been addicted to her mobile. Now she wondered why she'd spent so much time obsessing about what people she'd never met were doing and how they looked.

She even enjoyed the domestic chores. Especially weaving. It gave her a purpose she could never find at home. Best of all, she'd lost weight. Week by week, the hated flab had melted away and a new lithe figure had begun to emerge. She'd even started to draw the attention of the young men at the fort. It stirred instincts that she'd previously suppressed. She smiled. *Fancy me feeling sex*y. Then she frowned. *What a shame James only had eyes for Emma*.

Emma and James indulged themselves in some heated snogging before Emma disengaged. She smoothed down her dress and strolled along the footpath leading back to the village. James followed, pawing at her like a lovesick puppy, but Emma pushed him away and held out a wooden dish. "We're supposed to be collecting blackberries, naughty boy," she said flirtatiously.

"But I hardly see you. You're always too busy."

"That's not my fault," Emma said. "The whole tribe's busy. There's only two weeks to go before the fair. Everyone is excited."

"Samhain isn't just a fair; it's a religious festival like Christmas."

"I know what they call it," asserted Emma, "and I don't think it will be anything like Christmas. It's the festival of the dead!"

James laughed. "Imagine Mordred as Father Christmas! He'd steal the kid's presents and sacrifice Rudolph the Red-Nosed Reindeer!"

"Don't joke about him, James," said Emma seriously. "That man is bad news."

"Hey, lighten up. We've only got a bit of time together; let's not argue."

Emma smiled and handed James the empty collecting dish. "Let's fill this up, then we need to talk."

They picked in silence for a few minutes, quickly filling the container with fat, juicy berries. Emma examined her blackberry-stained fingers. *Disgusting*, she thought, looking at the broken nails and leathery skin, shocked at how Iron Age life had wreaked havoc on her once manicured hands. Grinding flour was the worst. The constant chafing of the granite quern had made the skin on her palms like leather.

James waited expectantly. Something was troubling Emma, but she needed to get it out of her system in her own time.

"I'm worried about Rhydderch," Emma said at last.

James was immediately furious. "What about Rhydderch? Has he been following you again? Because if he has, I'll belt him!" James snarled. He rolled his tongue menacingly.

"Don't be an idiot!" snapped Emma. "He's the chieftain's son, you can't hurt him and get away with it. These people have absolute power. And God knows if anybody should thump him it's me!"

"So what's he done now?"

"Nothing in particular. He doesn't try to come near me anymore."

James laughed. "After you kneed him in the bollocks, it's no wonder! So what is it?"

"He follows me at a distance and stares at me. It gives me the creeps. What really worries me is he told Tegwedd that I am his woman, and that Mordred has foretold we will be married."

James frowned. "Rhydderch is a nasty bit of work, but I don't think he can marry you against your will?

"In theory, no."

"So what's the problem?"

"I don't know. I've just got a feeling that Rhydderch and that Mordred are planning something, and it scares me."

James placed his arm around Emma's shoulder, but she pushed him away.

"Find me a knife," she pleaded, "and teach me how to use it. I don't think it'll be long before I'll need it."

Chapter 34

Samhain was two days away, and preparations for the festival had reached a fever pitch. Everyone was involved. Everyone, that is, except Tegwedd. She'd started her period a few days earlier and had been banished to the house of confinement, a tiny dwelling on the edge of the village. Wrinkling her nose in disgust, Emma pushed a bowl of ash and stale urine under the door of the hut. A pair of hands excitedly grasped the noxious offering.

"Will it work?" Emma asked doubtfully.

"Of course it will," insisted Tegwedd from the gloomy interior. "My mother did it when she became high priestess. Anyway, we bleach wool all the time and hair's no different."

"But how could you do it? That stuff stinks! No boy will come near you for weeks."

Tegwedd giggled. "I'll wash it off before I come out, silly. Which reminds me, bring an extra pitcher of water and some of the plants I showed you near the river. You know, the ones with those little pink flowers. I'll need them to wash the dye out of my hair when I've finished."

Emma smiled. Her mother would have a fit if her hair stylist bleached her hair with piss! And God forbid what Mummy would say if she was shut up in a darkened hut every month and made to use moss instead of sanitary towels! The thought made her laugh out loud.

"What are you laughing at?" asked Tegwedd.

"Nothing," replied Emma, still sniggering. "I was just thinking how different things are where I come from."

"Did many of the girls have golden hair like you?"

"Quite a few, but lots of them dyed their hair blond like you, only we didn't make our dye from sheep's urine, ours came in special bottles."

"Where did you barter for these bottles?" asked Tegwedd.

Emma was perplexed. How could she explain to a girl from an isolated Iron Age community how plastic bottles of hair dye are sold in high street shops? There were no shops here, no plastic bottles, no credit cards. Money hadn't even been invented. People either made their own things or swapped stuff for the things they couldn't grow or make. She decided not to explain.

"My mother traded them," she said simply.

Tegwedd didn't reply. Presumably the explanation was sufficient.

"Have you got enough moss in there?"

"Yes, don't worry about me; I'll be out in a couple of days with beautiful new hair. The other women will make sure I have everything I need.

"I don't know why you put up with this," said Emma. "I can't see what's so wrong with having a period; we all have to put up with it. I don't understand why you have to shut yourself away."

Tegwedd sighed. "I can't believe your mother did not tell you the truth of such things! The song of creation tells us the story. The first woman that walked the earth, Ara, was the most beautiful that ever lived. She was so beautiful that Tanu, the God of the trees, fell in love with her. He begged her to lie with him, but she refused. In a rage, Tanu cursed her, declaring that from henceforth, she and all her daughters would bleed every moon as a reminder of the tears that he had shed. Women have hidden their shame from Tanu ever since."

"You don't really believe that, do you?" asked Emma.

"Of course! Anybody will tell you. And take care the Tree God does not hear you question his word; it will bring bad luck to us all."

Emma bit her lip. She'd had this kind of discussion with Tegwedd before, and she knew it was pointless arguing, so she decided to change the subject. "Does anybody else know you're dying your hair?"

In the darkened hut, Tegwedd smiled. "No, it's our secret. I don't want anybody to know until my time of confinement is over. Hopefully I'll be out in time for Samhain. Then I'll shock everyone with my gorgeous new hair.

Emma grinned. "It's hardly worth the bother; your hair's lovely as it is, and all the boys will be too drunk to notice. But I promise I won't say a thing."

Chapter 35

As Tegwedd prepared to dye her hair, families from the outlying farmsteads began to arrive at the fort, the children running excitedly ahead while the adults, weighed down with huge backpacks. plodded behind. Judging by the quantity of food and numerous pitchers of home-brewed alcohol, they'd come prepared to party hard.

As each family arrived, the excited chatter reached a frenzy as the close-knit community greeted their fellow tribe members and caught up on the gossip.

"How was the harvest this year?"

"Terrible shame about Illytyd falling off the cliff."

"Serves the old bugger right. He was always pissed."

"Have you got cloth to trade this year?"

Over the top of this hubbub, hordes of children were running around the camp screaming like banshees. Presiding over the chaos like an inebriated impresario was Maelog. He was having a whale of a time.

As the families arrived, he shouted greetings, his booming voice carrying over the general babble.

"Welcome Erywlls, you old sheep shagger! ... Hey Llydan, I hope you've brought enough beer this time!" The men, some of whom had already been drinking, seemed to find these pearls of wit hilarious. They clearly loved their aging chieftain.

The women seemed less impressed. Guided by the chieftain's sober and efficient wife, they began to chivvy their menfolk into the houses where they were to stay for the next few days. They knew from experience that they'd better get unpacked and prepare a meal before night fell and the heavy drinking began.

James and Tom viewed the spectacle with amusement tinged with excitement.

"It's like a scene from Asterix the Gaul," quipped Tom.

"It's certainly comical," laughed James.

They'd stumbled across a debacle between one of the older warriors and his wife, who'd caught him sneaking out of a round house with a jar of booze. She was clearly a woman not to be crossed and was belting her husband on the arse with a length of firewood.

James shook his head. "I've never seen people as stir crazy as this before."

"You've never been in Swansea on a Friday night," replied Tom. "We Welsh know how to have a good time!"

"But this is only the first night," observed James, as raucous singing rang out from a roundhouse near the gate. "This is supposed to on for three days and nights. If they get out of their heads on the first night, they're not going to stay the course."

Tom grinned. "These are professional pissheads and they'll want to have want to have clear heads in the morning. Remember, tomorrow's fair is a serious business. They've waited all year to trade that itchy old woollen cloth they've been producing. And the iron-smelting people are supposed turn up tomorrow. It's all the warriors have been talking about for weeks. They need good quality crude iron to make new weapons. Apparently, the local stuff that Cllyneth makes is crap."

"Is that why the practice swords bend?"

"I reckon so."

"Where does the iron come from?"

"Somewhere down south. They come here every year to trade iron nuggets. Sometimes they bring brooches and other stuff with them."

The boys were interrupted by another gale of laughter, accompanied by high-pitched squealing. Three farmers, all the worse for wear, were dragging a pig to the edge of the village to be slaughtered. They stopped under an apple tree and one of them slung a rope over a branch. The pig seemed to know what was coming and was struggling wildly.

"Get that bloody rope round its legs!"

One of the drunks cried out as the pig bit him on the knee.

"In the name of the Gods, tie its legs!"

Eventually, they managed to haul the pig up in the air and placed an earthenware dish underneath. The pig surveyed its captors through panic-stricken eyes. The squealing was deafening. Several high-spirited spectators appeared. Everyone apart from the pig seemed to be enjoying the gruesome comedy act.

"Get on with it, Grygaleth," someone jeered. A man brought out a knife and waved it like a conductor's baton.

"Watch out, you'll cut us!" yelped one of the other men, jumping out of the way.

There were more hoots of derision from the spectators as Grygaleth plunged the knife into the unfortunate animal's neck. The pig's front legs paddled aimlessly, and the squealing was replaced by a gurgling sound. As the blood jetted into the waiting dish, the pig's eyes dimmed, its body twitching. Grygaleth wiped the blade on the grass and waited until the pig was still. The spectators disappeared as the men set about the task of gutting the pig and preparing it for spit-roasting the following morning.

Not a morsel wasted, thought James, as the men washed out the intestines to make sausages and sorted the various other internal organs for processing. *I wonder what kids from home would make of that*, James reflected. *Most of them never gave a thought how their bacon arrived on their plate. I guess most of them think meat comes from plastic dishes in supermarkets.* Life here was basic, brutal.

Chapter 36

It was still dark when the village cockerel woke James from his slumber. He turned over in his cot and groaned.

His head was pounding. The drinking the previous night had been monumental. He chuckled. *At least I didn't puke*, he glanced at Tom, sprawled like a dead man on the floor nearby, *unlike some*. He sat up, his head felt like a lead weight. *I need a paracetamol. No chance of that though,* he thought wretchedly, and staggered outside.

It was a damp morning with a faint breeze coming off the sea. He leant against the roundhouse and had a long, satisfying pee. The cockerel looked down regally from his vantage point at the apex of the thatched roof. "Cock-a-doodle-doo!" it screeched.

Bloody bird, thought James. *One day I'll wring it's neck!*

Gingerly, he wandered towards the gate. Cai was fast asleep, cuddled up to a pitcher of beer. Another warrior lay sprawled out on the damp grass. *Useless twits!* thought James. *Goodness knows what would happen if the Du Tarian arrived now, there's nobody on sentry duty.*

He climbed up the rickety ladder leaning against the wooden palisade and swung himself onto the parapet. He leant over the massive timber wall and gazed down at the tree-lined valley. Wisps of woodsmoke clung to the lower contours of the vale, betraying a group of houses nestling amongst the trees. One of these houses was where Emma lived. *I wonder if she's still asleep.* The thought precipitated a plethora of alluring images.

He didn't know what was getting into him; it was impossible to get her out of his head. By nature, he was a pragmatist not given to sentimentality, now he was all over the place. One minute he was dreaming up romantic notions, the next he was swamped by testosterone fuelled fantasies. "I must be in love," he announced to the silent fort.

Feeling foolish, he glanced at the two sleeping warriors. Thankfully neither had overheard.

He and Emma had made love for the first time the previous evening. They'd given Birieth the slip and sneaked into one of the grain stores. James closed his eyes. He could almost feel the softness of her breast in his hand and the warmth of her hungry mouth on his belly. Even hung-over, the thought made his pulse quicken. Then his hand flew to his temple as blood pumped around his dehydrated brain. *My head's splitting.* He groaned and cursed the lack of modern medication.

Emma lay in her lumpy little bed and looked up at the smoke disappearing through the thatch. Like James, she'd hardly slept. She'd wanted him desperately last night, so despite the risk of getting pregnant, and the terrifying prospect of delivering a baby without medical assistance, she and James had gotten carried away.

I just hope he pulled out in time. She shuddered, remembering the tragedy she'd witnessed soon after arriving at the fort. A woman in the next-door roundhouse had given birth and they'd listened to her screams all night until at last the child had been born. It had been a little boy. But the joy had been short-lived. After the birth, the woman started to haemorrhage. Mordred the druid was called. He'd wandered around the house waving his oak stick and mumbling his stupid rituals, but of course it had been no good. The poor woman had bled to death and the baby died the following day.

Mordred presided over the funeral. They'd laid the bodies out on a platform for the birds and animals to eat on a hill behind the fort. The experience had had a profound influence on her. It was the first time she'd seen a dead body. The milk-white face of the unfortunate woman still haunted her. The message was stark; sex here was never casual. Without contraception or modern healthcare, sex was a dangerous business. *But that doesn't stop me wanting him.* She sighed.

By the time James had walked back to the apprentice's house, the fort was beginning to stir. Two men, supervised by a ferocious looking woman, were placing the pig they'd slaughtered the day before on a spit.

"Don't drop it in the fire, you idiot," the woman scolded. "You'll get ashes all over it."

"Sorry, Cariad," one of the men whinged. "I'm not feeling myself this morning."

"I'm not surprised!" snapped the woman. "Only the Gods know how much ale you drank last night."

The man was wise enough not to reply. Instead, he made an ineffectual attempt to insert a metal spike into the pig's mouth.

"Hurry up," she nagged. "At this rate it won't be cooked in time for the feast."

Other members of the community were busying themselves in preparation for the fair. Some, mainly women, were setting up trading stalls. They were simple affairs: a crude wooden bench or table with products for sale displayed on the top. James watched them lay out their wares. The range of produce on offer surprised him. There was local farm produce of course. Cheeses wrapped in hessian cloth, thin strips of dried meat, dried herbs tied in bunches, unidentifiable fungi, desiccated roots, honey in earthenware jars, or in the comb and cut into sweet, sticky pieces. The beekeeper held up a square for James to try but he shook his head and moved on. He watched a woman place oatcakes on a wooden platter made from birch bark. She was chatting to her neighbour, who was stirring a pot which smelt like fish stew.

James noticed there was some logic in the way the fair was organized. Stalls offering similar wares congregated together. Soon he found himself amongst stalls trading leather belts, baskets, and wooden bowls. James watched a woman arranging bronze pins and jewellery made from amber beads on a bleached linen cloth.

There were a great many stalls displaying the multi-coloured, hand-woven cloth for which the locality was famed. The wool was gleaned from the bushes and from stripping the wool from the sheep by hand. The wool was combed, dyed, and spun, then woven on looms. Nearly every house had a loom. The process, almost entirely carried out by the women, was laborious and highly skilled. James had been told it was this highly-prized cloth which attracted traders from further afield, including the Iron Smiths from the south.

The smiths came to the fair each Samhain Eve to trade ingots of high-quality iron for local cloth. Their arrival each year was eagerly awaited, as it was one of the few occasions most people had to meet people from another tribe. It was also one of the few opportunities to trade for a highly crafted gold or silver brooch, or other trinkets, which the Iron Smiths had also brought for sale.

Tom, looking dreadfully hung-over, met James at the gate as a group of eight tough-looking smiths arrived. They were travelling on foot accompanied by two heavily-laden little ponies. The leader, a barrel-chested bull terrier of a man, halted at the entrance of the fort and looked up at the gate man. Cai looked down at the grizzled smith and gave a weak little smile of recognition.

"You look terrible Cai," grinned the smith. "Too much barley beer, I daresay!"

Cai gave another little smile. He looked like he might be sick. "Greetings, Gwilym! Have you come to trade iron or just insults?"

The smith ignored the question. "How is your esteemed leader? Has he managed to get his arse out of bed yet?"

"Yes he has, Gwilym, you cheeky sod!" roared Maelog, who'd appeared to greet his important trading partners. "How are you?"

"Very well, my Lord. But as you know, it is many days walking from my village, and we are tired and in need of refreshment."

"Have you brought the gift I asked for?" enquired Maelog.

"Of course, my Lord." The little man smiled broadly, then continued in a conspiratorial tone. "Though I don't know why! I come here each year and it's always the same. I end up giving away top-quality products in return for a little poor cloth."

Maelog looked up at the sky. "I wonder why the Gods have not struck you down for such lies." He sighed theatrically. "But come. Tell your men they may enter the fort. You are welcome to our hospitality."

Maelog led them, followed by a goggling crowd of tribespeople, to the central area of the fort, where Mordred was waiting to conduct a ceremony of welcome. The druid cut an impressive figure. His tattooed skin was oiled with goose grease that glistened in the October sunshine as he stalked around the circle of people that had formed around him. To start with, his audience seemed mesmerized, watching the druid's every move as his rich baritone voice sang the welcoming rituals, brandishing his staff of office, but after a while, some of the younger people started to get fidgety. It seemed Mordred was too fond of his own voice.

"What a bore!" said Tom in a stage whisper, and several of the young warriors stifled giggles. Mordred paused and stared at the young man who had dared to mock him. The look was venomous. Tom felt the druid's eyes burn into him. The eyes seemed to say 'I have marked what you said, and I will make you pay for your disrespect.' The crowd shifted uncomfortably. Tom ducked out of sight, his face burning. Mordred smiled menacingly, then continued with the ceremony.

After the formal proceedings were over, the smiths set about unpacking saddlebags from their relieved-looking ponies and displaying the contents on a large piece of cloth. The crowd gathered around excitedly.

"Be patient! Stand back!" shouted Gwilym, glancing anxiously around him. He knew it might be difficult for some to resist the temptation to filch one of the exquisite little trinkets being laid out for sale. A farmer's wife grabbed a silver hair clasp and one of Gwilym's men fingered his sword nervously.

Gwilym shook his head, and the man dropped his hand. "I see you have great taste, madam," said Gwilym tactfully. "Do you wish me to reserve it for you? I can let you have it for a yard of good cloth."

The woman shook her head sorrowfully and handed back the clasp. "I shall ask my husband," she said. "Perhaps he can come to an arrangement with you."

"Ignore her," cackled one of the other women, "her husband's a skinflint!"

"Have you brought any nice brooches this year?" asked another woman.

"What about knives?" shouted a man from the back of the throng.

Gwilym put his hand to his mouth like a loudhailer and yelled, "Everybody, stand back! There'll be no trading until we've finished unpacking!"

Tom and James watched the scrum around the smiths' stall with amusement.

"It's like when we did that car boot sale," observed Tom. "You know, when we arrived and all those people tried to nick our stuff? Vultures, Mum called them."

"I remember," laughed James. "This is a car boot sale without the cars."

One of the men lifted a strange looking object out of one of the saddlebags. It was about the same size and shape as a small lump of horse manure. It was obviously heavy.

"That must be the iron they've been talking about. It doesn't look impressive, does it?"

"It's supposed to be more valuable than gold," replied James.

"You're kidding!"

"No, straight up," said James. "Eglwis told me yesterday. He was saying how difficult it was to get the furnace hot enough to melt the iron rock properly. Apparently, these guys have a special way of getting it hot enough using... 'black rock' he called it."

"Coal," Tom replied shrewdly. "These guys come from South Wales. There's coal there."

"However they make the stuff, it's a gold mine for them. They swap the iron nuggets for pretty much whatever they want because the other tribes need it to make tools and weapons. I'm surprised no one tries to steal it," James mused.

"I expect they do. But those guys look like they can handle themselves," Tom replied, as one of the iron traders heaved a huge bag off the back of one of the ponies. "That bloke there has got forearms like turkey drumsticks."

The boys were so absorbed in watching the traders they didn't notice Delyth and Emma until Emma slipped her arm around James' waist.

"Hi," Emma ventured softly. Remembering how they'd made love the previous night made her strangely shy under James' gaze.

James felt his heart skip a beat. *God she's beautiful*.

"Hey! Put him down for a minute!" Delyth exclaimed, laughing. "We're supposed to be looking round the fair. Tom and I are fed up with you two mooning over each other all the time."

James grinned sheepishly. "Sorry. We didn't mean to make you feel like spare tires. We'll try to keep our hands off each other for a bit."

Emma looked sharply at Delyth; she knew her friend's feelings for James and recognized the jealousy that lay behind her jovial remark.

Tom, blissfully unaware of the dark undercurrents, put in his two-penny's worth. "Yeah, cut it out for a bit. Let's have a look at those daggers. I wonder if I could swap my boots for one of them."

Reluctantly, Emma let go of James, and the four of them pushed to the front of the stand. The woman with the skinflint husband was still haggling with one of the traders over the silver hair clasp. She was determined to have it, but the bolt of cloth she was offering in exchange was not to the trader's taste. Realising she was getting nowhere, she began to wave her arms about and shout. The youngsters laughed as the woman stomped off.

James picked up one of the daggers laid out on pigskin. It was around fifteen inches long with a razor-sharp double-edged blade and a heavy bone handle. The blade was beautiful; oily smooth and patterned with swirling blue shapes.

"It's the way we beat out the iron that gives the blade those patterns," said one of the smiths proudly. "I made that knife myself. It's made of three strands of the purest iron twisted together and beaten flat, then twisted and beaten flat again. That knife will hold its edge longer than any blade you've ever held."

James couldn't help smiling at the barrow boy patter; back home this guy would do well flogging stuff on TV.

"Well, son," the man went on, "are you interested in trading or just looking?"

On impulse, James reached into the leather pouch he hung from his belt and pulled out the Swiss army knife he had taken into the cave. It had been a fifteenth birthday present from his dad. It seemed like a lifetime ago. His birthday was the tenth of November. *Damn*, he thought, *almost a year ago*. He missed his mum and dad and wondered how they would be celebrating his birthday. *God knows how they would be feeling*. The trader watched with interest as James flicked open one of the blades. "What do you think?" James asked, holding out the shiny red pocketknife.

The trader took the knife and looked at it in wonder. The little stainless-steel blade shone like a mirror in the autumn sunshine. "How was this blade forged?" he asked, barely able to conceal his excitement.

"No idea. It was a gift."

"Then you must be of high birth," replied the trader, "for I have never seen its like before."

"Have a look at the gadgets," suggested James, showing the man how to open up the tools folded away in the handle. By now a little crowd had gathered around to watch as James tried to explain what each of the gadgets were for. They gasped in wonder as James demonstrated how the little scissors worked by cutting a length of hemp twine.

"Tell them you don't want to sell it," whispered Tom in English.

"But it's not very practical; I'd rather have that dagger."

"I know that you pillock!" Tom hissed, exasperated at his friend's lack of guile. "He obviously wants your knife; if you tell him you want to keep it, he'll offer you more."

Tom grinned as the sense of what he'd said dawned across his best mate's face. James could be incredibly naïve.

"You have a go then," said James truculently. "If you can swap my knife for that big one, I'll be happy."

A short time later, the four of them walked away from the stall carrying the dagger, a silver cloak clasp, and a necklace made of amber and little black stones, which Delyth thought were jet.

James was ecstatic. "How did you manage that?" he laughed.

"My dad's a farmer," Tom replied. "Haggling is bred into us!"

"What are you going to do with the knife?" asked Delyth.

"It's not for me. It's for Emma." He glanced at her.

"That's hardly a romantic gift!" Tom smiled. "What's she going to do with it, stick a pig?"

"Don't refer to me as 'she,'" snapped Emma. "And sticking pigs is exactly what I have in mind… that is if the pig in question doesn't leave me alone." She wrapped her arms around James and kissed him on the lips.

Tom raised his eyebrows in mock horror. "I can guess who the pig is."

"She's being melodramatic," said James. "Rhydderch has been hanging around and she wants to give him a scare if he gets too familiar."

"If he's got any sense, he'll back off," laughed Tom. "If you don't kill him, Emma will slice his balls off!"

Chapter 37

A cough echoed around the damp cave walls. It was a rattling wheeze that spoke of an infection lodged deep in the lungs. Myrleduin spat the sticky mucous that clogged his throat onto the cave floor and examined the blob of sputum in the flickering candlelight.

The Goddess be praised, he thought. *The blood has gone, the curse is passing.*

The druid had been sheltering in the cave since pneumonia struck two moons ago. He'd come here to die, but somehow, he'd clung to life. It was the boy Artur who'd saved him, keeping the little fire going and bringing honey cakes and fresh spring water. Thankfully, he'd managed to persuade the lad not to tell his mother about his visits, so Heulwen remained unaware of his presence.

With his health improving, Myrleduin knew it was time to search for the girl in the Cup of Knowledge. He'd have liked longer to recover his strength, but tonight was the Eve of Samhain, the night of the dead. The night when the partition between life and death was meniscus thin. The night when the spirits of the dead walked freely amongst the living.

Myrleduin heaved himself from the straw palliasse where he'd spent so much time in recent weeks.

"Give me strength," he muttered. He shuffled across the cave and reached into a secret recess in the rock.

He grunted as he lifted the metallic dish from its hiding place.

Myrleduin held the bowl in both hands with a mixture of reverence and fear. The origin of the Chalice known as the Cup of Knowledge had been lost in the mists of time. Legend had it that the Smith Gofannon smote Mwnt Dinas with his hammer and fashioned the bowl from the molten iron that flowed from the rock. The druids claimed the cup had been cast by one of their own Men of Knowledge.

Whether fashioned by a god or man, they had been a master of their craft. The ancient iron, darkened by time and polished by many hands, shone in the candlelight. It was a thing of beauty, simple in form yet wondrously decorated. Maidens danced around the base, their lithe figures sculpted to perfection, while a woman's face looked on from the main body of the Cup, her expression serene and inscrutable. The line of sword motifs around the rim affirmed the bowl was dedicated to the Goddess Cliodna.

Myrleduin dipped the cup into the pool and set it on a makeshift altar. Few men had harnessed the Cup's power, and fewer still had lived to enjoy its secrets for long. The Master had explained the dangers. The Cup of Knowledge destroyed all that entered its mind changing waters. The effect was cumulative; the hallucinogenic toxins ate at the brain until finally death became a welcome release.

Such is the fate of those who seek the Knowledge, Myrleduin fretted. *But I shall not die tonight. My destiny is still before me.* That much the cup had already shown. He felt the cold sweat of anticipation moisten his palms as he gripped the Chalice.

"I drink this cup in your name, Cliodna, Goddess of the Lake," he proclaimed, putting the rim of the chalice to his mouth. "Protect me and illuminate the path before me."

He gulped down the contents quickly, grimacing as the familiar bitter taste of spring water laced with fungus hit the back of his throat. When the cup was empty, he refilled it, placed it on the floor in front of the altar, and sat down cross-legged to meditate while the mycotoxins took effect.

The first cramping pain hit his stomach soon after swallowing the first draught of sacred water. Breathing deeply, focusing on the water in the Chalice, he blocked out the pain and allowed his thoughts to float free. Suddenly, the toxins entered his brain, and he felt himself spiral down into the swirling water. He felt a brief moment of ecstasy as he burst through to the other side and fought the wild urge that sought to plunge him headlong through time and space. His years of training were not in vain, and he soon found control, homing in on his target. Watching, listening, controlling.

He could see where the girl would be waiting now, and watched the bloody events that would bring her to that place. He felt a stab of pity for his people, but he knew there was nothing he could do to change their fate. He shook his head. He couldn't change what was to pass that night, but at least he now knew where to wait for her. The time had come for the virgin bearing the sign of Cliodna to fulfil her destiny.

Chapter 38

As the autumn sunlight faded, the party at the fort began to hot up. Everyone was congregated around a huge pile of logs and dry branches piled up in the centre of the warrior-training field. Most people, old and young, had been drinking. The interlopers from the twenty-first century were no different, and all four were slightly worse for wear.

"When are they going to light the fire?" shouted Delyth over the excited chatter.

"I think something's happening now," James yelled back.

A trumpet sounded, and figures began to emerge from the big house where Maelog and his close family lived. Somebody struck up a beat on a drum, and a group of strangely dressed people began to process towards the fire. Mordred led, carrying his staff;

everyone else in the procession held a burning brand and wore a headdress with antlers. The crowd fell silent as they approached.

"The guys dressed as stags represent Arawn, the God of the Otherworld," whispered Delyth.

James nodded. He'd already been told what to expect. The reality was even weirder than he thought it might be. The light from the firebrands cast alarming shadows of the men in their bizarre headdresses. When they reached the bonfire, the deer men fanned out and surrounded the bonfire. One of them was decidedly unsteady on his feet.

James recognized him. "That's Maelog," he whispered. "He's pissed!"

When all the stag men were in place, each holding their torch, Mordred stepped forward. The druid gazed at the expectant people. Tattooed from head to foot and smeared with goose grease to ward off the cold, his muscular physique cut an impressive figure. "We are gathered together at the beginning of this special day to welcome the spirits of our ancestors into our midst," Mordred began in a booming voice. "Samhain is the time when…"

But James wasn't listening; Maelog was swaying, his antlers drooping. James dug Tom in the ribs, "He's going to fall," he hissed.

As Mordred addressed the crowd, the chieftain lost his battle with gravity and landed with a crash in the bonfire, torch in hand, and the tinder dry twigs caught with a *whoosh*.

A child standing near James laughed as two of the stags rushed forward and pulled Maelog out of the fire. The stare Mordred gave Maelog was venomous. Everyone else looked on in horror. This was not part of the script. The lighting of the Samhain fire was a solemn occasion. Arawn would be offended.

Maelog pushed away his helpers and glanced toward the druid. He looked chastened. "I'm sorry," he said. "Too mush to drink. Please carry on."

Mordred nodded. "As you please, Lord."

Maelog, trying to muster some dignity, drew himself to his full height, stalked towards a wooden bench and sat down.

"Don't laugh," whispered Tom. "He'll kill you."

The tribespeople looked on awkwardly, their faces bathed in light from the rapidly spreading fire.

"The fire is lit," Mordred announced to the crowd balefully, "so we will dispense with the lighting ceremony and move directly to the rites of passing." The druid nodded to a drummer, who started up a slow beat on an ox skin drum. After a few moments, a woman struck up a haunting melody on a bone flute and the Stags started to dance. Mordred began to sing, his rich baritone voice carrying over the sound of the instruments and the crackling of the fire.

The song was the song of the dead: a song of welcome to Arawn the Stag King of the Otherworld and the spirits of the ancestors. At the end of each verse, the people joined in the chorus. "Hir yw'r dydd a hir yw'r nos, a hir yw aros Arawn." *Long is the day and long is the night, and long is the waiting of Arawn.*

The sound was extraordinary. It made the hair on the back of James' neck stand on end. "This is amazing," he said in English.

"Beats Fireworks night," grinned Tom.

"It's scares me," said Emma. She shut up as a woman in front of her turned and gave her a hard stare. Chastened, they watched the proceedings unfold in silence.

The drumbeat became more insistent with each passing verse, and the dancing of the stags more frenetic as they pranced and leapt around the fire. Facing the crowd with his back to the fire stood Mordred. His oiled skin glistened in the flickering orange light.

When the final chorus came to an end, Mordred motioned to the assembly and the atmosphere became tense. James noticed people moving through the crowd carrying wicker caskets that looked like the hampers expensive department stores sold at Christmas. The stag men continued to dance to the drum and bone whistle as the caskets were brought forward.

"The baskets have got peoples bones in them," whispered Tom, risking the wrath of the woman in front. "There's Carrad. He told me his auntie would go to the Samhain fire today. He went with his family to the field of the dead a few days ago to collect her remains."

"Gruesome." Delyth shuddered.

"It's not that odd," said Tom. "Grandma was cremated."

"She wasn't left outside to rot first," Delyth pointed out.

Their conversation was brought to an end as the first funereal basket was cast on the fire and a cry of anguish went up from a section of the crowd.

There were nine baskets cast into the flames. The last to be thrown onto the bonfire was carried by a warrior; a grey-haired woman supported him. The warrior bore the casket as though the weight of the world was on his shoulders. The older woman gripped the warrior's arm as though she might collapse. As the basket was thrown on the fire, the woman began to ululate. Her cries of desolation were infectious, and many in the crowd joined in. The raw emotion amongst the tribespeople was almost overwhelming.

Emma squeezed James' hand; her eyes were wet. "That's the girl who died having a baby. The guy carrying her basket was her husband."

James swallowed. Things had gotten out of hand last night. The idea that he might have made Emma pregnant terrified him.

"Now what?" whispered Tom as Mordred held up his hands and the music ceased. The stags stopped dancing and the crowd fell silent, their heads bowed.

James didn't reply, he was lost in his own thoughts. He should never have put Emma at risk. What if she died giving birth?

The fire was roaring, and although it was thirty metres away, he could feel its heat on his face. He watched the flames devour the earthly remains of the girl and her baby. Sparks flew up into the night sky. James watched as they were snuffed out in the vast darkness. *Are we just burning embers to be extinguished after we die?* he wondered. *Or is there something else? Some part of us that goes on into the future?* His Mamgu believed so, she was a Christian. *I hope she's right*, he thought.

James was jolted out of his imaginings by the druid.

"We have offered up our loved ones to the fire," Mordred told the people in a sombre voice. "We implore you, great Arawn, Lord of the Otherworld, to accept their souls, and ask that they might dwell under your protection in your kingdom forevermore. Mordred turned to the fire, his face lifted to the sky, his arms outstretched. "We ask you and your people to join us as we celebrate this special night of Samhain. We have prepared food and ale, let flesh and spirit feast and drink together!" The druid turned to the crowd, and with one accord, the people began shouting the names of their dead loved ones, calling them to the feast.

Then the mood changed. Everyone began dividing into family groups and chattering. Food was brought forward on massive platters, and jugs of frothing, still-fermenting ale were distributed. James, Tom, Delyth and Emma had no relatives at the fort, so they had been invited to join Tegwedd's Aunt Birieth and her family for the feast.

"Where's Tegwedd?" asked Tom.

"She's not allowed," Delyth said sadly. "She's still shut up in that stupid women's period hut."

Tom looked shocked. "You're joking. Surely this is a special occasion?"

"You know what these people are like with their superstitions," Emma explained, "Birieth's very strict about isolating. She says it offends the gods for a woman to mix with others while she's bleeding. She insists it's unclean."

"Bloody mad, I say. Pun intended." Tom grimaced.

"Bloody ignorant more like," added Delyth, still cross at how Birieth had shut her away when she had started her period.

"Somebody will take her some food, won't they?" asked Tom.

"Tegwedd said Birieth would take her a plate. She told me they set out places for dead family members as well."

"That really is weird," said James. "And what a waste of food."

Tom grinned. "We leave out mince pies and brandy for Father Christmas."

Delyth frowned. "This is different. This business of the ancestors coming back from the spirit world freaks me out."

Emma bit her lip. "I know what you mean. It's superstitious crap, but when you look away from the fire, the darkness creeps up on you, and before long you're beginning to wonder if something is out there."

"There's plenty of grub," interrupted James, eying the roasted pig being carved up. "Look at that crackling! It's mouth-watering. I haven't seen so much meat since we got here."

"We'd better be quick," said Tom, jostling forward. "Those vultures will strip the meat off that pig in no time."

"Get me some!" shouted Emma as the boys disappeared into the crowd, armed with bark plates.

Emma and Delyth stared into the glowing embers of the Samhain fire.

"Do you still think we'll wake up and it'll all have been a dream?" asked Delyth.

"Sometimes," Emma paused. "But not as often as I used to. Most of the time I'm too busy to think about it."

"I do," said Delyth. "Every day. Waking up is the worst. I expect to be at home with mum shouting at me to get out of bed and get ready for school. Then I look up and see that horrible dirty thatch." Tears welled in her eyes and Emma put her arm around her friend. When the boys returned, their wooden plates heaped with pork, the girls were huddled together, sobbing.

"We want to go home," explained Emma.

"Me too," sighed James, squatting beside the girls. "But right now I'll settle for eating this lot and getting pissed. We can't go home, so we may as well enjoy the evening and try to forget. At least for a while."

Emma brushed away her tears and managed a brittle smile. "You're right." She sniffed, pointing to a jar. "Give me a swig of that stuff. It's horrible, but it's alcoholic."

The next few hours passed in a whirl of eating and drinking, and by midnight the four friends found themselves amongst the throng of tribespeople, dancing frenetically in the firelight.

"This is the craziest party ever!" laughed Tom, shouting to be heard over the singing, stomping mob around him.

"Watch it, mate!" yelped James as one of the Iron Smiths, pogoing like a demented punk rocker, careered into him. The man, lost in an alcoholic stupor, smiled inanely, and staggered off into the crowd.

The music was incredible. James closed his eyes, allowing his body to absorb the visceral beat thumped out by two huge drums and a crude bagpipe. But good as the primitive instruments sounded, it was the singing that set the hairs on James' neck shivering.

The voices, mostly male, blended in effortless harmony, the primal, aggressive undertones of the bass driving the rhythm forward, and beautiful clear tenors soaring over the top. The effect, which sounded like a fusion of Afro beat and Welsh male voice choir, was electrifying. James closed his eyes and drifted into a vortex of sound.

A pair of warm arms being wrapped around him broke the spell; he opened his eyes to find Emma gazing at him, her pouting lips moist with promise. "May I have this dance, kind Sir?"

"Why not," James replied, clasping her in his arms, "I guess this is the closest we'll get to a slow dance."

Delyth smiled at her two young friends as they smooched to the tribal music. She'd long gotten used to the idea of James and Emma as a couple, but she still felt twinges of jealousy. Especially at moments like this when their love was so evident.

"Bugger both of them," she muttered to herself. "I'm going to have some fun for a change." She took another swig from the jar and scanned the crowd, seeking out one of the boys she'd caught looking at her a few days ago. It was then she noticed Rhydderch.

He was staring at James and Emma; his lips were twisted in a triumphant smile. The chieftain's son turned and locked his hard blue eyes on Delyth. The look of pure spite hit her like a slap in the face, and she gasped with shock. Then, as abruptly as he had appeared, Rhydderch slid out of the firelight, back into the shadows.

"What's that arse Rhydderch up to?" whispered Tom, who'd witnessed the whole screenplay.

Delyth bit her lip. "No idea, but I've got a horrible feeling something bad is about to happen. Call it a premonition or whatever. I just know something's wrong, and I'm sure Rhydderch is at the centre of it."

"Well, if he's up to something we'll know pretty soon. One thing I've learned about that arrogant turd is he has no patience and..." Tom trailed off.

The drumbeat came to an abrupt halt and the singing petered out as Maelog strode into the firelight. He had sobered up and changed out of his stag outfit. Dressed in his finest clothes, with a gold torc around his thick neck, he cut an impressive figure. By his side stood Mordred, still almost naked despite the chill night air. His tattoos shimmered menacingly in the light from the fire.

The chieftain raised his hand. "Samhain is upon us," he announced, "and as we feast and drink with those that have passed, we are reminded that another year has come to an end and a new year begins."

Several of the warriors stamped their feet in approval. Maelog ignored them.

"Tonight is a time to think of the future." More stamping followed. Maelog paused for effect, smiling at his wife. "As another year passes, I am reminded that I am getting older, and the time has come for me to name my successor."

A deathly hush fell on the crowd, and everyone stared at Rhydderch who had stepped forward to stand in front of his father. Maelog appraised his son before turning to the crowd.

"This is my son, Rhydderch. He stands before you a grown man who he has passed from the house of training and is ready to enter the house of warriors. He will be our future, before the Great Oak God, Tanu, I name him as my successor!" The chieftain glared at the tribespeople gathered before him. "If there are any here who would challenge his right to succession, let him come forward now."

James looked around the crowd. Everyone hated Rhydderch. Surely somebody would say something. There was a lot of shuffling of feet and one or two of the younger warriors started muttering. The older warriors and farmers stood in mute acceptance, none of them willing to defy their chieftain.

"It is settled then," announced Maelog. "When my spirit starts its journey to the Otherworld, Rhydderch will take my place as your chieftain. May he rule wisely and courageously."

A triumphant smile crept over Rhydderch's arrogant features. He glanced meaningfully at Mordred, who nodded and stepped forward to address the chieftain.

"My Lord," the druid said, clearing his throat, "perhaps this is the moment to announce the news of your son's betrothal."

Maelog nodded solemnly. "Yes of course," he said, turning to face Rhydderch. "Your mother and I were troubled when you first told us you wanted to marry outside the tribe, but we have been watching the girl you have chosen. She has spirit and beauty and will breed fine sons."

A shiver of ice ran up Emma's spine as scores of eyes swivelled to gawp at her. She shook her head slowly as Rhydderch swaggered towards her, his cruel lips twisted into an exultant grin.

"Take your place at my side, Emma, so the tribe may see who will be my wife and know that I have chosen well."

"Fuck off," spat Emma.

"You will soon learn to curb your- urgh!"

The young noble was cut off by James' shoulder crashing into his ribs. For the second time in their short acquaintance, the two young men rolled together on the ground, locked in combat. This time, James had the element of surprise, and Rhydderch was powerless to defend himself from the savage blows that rained down on him.

"Stop!" shouted Maelog, but James couldn't hear him. A red mist had descended, blocking out everything except the need to slam his fist into Rhydderch's face.

A huge hand grabbed the back of his collar. Instinctively, James jabbed his arm backwards and felt the hard, bony tip of his elbow connect with the soft cartilage of a nose. Leaving the now limp Rhydderch, he turned on his new assailant, tearing at his face like a wild animal.

The ferocity of James' attack caught Maelog off balance and he fell back, clutching his bleeding nose. His attack was short-lived. Several strong, burly warriors descended on the violently flailing James, dragging him to the ground. He writhed in their vicelike grip.

Maelog loomed over the struggling boy, his face twisted with rage. A deathly hush fell over the crowd. The chieftain drew his sword and wiped the blood from his face with his sleeve.

"Please," screeched Emma, "he didn't mean it!"

"Shut up, girl!" snarled Maelog. "Give the boy a sword! I'm going to cut the impudence out of him one piece at a time." The crowd drew back and James, breathing heavily, was allowed back onto his feet.

"My Lord," Mordred moved into the centre of the circle formed around Maelog and James, "why give the young cur the honour of a warrior's death? He has turned his hand against his clan chief. The law demands he suffer a traitor's fate!"

Maelog paused. The crowd waited expectantly while James stared at the chieftain like a cornered tiger.

"You are right. We'll let the Gods decide." His voice was cold. He turned to the Pig. "Take him out of my sight and bind him well. Tomorrow he'll face the pit. If the stakes spare him, he'll return to the house of training. If not... cast his body outside the gates and let the dogs gnaw on his treacherous carcass. He turned to his son. "And Rhydderch, take that bloody girl outside and screw some manners into her. I like a feisty wench, but her tongue needs taming before she'll make a worthy wife."

Once again, James felt hard hands pin him to the ground, but this time he let his body go limp. It was no use trying to struggle, he would bide his time and try to escape later.

He fought back the surging panic as the Pig began to wind coarse hemp rope around his wrists, pressing his face into the muddy soil.

"Steady, boy," grunted the old warrior. His alcohol-laden breath wafted in his captive's face as he yanked the bindings tight. James winced in pain as the Pig dragged him to his feet by his hair.

Standing in the flickering light from the fire, he found himself face to face with Rhydderch. To James' satisfaction, his eye was swollen, and his split lip was smeared with blood. Rhydderch had been drinking heavily and was swaying slightly. He burped. One of the younger warriors in the crowd sniggered as though the future chieftain had just cracked an incredibly funny joke.

James said nothing. There was nothing to say and absolutely nothing he could do. Bound and held secure by two muscular warriors, he braced himself for the inevitable. Rhydderch didn't disappoint. He jabbed his fist into James solar plexus, then, as James doubled up, gasping for breath, he brought his knee savagely into his unprotected face.

James' world exploded into stars as he slipped into unconsciousness. His head lolled at an impossible angle. Only the two warriors holding his arms kept him on his feet.

Rhydderch drew back his arm for a second punch, but the Pig restrained him. "That's enough, my Lord," he advised. "Is it not enough that he dies in the morning? Take the girl and forget him."

"You're right, why waste effort on this piece of shit" he sneered drunkenly. "I'll need all my strength for Emma."

Chapter 39

When James regained consciousness, his hands were tightly bound behind his back and his arms were a mass of pins and needles. He clenched his fists to try to improve the circulation, but the hemp rope bit into his wrists. His cheek hurt. It was pitch black.

For a moment he thought was back in the cave, then the memory of the encounter with Rhydderch and his father came flooding back.

The thought of what awaited him at first light made James' guts constrict. He and Tom had been shown the pit soon after they arrived at the fort. The Pig had delighted in showing the boys how miscreants who betrayed the tribe or committed serious crimes were put to death. James remembered peering over the safety barrier of willow hurdles at the rows of stakes driven into the floor of the pit three metres below. The stakes, positioned about two feet apart, were sharpened, and some were stained rusty brown by what was clearly blood.

James remembered how he and Tom had listened, horrified, while the Pig described how condemned men or women would be blindfolded and thrown into the pit to take their chances on the pointed stakes. The positioning of the stakes was calculated to give the victim a chance, albeit small, of emerging unscathed. Most were impaled on the sharpened points and received horrific injuries. The Pig said many screamed for hours before they succumbed to their wounds. If they survived three days in the pit, they were deemed spared by the Gods and pulled out.

For a while, all James could do was lie in the dark, waves of panic washing over him as he imagined himself writhing on the sharpened stakes. The image rendered him temporarily helpless. He'd always wondered why terrorist hostages he'd watched on TV newsreels meekly accepted their fate as their captors prepared to execute them. Now, with tears of self-pity running down his cheeks, he thought he understood.

His stomach churned. *I'm going to throw up.*

He remembered the last time he'd been sick. He and some mates had stolen a bottle of his dad's brandy and downed the lot in the park. When he got home, he'd puked all over the living room carpet. His father had been furious. If only Dad was here to help him now.

He swallowed the bile in his throat and sniffed. The reassuring image of his father gave him strength. He pictured his strong hands hauling him to his feet, exhorting him not to be a wimp, to get up and fight. He bent his knees and pulled himself into a sitting position. His back was stiff and bruised, but just the act of sitting made him feel better. He began to breathe more easily and started assessing his situation rationally.

Thin wheat grains slipped between his fingers. *I must be in one of the grain stores*, he thought, visualising the cluster of small, round huts on the edge of the settlement. *I wonder if I can get this bloody rope off my wrists.*

He wriggled, trying to pass his hands under his butt in an attempt to get his hands in front of his body, but the bonds were too tight and after a few minutes he was forced to accept that this wasn't possible. He began to cast around for something sharp to cut the rope. Maybe there was a shard of flint lying on the earth floor? He shuffled his way around the hut on his buttocks, feeling around for anything he could lay his hands on.

A thought occurred to him, and he froze. Had they placed a guard outside the door? He listened for signs of life outside but heard nothing. He decided to continue his search, moving with extreme care. He couldn't afford to be overheard while his hands were still tied. But if he could just get them free, he had a chance to open the door and surprise the guard... or even break through the wattle and daub wall on the far side of the door.

His ankle banged against a large, solid object. His hands groped excitedly. His fingers connected with rough granite. A spark of hope fanned into a glowing ember. A grindstone! He'd have to work quickly; there couldn't be much time. Planting his butt on the stone, he began to rub the hemp rope against its rough edge.

Then he heard the sound he'd been dreading. Up on the roof of the apprentices' hut, the cockerel put back his head, opened his beak, and crowed his welcome to the approaching dawn.

Chapter 40

Emma lay in a crumpled heap on a stinking sheepskin rug in Rhydderch's living quarters. The Pig had dumped her there before barring the heavy wooden door of the roundhouse behind him. It was hard to believe that earlier that evening she'd been dancing happily with a boy she loved and dreaming about their future together. How quickly those hopes had been dashed, and how rapidly her emotions had spiralled from love and desire to disbelief, rage, hate, and finally terror.

She knew she didn't have long before Rhydderch tired of drinking and came looking for her. She clasped the bone handle of the knife she'd secreted beneath the folds of her tunic and fought back the tears. *I'll kill him if I have to*, she vowed. *I swear I won't let him take me.*

A mental picture of James' battered and bloodied face played across her mind. This time the tears flowed freely. "They're going to kill him," she sobbed into the oily sheepskin. "He was trying to protect me and now they're going to kill him." She sniffed, wiped her eyes with the back of her hand and tried to think. "What am I going to do?" she muttered.

There was a movement outside. Shuffling feet. She stiffened in alarm. The timber bolt was being drawn back. No time left! Her heart felt like it would leap from its chest. She lay very still. The door swung open, and a shadowy figure staggered into the room.

"Damn!" The man caught his shin on a wooden bench. He was very drunk. Emma gripped her knife and played possum.

"Where are you, *cariad*?" As the man neared the fire in the centre of the room, Emma could make out Rhydderch's' features in the glow from the embers.

"There you are!" Rhydderch swayed slightly, then started to unbuckle his belt clumsily.

Emma, curled up in a foetal position, was a coiled spring waiting to strike. Rhydderch got the belt undone and grunted in triumph as he dropped his trousers. Then, with his breeches around his ankles, he shuffled towards his victim. She felt his hand on her ankle. His skin was cold from the night air. His hand reached beneath her skirt and began to grope its way up her leg. Emma felt sick with fear and loathing; she steeled herself to plunge the knife into Rhydderch's back.

Suddenly the hand was withdrawn. "You've put a curse on me you witch," he groaned. Emma gripped the knife and retreated to the shadows at the far end of the room.

Rhydderch looked down at his crotch, his face contorted into a comical mixture of fury and shame. In any other circumstance, Emma would have laughed out loud. Hanging between his legs, limp and pathetic, Rhydderch's penis had a bad case of brewer's droop. For a moment, Emma was convinced he was going to hit her, then, with a cry of anguish, he pulled up his trousers and slunk out of the door.

Emma slipped the knife back into her tunic. That bastard would never know how close he'd been to death. She lay back on the bed to allow her heart to steady. Wild, desperate escape plans, each more implausible than the last, danced around her head.

"Where are you, James?" She asked the thatched roof above her head. Now he wasn't there, she realised how much she'd grown to rely on his broad shoulders for support. On the far side of the fort, perched on the roof of the apprentices' hut, a cockerel began to crow.

Tom and Delyth sat shivering under the eves of the apprentices' hut. Dew had condensed on the roof and icy drops of water dripped onto the two youngsters, who were oblivious to the discomfort. Huddled together for warmth and consolation, they talked in fearful whispers.

"No one will help us," Tom grumbled. "I don't understand it. The whole tribe hates Rhydderch's guts. Everyone knows he's a complete shit, but they won't do anything! I thought they were our friends."

Delyth wiped her cheeks. She'd been crying. "Don't blame them," she said softly. "It's not their fault. What the chieftain says is law here, you know that. They're not going to cast aside their customs and beliefs to suit us."

Tom put his arm around his sister and bent to kiss her wet cheek. "You're right, the tribe are never going to question Maelog's decision." He glanced at Delyth. His jaw was set, his eyes glittered. "So we're going to get them out of here ourselves. We'll start with James, then go find Emma."

"But how? How are we even going to get past the guard outside James' hut, let alone get out of the fort without being caught?"

"I don't know. Maybe I'll kill him. They've taught me how to do it. I'll creep up behind him. It can't be so difficult; he's bound to have been drinking and it's pitch black." Tom hesitated, contemplating the enormity of what he'd proposed. What if the guard was one of the apprentice's dads? Could he cut a man's throat in cold blood? Self-doubt crowded in. *What we need is a diversion*, he thought.

Just then, the cockerel crowed from the roof above their heads. Tom and Delyth nearly jumped out of their skins.

Chapter 41

Cai the Gate opened his eyes and groaned. His head felt like someone had tried to cleave it in half with a war axe. He wished he'd not started drinking Girieth's gut rot cider. "I should know better at my age," he grumbled. "That cider's always the same; tastes like apple juice, then kicks you in the head."

He ran his fingers through his thinning hair and massaged his pounding skull. It was still dark, but across the valley to the east, a faint yellow glow heralded the approaching dawn. He looked down at his mate Girieth. He was fast asleep, curled into a tight ball and snoring like an old boar.

Down in the valley, some dogs began yapping. "Stupid mutts," he moaned. "I wonder what's stirred them up." Still puttering to himself, Cai poked his little fire with a stick. Enriched by oxygen, the embers glowed then spluttered into life. Cai sighed with pleasure as the orange flames licked around the partially burnt logs, radiating warmth into the damp dawn air.

Suddenly, the old gatekeeper sat up. "What was that?" He sat still and listened hard. Something was moving outside the fort walls. He gave Girieth a nudge with his foot. He might as well have tried to wake a corpse, "*Meddwyn*," Cai grumbled sourly.

Another dog barked. This time it sounded nearer. *They'll be squabbling over scraps*, he reasoned, *but I'd better have a look.*

The aging gatekeeper dragged himself away from the warmth of the fire and squinted over the wooden parapet. The sun hadn't yet risen over the hill behind the fort, but the light was just strong enough to make out the tops of the trees crowding the valley below. They were wreathed in a thin mist. The dogs were still making a fuss. Something about the pitch of their barking made him suspicious.

Cai stared out across the valley, scanning for movement. "Nothing," he said to himself. A cockerel added its voice to the cacophony; he sighed and looked to the heavens in exasperation. "Bloody chicken!" he complained. "What is it with the damn animals round here? Can't a man get any peace?"

Still whinging, Cai turned to go back to the fire. He didn't hear the arrow as it sped towards him from the trees below. It whistled through the air in a graceful arc and, with a thud, embedded itself between his scrawny shoulder blades. The force of the impact knocked the wind from the old man's lungs, and, with a wheeze of surprise, Cai arched his back and crumpled to the ground. He lay on the damp grass, paralysed. The arrowhead buried deep in his vertebrae had severed his spinal cord. Conscious but unable to move, he felt no pain as he watched the Du Tarian warriors swarm soundlessly over the palisade.

He prayed his family would forgive him for not raising the alarm. *Damn Girieth's bloody cider*, he thought, as a warrior carrying an axe stood over him. Cai closed his eyes as the man lifted the weapon.

James rubbed the rope binding his wrists against the grindstone like a madman. He knew he didn't have long before they came for him. *I'll have to free my hands and get out of here before it gets light*, he thought. He could hear dogs barking, and something else. He looked up, alarmed, listening intently. He could hear shouting.

"No," he whimpered. "Not yet!" He tugged desperately at his bonds, but they held firm. The shouting was getting louder, and now he could hear the clang of iron hitting iron. What the hell was going on? A scream rang out across the sleeping fort.

Tom's done something, thought James grimly. *Stupid, brave, little bugger!*

Gripping the edge of the stone, he worked feverishly on the stubborn hemp rope. The sounds of warfare were getting nearer. He could hear people running past the hut and shafts of orange light danced around the cracks in the doorway.

There was a crackling noise, then a great *whoosh*, and James looked up. The roof was alight. He had to get out. He abandoned his efforts to cut through the rope and hurled himself against the door. It wouldn't budge.

He choked; smoke was beginning to filter through the thatch into the room. James decided to smash his way out through the wattle and daub wall.

As he drew back his foot to kick the wall, the door swung open. James had never been so pleased to see anybody in his life.

"Tom! Thank God!"

"Quick! All hell's broken loose." Tom deftly cut through James' bonds with a knife. "It's the Du Tarian! We've got to–" A blood-curdling shout prevented Tom from completing the sentence. Startled, Tom and James swivelled to face the source of the sound.

A huge warrior was standing in the doorway. His helmet glowed orange in the reflected light of the dancing flames. James gasped. He'd lived this moment before; this was the demonic man from his recurring nightmare.

James and Tom froze as the red-bearded giant burst into the hut, swinging his sword like a reaper harvesting corn. Tom was the first to react. He yelped as the blade whistled past his ear, then darted into the smoke filled shadows at the back of the hut.

Denied an easy victory, the warrior turned towards James.

The Du Tarian warrior, his face painted blue for war, presented a terrifying apparition, James backed away, but there was no place to run. Beneath the tangled beard, the warrior's lips cracked into a triumphant smile. The man said something. James didn't understand what he was saying, but the voice was harsh. These were not words of endearment. As the warrior raised his sword to strike, James felt like someone had pressed the pause button on a video. Time stood still. This is where his nightmare would end.

Stupefied, James waited for the dream to explode into a burst of red, but it didn't happen. Instead, the man grunted, his mocking smile replaced by a look of incredulity. The sword slipped from his hand and his knees buckled. As he fell, James saw Delyth framed in the doorway. She was holding the shaft of a spear. Its business end was embedded in the warrior's back. As she withdrew the bloodied spearhead, her expression was one of horror.

Delyth and James locked eyes in stunned disbelief. For a moment the only sound was the roaring of the flames tearing through the tinder dry thatch. Then, over the noise of the fire, James heard Tom shout a warning and turned. The Du Tarian giant, blood welling from a tear in the back of his jerkin, had got up on one knee. He made a grab for his sword. James, waking from his reverie, was too quick. He kicked the weapon away from the stricken warrior, then scooped it up. The warrior staggered to his feet, fumbling for his dagger. He was bellowing like a wounded bull.

"Kill him!" screamed Tom.

James hefted the sword; despite its size, it felt light in his hand, its balance perfect. James was pumped up. Everything seemed set on super slow motion. In the microseconds that followed, James debated whether he was capable of killing another human being. *Yes*, he decided, and brought the sword down in a vicious slicing motion.

James felt the razor-sharp iron bite into the side of the man's neck. The impact dislodged the warrior's helmet. It clattered across the room like a saucepan dropped on a kitchen floor. James watched the big man slump onto the packed earth of the granary floor. The three youngsters stared transfixed as blood pooled around the dying warrior's head.

Tom was the first to come to his senses. "Get out! Get out!" He screamed. "Take the sword and get out!"

They bolted for the door. Tom nearly tripped over the prostrate warrior, his feet sliding on the blood-slicked floor. On the way out, James caught Delyth's arm and pulled her away from the burning hut.

Standing in the open, James sized up their situation. The grain store behind them was a roaring inferno; billows of black smoke and burning cinders filled the air. James peered into the gloom, trying to get his bearings. Screams rang out from around the settlement, many other buildings were alight, and people were running in all directions in the smoke-filled half-light. Wherever he looked, painted Du Tarian warriors were charging through the fort like demented cattle.

"Where's Emma?" yelled James over the bedlam. Delyth looked at him blankly; she was in a state of shock.

Tom answered for her. "She was locked in Rhydderch's roundhouse last night. The Pig took her there after you were shut in the granary."

James rolled his tongue in anger. "Bastard!" he growled.

A dark shape loomed out of the smoke and bore down on them menacingly. James didn't give the Du Tarian a chance. Months of weapons drills took over and, without thinking, he found the gap under his assailant's shield and buried his sword deep in his ribcage. The man collapsed, choking.

James wrenched his blade out of his victim's chest and ran towards the far side of the fort. Delyth and Tom followed.

Rhydderch slunk out of the roundhouse, holding his trousers round his waist. He was too distracted to notice the raucous crowing of the cockerel sitting on the apprentices' hut at the far end of the fort.

"Bitch," he muttered angrily. "Bloody bitch!" Frustration, anger and shame jostled for pole position in his mind. Then he remembered he'd left his belt in the house. He glanced at the open doorway, then looked away. *I'm not going back in*, he thought. The humiliation would be too much to bear.

A horrible thought crossed his mind. "I'll strangle her if she tells anybody," he muttered murderously. He wandered over to the dying embers of the fire and sat down. His head was fuzzy from too much cider; his stomach roiled. He thought he might be sick.

Shouts rang out from over near the main gate. He looked up. It wasn't unusual for arguments to break out after the Samhain celebrations, perhaps somebody was having a row with his wife. Then he saw flames coming from the direction of the apprentices' quarters and heard the first clang of steel.

Above the melee, he heard the unmistakable bellow of his father. "To me! To me! The Du Tarian are upon us!"

Rhydderch got to his feet and jogged towards the sound. As he rounded the forge, he stopped in his tracks. A man lay spread-eagled on the ground. He recognized the corpse; it was one of the Iron Smiths. He'd been gutted like a deer. His entrails lay steaming on the grass. Fear engulfed Rhydderch like a sodden woollen cloak weighing him down. He knew he should go to his father, but his legs felt like jelly. His eyes darted across the compound. He didn't know what to do. He ducked under the eves of the forge.

Thick black smoke was pouring across the weapons ground. A shadowy form charged past, his clogs churning up the mud. Rhydderch cringed in the shadows. He could hear the sounds of warfare drawing closer. Another thatch caught alight. As it burst into flame, he saw his father illuminated in the flickering light. He and a tightly-knit group of warriors stood at bay in front of the apprentices' hut, their shields forming a defensive wall. Maelog was naked to the waist and splattered with blood. He'd been slashed across the chest, yet still wielded his massive sword as if it was a willow switch. He was a fearsome sight. The Du Tarian circled like a pack of wolves closing in on a wounded bear.

Rhydderch recognized some of his fellow apprentices amongst the warriors fighting alongside Maelog. They fought as bravely as the men, but one by one they were hacked down. At last, with only three warriors standing with their chieftain, the wolves rushed in, and with a final howl of rage, the old Bear went down under a hail of blows.

Shaking like a leaf, Rhydderch knew this was his only chance to escape. With his father dead, the Du Tarian would swarm through the fort unfettered, killing at will. By the time the sun had risen over the mountain, the settlement would be nothing more than a charnel house. He decided to make a run for it. Clasping onto his breeches, he sprinted for the gate; he'd covered fifty paces when a shout went up from one of the Du Tarian. Aware he'd been spotted, he panicked and let go of his waistband, allowing his trousers to droop halfway down his pistoning thighs. The Du Tarian archer posted outside the fort needed no further invitation; the target was too good to be true. He pulled back the bowstring and took careful aim. He chuckled with delight as the arrow thwacked into the boy's milky white buttock. Rhydderch's scream pierced the air, but he kept running.

The archer shrugged his shoulders as the boy staggered into the woods. It was a bloody good shot, he thought, and it wasn't often you got to shoot a naked arse! So what if the coward got away? He'd be dead in a week.

Chapter 42

Tegwedd and Birieth watched with dismay as Rhydderch left his hut.

"It's too late," muttered Birieth angrily, noting the young man was holding up his trousers. "The little brat has set his seed. In the name of the Goddess, I ought to kill him myself!"

Tegwedd restrained her aunt. "We've come to help Emma escape, not to seek revenge. If we harm Rhydderch we'll put a stick in a hornets' nest. Maelog would never rest until he'd run us to ground."

The older woman sighed. "You're right, *cariad*," she agreed reluctantly. "We must get Emma away and let the Gods seek their own retribution."

The two women waited in silence as Rhydderch wandered off and sat on a bench. Then as the cockerel crowed, they slipped into the darkened roundhouse. From the corner there was a muffled cry of alarm.

"Quiet now, child," insisted Birieth kindly. "We don't have much time."

"Birieth?" Emma whispered hopefully.

"And me," added Tegwedd.

Emma sat up. "Tegwedd? Oh, I forgot! Your hair. It looks different."

Tegwedd pushed back her bleached blond locks impatiently. "Forget my hair. Are you alright?"

"Yes. He couldn't do anything, he was too drunk. I'd have killed him if he tried!" Emma held out the dagger.

"The Gods be praised!" exclaimed Birieth. "Nothing happened! Come, we've no time to waste. We must be away from here before it gets light. Now is our best chance, the sentries are drunk as pigs. If we get a move on, we'll be half a day's walk away from here before anyone realizes we're gone."

Emma shook her head slowly but emphatically. "I'm not leaving without James," she insisted. "We have to help him escape."

Emma's cheeks were stained with tears, but Tegwedd could see the determined set of her friend's jaw. She knew it was a waste of time to argue. She nodded to her aunt. Birieth opened her mouth, but before she could respond, sounds of fighting pierced the dawn. They exchanged startled looks.

Birieth was the first to speak. "Hurry," she said. "The whole fort will have heard that." She hesitated, debating the options, then continued; "They've shut James in one of the grain stores. With a bit of luck, we might still sneak past the guard." Another shout went up and they made a dash for the door. By the time they got outside, two houses were alight and dark figures brandishing torches were running across the open space in the centre of the settlement.

With a cold feeling of dread, Tegwedd knew what was happening. The sights and sounds of the attack at the lakeside settlement came flooding back. She was a little girl again, standing in the dawn light, watching her loved ones cut down. "They're back," she gasped. "The Du Tarian are back!"

It was Birieth who took the initiative. "Run for the forest path," she hissed, grabbing Emma's hand. "Keep running and don't stop for anything!"

Emma twisted free. "I said I'm not going without James. You do what you like, but I'm going to find him!"

Birieth opened her mouth to argue, then froze. A Du Tarian warrior had appeared from behind the roundhouse. He advanced on them, sword in hand. The blade glinted menacingly in the early morning light.

"Run!" Birieth shouted. "In the name of all the Gods, run!" Then she turned to face the warrior. Bringing herself to her full height, the tiny woman looked her adversary in the eye. "I'm not afraid of you," she scolded, wagging her finger at the bearded brute.

For a moment the warrior was taken aback. Then he grinned, revealing a set of crooked yellow teeth. Still smiling, he brought his sword down on the unarmed woman. Birieth collapsed like a doll thrown to the ground by a thoughtless child. The last thing she saw was Tegwedd and Emma running into the black smoke.

The acrid taste of burning thatch assaulted Emma's senses and made her eyes sting. The swirling black smoke made it incredibly difficult to see, and as they careered through the settlement, she was afraid that she'd lose Tegwedd. All around she could hear the sounds of fighting.

Birieth's dead, was all Emma could think. *He killed her! The bastard actually killed her!*

Blind fear kept her running, the adrenaline pumping through her body like high-octane fuel.

When they reached the grain store, the thatch was ablaze and roaring like a mountain torrent. A body was sprawled in the entrance. The man was a Du Tarian, and, judging by the quality of his attire, a high-ranking one. The enemy warrior was still alive, just, his eyes wide in mute appeal. Fresh blood, red and sticky pooled on the ground around his bearded head like a halo.

Emma stepped over him and went to enter the burning hut. "James!" she screamed. "Are you in there?" The heat was intense. "James! James!" She could feel the skin on her hands and face blister. "Are you in there?" Her hair began to singe. The smell was awful.

Tegwedd tugged her arm. "We've no time! We must run now!"

Emma shook her off. The flames wouldn't allow her to get closer, but she couldn't bring herself to leave.

"Emma!"

Emma wasn't listening, "I love you," she screamed into the flames. Then she stopped, someone else was screaming. The wailing grew higher, then stopped abruptly. She looked up. Shadowy figures were moving through the smoke.

"Run!" shouted Tegwedd. She bolted towards the gate.

Emma took one last look at the grain store where James had been incarcerated, then her instinct for survival kicked in and she sprinted after her friend. Both girls passed through the entrance unseen, but as they reached the woodland, an arrow whistled past them and clattered into the undergrowth nearby. Galvanised by the close miss, the girls ran up the muddy path that wound along the valley floor. They didn't stop until they'd climbed to the head of the valley and emerged from the woodland onto an area of open pasture littered with rocks and gorse. A stray sheep looked up in alarm and trotted away bleating.

Emma stopped. Her lungs were heaving and her legs felt like jelly. She bent, hands on knees, gasping for breath, and looked back across the valley towards the fort. The sun had climbed above the hills, bathing the landscape in golden autumn light. Far below, plumes of smoke were rising into the clear blue sky.

"They're all dead, aren't they?" said Emma.

"It is in the hands of the Gods," replied Tegwedd. "Many may have escaped."

Emma opened her mouth to reply, but the words wouldn't come. She sobbed brokenly.

Tegwedd put her hand around her friend. "We will go to my mother. She'll know what to do."

Chapter 43

James led his two friends through the smoke-smothered fort.

The settlement was in uproar. Screaming women and children scattered before the Du Tarian warriors, while their menfolk, still stupefied from the night's heavy drinking, fumbled for any kind of weapon.

In the confusion, the three youngsters managed to reach Rhydderch's roundhouse without attracting the attention of the invading warriors.

James darted through the door; a quick look was enough to confirm Emma was not inside. He emerged from the hut and shook his head. "She's not there."

Tom glanced at his sister, then back at James. "We'll never find her," he shouted above the cacophony of war.

James hesitated.

Tom grabbed his sister's hand,

"We're getting out of here now! If Emma's alive, she'll have made a run for it already. Get real, James, if we don't leave now, we're dead! Are you coming or not?"

Delyth looked at James, pleading with desperate eyes. "We need you," she begged.

James stood, wavering, torn by conflicting loyalties. The sounds of battle intensified as Maelog made his stand. "Head for the gate," James shouted. "We don't have much time!"

They charged through the gate unchallenged and sprinted down the woodland path heading along the valley bottom. They had no plan, they just knew they had to get as far away from the fort as possible.

They ran about a mile before Delyth stumbled to a halt. "Please," she panted, her lungs bursting, "I'll have to stop. You go on, I'll catch up to you later."

"You can't stop here," hissed Tom. "Anyone could come down this path."

"She can't help it!" snapped James. "But you're right, we're sitting ducks here. Let's get off the path before we meet any warriors." He gripped Delyth's hand. Her palm was slick with sweat, her whole body trembling. "Come on," he said encouragingly. "Only a bit further and we'll hide and rest for a bit."

Delyth smiled weakly and squeezed James' hand in accord.

Tom glanced nervously back up the path towards the fort. "It's clear," he whispered. "But we'll have to make sure we don't leave a trail to follow."

James nodded, then, taking care not to disturb the carpet of leaves that littered the woodland floor, he led them into a stand of coppiced hazel. Soon they were screened by a wall of beanpole-sized sticks, poking up out of ancient stumps like candles sticking out of a birthday cake.

They sat down on a mossy hazel stub and considered their next move. The full horror of the morning's attack was sinking in, and it was a while before anybody said anything.

"We'll have to put as much distance between ourselves and the fort as possible," Tom said, trying to remain calm and logical. "Whatever happens now, we can't go back. If Maelog wins, he'll kill James and probably me as well, and if the Du Tarian win, they'll kill us anyway."

"I'm not going very far," insisted James. "What about Emma? We can't just run off and leave her!"

Delyth's pleasant oval face was ugly with anguish. "Forget her, James," she said. "She's probably dead!"

A twig snapped. To their adrenaline-heightened senses, the dry crack sounded like a gun going off. They cowered under their umbrella of hazel, watching and waiting. A groan broke the silence. James and Tom locked eyes. Tom inclined his head at a large blackberry bush twenty paces or so to their right, where the sound had come from. James gripped his sword and nodded to Tom. They rushed towards the bush.

They had no idea what to expect, but what they found took the boys by surprise. Cowering under the scrubby brambles was Rhydderch. His trousers were pulled down to his mid-thigh. He'd been trying to remove an arrow from his left buttock. He'd snapped off the shaft, but blood oozed from the wound where the barbed head was embedded deep in his flesh.

When Rhydderch had crawled under the blackberry bush, it had seemed the perfect place to hide. Now, as James' approached, he realised it had become a trap. He clawed at the tangle of brambles in a feeble attempt to rid himself of their prickly embrace, but escape was impossible. "No. Please," he whimpered.

James regarded Rhydderch with all the compassion of a child about to squash a fly. He waded into the brambles, white-hot anger rendering him impervious to their razor-sharp thorns.

"Don't, James," begged Delyth. "He's not worth it."

James ignored her and, treading down the barbed brambles on top of Rhydderch, placed his booted foot against his enemy's windpipe. Rhydderch's eyes widened as James swung the sword, as if testing the balance of a new cricket bat. The blade, glistening with the half-congealed blood of the Du Tarian warriors James had killed earlier, seemed to have acquired a menacing persona all of its own.

Tom gripped his friends' elbow. "For God's sake, James. You can't kill him."

"Why not? The bastard wanted me dead." James' faced darkened. "And he's probably raped Emma. Now the little shit's going to pay."

They watched in horror as James lowered the point of the sword so it hovered over Rhydderch's left eye.

"His trousers have come down," squeaked Delyth, "and he's been shot!"

"For Christ's sake James!"

James held the sword to Rhydderch's face a few seconds more, then thrust it angrily into the ground. He'd known all along he couldn't kill him in cold blood. He loathed Rhydderch, but he could never bring himself to hurt anyone when they were helpless. He'd never thought about the rabbits he shot, but murdering a person was different. He looked at the sword; it glinted back at him knowingly.

His stomach churned, suddenly he felt sick. He'd killed two men with this sword. In his mind's eye, their faces stared at him accusingly.

In the heat of battle, it had seemed easy to slide that razor sharp blade into their bodies; there hadn't been time to think. He wondered if the men had wives or children, and what would happen to them now. He wondered what Mum and Dad would say if they knew what he'd had done. For the second time that morning, he could taste bile in his throat. This time he couldn't hold it down; retching, he leant over and emptied the contents of his stomach onto the woodland floor. He needed his dad, and his heart ached for Emma.

"James?"

James felt a hand grasp his elbow. He turned to see Tom staring at him with troubled eyes.

"James, are you OK?"

James wiped a smear of puke from the corner of his mouth with his sleeve and shook his head. "Can I ever be forgiven?" he asked.

"What?"

"I've killed two people," James insisted, his voice cracking. "That's a terrible sin. Do you think I'll go to Hell?"

"You had no choice," Tom replied quietly. "If you hadn't acted as you did, we'd all be dead."

James stared down at the sword with a mixture of wonder and revulsion. "It sounds crazy, but it almost felt like the sword was doing it. Like it has a life of its own."

Delyth reached out to the boy she still loved. "I did something bad too," she said. "It was me who speared the guy, remember?" Her voice was steady, but her shaking hand betrayed how close she was to breaking down. "What happened last night is going to be with us the rest of our lives, but now isn't the time to think about it. If we want to live, we've got to get as far away from here as possible."

James nodded, then turned to stare at Rhydderch. The lust for revenge that had consumed him earlier had seeped away like poison from a lanced boil. It left him hollow and deflated.

"We've got to keep moving," insisted Delyth. "We don't know who might find us if we stay here."

"Where are we heading for?" asked Tom.

James looked at him thoughtfully. "We'll steal a boat from the beach and head north. We can stop at Heulwen's house to check if Emma's there, then decide what to do after that."

"And what about him?"

"Pull that arrow out of his arse and leave him here. We can't take him with us; he'll slow us up. He'll have to fend for himself. After what he did, he's lucky I didn't finish the job for the Du Tarian."

Chapter 44

The autumn sun had burned off the last tendrils of morning mist when Emma and Tegwedd reached the track leading to the collection of thatched buildings that Tegwedd called home. Recent rain had made the path slick with mud and the girls, still fearful they were being followed, were unsteady in their haste. Emma's leather moccasins slid on the mud. She cried out in pain. Then, fearing she might have alerted a pursuer, she clapped her hand over her mouth.

Tegwedd stretched out her arm to support her friend. "Are you alright?"

Emma nodded shakily. "Yeah, I'm okay. I just turned my ankle. It'll walk off in a minute."

"It's not much further," Tegwedd encouraged. "Mam will know what to do."

Emma grimaced. *My mum would be worse than useless here*, she thought wryly.

She imagined her mother teetering down the narrow track in her high heels and best frock. At another time and in another place, the thought would have made her laugh. Now it just made her sad. A sense of loss threatened to overwhelm her. She was alone now. Her friends were probably dead.

Emma brushed aside her last friend's helping hand; she didn't want Tegwedd to see her cry. "You go ahead," she insisted.

Tegwedd took one look at Emma's rapidly swelling ankle and shook her head. "If you put weight on it, it will take longer to heal. It's only a short distance, let me help you."

By the time the girls limped into the clearing surrounding Heulwen's roundhouse, Emma's ankle was puffed up like a balloon.

"How's it feeling?" asked Tegwedd, whose shoulder was numb from supporting her friend's weight.

Emma tentatively placed the ball of her injured foot on the ground. She gasped as a bolt of pain shot up the side of her shin. "Not great," she admitted. "I'm lucky I don't have to walk any further."

Tegwedd smiled wearily. "We're safe here. Why don't you wait while I get Mam; she'll want to take a look at that ankle."

Emma eased herself onto a log bench placed at the edge of the compound. She could never remember feeling this drained before, but a sense of relief washed over her as she stretched out her leg and watched her friend run towards her mam's house.

Tegwedd's spirits lifted the moment she passed through the protective thicket of thorns that cocooned her childhood home. All morning, she and Emma had kept glancing back, expecting warriors pounding up the track behind them. Now, Tegwedd, for the first time that day, felt safe. Almost skipping with relief, she ran forward and ducked under the lintel of her home. "I'm home, Mam!" she shouted excitedly. Then she froze.

On the far side of the smoke-filled room, a woman lay gagged and trussed like an animal awaiting slaughter, her eyes wide in warning. In the split second that mother and daughter locked eyes, Tegwedd realized it was a trap, but it was too late. An oak club arced towards the back of her head, leaving her only enough time to scream before her world went black.

Emma heard the shriek and, sobbing in pain, broke into a stumbling canter, running blindly like a wounded deer. She'd covered less than twenty paces before the huntsman brought her down. She fell heavily and her face squelched into the smelly mud behind the latrine. Then a vicelike hand gripped her injured ankle. She screamed in pain and twisted over to face her attacker. She scrabbled for the dagger James had given her.

She caught a glimpse of a tattooed face before the oak staff bludgeoned her into darkness.

"Why didn't we leave him?" grumbled Tom bitterly as he helped James drag Rhydderch down to the shoreline.

"Because I'm soft in the head," James replied tersely. "I couldn't just leave him to die, no matter what a bastard he is." Rhydderch moaned as they heaved him over the side of the boat that one of the local fishermen had conveniently left on the foreshore. The craft was essentially a sea going coracle, made from a frame of woven willow wands, over which ox hide painted with pitch had been stretched. Unlike a peanut-shaped coracle, the boat was elongated and looked like a very large canoe. The lightly-built vessel bobbed up and down in the swell like a cork.

James, standing thigh-deep in the icy autumn sea, grasped the wickerwork gunwale to prevent it floating into deeper water. His legs were freezing, and he looked impatiently towards the beach where Delyth was hitching up her skirt. High above the cliff line, he could make out the outline of the fort. It was wreathed in black smoke. "Get a move on," he hissed. "They could be here any moment."

Delyth hesitated. She'd shown amazing courage spearing the Du Tarian warrior, but she hated cold water, and the physical and emotional strain of their escape was taking its toll.

"Come on!"

"Alright!" Delyth splashed her way out to the boat and allowed James to shove her onboard.

James was the last to haul himself in. His weight made the boat rock alarmingly. For a moment, the four fugitives floundered like kittens in a basket. Then, just as it seemed the boat might tip over, James dipped his paddle in the water and steadied it.

"That was close," muttered Tom. "Where's the other paddle?"

"Delyth's sitting on it!"

The craft wobbled while they extricated the lost paddle from under Delyth's behind.

"We're supposed to sit on the planks," said Tom.

After a few more wobbles, James and Tom managed to manoeuvre into position on the oarsman's seats with their knees tucked under them.

"Ready?" asked James.

Tom gave James the thumbs-up, then grimaced. The willow wands which formed the interwoven framework of the boat were digging into his knees.

"Let's go."

James and Tom leant forward and dragged their paddles through the water, and the craft began to move. Once moving, the boat became more stable. James was surprised at how responsive it was, and how quickly it cut through the water.

They paddled steadily out of the cove and headed into the choppy waters beyond. As they rounded the headland, the ebb tide caught them in its twice-daily rush north. The boys knew it was futile to fight the tide; in any case, it was taking them in the direction they wanted to go. All they had to do was paddle gently to ensure the boat remained steady, and to keep the prow heading north, parallel to the shore.

Once they had negotiated the rough water around the headland, James looked back. He could still make out a smudge of black smoke rising from the fort, but it quickly receded into the distance as they glided along on the powerful current.

A splash to the landward side of the boat caused James to glance over his shoulder.

He found himself looking into the dark eyes of an inquisitive seal. With a jolt, he was carried back – or was it forward? – to the kayak trip. *Emma loved seeing that seal*.

He bit his lip and prayed that she'd made it out of the fort alive. Perhaps, he thought, he'd wake up and find that this had all been a dream. The seal slipped leisurely back into the chilly waters, breaking the spell.

James scooped up a handful of seawater and splashed it over his face. *This is no time to get philosophical*, he told himself. *If I keep trying to work out whether this is real or whether it's all some kind of dream, I'm going to go crazy.* He tried to clear his mind and think about how they were going to survive the next few days.

Chapter 45

Myrleduin sat back on his haunches and studied his new captives pensively. The two girls, gagged and bound, stared back, wild-eyed. He stroked his matted white beard. "Two maidens," he mumbled. "This was not foreseen." His ruminations were interrupted by a bout of coughing.

The girls watched the druid like a pair of mice mesmerised by a viper.

When the paroxysms subsided, Myrleduin cleared his throat and spat a globule of green mucous on the floor. Then he smiled, revealing a set of rotten teeth. "Well this is a pleasant surprise, Tegwedd, but why are you here?" he asked gently.

Even if Tegwedd hadn't been gagged, she would have been too frightened to reply. Just seeing her father was her worst nightmare.

Myrleduin reached out and stroked his daughter's hair with a grubby finger. Then he laughed as if at some private joke and shuffled close to Emma. Emma recoiled – his breath was awful – but the druid held her face close. "You are the chosen one who will honour The Goddess. But of course you know that, don't you?"

Emma knew nothing of the kind. She almost choked as the putrid smell of halitosis wafted up her nostrils. The druid rambled on. "But where is the sign? The charm I have seen in the waters?" Emma looked up at her captor. His eyes shone with a fanatical light. *He's mad,* she thought.

Without warning, Myrleduin brought out a knife and hacked at the rough spun fabric of Emma's tunic. With a ripping sound, the cloth gave way, and Emma's soft white breasts spilled out. "Well, girl? Where is it?" he demanded, staring at her chest.

A tear rolled slowly down Emma's cheek. Myrleduin put the knife to her face and sawed at the strip of cloth he'd used to gag her mouth. The knife was blunt, and it took a while before the gag fell away. Once it had gone, he repeated the question. "Where is it, girl?"

Emma was a rabbit caught in headlights. She knew the filthy old man was asking where her gold cross was, and she was determined not to tell him. "I don't know," she croaked. "I lost it."

"Idiot!" Myrleduin's eyes blazed. He raised the knife.

Emma fainted.

When Emma came around, she was on the floor. Instinctively, she lay still, not daring to move a muscle, expecting the druid to continue his inquisition, but the questions never came. Instead, the old man was clattering around the hut talking to himself in his wheezy, high-pitched voice.

Emma opened an eye; Myrleduin had suspended a cauldron over the fire and was pouring a small quantity of barley onto the quern Heulwen used to grind flour.

Emma glanced at Tegwedd. Like her, Tegwedd's hands were tied behind her back. She was sitting with her back against one of the timber posts that supported the roof trusses. Emma groaned. She could see her gold chain peeping over the collar of Tegwedd's woollen tunic.

Emma sneaked a look at the druid. Surely the old man would notice? But the druid appeared completely engrossed with his strange preparations. Emma resolved to make sure his attention continued to be distracted. "What are you doing?" she asked in her best Iron Age Welsh.

Myrleduin looked at her as a spider would look at a fly. "You have learned our language well," he condescended, "but I see you have not troubled to study our customs." He poured a handful of what looked like pomegranate seeds on top of the barley and started to grind.

"What are those pink things?"

"You don't know, child?" Myrleduin sounded surprised. "I forget you are not of our world." He picked up an ergot grain between thumb and forefinger. "These are the fruit of the harvest God; they will ease your passage to the next world. We druids are not cruel men; I do this only to serve the Goddess. I promise when you pass, you will feel no pain."

Emma's skin crawled.

Myrleduin smiled and patted Emma on the head as if petting a dog. "I do not expect you to understand, these are ancient rites. But tonight you will give your life so the Goddess of the Lake may dwell amongst us in a physical body. It is a privilege you will thank me for, should we meet in the Otherworld. Now hush, child. There is little time left, and I have much to prepare." Myrleduin paused. Then his wrinkled face lit up. "You will have flowers for your hair," he announced brightly. "But what to pick at this time of year, eh?"

Emma had little interest in flowers. Her fingers closed around the little knife that the druid had carelessly dropped. She rubbed the twisted hemp that bound her wrists against the upturned blade. The knife was blunt but, given enough time, she would cut herself free. She shot a wary look at the druid; he was busying himself with his poison kit. *I've got a chance*, she thought, *but how long before...?* She couldn't bring herself to think about how she might be sacrificed.

Chapter 46

The ebb tide had run its course, and the sea took on an oily stillness in the slack water.

"He should take a turn with the oar," complained Tom, rubbing an angry red mark on the palm of his hand. "I've got a blister."

James sat up and stretched. His back was sore. "I'd rather he did his share too, but he couldn't swat a fly at the moment, let alone take a turn paddling."

James and Tom stared at the chieftain's son with undisguised loathing. Rhydderch was lying on his side in the bottom of the boat; he was as white as a ghost and shivering. He seemed to be in a lot of pain, and he groaned every time he moved.

"We shouldn't have brought him after what he did," said Tom.

James clenched his jaw. "We've been through this before, Tom," he said sharply. "Stop griping and get on with it! It won't be long before the tide turns against us."

"Please don't argue," begged Delyth. "It's bad enough losing Emma without you two fighting."

Emma's name was enough to sting James into silence. He grasped his paddle and grimly returned to his task. With four people crowded into the wicker craft and only two paddling, it was difficult to make headway without the assistance of the tide, so when they reached the entrance of the cove that would one day be called Abereiddy Bay, the muscles in James' arms were burning. By the time they reached the beach he was at the limit of his endurance.

"Thank God!" said Tom, slinging his crudely fashioned paddle into the bottom of the boat and jumping into the gentle surf. "I don't think I could have paddled any further."

"We're not finished," said James. "We can't leave the boat here. We'll have to carry it up the beach or we'll lose it." Tom groaned; the tide was out, so they'd have to drag the boat seventy metres over the sand before they reached the line of seaweed that defined the high tide mark on the steep shingle storm beach. They'd carried the boat about half that distance when they heard shouting. They looked up, startled. A boy was running full pelt down the beach towards them, his arms windmilling.

Delyth recognised him first. "It's Tegwedd's brother!"

Tom and James put the boat down while the boy caught his breath.

"What's the matter?" asked Delyth.

The boy was very agitated. "Come quick!" he panted, pulling at Delyth's arm. "He's got my Mam!"

Artur was wild-eyed, and for a moment James thought he might run off. "Artur," he said gently, "you need to tell us. Where is your mam and who's got her?" James kept his voice level, but his heart was thumping. Something was seriously wrong.

Artur managed to calm himself a little. "He must have come while I was fishing in the brook. When I got to the gate, I could hear them arguing."

"Who was arguing?" demanded James, exasperated.

Delyth gave James a sharp look and smiled at Artur. "Go on," she said encouragingly.

The boy nodded and turned to James, his eyes wide. "Mam and the druid were arguing. It happened last night. It was getting dark, and I couldn't see properly, but it was Myrleduin. I heard Mam say his name."

"What happened?"

"Mam shouted and he hit her with something. Then she fell and he pulled her inside the house."

"What did you do?"

The boy's freckled face crumpled. "I ran and hid in the gorse on the top of the hill. When I saw you paddle into the bay I thought you were fishermen and ran to the beach. I didn't know what else to do." Tears flowed down his cheeks. "And- and I can't find Bregg! Something must have happened to him as well."

Delyth did her best to console the boy while Tom and James conferred. "You stay with the others," said James. "I'll go find his mother. I won't be long; their house is only half a mile away."

"No way," insisted Tom. "You can't go on your own. The druid might be old, but he's dangerous." He paused. "We'll have to leave him here," Tom indicated Rhydderch, who was eying James' sword as a wolf would watch a burning stick. "He can look after the boat."

James looked doubtful, but Tom knew how to convince his friend. "What if the Du Tarian rock up when you're gone? It'd be pretty dicey. I can't protect Delyth and the boy without you; I haven't even got a weapon! We need to stick together."

James nodded. "Okay," he said. "We leave Rhydderch here and go together. But if it comes to a fight, you have to promise you'll leave me and leg it with Delyth and the boy."

"Fair enough."

"You hear that, Rhydderch?" James pointed his sword at the chieftain's son. "You stay and guard the boat while we find the boy's mother. And don't think about stealing it, or you'll have me to answer to. Understand?"

"Yes, my Lord," Rhydderch replied, hardly bothering to hide the sarcasm in his voice.

James bridled. After taking pity on his enemy, Rhydderch's insolence was too much. He was tempted to smash his fist into the chieftain's son's arrogant face, but he decided to let it rest. He turned his attention to Artur. "Come on," he said kindly. "Let's go find your Mam."

James led Tom, Delyth and Artur towards Heulwen's house in single file. When they reached the edge of the clearing, James crept up to the stock proof hedge and peered through its densely laid branches towards the entrance. Smoke was wafting lazily up through the thatch, but the building looked deserted. A flock of sparrows chirruped in the doorway, picking for titbits in the rushes that sufficed as a doormat.

As James popped his head over the gate, the birds flew off, chattering in alarm. Fearing discovery, James ducked back behind the gate. When no one came to investigate the birds' flight, he pushed aside the gate and tiptoed across the muddy compound.

It was then that he discovered the knife. He picked it up and wiped the blade with his sleeve.

James' heart soared. *It's Emma's*, he thought, *she must've made it out of the fort*. Then he stopped. Why did she drop it? Then he noticed a body-sized depression in the mud. He looked around warily.

Tom crept up beside him. James silently handed him the knife and gave his friend a meaningful look. Tom's facial expression registered understanding, and he swivelled his eyes towards the house. James nodded. Together, they sidled up to the building and took up positions either side of the door.

At a signal from James, the boys burst into the round house. James was first through the doorway, sword in hand, while Tom covered his back with Emma's knife.

"Myrleduin," growled James.

There was no reply and no sign of movement. It felt like an anticlimax. They lowered their weapons and looked around sheepishly. Embers were glowing in the central fireplace; a small length of hemp rope lay discarded, and a bowl lay broken, porridge was spewed across the floor.

"There's nobody here," declared Tom.

"Wait a minute!"

A huddled form stirred in the shadowy recesses of the smoky room. James raised his sword and approached the mystery object. Whatever or whoever it was, it was covered in a tatty woollen bed cover. Using the tip of his sword as a hook, James flicked the blanket aside. He gasped. "Tom, look!"

A woman lay sprawled across a straw cot. Her head lolled over the side of the bed and her long dark hair, streaked with grey, cascaded onto the floor. Beside her, curled up at her feet, lay a huge, shaggy dog.

"It's Heulwen," said Tom.

Bregg looked up groggily. He gave a half-hearted growl, then flopped on his side. The boys jumped at the dog's warning, but having discovered Emma's dagger outside the door, James was not deterred.

Keeping half an eye on the sheepdog, he examined the unconscious woman; Heulwen's breathing was shallow but there were no obvious signs of injury.

Delyth joined them. She looked at the broken bowl by the fire, then at the woman and dog. "They've been drugged," she observed.

"And her hands are tied behind her back," added Tom.

"Well untie them then!" demanded Delyth. "It must hurt."

James rolled Heulwen's body on its side while Tom used the dagger James had found in the yard and sliced through the roughly twisted hemp bindings.

"What now?" asked Tom as the bonds fell away.

James' frowned. "I think Emma's been here today, and maybe Tegwedd too." He cradled Heulwen's head. "We need to bring her round and find out what's happened,"

"I'll fetch some water," said Delyth. "You try to make her more comfortable."

James and Tom got Heulwen into a sitting position while Delyth fetched a pitcher of water and splashed some on the unconscious woman's face. Almost as soon as the water touched her skin, Heulwen's eyes opened and her mouth twitched. For a moment it seemed she was about to talk, then she groaned and threw up all over herself. The youngsters fell back as vomit splashed over Heulwen's tunic and the unfortunate Bregg.

"Get her on her side or she'll choke!" ordered James, remembering his first aid classes.

James and Tom manhandled Heulwen into the recovery position, but not without Tom getting sick on the back of his hand.

It was a pink and sticky with mucous. Tom gagged; it was as much as he could do not to throw up himself. He wiped the vile smelling goo onto the blanket.

James examined the mess with disgust. "I think you're right, Delly. She's been poisoned."

"Agreed," said Tom. "But what the hell can we do?"

Delyth dabbed a trickle of sick from the side of Heulwen's mouth. "I can't remember everything they said in first aid, but it's good she's thrown up, surely? She'll have sicked up most of the poison."

Tom looked doubtful. "Who knows. I suppose we'll have to wait for her to come round. It'll be a while. She doesn't look like she'll be in a fit state to tell us anything for ages."

"We haven't got time," interrupted James. "Don't you understand? The druid has been seen here, we've found Emma's dagger, the pieces of cut rope, the poison…" James' face was set hard. "Emma's in trouble. Chuck the rest of the water on her and see if that livens her up."

Delyth stared at James, shocked by the aggression in his voice. James snatched the water jar and tipped the contents over Heulwen's head.

"James, you bastard! There was no–" Spluttering interrupted Delyth's tirade. The cold shower had had the desired effect. Heulwen seemed to be coming around.

"Dry her off with the blanket," snapped James. "And get Artur in here before the dog comes round and takes a lump out of one of us."

Suddenly they were all rubbing and fussing over Tegwedd's mother and dragging her into an upright position. Artur, who'd been eavesdropping outside, rushed in and stood, white-faced, next to his mam. As her eyes fluttered open the lad squeezed her hand. Heulwen smiled.

James leaned forward. "Heulwen," his tone was urgent, "has Emma been here?" Heulwen didn't reply. Her puzzled expression indicated she was trying to register what James was saying, but the message wasn't getting through. James became frustrated. "Where's Emma?" he demanded. "Has Myrleduin got her?"

This time the cogs in Heulwen's brain connected, and she shot upright. "Hurry!" she screamed, her eyes wild in panic. "He's taken her to the Lake! He means to kill her! In the name of the Goddess, hurry before it's too late!"

James leapt to his feet. "I knew she'd been here. Tom let's go. Delyth, you stay here with the boy and Heulwen."

Delyth's eyes flashed angrily. "For fuck's sake, James!" she snapped. "Emma's my friend too. I'm coming."

James stared at Delyth in surprise; his meek childhood playmate had turned into a lioness. He nodded. "We need to hurry," he said, as he ran out of the door.

Chapter 47

When Myrleduin reached the lake, the sun was a red disk hovering over the treetops, it's fading light painting the water with bold brushstrokes of pink and orange. But the druid had no time to enjoy the view; he'd carried the girl all the way from the house, and her drugged body was a dead weight. Now the muscles in his scrawny body were screaming for him to put the girl down, but he dared not rest. He risked a look along the path towards Heulwen's farmstead. The spirits were telling him the boy James wasn't far behind. He glanced at the girl sleeping peacefully in his arms. The deed had to be done quickly.

"Not much further, *cariad*," he whispered as he stepped onto the wooden platform leading out into the lake. At the far end of the platform stood the henge, its circle of oak pillars reared out of the peaty water like giant wooden sarsens. "Careful!" The druid's foot slid on one of the roughly hewn boards, and he almost dropped his precious load into the water. "Not yet," he muttered to the girl. "Patience, child. Your time is almost here."

Somehow, Myrleduin found the strength to reach the end of the pier and place the girl on the raised wooden altar. He looked around exultantly. The altar was at the centre of the circle of brooding pillars. In his madness, he could feel them watching and sensed their power. His tired body tingled with renewed energy. The Goddess was there. He knew it!

Myrleduin raised his arms; this was his moment of triumph. "Cliodna, Spirit of the Lake, I have fulfilled my promise!" he yelled across the water. He paused, relishing the way his words bounced off the pillars and echoed around the primitive temple. "Behold the girl spoken of by the prophets. A golden-haired virgin bearing your sign." The druid ran his tongue over his lip and gazed at the unconscious girl; her long blonde hair flowed over the edge of the carved wooden table. "You are even more beautiful than I imagined," he whispered, as though speaking to a lover. "Truly a fitting sacrifice."

Myrleduin looked up. A flicker of fear crossed his lined face. "I must hurry," he muttered irritably. "The boy will be here soon."

He reached into a bag and brought out a coil of sinew. The sinew was oiled and knotted, and wooden handles were tied on each end. He carefully unwound the coils and placed the ligature on the table alongside the girl. He took a deep breath. Now that the moment had come, he felt strangely reluctant. He looked to the west. Wisps of cloud tinged with purple and pink floated overhead. Tomorrow would be a sunny day.

Smiling, Myrleduin wrapped the garrotte around the girl's neck and began to pull. "Quiet now, child," he murmured as the girl's hands flailed and her back arched and twisted. He felt the knotted sinew cut through soft skin and into the flesh below. He kept applying pressure until the girl's body stopped twitching and lay limp on the altar.

When he was sure she was dead, Myrleduin dropped the garrotte and looked down at the girl. He was surprised how easy it had been to kill her. He felt no regret. Why should he? The girl was with the Goddess now.

He glanced at the far bank of the lake. There was no time for the ritual. He had to commit the body to the water immediately. He dragged the girl to the edge of the platform and rolled her off. She hit the water with a dull splash. At the moment of impact, her arms spread wide as if in a mute gesture of appeal.

Myrleduin knelt on the wooden deck and watched as the girl's face, encircled by a tangle of golden hair, stared up at him from the peat-stained water. The last he saw as she slid into the depths was a glint of gold.

"It is done," he sighed. He heaved himself to his feet and stood, facing the altar, to address the Goddess. "Lady of the Lake," he shouted, his high-pitched voice carrying over the water. "A maid has been offered to the water according to the ancient laws. May her sacrifice be acceptable to you and her body prove a fitting temple for your gracious spirit. Inhabit her mortal remains, I pray, and feed on her soul so you may dwell amongst us again in body and in spirit."

The wooden henge looked on in silent approval as the invocation came to a close. Then Myrleduin looked up, startled. Angry shouts rang out across the water. He had to run.

Chapter 48

Tom, with his wiry physique, reached the lake first. James, who'd been keeping pace with Delyth, lagged way behind. Tom waited for them next to a belt of reeds that screened the lakeside. He stood, hands on hips, for a moment, catching his breath. He looked up. Someone was shouting. He pushed his way through the reeds and found himself standing at the edge of the lake; he was only a stone's throw away from the circle of massive posts that marked the perimeter of the henge.

The druid Myrleduin was standing in the centre of the circle, shouting like a maniac. Something about a virgin and a lady. With a start, Tom noticed a person, a girl, was laid out on a raised wooden altar. The druid stood over her like crow inspecting a carcass. The girl's long blonde hair hung over the edge of the altar. Her neck was twisted to one side at an impossible angle.

Tom's heart stopped. "Emma!" he screamed. He looked back down the path; James was nowhere to be seen.

The druid must have heard him because he stopped yelling, grabbed the girl under the arms, and dragged her towards the edge of the platform. Her body flopped like a de-boned chicken. Tom stared in horror at the unfolding tragedy, then glanced back down the path again. James wasn't coming. He had to act. He frantically assessed his options; should he swim or sprint around the lake to the causeway?

The body hit the water with a splash.

No time to think. Tom ran to the water and waded in, then stopped. Emerging out of the trees on the far side of the lake was a party of warriors painted for war. Their black, circular shields marked them as Du Tarian. Tom stood knee-deep in the water, his expression one of incredulity and indecision. What should he do now? Suddenly, James and Delyth were on the bank beside him. "He's mad," said Tom. "He's killed her!"

James looked from the druid to the approaching Du Tarian warriors. Then he saw the ripples spreading out from the end of the wooden platform. "Emma!"

"James, don't!" shouted Tom, but James was already running down the bank.

Delyth caught James as he entered the water and pulled at his tunic. "Stop him, Tom!" she screeched. "We've got to get away."

Tom hesitated. A shout went up from the other side of the Lake; the warriors had seen them. Tom decided to act. He launched himself at his friend, his shoulder hitting him in the side of the thigh as he'd done in countless rugby practices. James went down like a sack of potatoes and the two boys wrestled in the shallow water.

Delyth waded in after them. "Stop it!"

In a moment of fist-flailing lunacy, the two boys were oblivious to the danger posed by the warriors jogging along the shore towards them. Delyth brought the madness to an end. She slapped James across the face. "Run," she yelled and sprinted up the bank. Tom was straight after her. The warriors charged in pursuit, whooping like a pack of hunting dogs.

James raised his sword, and for a crazy moment, he considered attacking. Then the red mist lifted. He took a final anguished look across the lake, then sprinted up the path after his friends.

Delyth usually came last in school cross-country runs. Perhaps if her games teacher had threatened to hack her to pieces with a sword, her times would have improved. Certainly, being pursued by armed warriors had Delyth scampering down the woodland path towards the bay at a pace she'd never believed possible. Sweat beaded on her forehead and dripped off her nose.

James ran beside her. "We're losing them," he panted, glancing back up the track. Delyth was too breathless to reply.

Tom, who'd bounded ahead, slowed to let them catch up. "What's the plan?"

James didn't have a plan. His mind was numb. He was struggling to process what had happened at the henge, let alone think about an escape route. He thought for a moment, "We'll get away in the boat," he said. Then he remembered the boy and his mam. "We need to warn Artur and Heulwen. You're fastest, Tom. Go to the house. We'll meet you on the beach."

Tom nodded. "I'll be careful," he said. He took off like a scalded cat, his stringy runner's legs covering the ground effortlessly.

James watched him go, then glanced at Delyth. Her face was bright, and she was blowing heavily. "You alright?"

Delyth returned a tired smile. "Don't worry about me."

Suddenly James was crying. "You are amazing, Delyth. You know that don't you?" He reached out his hand.

Delyth shrugged him off. "Not now," she said firmly, "there's no time. We need to get away. Emma would want that."

James swallowed, then nodded.

Delyth smiled again. "Good," she said decisively, and shot off.

James hesitated, then looked over his shoulder. There was no sign of the Du Tarian. Maybe they'd given up and gone back to find the druid. The thought of what the warriors might do to Myrleduin brought little comfort; no amount of suffering meted out to her killer was going to bring Emma back. *There'll be time to grieve later*, he told himself. He sprinted after Delyth, who'd disappeared around a bend in the track.

It took James a while to catch Delyth, who'd set a blistering pace down the narrow woodland track. In places the way became muddy and treacherous, and on more than one occasion, Delyth stumbled on the many slippery roots that snaked across the path. Fortunately, James' strong arm was there to prevent her falling and risk twisting an ankle. As they approached the beach, the scrubby oaks and mountain ash petered out. Soon they were squelching through marshy grassland behind a ridge of stones and coarse gravel thrown up by the winter storms.

Tom caught them as they were about to climb the ridge. "They aren't there," he panted.

"They must be. We left them less than an hour ago!" said James.

"Well they're not there now," insisted Tom. "I looked inside the house and they've gone. The dog too."

James raised his eyebrows. "There were no signs of the Du Tarian?"

"Nothing."

James sighed. "You've done your best. It looks like Heulwen has recovered enough to hide. She and Artur know these woods like the back of their hands; they'll lie low until the war party have gone."

The three youngsters reached the top of the storm ridge and looked down at the beach. The sun was sinking into the sea and the light was beginning to fade. Most of the beach had been covered by the incoming tide. They scanned the remaining sand; there was no sign of Rhydderch or the boat.

Look!" Tom pointed at a black dot rounding the headland. "He's taken the boat."

"Damn!" James grimaced. "You were right. I should have left him where we found him." He looked back to where the path emerged from the woodland. There was no sign of the Du Tarian, but they could appear at any moment. He held the heel of his hand against his forehead in despair. What were they going to do now? He was starting to panic. They couldn't stop here; they were too exposed!

He turned to face his friends. They looked back at him expectantly. The weight of responsibility felt like a millstone round his neck. This was his fault, he thought. He'd failed them.

"What next, James?"

"Why is it always me who decides?" he snapped.

Delyth looked like she'd been stung.

"There's no need to have a go," said Tom angrily.

James felt awful. "I'm sorry it's just..." There was a lump in his throat. The words trailed off.

Delyth stroked his cheek with the back of her hand. "It's okay," she murmured. "I understand."

James stared at Delyth as though it was the first time they'd met. He swallowed hard. This gentle girl had saved his life today. It was incredible; he'd known her since they were toddlers, and yet it seemed he'd never really known her at all. Who'd have guessed at the courage hidden under the baggy clothes and giggles? It was all he could do not to cry. He took a deep breath. "We'll hide in the cave," he said decisively.

Tom looked appalled; the thought of going back into that cold, dark hole terrified him.

James read his thoughts and pointed an accusing finger at his friend. "You were the one who asked me what to do."

"It's not safe," Tom said.

"It's a lot safer than being caught. If we climb round rather than take the cliff path, nobody will see us."

Tom didn't reply.

"You're scared, aren't you?"

"I can't help it. That cave gives me the creeps."

Delyth intervened. "James is right; the cave is the safest place and it's close by. We don't even have to go in, we can hide up in the entrance. And it will only be one night. We'll sneak back to the house tomorrow morning and look for Heulwen and Artur. With luck, the Du Tarian won't have found the farmstead, and the food stores will still be intact."

Tom nodded. The plan made sense. He was starving hungry, and the thought of food – any food – sounded good.

Chapter 49

It was dark when they climbed down onto the little beach below the cave, and it was already chilly.

Tom shivered like a whippet that had fallen in a river. "Do you think it's safe to light a fire?"

James was doubtful. "I'm not sure."

"It's going to get a lot colder," Delyth pointed out. "We'll be freezing by morning. We can make a small fire in the cave. Nobody's going to see it in there."

"We'll have to light it well inside the cave," James observed, glancing towards the sea. "The tide's still coming in. The beach will be flooded in a minute!"

The three exhausted youngsters searched amongst the boulders at the base of the cliff, hunting for driftwood. James had a vague memory of flotsam lodged in a cleft in the rock at the cave entrance and checked it out. "Hey! Look what I found." He held out two strange looking pots.

"Great!" said Tom. "Just what we need." Then he frowned. "Someone must be using the cave."

"Myrleduin," growled James. "If–"

"Don't!" interrupted Delyth. "There's been enough killing already. Anyway, what are those things?"

"Lamps." Tom held out one of the strange objects. "Look, the saucer is filled with fat, and this," he pointed to a piece of twine poking out of the sheep tallow, "is the wick. This bit with holes is a lid that goes over the top. Clever, eh?"

Delyth was too drained to consider how Iron Age lamps functioned. "Just light it," she said abruptly.

Tom glanced at his sister. It wasn't like her to get irritable. "Don't get ratty," he grumbled. "Things are bad enough as they are, eh, James?" James didn't reply; he was busy thinking violent thoughts about Myrleduin.

Tom shrugged and took his fire lighting kit from a pouch around his neck. He placed the contents of the kit – a quartz stone and a dried bulrush seed head – on a flat stone, then picked apart the seed head with his fingers, heaping the fluffy fibres into a pile on the stone. He set about striking the quartz against the flat of his dagger until a spark ignited the carefully prepared pile of tinder. Within moments, he had a small pile of twigs alight. Tom grinned. Even in these dreadful circumstances, he took great delight in this newfound skill. The orange glow radiated by the burning twigs lifted the mood.

"Let's get the lamps going," James suggested, "then move further into the cave before the tide gets any higher."

Half an hour later, the three fugitives were warming their hands on a blazing fire laid on the dry sand at the base of the chimney. It all worked well to start with; the smoke gently rising to the roof and drifting across the beach. However, as the temperature outside fell, an onshore breeze started blowing fumes back inside the cave. Soon they were choking on acrid smoke.

"Shit!" gasped Tom, his eyes stinging. "We're being smoked like kippers!"

"I could murder a kipper," said James, whose thoughts had moved from murdering druids to his empty stomach.

Delyth put another lump of driftwood on the fire. She too was hungry. "We haven't eaten since last night," she said. "We need to eat tomorrow, or we'll start feeling ill."

"We could find some limpets. And maybe there'll be some mussels in the rock pools."

Delyth wasn't impressed, "You'll have to do better than that, James."

James poked the fire with a stick angrily. Burning embers shot up into the blackness, and they were treated to another dose of choking smoke.

"You idiot." admonished Delyth, flicking a smut out of her hair. "You burnt me!"

James' emotions boiled over. He knew it was irrational, but he couldn't stop thinking their misfortunes were his fault. "I'm sorry, okay?" he snapped. He poked the fire again savagely. He had to get away and straighten his head out. "I'm going for a piss," he announced, and stalked out.

Delyth went to stop him, but Tom grabbed her arm. "Let him go," he advised. "It's not your fault. It's just his way of coping."

The tide had almost reached the top of the little beach, and James hopped between half-submerged rocks to avoid getting his feet wet. The lapping of the waves on the gravel was a balm. He breathed in the ozone-rich sea air; it tasted like nectar after the smoky atmosphere in the cave. He placed the lamp he'd taken from the cave on a rock and fumbled with his breeches.

Why haven't these people invented flies? he thought. Then he stopped; a stone clattered down the cliff and landed with a splash in the shallow water a few paces to his left. Suddenly having a piss wasn't a priority. He quickly blew out the lamp. Something was moving around above him. He heard voices. He wasn't sure, but he didn't think the language was Welsh.

He squinted up at the cliff face. Two figures were descending the little goat track. They were moving slowly, picking their way down the screed slope in the darkness. He wondered if they'd seen the lamp and concluded they had. He had to warn the others. With exceptional presence of mind, he scooped up the extinguished lamp and blundered back into the cave, groping his way towards the glow of the fire. "There are people outside," he hissed. "Two of them, climbing down the cliff."

"Du Tarian?"

"I didn't ask," replied James, grabbing his sword. "We have to assume they are. We need to hide!" He thrust his lamp into Delyth's hand, "Light it," he ordered, "and get climbing. If they come in before you reach the top, I'll hold them off."

Tom and Delyth threw themselves at the side of the cave and started scrambling up the chimney. It was a lot easier than the climb they'd made with Rick way back in their old lives. The stone steps were freshly cut, and the recent dry spell meant the rock wasn't slippery.

James kicked out the fire and clambered after them, his eyes stinging from the plumes of acrid smoke. He could hear his friends coughing and choking above his head. "Keep going," he hissed at the bobbing lights.

There was no reply; Tom and Delyth were too busy climbing and trying not to choke. Despite juggling with the lamp, Tom reached the ledge in double quick time, where he waited for his friends. The air here was clearer, so he put the lamp on the floor and took a few deep breaths. As soon as he stopped, he felt the first prickling of claustrophobia. The fear crept up on him like a big cat stalking him in the darkness. Beads of sweat prickled on his forehead. "I can't believe I'm doing this again," he cursed.

Delyth crawled onto the ledge beside him and held him tight. "Try to stay calm," she said. "They won't come in after us. We'll wait here till they're gone."

"I'm not frightened of the bloody Du Tarian," he lied. "I just don't know if I can stay in here much longer." Delyth didn't reply. The cave didn't bother her, but she was absolutely terrified of the Du Tarian.

The twins huddled together until James joined them a couple of minutes later. His throat was dry from the smoke. "Are you okay," he wheezed.

Delyth ignored the question. "Are *you* okay, more like? You've got asthma, haven't you?" she asked, concerned.

"No, it's just the smoke. How's Tom?"

"Oh bloody brilliant," quipped Tom.

"Well everything's super then," riposted James.

"Shut up," hissed Delyth. "They'll hear us."

Chastened, the boys went quiet and listened intently. The silence was ear-poppingly deafening. Then something scraped against the cave wall at the bottom of the chimney.

"Shit!" Someone was moving around in the cave. Panic ensued and all three scuttled soundlessly down the passageway, only stopping when they reached the tunnel that led into the Blue Cavern.

James held out his lamp. The narrow entrance looked slimy and menacing in the guttering candlelight.

"Don't make me go down there," whined Tom.

"Nobody's going to make you," replied James. "But trust me, it's the safest place. If they try to get through, they'll only be able to squeeze through one at a time, and I promise you that's the last thing they'll ever do." James held up his sword as assurance.

"Bollocks! It's no safer in there than anywhere else in this cave," argued Tom. "We're trapped and you know it. If they want to, they can starve or freeze us out. We can't stay here forever. Anyway," he had a horrid thought, "the lamps will only last a few hours."

"He's got a point," said Delyth. "We can't stay here for long. Remember how cold we got!"

"I know all that. I'm not a complete dickhead. I thought we'd just hide up and hope they get bored and clear off in the morning."

Tom sighed. He might as well give in; James was determined to get his way. He'd have to go down that nasty hole sooner or later, so he might as well just get on with it.

He lay on his back in the sloppy clay and slithered headfirst into the tiny passageway. He was terrified. *I must be bonkers*, he thought.

"I told you it'd be easier this time," said James later.

The three of them were sitting in the Blue Cavern on a ledge next to the spring. To conserve fuel, only one of the oil lamps was burning. Its yellow glow illuminated a tiny fraction of the massive cavern; a bubble of yellow light in an inky sea of darkness. Huddled in this island of light, the little group was united in their misery.

"We'll have to take turns to guard the tunnel," James told them.

Tom was apologetic. Like the others, he'd had no sleep for forty-eight hours, and the cold was seeping into his flesh. "I'm sorry, James, I'm just too knackered. I've got to get some kip."

Delyth put her arm round her brother. "I'm feeling alright at the moment," she lied. "I'll keep an eye out if you like."

James smiled. "Thanks, Delyth but you look like shit," he said kindly. "I'll take the first watch. You guys get your heads down. I'll wake you later."

James looked enviously at Tom and Delyth, curled up in their heavy woollen cloaks.

He sat on the damp rock and listened. The only sound was the gentle breathing of his two companions. His eyelids felt heavy; he was very tired. Perhaps he'd just lie down for a bit.

Chapter 50

The Jag crunched to a halt on the gravel drive outside Myrtle House. The driver's door opened, and a thick-necked young man in a suit stepped out. Kingsley-Smith's personal protection officer scanned the courtyard, nodded to the policeman stationed outside, then opened the passenger door. Emma's parents climbed out. Her mother had been crying, her perfectly applied foundation and mascara was smudged. Emma's father's face was impassive.

The policeman met them at the front door and ushered them inside. A tall man in a creased suit was waiting for them in the hall. "Good evening, sir," he said ignoring Emma's mother. "I'm Chief Inspector Reid, incident commander."

Benjamin Kingsley-Smith gave the inspector a cool stare. "I know," he said. "Are the other parents here?"

"They're waiting in the lounge, sir," Reid said stiffly.

Tom and James' parents were sitting squashed together on a tatty three-seat chesterfield; they stood as the Kingsley-Smiths entered the room.

As the introductions were made, Emma's father found it difficult to engage. The thought of his daughter trapped in a cave filled him with anguish and fury. Listening to Lucinda's sobbing in the car hadn't helped; he couldn't resist reminding her that it was her idea to allow Emma to come to this dump.

He studied the other parents. *They look shell-shocked*, he thought. He wondered if they felt as frustrated and helpless as he did.

The policeman was blathering on. "I'm sorry to meet you under such difficult circumstances. I expect you're tired after your long drive. Please sit down. Would you like a cup of tea?"

Kingsley-Smith looked up. He needed to pull himself together. The bloody copper was staring at him like a spaniel waiting for its next command. "Eh, tea? Yes that would be great." He glanced at his wife who nodded her head and sunk gratefully into a worn armchair next to Anne Cordle.

"Two teas please, Rees," ordered Inspector Reid.

Anne Cordle reached out a sympathetic hand to Emma's tearful mother, while Lizzie Rees, the family liaison officer, went to put the kettle on.

Kingsley-Smith remained standing. He'd come here for answers, not to be fobbed off with tea and sympathy. He came straight to the point. "When do you expect to break through?" he demanded.

The Inspector's response was carefully worded. It wasn't often he had to deal with a Cabinet minister. "The team is still clearing the main fall, Sir. They've been working around the clock, but the material is unstable. One wrong move and the whole lot could collapse."

"There are four children in that cave, Inspector. It's been forty-eight hours now."

"I understand your concerns, but we can't move any faster. We have to think about the team. There are safety protocols we need to follow."

Kingsley-Smith's expression hardened; he was used to getting his own way. "Health and safety be damned! It's my little girl in there."

Reid was adamant. "I can't put any more lives at risk. We don't know what we might find when we break into the cave. For all we know, this is already a recovery mission."

Kingsley-Smith stabbed his finger at the inspector. "Your job is on the line, Reid. Pull your finger out and get them out of there! And interview that bloody idiot who took them in there in the first place. I want a statement from him and his girlfriend. They've got a lot of questions to answer."

Anne Cordle had heard enough. "That girlfriend you're slagging off is my sister, and you're not the only one with a child in that cave. This is bad enough for everyone without you throwing your weight around. The Inspector and his team are doing their best, so why don't you sit down and shut the fuck up?"

Kingsley-Smith opened his mouth to reply, but his wife intervened. "Anne's right. Sit down, Ben, and stop acting like a prick."

Kingsley-Smith gaped. In twenty years of marriage, she'd never spoken to him like that.

Chapter 51

Owain was knackered and he was only an hour into his new shift. He sloshed though the ankle-deep water and dropped the boulder he was carrying on the heap of rubble piled up at the top of the beach. He wiped his brow with the back of his gloved hand and smeared his face with mud. He looked back towards the cave.

People in hard hats swarmed in and out of the entrance like ants, their muddy high-visibility waistcoats streaked by soft, persistent Welsh rain.

He looked up. A group of forlorn onlookers and thoroughly fed-up newspaper reporters were still standing guard on the clifftop. Owain wondered at their tenacity. Some, like him, had been here off and on since the beginning.

He looked at his phone; eight-thirty AM. The kids had been trapped for almost three days. Surely there was no way they could have survived in there for that long?

Owain heard shouting, and then a ragged cheer came up from the gaggle of tired rescuers gathered at the cave entrance.

"What's up?" he called.

"We've broken through!"

Owain switched on his headlamp and hurried back into the cave. Everyone was grinning. Owain barged his way past his fellow rescuers and made his way to the mound of scree at the site of the rock fall. A group of guys were peering up into a void between the top of the pile of rubble and the chimney wall.

"Can you see anything?" asked Owain.

"No, just a big empty space."

"Wait a minute," one of the men squinted upwards. "There is something. It's the end of a rope."

"Any sign of the kids?"

"Nothing."

"They must be further in," Owain mused. "Or they'd have heard us by now."

"Or they haven't made it."

The men fell silent as they considered what they might find when they finally entered the cave.

Owain looked up at the narrow aperture, then at his fellow rescuers; they were big lads. Most looked like they'd spent too much time in the pub or eating fast food. "I'm skinny," he said tactfully. "I reckon I could squeeze through. Why don't I take a look while you carry on clearing?"

The men looked doubtful. "Even if you can squeeze through, how are you going to climb up to the passage they told us about?"

"Same way as the kids," retorted Owain. "If they can get up, so can I."

"You'd better give it a go then," said Alan Evans, a bull of a man whose stomach tested the seams of his boiler suit. The big man turned to the others and shrugged. "None of us are going to get through that gap, and it'll take another hour to clear a bigger hole."

Owain needed no further encouragement. He'd been at the cave since the beginning of the operation, and after finding Rick it wasn't a job, it was personal. He nodded to Alan. "I'm going to need a bump up."

"*Pob lwc*," grunted Alan, as Owain trod on his shoulder with a muddy boot and scrambled up the loose scree.

As he reached the gap, Owain steadied himself against the side of the cave wall. He was breathing heavily. His foot began to slide, and several rocks clattered down behind him, eliciting curses from Alan and his friends below.

Owain paused to catch his breath, then hauled himself upwards again, his feet scrabbling for purchase on the rubble. Soon his head was poking through the hole, then his elbows. Finally, he was able to wriggle through, and found himself standing on the top of the heap. He looked up. In the beam from his headlamp, he could see the roof of the cave and the rope Alan had spotted. There was no sign of the trapped youngsters.

"Hello! Can you hear me?" he called up towards where the rope disappeared.

"Yes," shouted one of the blokes from the base of the chimney.

"Not you, you dickheads!" yelled Owain.

There were laughs and expletives from below. Owain grinned; he'd gotten to know these men over the last couple of days. Some, like him, worked in the emergency services, others were local volunteers, and a few were from caving clubs and had travelled many miles to be here. All of them had given their time cheerfully, working in gruelling conditions. He smiled. When this was over, he'd join them for a few beers. Then the smile died on his lips. What if there were four young dead bodies up there?

Owain shook his head. *Don't be negative*, he thought, and turned his attention to scaling the chimney.

"Got you!" he grasped one of the metal rings mentioned in the briefing, then clipped his safety line to the ring and looked up. There was a second ring a couple of metres above his head and a series of footholds cut into the rock. Owain smiled; this was going to be a piece of cake.

He was a competent climber, and when he made it up to the top a few minutes later, he was hardly out of breath. He crawled onto the ledge that marked the entrance to the horizontal shaft then hesitated, suddenly nervous. Bracing himself for the worst, he took a deep breath and pointed his lamp down the passageway. He was half expecting bodies, but there was nothing. He exhaled in relief, surprised at how fast his heart was beating. It was then that he noticed the rocks arranged on the cave floor.

'WE ARE HERE,' somebody had written in stones. There was an arrow pointing further into the cave.

Owain peered into the shaft. 'We' meant more than one of them must have survived the fall. And they'd had the presence of mind to tell the rescue team where they were. Perhaps they'd been resourceful enough to stay alive.

A beam of light was dancing on the roof above the chimney. He looked towards its source. One of the cavers, a lad called Nick from Derbyshire, had squeezed through the gap at the top of the rock pile. Owain decided to wait for the guy to catch up before venturing further. He wasn't sure if he could face stumbling across another dead or injured person on his own.

Owain and Nick peered into the entrance of the tunnel that led to the Blue Cavern. The tunnel was slick with grey, slimy mud.

The young caver looked at Owain quizzically. "You sure you want to go first? You know what you might to find."

Owain nodded. "I want to see this thing through. And it's too soon to write them off. You saw the message; they must have left that message after the roof fall, so there's a chance they're still alive."

"As long as you're sure you can handle it. Finding a dead kid wouldn't be an easy thing to forget."

The voice relayed from the surface was impatient. "When you two have finished your heart to heart, will one of you go and find those kids!"

"Yes, Boss," Owain replied sheepishly into the radio mic. "I'm moving into the tunnel now."

Owain emerged into the Blue Cavern with mud smeared all over his headlamp. He sat on the cave floor and wiped the headlamp with his sleeve, then scanned the cavern for the trapped youngsters. He saw the first body immediately. It was lying curled up just to his right. Then two more huddled together on a slab of rock next to a pool in the centre of the cave. "I've got three of them!" he shouted into the mic.

"How are they?" crackled the voice in his earpiece.

"There's no movement," Owain asserted. "I'm having a look now." He knelt by the boiler-suited figure by the tunnel entrance. It was one of the boys; a pale moonlike face gazed up at him. His eyes were wide open. There was no sign of movement.

"It doesn't look good." Owain pulled off his neoprene glove and placed the fleshy tip of his index finger to the lad's neck. The boy's skin was cold to the touch. "I think this one's dead," he said to Nick, who had joined him. "We'd better have a look at the others. Wait!" He felt a faint movement under his finger. "I've got a pulse," he said excitedly. "Check the others, they might be alive as well!"

While Nick went to the two bodies by the pool, Owain spoke into his microphone. "Where are you with those stretchers?" he demanded.

"We're still climbing the bloody chimney. We'll be with you in a few minutes. Over."

Owain loosened the boy's collar and his head lolled around alarmingly. Owain ran his hands over his patient, searching systematically for any injury. "No sign of trauma on this one. I think he's hypothermic, but there's something else really strange going on."

"What do you mean? Over."

Owain held James' head between his hands and examined his face. "His eyes are odd. They're wide open and the pupils are massive. It looks like he's tripping out. Do you reckon it's a reaction to the cold?"

"No idea," said the disembodied voice from the surface. "How are the others?"

"The others are the same," said Nick. "It's like Sleeping Beauty in here."

"That's not funny," said the voice irritably. "I've got their parents and God knows how many journalists out here. Please confirm their status. Over."

"We have three young people. Two male, one female. I can confirm all three are alive, but severely hypothermic," Nick replied, chastened. "They all look drugged," he added. "Over."

"Thank you. Make them as warm and comfortable as possible and wait for the stretcher group. Are you sure the second girl isn't there? Over."

"Positive, Boss," Owain said hurriedly. "We've checked the whole of the inner cave, she's not here."

"Damn!" said the boss. "If it's the politician's girl that's missing, there'll be hell to pay."

Chapter 52

James' eyelids fluttered. The harsh fluorescent light was a shock after the darkness of the cave.

"I think he's waking up," someone said excitedly. With a start, James opened his eyes. A gentle but firm hand prevented him from struggling to a sitting position.

"It's okay, James. You're safe now." The voice was familiar.

"Dad?" James' brain felt like it had been pureed. He tried to sit up again and nearly knocked over the stand, which suspended a drip connected to his right forearm. "But how can I…"

"Steady, James. It's all over. They got you out."

A nurse bustled into the room. "I see you've decided to join us." She smiled. "How are you feeling?"

James hesitated; he didn't know. He had an awful taste in his mouth, his throat was dry, and his head felt like someone was inside his skull, treading all over his brain. "I'm okay," he lied croakily. "I've got a bit of a headache."

The nurse wrapped the Velcro band around his bicep and started to take his blood pressure. "I'm not surprised. From what I've been told, you must have a world class hangover!" She looked at the pressure reading. "One-hundred-and-twenty over seventy-five; bang on. No problems there."

James hardly heard her; his mind was spinning like a top. Was he really back home? Had it all been a dream? He grabbed his dad's arm like a drowning man clinging to a life ring.

"What about the others?" James jerked upright. This time he did knock over the stand, which crashed to the ground; fortunately, the saline drip remained intact.

The nurse was about to make a fuss, then she read the warning look in Richard Cordle's eye and thought better of it. She sorted out the drip, tut-tutting, while Richard groped for the words he needed to tell his son. He knew James hated bullshit, so he decided to be entirely truthful. He reached out and held his son's hand. "Tom and Delyth are doing fine, they are in hospital and are expected to make a full recovery," he said, as if addressing a funeral. "But they haven't been able to find Emma."

James sat in silence. So it was true. She *had* died. He gripped his dad's hand very hard. His eyes watered, but he bit down on his emotions, refusing to allow the tears to come. Richard pretended not to notice. He knew any overt sign of affection at this moment would make his son angry. He waited for James to compose himself.

"So she's dead."

Richard assumed this was a question. "We don't know, son. The police have searched the cave with a fine-toothed comb, and there's no sign of her. They told me they want to ask you some questions when you feel a little better. They need to know what happened."

James hesitated. "Have Tom or Delyth said anything yet?"

His dad looked worried. "They've been saying some very odd things," he said seriously. "Did Rick give you anything strange to eat? Like pills or mushrooms?"

James shook his head.

Richard stared intently at his son. James never lied. He could be stubborn as hell, and on rare occasions aggressive, but he always told the truth. "You must tell us what happened in the cave."

"Not now, Mr Cordle," said the nurse. "He needs to rest."

James was insistent. "I want to talk to my dad!"

The nurse scuttled away.

Once they were alone, James took a deep breath. "Dad," he began hesitantly, "something weird happened in that cave, and I don't know if it was a dream or if it really happened." His brow furrowed; a thought had occurred to him. "How long were we in the cave?"

"Three days. We all thought you'd died. They said you wouldn't survive the cold." This time it was his dad's turn to fight back the tears.

"Yes, the cold," murmured James distractedly. He turned to face his dad, a haunted expression on his face. "I thought I'd been away for months," he said. "If I told you where I'd been, you'd think I'd gone mad."

"Try me."

James paused for a moment, summoning the courage to speak.

"For the last few months, Tom, Delyth, all of us," he couldn't bring himself to say Emma's name, "have been living in another time." He glanced anxiously at his dad, aware how ridiculous he sounded. "We thought we were dreaming at first," he said. "Then after a while we came to believe it was real. I killed a man, Dad. And I know why Emma is missing. The druid killed her. Tom watched him throw her in the lake. I wanted to go in after her but there was nothing any of us could do."

Richard tried not to show how much these revelations worried him. The consultant had warned him James might behave strangely for a while. He prayed that there wouldn't be any long-term damage.

"James," he said quietly, "the doctors found a dangerous drug in your blood. If you say you haven't taken the drug intentionally, then I believe you, but you must understand that these things you think happened while you were in the cave might *seem* real, but they were just dreams. It's the drug that made you think them. That's what it does. It makes you hallucinate."

"So what bits were real?" asked James. "Did Rick die in the rock fall?"

His father's eyes narrowed. "Rick didn't die, though I reckon he's going wish he had. The police have got some tough questions to ask him when he's well enough. Things don't look good for him at all."

James lay back on the crisp white linen pillow. His head hurt.

Chapter 53

"What a mess!" Chief Inspector Reid was beside himself. "Are you absolutely sure that the girl is not in that cave?"

"One-hundred percent, sir," replied the officer drafted in from Cardiff. "Forensics has combed every square centimetre. All they've found is muddy footprints which correspond with the footwear worn by McFarlane and the kids, and a few bits of old pottery."

The Inspector slumped in the cheap swivel chair and brooded over his tea mug. "What's the prognosis on McFarlane?"

"Oh, he'll make it, sir. The hospital is expecting him to come round any time now."

"Who have we got over there?"

"Evans, sir."

The inspector regarded his officer from underneath his beetling brow. His expression was murderous.

"Tell Evans to grill McFarlane's girlfriend again. We've only got her word that the Kingsley-Smith girl went into the cave at all." He pointed his index finger at the officer from Cardiff. "You mark my words, Jones, McFarlane and that woman are in it together, and I'll screw the truth out of them even if we have to tear up the rule book page by page! Hell. The girl is a bloody Cabinet minister's daughter!"

The senior officer leant back in his chair, his eyes half closed, as if in pain.

"I've had the Home Secretary on to me this morning, asking where his friend's little girl has got to. And as for that lot," he said, looking out of the window at the bored group of waiting journalists. "What the hell am I going to tell them?"

Officer Jones stood in silence, waiting for the tirade to finish.

Inspector Reid continued unabated. "I'll tell you what I *can't* tell them. I *can't* tell them the kids were high as kites on bloody magic mushrooms when they found them. And I *can't* tell them Emma Kingsley-Smith was sacrificed to a lake goddess by an Iron Age druid!"

"I see your point, sir."

Reid looked up. "Have the results come in from forensics yet?"

"Yes, sir. McFarlane's house is clean. No sign of anything that matches the substance the doctors found in those kids. In fact, there was nothing at all, sir. The place was as clean as a whistle. Not so much as a whiff of weed."

Reid arranged the statements from Mags and the three youngsters on the desk in front of him. "What do *you* make of this, Jones?"

The officer chose his words carefully. "The whole thing's off the wall, but the similarity between the three kid's statements is striking. It makes me think they did witness something at that lake." He paused watching his boss' expression.

Reid was impatient. "Spit it out, Jones. What do you think happened?"

"I don't know, sir, but I don't like this at all. The unusual drug. The kids babbling on about druids and a sacrifice. My hunch is the kids were drugged and the girl was killed at the lake in some sort of ritual. Then McFarlane and his girlfriend threw the girl in the lake and dumped the others in the cave. The cave was a cover up that went wrong." The young officer warmed to his subject, "I wouldn't be surprised if McFarlane staged that rock fall and got caught under it. Serves the bastard right!"

"My thoughts exactly!" Reid concurred. "But until we have a body, we haven't a shred of evidence. All we've got is a hypothesis that's more improbable than a Midsomer Murders mystery." Reid pursed his lips. "The lake is the key; something very strange has been going on at the lake. That officer, the local guy, what's his name?"

"Evans, sir."

Reid grimaced. "Not another bloody Evans. Why can't you Welsh be more imaginative with your names?"

Jones remained impassive.

"Yes. Evans," continued the Inspector. "He tells me there's been trouble at that lake before; reports of girls being watched."

"Yes, sir. The locals say the lake is haunted."

Reid looked irritated. "Bollocks! Dig out the reports and get a description of this mystery girl-watcher. I'd lay odds it matches McFarlane. And Jones..."

"Yes, sir?"

"I want that lake searched. Frogmen, the lot. Drain it if necessary."

"Right, sir."

Chapter 54

Sergeant Evans gazed at the pumping equipment in bemusement. "The whole thing's a bloody circus," he observed. "Why drain the damned lake? The girl's not there; we had a team of divers in there all day yesterday. They didn't find a thing."

Detective Jones took a leisurely drag of his cigarette and looked out at the crime scene. The once secluded beauty spot had become a sea of mud, polluted by unhappy coppers clad in waders and waterproofs. "It's not every day the Minister for Pension's daughter gets mislaid," he said philosophically. "Reid said no stone would be left unturned and he meant it. If he doesn't get a result on this one, his balls are on the line."

From the comfort of the Land Rover they were sitting in, they watched a fresh-faced English police sergeant line up the gum-booted rank and file at one end of the quagmire that was Abereiddy Lake. The coppers eyed the mud with distaste.

Detective Jones sniggered in anticipation as the young sergeant blew his whistle for the search to begin. "Over the top boys." Jones attempted an upper-class English accent.

Sergeant Evans smiled. "Rather them than me." They watched as the ragged line of reluctant volunteers waded across the drained lake, poking their walking sticks deep into the mud.

"It looks more like the battle of the Somme than a police investigation," observed Jones, blowing a plume of smoke out of the car's partly open window. He almost choked mid-drag, "I don't believe it!" he cackled. A ripple of laughter went up from the coppers in waders. The young sergeant had toppled face first into the slime.

Evans sniggered. The two officers in the Land Rover laughed as their young colleague floundered.

Suddenly, one of the volunteers shouted excitedly. Jones sat up and peered through the windscreen. "Hey! It looks like they've found something."

The two cynics left the comfort of their vehicle to take a closer look. What they saw took both of them by surprise.

Detective Jones took one look at the hand sticking up out of the mud and reached for his mobile. He nudged his colleague. "Tell them not to touch anything. And tape the area off; I don't want anyone other than forensics near that body. I'm phoning the coroner's office. You know what that old codger Padmore is like. He'll have our guts for garters if anybody so much as farts near that crime scene."

When Doctor Padmore arrived forty minutes later, a stripy green and white tent had been erected over the outstretched hand, and the lake had been cordoned off with striped police tape.

Padmore looked over his spectacles and appraised the crime scene critically. "Has anyone touched the body?" he demanded.

"No," Detective Jones replied, his expression angelic. "I phoned your office the moment we found the body. All we've done is secure the crime scene."

"Mmm." Padmore seemed mollified. He produced an archaic Dictaphone from the top pocket of his brilliant white overalls. "August twenty-third." he said into the machine, which, like it's owner, was yellowed with age. "Abereiddy Lake, thirteen-hundred hours. Crime scene secured. Officer in charge of investigation: Detective Sergeant Jones."

Jones tried not to let his frustration show. He wished the old bastard would retire.

The aging pathologist approached the body, his long skinny legs and slow movements reminiscent of a praying mantis closing in on its victim. He bent down and examined the hand, gently manipulating its tobacco-coloured digits with his own rubber-gloved fingers. "Remarkable," he muttered. "Truly remarkable." He pressed the record button on the Dictaphone. "Left hand exposed two centimetres below the wrist joint. No obvious sign of injury. Skin stained dark brown, indicating significant time has elapsed since internment."

Padmore stood up. The group of muddy officers on the bank waited with bated breath. "Gentlemen," he said, relishing their rapt attention. "You'd better continue your search for Emma

Kingsley-Smith elsewhere. This person has been dead for a long time. Possibly a very long time indeed."

The assembled police officers looked crestfallen. Doctor Padmore paused for effect. "Quite honestly, I think this is the most interesting find I have ever attended." He looked around the group and his eyes landed on Detective Jones. "This discovery is unlikely to result in any sort of police investigation. However, please instruct your colleagues that nothing in the immediate area is to be disturbed." Padmore, puffed up with his own self-importance, paused again. "Meanwhile, I will be contacting the National Museum of Wales. In my humble opinion, this particular investigation would be better carried out by an archaeologist, not a practitioner of forensic science!"

Evans and Jones stared at the pathologist as he sloshed his way back to his waiting pickup.

"I've never seen him so excited," said Jones.

Chapter 55

James, Tom and Delyth watched a squirrel snatch an acorn and scamper towards the formal rose garden. The spot where they were sitting, a bench under the shade of an oak tree in the grounds of Swansea Hospital, had become a refuge from the anxious gaze of parents and medical staff.

"They all think we're mad." James sighed. "I don't know how much longer I can watch mum staring at me like I've sprouted an extra head or something." The others looked glum.

"Have you seen some of the things people are posting on Facebook?" said Delyth.

"I don't care," James lied. "And no, I haven't. Mum made the whole family delete their accounts."

"Your mum's probably right," said Delyth. "Some nutjobs are posting really crazy stuff."

"As crazy as what happened?" asked Tom. They sat in silence for a few minutes, soaking up the warmth of the morning sun, and thinking.

Tom broke the silence. "So the Iron Age thing really happened?"

Delyth shrugged her shoulders. "I don't know," she said. "It all seemed incredibly real but maybe it was the water we drank after all. Doctor Perkins told me the hallucinations could–"

James cut her off. "I don't care what that bloody shrink says, it happened! There's no other explanation. There was no way out of that cave. That chimney was blocked by tons of rock. So how come only three of us were found?" James glared at Delyth. "Go on, you tell me. If the druid didn't kill Emma, where is she? And how do you explain that we all had exactly the same dream?"

Delyth didn't respond. She didn't want to make James even more agitated than he already was.

"And how come I can speak Welsh?" James demanded. "According to them, we were in that cave three days. I'd have to be a bloody genius to learn a language in that time. I've been doing French since year six, for fuck's sake, and I'm still completely shit!"

Tom intervened. "Leave her alone. It's not her fault."

James grasped Delyth's hand. "Don't you see we have to stick together?"

Delyth shook her hand free. "It doesn't matter what anyone else thinks. The important thing is that we're home and safe."

"But Emma's not!" James snapped. His tone was harsh, but his face was anguished.

Delyth held James' gaze. When she replied, her voice was tender but firm. "If we try to make sense of it all, we're going to crack up. You need to stop beating yourself up. It's not anyone's fault

Emma didn't make it. You have to move on. You have the rest of your life to live."

James buried his head in his hands. "Mum says the police are going to question us again. And I think Dad's still convinced I've been taking drugs."

Tom interrupted. "They know we didn't do any drugs. The blood tests proved it was a fungus in the water, and we've told them Rick had nothing to do with Emma's disappearance. What else can we tell them?"

"I dunno."

"Well then."

James started to cry.

Richard and Anne and Doctor Perkins scrutinized the youngsters through the psychiatrist's office window.

"They look so vulnerable," said Anne. "Are you sure they're ready to come home?"

Dr. Perkins removed her glasses and faced James' parents. They looked shattered. "I understand your concerns," she said kindly, "but we've been through this before. They'll recover better in the familiar surroundings of their own homes."

"The consultant said the effects of this poisoning could reoccur at any time," said Anne.

"That's true," Doctor Perkins replied. "I'm afraid recurring events are an unfortunate symptom of this kind of toxin. It can remain dormant for months, even years without any effect, then without warning, the patient suffers another episode."

The Cordles looked horrified.

Doctor Perkins was quick to reassure them. "Fortunately, the medics believe the amount of mycotoxin they ingested is not sufficient to have long-term health implications. So, given time, they're all expected to make a full recovery."

Richard remained unconvinced. "So you're sure these dreams were the result of the water they drank in the cave? Because the police have been working on the assumption they'd been given drugs."

"Yes," said Doctor Perkins unequivocally. "The toxins in the water exactly matched the markers found in the children's blood. It's also consistent with their belief that the hallucinations they had in the cave are real." She hesitated. "What makes this case problematic, of course, is the disappearance of their friend."

"Yes," agreed Richard. "Until the police get to the bottom of what's happened to Emma, they'll find it difficult to get closure."

"Quite. And because James believes he had a relationship with Emma, this fantasy about a druid strangling Emma has affected him worse than the others."

Anne squeezed her husband's hand tightly. The events of the last month had stretched her reserves to the limit. The TV coverage and social media interest had been relentless. They still had newspaper reporters camped outside their house. Only this morning, a man had knocked on the door offering a large sum of money for an exclusive interview with James. She was rattled and needed encouragement. "How long before he gets over this, doctor?"

Doctor Perkins met Anne's troubled gaze. "It's impossible to give you a meaningful timetable," she answered honestly. "The involvement of Mycotoxins makes this an unusual case, but James is displaying all the classic symptoms of PTSD." She glanced at the Cordles, gauging their response, then continued. "You can expect him to have reoccurring nightmares, and there'll be times when he'll become moody, perhaps aggressive, but," she smiled encouragingly, "James is a very sensible young man, and he has a loving family to support him. So, while he may find life difficult in the short-term, over the next few weeks and months, the nightmares and mood swings will become less frequent. The human mind has a tremendous capacity to heal itself. Within a year, with your help, I'm sure he'll have returned to his usual happy-go-lucky self."

Chapter 56

Inspector Reid gazed down at the newspaper article in dismay. A photograph of the hand sticking out of a muddy lakebed waved back at him under the headline: *Bungling Coppers Find National Treasure.*

"The words 'balls' and 'chopping block' spring to mind, Jones."

"Yes, sir," Detective Jones replied warily, expecting a tirade. But the outburst never came.

"So where do we go from here?" Reid asked helplessly.

"Difficult to say, sir. The statements from Richard McFarlane and Margaret Edwards both match what the kids have already told us. So far, we've not got a shred of evidence against either of them. And the drug theory is a dead duck. The hospital reckons it was the water the kids drank in the cave. Mycotoxins or something."

"So where the hell is the girl?"

"That's the million-pound question. There's been a limited response to her father's TV appeal last night, but no useful info, just the usual cranks."

At the mention of Emma's father, Reid pursed his lips. He'd already spoken to Kingsley-Smith twice this morning. He couldn't blame the man for throwing his weight around, he'd probably do the same in his shoes, but what could he say? The girl seemed to have disappeared into thin air. He'd run out of leads and had no idea where else to look. "Christ, man! Somebody must have seen *something*?" He looked at his detective sergeant in desperation.

Detective Sergeant Jones shrugged his shoulders. "At least those university people seem pleased."

The people from Aberystwyth University were ecstatic. They hovered around the half-exposed body like a flock of wading birds picking over the mud at low tide.

One of them, a man with a long, grey beard that would have shamed Gandalf, could hardly contain his excitement. "I can't believe it," he raved. "She's amazing. Simply amazing. Just look at her hair!"

A young woman in a tatty Barbour was busy scraping away black peaty deposits from around the body. She looked up in surprise. "Are you sure it's female, Professor?"

Professor Carrington squinted at her over his bifocals. "Of course!" He replied, affronted. "Look at the shape of the cranium. And the jawline. We're looking at a female, and a young one at that."

They stared at the shockingly well-preserved remains. The flattened face was stained nutty brown. With the peaceful expression on her face, she looked as if she were sleeping.

"Go on, sir," piped up one of the other students. "Have a guess at her age."

The professor smiled indulgently. "It's too early to start making wild guesses. We'll have to wait for the results of the carbon dating. But that hair clasp," he pointed to an intricately-carved bone comb. "That's very old."

"So, you think we could be looking at an Iron Age bog body?"

The professor nodded. "Quite possibly." He grinned.

Chapter 57

James lay on his bed in his parent's holiday cottage in St. Dogmaels. He was bored.

He stabbed the off button on the TV remote and chucked it angrily into the corner of the room. It lay on the sea of dirty clothes and miscellaneous detritus that covered the bedroom carpet. He opened the top drawer of his bedside cabinet and, for the second time that day, pulled out the crumpled newspaper cuttings from where he'd secreted them and laid them out on the bed. He kept them hidden – he didn't want his mum and dad to know he still looked at them, they'd only worry. They'd all insisted the bog body had nothing to do with Emma's disappearance, but he knew better.

He looked down at the grainy black and white photo; a group of people were lifting the blackened corpse from the embrace of its muddy grave. The scruffy archaeologists grinned at the camera like big game hunters holding up a trophy. James felt sick every time he looked at the photo, but he still felt compelled to stare at the grisly remains, sometimes for hours.

For a time, the newspapers had been full of the find and the disappearance of Emma. As the months had passed, the media had moved on. But he and the others were still struggling to come to terms with the events of the summer.

James threw the newspaper down in frustration. If only people would try to understand! The paper fluttered down to join the clothes porridge on the floor. James sighed. Of course they couldn't be expected to get their heads around what happened in the cave, it was all too weird. They meant well. Even that smiling psychiatrist woman, Doctor Perkins, although he didn't know whether he could face yet another interrogation about his feelings

He leant down and retrieved the newspaper cutting from on top of a pair of dirty pants and glanced at his mobile; they were due to arrive any minute.

He clicked his knuckles nervously. It had been his suggestion to visit the university in Cardiff, but now the moment had arrived, he didn't want to go through with it.

No chance of chickening out now, he thought. Doctor Perkins had persuaded all their parents it was a good idea.

He smoothed the cuttings down and slipped them back into the drawer, just as a car door slammed outside the cottage. He thundered downstairs and flung open the front door to see Tom, Delyth and Dr Alice Perkins disembark from a red people carrier. Running outside to greet his friends, he did a double take.

Delyth had lost weight. She'd also ditched the sloppy jumpers and jeans in favour of a short skirt and high heels. Her hair had been professionally cut. She was even wearing makeup.

James gawped. "Have you fluffed up your hair or something?"

Tom grinned. James hadn't seen his sister since her transformation from ugly duckling to graceful swan.

Delyth blushed and flicked back her hair. "Mum and I decided to go on a keep fit campaign," she explained. "It was a New Year's resolution. The clothes are a reward for losing weight."

"You- you look great!" stammered James.

Tom pouted. "What about me, James. How do I look?" He pranced around the front lawn like a model.

James grinned; Tom always managed to lift his mood. He slapped his friend on the shoulder, "You pillock!" He grinned. He glanced shyly at Delyth. "It's good to see you."

Anne Cordle met them at the front door and ushered them into the house. The youngsters piled upstairs to chat while Doctor Perkins and Anne gravitated towards the kitchen.

"Have you got time for a cup of tea?" asked Anne.

Alice smiled. "I'd love one," she said, perching on one of the wooden stools at the breakfast bar.

"It's good of you to give up your time," said James' mother, busying herself with the kettle. "You must be busy."

"It's a pleasure. I really mean that. They're great kids, and I've enjoyed working with them. And today, well it's a perfect excuse to get out of the office. It's not every day you get to see a national treasure up close!"

Anne placed two mugs on the breakfast bar and looked closely at the young psychiatrist. "Are you sure this is the right thing to do?"

"Absolutely. They're still clinging onto the idea that the bog body is Emma. Seeing it up close will be a reality check."

"I'm worried it'll make things worse. Surely it would be better to forget?" Anne dropped a teabag in each mug and went to get milk out of the fridge.

Doctor Perkins shook her head. "It'll be for the best, Anne," she said gently. "Tell me, how has James been recently?"

"He still doesn't talk to us. He lies in bed for hours. Sometimes he goes out for the whole day. He says he's going fishing or shooting, but I think they're just excuses to be on his own."

"How about the nightmares?"

"They seem to have stopped, but I'm worried about the photos he keeps in his bedside drawer."

Alice raised her eyebrow suggestively.

Anne coloured. "No, not those sorts of photos! Though I think I'd prefer that to those ghoulish newspaper cuttings he keeps staring at."

"Photographs of the bog body?" guessed Doctor Perkins.

"Yes. He thinks I don't know about them. I thought it would be best that way. Not to confront him with them, I mean. He'd only get angry." Anne poured hot water into the mugs and waited for the tea to brew.

Doctor Perkins leant over and poured the milk. "Trust me," she said, "this visit is just what he needs. And having his friends with him will be a great tonic."

Anne squeezed a teabag against the side of one of the mugs with a teaspoon, but as she went to scoop it out of the finished brew, it fell back into the mug with a splash. Suddenly, she burst into tears. "I just want my happy little boy back," she sobbed.

Doctor Perkins waited while Anne mopped up the spilt tea and brought her emotions under control. She decided now was not a good time to point out that Anne's 'little boy' was a hulking, six-foot, three-inch, seventeen-year-old that needed to shave more often. "Give it time," she said soothingly. "He'll be okay."

Chapter 58

Rick sat on the wooden bench overlooking the bay and sucked in the clear sea air. It felt good to be out and about after all those months in hospital.

He looked down at the inert plastic where his lower legs used to be. The prosthetic limbs reminded him of the Action Man doll he'd had as a kid, 'featuring real hair and moving limbs,' he'd joked with his surgeon. He smiled. *I must be getting used to this*.

"Fancy a beer?"

He twisted around. Mags had guessed where he was and wandered down from the house with a couple of cans. "You star," he replied. Mags smiled and silently handed him a beer. He tore open the ring-pull and watched the golden liquid froth onto the rim. He closed his eyes and took a long, satisfying quaff of cold lager. "Did I ever tell you that I love you?"

"Are you talking to me or the beer?" Mags shot back.

Rick grinned. "That's why I love you," he declared, putting his arm tenderly around his partner. "You make me laugh."

"Well, you haven't had a lot of laughs recently," she replied.

Rick squeezed her arm. "I couldn't have made it without you."

"Nonsense. You're tough as old boots."

"No, I mean it Mags. You're the only one who believed in me. Those coppers were convinced I'd murdered Emma. They'd made up their minds to put me inside and chuck away the key. If you hadn't stuck by me, I'd have gone down big time. Christ, even the nurses looked at me like I was Peter Sutcliffe!"

"It wasn't just me," protested Mags. "The kids all backed you up. And remember the police thought I helped dispose of the body?" Mags shuddered. "They had us down as a couple of Pagan psychopaths. God! What an imagination."

Rick took another swig of beer and looked back out to sea. Gulls wheeled over the headland, riding the faint onshore breeze with effortless grace. "Do you think we'll ever find out what happened to her?"

"I've no idea, darling. But it looks like the police have run out of ideas and given up searching."

"That's the only reason the police let me go. That inspector told me that without a body he couldn't charge me with anything." Rick frowned. "They still think I did it."

"So what?" countered Mags. "We know we didn't hurt Emma or spirit her away, so fuck the lot of them! We've got each other. That's what matters."

Rick grinned. "Us against the world, eh Mags?"

Mags smiled back at her man; the scars on his face were still an angry purple. The Doctors said they'd fade; she wouldn't mind if they didn't. They made him look rugged.

She snuggled closer and planted a lingering kiss on Rick's lips. He kissed her back hard, and she pulled away, pleased with herself. "Steady boy," she said. "Or I'll leave you to walk home on your own."

Rick smiled again and reached up under her blouse, but Mags pushed him away, suddenly serious. "Rick," she said, "I've been thinking. You realise there won't be any more adventure holidays, don't you?"

Rick looked down at his plastic feet. "That's pretty obvious."

Mags looked relieved. "Well," she continued hesitantly, "I had a little chat with the head archaeology guy, Professor Carrington, at the lake. They want to build a visitor centre here when the excavation is finished. And, well, Myrtle farm is perfect for them. He seemed to think the National Trust might make us an offer. Apparently, the wooden circle they've found makes this the most important Iron Age site in Wales. Possibly Europe. They're already calling it the wooden Stonehenge. They say there'll be thousands of visitors."

"I'm not selling!" Rick insisted. Then he winked. "You must think I'm a wooden top," he teased. "I've had a chat with a guy at the council. He thought we'd get planning permission to convert the farm buildings into a display area and tearooms. We might even get grants for the building work. We'd be mad to sell. With all those visitors, Myrtle House would be a goldmine. Besides," he laughed, "I can't think of a better place to bring up children."

Mags smiled and dug Rick in the ribs playfully with one of his crutches. "Come on, Rockefeller. Walk me home, and we'll have a think about making one of those babies you've been threatening me with!"

Chapter 59

Professor Carrington stared at the oversized clock hanging on his office wall. It was nine-thirty.

He wished that wretched psychiatrist hadn't persuaded him to show the children his bog body. Now they were late. He deplored unpunctuality. He drummed his fingers on the desk. If they weren't there by quarter to ten, he was going over to the lab on his own.

Having made that decision, Carrington looked for something to fill the time. He was tempted to go to the coffee machine, then he remembered he was trying to cut down on caffeine. Instead, he opened his desk drawer and took out the gold cross. He held the clasp between thumb and index finger, so it hung suspended by the heavy-duty gold chain. He stared at the object for a while, moving his hand so the cross swung to and fro like a pendulum.

Then dropped it into the palm of his left hand, squeezing it in his fist as though he hoped it would disappear.

The discovery of this piece of twenty-first century bling around the neck of his Iron Age bog body was, to say the least, a bit awkward. He'd interrogated everyone who'd assisted in the dig but of course, nobody owned up to planting it on the body. *I'd give odds it was Stevens*, he thought darkly. He'd taken a dislike to the postgrad after he'd placed live yogurts on the radiators in the common room and waited for them to explode. It was just the sort of irresponsible joke that young idiot would play. It was a pity the lad didn't have the guts to admit what he'd done.

Carrington glanced irritably at the clock. He pursed his lips. Thank God the team had agreed not to mention the cross in any of the reports or leak anything to the media. It was just a silly prank, but if the press got wind of it, it would be an embarrassment, and might cast doubt on their findings. Even worse, the university might withdraw their funding.

The Professor was just reconsidering his decision concerning coffee when there was a knock on his office door. He slipped the cross back into the drawer as a smartly-dressed woman and three teenagers filed in. "Delighted to meet you," lied the professor, standing up to greet his guests. He held out his hand. "You must be Doctor Perkins."

Perkins returned the handshake. "Thank you so much for agreeing to see us, Professor." she said. "Let me introduce you to the young people I've been telling you all about."

James, Tom and Delyth took their turn to shake the professor's hand, then, while the adults engaged in small talk, James checked out the Professor's office. The room was an uninspiring white-emulsion box with a cheap office desk at one end and a large picture window at the other. The window looked out over a grey and equally boring cityscape. The contents of the room were rather more interesting. The eccentric professor had packed it with an Aladdin's cave of dusty books and bizarre objects. James gazed around the clutter in amazement.

There were astonishing and grotesque things everywhere he looked; a mummified cat had been blu- tacked to the top of a computer monitor. A human skull used as a book stop stared down at him disapprovingly from one of the shelves. Curious pieces of stone, wood and pottery crowded every available surface, and stacks of papers lay everywhere. James' eyes were drawn to the papers on Carrington's desk. Some of them were related to the finds at Abereiddy. With a start, he saw a photo of the bog body. He stared at it in horror. Suddenly he was back at the lake, watching the ripples where Emma had been thrown in the water.

"James! James, we're going now!" James snapped out of his daydream.

"We're going to the laboratories," Delyth said impatiently.

James found himself trotting after the others down a long corridor. It felt like he was at school, running late for the next lesson.

The professor swept them through the corridor and down two flights of concrete steps. At the bottom of the stairs, Carrington fumbled in his pocket for a fob key. The security door into the basement clicked open and they stepped into a reception room. Ahead of them was a pair of double doors. Next to the doors was an intercom with a green button.

Carrington pressed the button and a woman in a white lab coat appeared, holding an armful of lab coats. She smiled; she had gap between her front teeth. "Please thign the vithitor book and put thith on," she lisped, holding out the coats, "then we'll take you through to view our exciting new find. I'm afraid you'll have to take potluck with the thizes."

James wrestled with the coats, but of course couldn't find one big enough. His bulging forearms and shoulders threatened to split the thin cotton. He glanced at Tom, expecting a sarcastic comment about the fit, but Tom was lost in thought, his eyes fixed to the floor. James hesitated. *What if it is really Emma?* he thought.

James caught Delyth's eye, and she reached out and held his hand. "Come on," she said. "Let's get this over."

Doctor Perkins watched the interactions between her charges closely. "Are you sure you're ready?" James, Tom and Delyth nodded in unison.

The lady with the gappy teeth smiled. "We'll go through then. You're welcome to ask any quethtions, but I mutht remind you that we are looking at extremely valuable archaeological material, so pleathe, *pleathe* do not touch anything." James gritted his teeth. He didn't like the body being described as archaeological material; whoever it was, it was a person.

The three friends, looking like extras in a washing powder ad, followed the professor and his toothy colleague through the double doors. The Archaeology laboratory, like the rest of the building, was painted brilliant white. Banks of tubelights bathed the room in fluorescent light. A long, stainless-steel worktop punctuated by stainless-steel sinks ran along the wall opposite the windows. It looked like something from NASA.

In the centre of the room, two technicians wearing white overalls and blue latex gloves stooped over a brown object lying in a shallow, stainless-steel bath. The room smelt like a hospital ward. As they walked in, the researchers looked up.

One of them put down the squeegee bottle he was holding and addressed them. "Hi. Please join us," he said in a lilting Irish accent.

Professor Carrington did the introductions. "This is Doctor O'Connell. He's over here from the National Museum of Ireland," he explained. "This is the first bog body discovered in Wales, so our Irish colleagues are helping us out. Doctor O'Connell here has worked on some very interesting finds, including the celebrated Old Croghan Man."

The youngsters weren't listening. They were all staring at the gruesome human remains floating in the steel tank. James watched, fascinated, as O'Connell's colleague squirted water into the tangle of orange-tinted fibres on top of the head and removed one of the hairs with tweezers.

Doctor O'Connell gave a running commentary. "We're having a second look at the hair. Microscopy detected some structural changes to the hair fibres. We think the changes may be consistent with the application of some sort of bleach or dye. Ned here is taking some more samples for analysis."

James was surprised how dispassionate he felt about watching the procedure. Perhaps it was because it was hard to imagine the blackened husk lying in the tank as Emma. *It looks more like a squashed doll*. Everything was there, perfectly preserved. Ears, lips, hair, everything. But distorted, flattened by years buried in peat. It looked like it had been run over by a bus. James paused, shocked he was no longer thinking of the body as Emma, or even a 'he' or a 'she,' but an 'it.'

Tom voiced James' feelings perfectly. "I'm not sad," he said. "I thought I'd cry. But this thing isn't Emma."

Alice looked over her spectacles, relieved at their reaction. "This can't be Emma," she said gently. "This girl lived three-hundred years before Jesus Christ was born."

"Near enough," agreed Professor Carrington. "Carbon dating of a bone comb this young woman was wearing when she died confirmed her as living in around three-hundred-and-fifty BC."

James stared at the ancient face; it was even possible to make out eyelashes.

"How did she die?" asked Delyth quietly. Even before she asked the question, she knew the answer.

"She was strangled with a leather garrotte," Doctor O'Connell announced cheerfully. "It's a method of execution in common with several other..."

O'Connell carried on talking, but James, Tom and Delyth had stopped listening; they stared at the body in silence.

James broke the spell. He shook his head angrily. "Alice is right! None of it happened! This person died two-thousand years ago. What's it got to do with us?" He looked at Tom, defying him to disagree.

Tom nodded in assent. "I've seen enough," he said. "This is too weird for me."

James squeezed Delyth's hand. "Come on. Let's get out of here."

They turned to go, but the professor called them back. "Don't you want to look at the reconstruction? I thought that's what you'd come to see?"

James shrugged; he felt he had to be polite. They crowded round the computer screen while Doctor O'Connell's fingers rattled over the keyboard. He located the file he was looking for and a 3D image of the bog body's face appeared on the screen. The flattened features stared out of the screen at them.

The archaeology wizard punched another set of keys and a grid of green lines appeared on the face. Gradually, the lines bent, and the bog body's squashed features began to fill out. Bit by bit, the computer breathed life into the crushed face, finally generating lifelike skin, hair and eyes.

James, Tom and Delyth gasped in unison at the two-thousand-year-old face staring back. "Tegwedd!"

Epilogue

Emma sat on the clifftop and watched the winter storm waves smash against the rocks; her eyes were stinging from the salt spray and her tears.

She felt the baby kick and placed her hands on her swelling belly. "Where are you, James?" She shouted. The words went unanswered, whipped away by the rush of the Atlantic gale.

Emma brushed the spray and tears from her face with a hand reddened from cold. She knew coming to the cliff above the cave was futile, but it was where she felt closest to her family, her friends, and especially to James.

A woman approached along the cliff path, her head bent into the wind. Emma hardly registered her presence, even when she felt her comforting arm around her shoulders.

"You can't mourn him forever, *cariad*," Heulwen yelled against the wind. "Come home. There is a fire and a dish of hot lamb broth."

Emma looked at the priestess she'd come to regard as a second mother. "Will I ever see him again?" she asked.

Heulwen held Emma close. "I do not know. The Goddess has not shown me," she answered truthfully. "But I believe in the power of love. If the Gods allow it, love will draw his spirit here as the moon draws the tide."

Emma nodded then glanced down at the foaming sea, "I'm tired, Mam. Let's go home."

Author's Notes

The setting

Reflections in Time is set in Pembrokeshire which is situated in the Southwest corner of Wales. It's an area rich with fantastical folktales, and the landscape carries the marks of people who inhabited it thousands of years before the Romans first landed on the shores of Britain. It is easy to understand why legends persist. The county is littered with archaeological treasures. Everywhere you look there seem to be Iron Age forts, Bronze Age burial chambers and Neolithic stone circles. Indeed, the blue stones that formed the original circle at Stonehenge were quarried from the Preseli Hills in Pembrokeshire.

Most of the locations mentioned in the book are real places. Abereiddy is a sheltered beach popular with holidaymakers. The Blue Lagoon, adjacent to Abereiddy Bay, is a flooded slate quarry that has hosted the world high diving championships, and Clawdd y Milwyr at St David's Head is the Iron Age fort that I envisioned as Maelog's stronghold. Some places have been re-imagined for the sake of the plot. There is a cave on the headland overlooking the Blue Lagoon, but it only extends a few metres into the cliff face, and the lake, which in the book occupies marshy ground behind Abereiddy beach, does not exist.

Celtic beliefs

In Iron Age Wales, around 350BC, the predominant religion was Druidism. A belief system based on the natural world, where gods and goddesses were worshipped in sacred places and sacrifices were made.

The Druids, who could be men or women, were the priests of the Celtic religion and held a very important position in Iron Age Welsh society, performing the roles of judge, doctor and scholar as well as their religious functions. The Celts did not have a system of writing and Druidic law prevented their religious beliefs being recorded, so Druids had to undergo a long education, committing all their knowledge to memory, probably in the form of songs and poetry. Accordingly, our understanding of their religion is sketchy and comes from Roman writings and conjecture based on archaeological remains and mythology.

The enduring fascination with the Celtic religion is that when the last Druid died, the poems and songs, which held the key to their beliefs also died.

So what do we know about Druidism?

Celtic Mythology is based on the earth goddess and fertility religion common throughout the ancient world. Some Celtic beliefs were probably rooted in much older Neolithic cultures, which worshipped the Sun, Moon and stars, and built the stone circles. Certainly, these celestial bodies were important to the Celts, who believed they were supernatural forces.

We know from Roman accounts that the Celts believed that the soul is immortal and that after death it passes to the Otherworld, where it stays until it returns to inhabit another body and live a second life. The Druids believed they were gatekeepers to the Otherworld and claimed to be able to foretell the future through meditation, the interpretation of dreams and natural occurrences such as the flight of birds.

The Celtic feast of the dead, Samhain, was the precursor to Halloween. It was celebrated at the midpoint between the summer and winter solstice, which for us falls on the first of November. The night of Samhain was when the Celts believed the barrier between the world of men and the Otherworld thinned, allowing contact between the spirits and humans. Ancestors were honoured and invited home, while harmful spirits were warded off. Bonfires were lit, and people wore costumes and masks to disguise themselves as harmful spirits as a means of avoiding them.

Watery places were of particular spiritual importance for the Celts, who may have believed water provided some sort of gateway to the Otherworld. The archaeological record shows that Iron Age people often threw weapons and other valuable items into lakes, rivers and bogs. Human sacrifices were also placed in bogs, and a number of remarkably well-preserved bodies bearing marks of ritual murder, such as Old Croghan Man discovered in Ireland, and Tollund Man found in Denmark, have been recovered from peat bogs.

There is so much we don't know about the religious practices of the Druids that an author such as myself has plenty of scope to invent their own 'facts' to support their storyline.

Inducing a trance by ingesting mycotoxins derived from fungi is a practice observed by shamans and holy men in tribes in Africa and South America. In these cultures, the trance is believed to facilitate contact with the spirit world to speak to the dead or divine the future. The blue fungus in the sacred cave of the goddess is a fiction, however the Druids would almost certainly have understood the hallucinogenic effects of Ergot and certain species of mushroom. Long-term abuse of hallucinogenic substances affects brain function, which is why Myrleduin goes mad.

Divining the future in a chalice filled with sacred water is an extension of the Celtic belief that water is a gateway to the Otherworld. The bowl of water is my Iron Age equivalent of a crystal ball.

We don't know if the Druids knew that placing their victims in peat would preserve the bodies or why such sacrifices were made. In my fictional depiction of Druidism, Myrleduin sacrifices Tegwedd at a wooden circle in the middle of a sacred lake and throws her into the peaty water. The ritual was intended to preserve the girl's body and bind her soul to the Goddess, so she can intercede on behalf of her people and allow Myrleduin access to the Otherworld. The idea has parallels with the practice of preserving the bodies of family members carried out by tribes in Papua New Guinea. In their case, the body is preserved by smoking to ensure their ancestor's spirit remains with them to intercede with spirits embodied in things around them, such as animals and trees.

Human bones are scarce in the Iron Age archaeological record and those that are recovered are often found in unusual configurations, including detached limbs, isolated fragments and skulls. This suggests bodies may have been buried, then exhumed, or been left in the open to decompose. I have assumed the latter, with the bones of loved ones being cremated in a ceremony for the dead held at the festival of Samhain.

My depiction of Samhain features men dressed as stags in the fire-lighting ceremony. The stags represent Arawn, the king of the Otherworld, a character in the Mabinogi – a series of Welsh folktales compiled in the 12th century, which are almost certainly based on much older oral traditions. Speculating that the story of Arawn might hint at the beliefs of the Celts over a thousand years earlier, I have included him in my Samhain festival.

The Welsh language

Welsh is widely spoken in West Wales, where many regard it as their first language. Welsh is derived from Brittonic, which was the common language of Iron Age Britons, and is related to the other Celtic languages; Irish, Scottish Gaelic, Manx, Cornish, and Breton. My father, a Welsh speaker, told me that when he went on holiday to Brittany, he was able to converse with the locals in Breton. Like all languages, Welsh has evolved over the millennia, but its similarity with other Celtic languages, especially Cornish and Breton, suggest it hasn't undergone the radical changes English has. This allows me to entertain the possibility that a Welsh speaking twenty-first century time traveller might understand an Iron Age Welsh tribesman

Glossary

Welsh names
  Tegwedd: *meaning 'fair of appearance'*
  Artur: *meaning 'river god' or 'bear'*
  Du Tarian: *meaning 'black shields'*
  Heulwen: *meaning 'sunshine'*
  Rhydderch: *meaning 'exalted king'*
  Maelog: *name derived from mael meaning 'prince'*
  Mordred: *meaning controlled / moderated*
  Cliodna: *Celtic goddess of water, wells and streams*

Welsh words / phrases
Pwy wyt ti: Who are you?
Nadu: No
Beth sy'n bod?: What's the matter?
Cariad: Darling
Pob lwc: Good luck
Meddwyn: Drunkard or pisshead

IF YOU ENJOYED **REFLECTIONS IN TIME**
YOU WILL WANT TO READ THE
SECOND BOOK IN THE **SERIES**

The Author, a Suffakated Welshman

Gwyn Jones was born in England to an English mother and a Welsh-speaking father.
He was educated in Suffolk but spent his school holidays in West Wales, a place he regards as his spiritual home.

After graduating he joined an animal feed company selling feed to farmers. This was the start of a career, which led to him marketing specialist feeds and nutritional advice across Europe and Russia. He retired in 2018 and divides his time between his home in Suffolk and a cottage in West Wales.

His hobbies include cold-water swimming, painting with pastels and ratting. Married for forty years, he has three children and four grandchildren. Reflections in Time is his first Novel.

Printed in Great Britain
by Amazon

50808541R00219